# The Platinum Briefcase

**sands press**
Brockville,Ontario

# The Platinum Briefcase

## Henry Cline

sands press

# sands press

A division of 3244601 Canada Inc.
300 Central Avenue West
Brockville, Ontario
K6V 5V2

Toll Free 1-800-563-0911 or 613-345-2687
http://www.sandspress.com

ISBN 978-1-988281-27-8
Copyright © 2017 Henry Cline
All Rights Reserved

Cover concept and Design by Kristine Barker and Wendy Treverton
Edited by Katrina Geenevasen
Formatting by Renee Hare
Publisher Kristine Barker

**Publisher's Note**

This book is a work of fiction by the author. Characters, names, places and circumstances are the product of the author's imagination and are used in a fictitious manner. Any relation to any persons, alive or deceased, place, location, event or otherwise is purely coincidental.

No part of this book may be reproduced in whole or in part, stored in a retrieval system or transmitted in any form or by any means, without the prior written permission of the publisher.

1st Printing October 2017
To book an author for your live event, please call:   1-800-563-0911

**Submissions**

Sands Press is a literary publisher interested in new and established authors wishing to develop and market their product. For more information please visit our website at www.sandspress.com.

Dedicated to all of the people who supported me in my long journey to get published. Please enjoy.

Henry Cline

# Part One:

Not Quite the American Dream...

# The Platinum Briefcase

# **Prologue**

In the early 1900s, immigrants from across the world began to seek refuge elsewhere. Somewhere that would help them succeed in life, somewhere that would make them great. That great land they sought after was America. Land of the free, and the home of the brave.

Sadly, a bunch of cowards and criminals started making their way over from European and Asian countries to corrupt the already not-so-stable America. These Europeans and Asians came over and started making gangs that were primarily family oriented, but as the fifties rolled around, these gangs started losing their family muscle and trust. And by the time the sixties came in, gangs were just a mix-and-match of whoever they could find. Sure, they'd be able to trust them in the beginning, but in the end, they'd have a knife in their back or a loved one lost. It was upsetting to the Italian and Sicilian gangs who started it all in New York, for they only wanted gangs that were based on family principles, morals, and trust. This story is about one gang in particular that had quite a falling out. A gang that thought it could muscle its way into the center of the motor city as it started to collapse. And that gang was rumored to have something so sacred in their possession that no one usually spoke of it. Unlike the other gangs out there in America, they had something known only as: The Platinum Briefcase.

**The Platinum Briefcase**

# Chapter One

I think we all wonder how things could have been different. How, if maybe I had gone home the short way instead of the long way, I would've avoided the terrible wreck that perverted the streets, or if I'd done better in school, I could've made something of myself? Or the classic, what if I was never born?

It would be dumb to say I never thought of any of those things, especially after Queen popularized the last one. Honestly, I don't know the answer to the last one. The other ones are easy: I would've avoided the wreck and I could've been a little more successful in my life, or at least, successful in an honest way. But then again, what successful person doesn't have somewhat of a hidden past or burning regret?

Whatever. It doesn't matter now. What's done is done, and there's no changing that.

My name is Victor Carez and I'm eighteen years old. I'm not Hispanic, or maybe I am somewhere down the line, but I don't speak Spanish and my skin has gone for a more olive tone rather than brown. I guess the story goes, some General for the Mexican Army found my great, great grandmother and did her near the Alamo and that's where the last name came from. But, my dad told me that story when he was drunk, which is not too uncommon nowadays.

But in the good days, it was uncommon.

The good days I refer to is anywhere from when I was born in January of 1958 right up until the gas crisis in 1973. My dad worked for a car and gas company he co-founded in '66 and my mom was a writer for the paper. We were living a great life and I remember everything remarkably well. Our giant house in Brighton with the elaborate furniture and silverware and it was just a small walk to the beach; our golden retriever Max and the beautiful front yard...

But see, that *would be* the American Dream.

Now, it's quite the opposite.

The gas crisis of '73 sent my dad's business plummeting into the ground and we lost a ton of money. He was once a happy-go-lucky, friendly, caring man who would never hurt a fly, but after the crisis, he turned into a miserable bloated drunk who couldn't stay sober for five minutes.

My mom, on the other hand, wrote an article over the whole thing and got fired over it since she blamed my dad's misfortune on American politics. The article also contained some foul language and nearly Communist remarks and... it just didn't end very well.

We moved from our house to downtown Detroit in a small apartment filled with every person I was told to stay away from as a kid. Well, it wasn't really that bad but I probably heard at least one gunshot every night, or a siren.

I remember Max didn't like the apartment at all. He always wanted to go outside for a walk but no one in the apartment had the morale for it. One day, because of my dad's new drinking habit, he left the door wide open and Max got run over right in front of the stairway to the apartment's lobby.

I hated my dad after that. It was like money really did buy his happiness and when it was taken away, my mom and I could never bring it back. Just a month or two after we moved to the apartment, my mom mouthed off to my dad, something she never usually did, and he beat her. When I interjected, he beat me.

That's when the Dad I used to know vanished.

It was so awful. I can remember that pain I felt as he beat me for the first time, but it wasn't even the physical pain, just the mental agony.

I also had to move schools after we relocated, and that also sucked. Because of our dramatic change in lifestyle and mood, when I moved schools, all the kids saw me as just some burnout no-life who had a shitty home life and no friends. I wore tattered band T-shirts and jeans every day with some deteriorating Converse and no one talked to me. I wore a jacket to school every day because the school was about three degrees Fahrenheit, but it made everyone think I was a cutter. I never did anything like that, but I did punch my wall sometimes. Because I knew if I hit my dad back, that would be the end.

The teachers would keep their eye on me too. Especially my English teacher, Mrs. Huffman, but luckily, she kept her eye on me in a more sympathetic way rather than a conniving way. She was sweet, and sometimes when I had bruises on me, she would pull me outside and ask what was wrong or where I got the bruises from.

For some reason, I never told her either reason as to why I had bruises, and yes, there were two reasons.

My dad was the main one, but there were also some kids who beat up on me after school. Some days when they weren't happy with their stupid perfect lives, they would find me and beat me down. The three of them couldn't do shit compared to my dad though...

My dad beat me about... Well really, there was no way to tell when he'd do it. It was very random, and sometimes it was just me, sometimes just my mom, but mainly it was both of us.

I hated to go home because I'd get beaten up there, but if I stuck around at school the kids would beat me.

The only thing that I think kept me going was my only friend at the time, Chief Ramzorin.

He was in his forties and he was actually friends with my dad before everything happened. But now, my dad wouldn't even talk to him, let alone look at him if the situation was there. Now, Chief Ramzorin was my friend, and we ate together every Wednesday at Michelangelo's Italian Grill.

In fact, I think that's where I should start this whole maniacal story.

## Chapter Two
Detroit, Michigan
Wednesday, March 3rd, 1976
6 P.M.

I walked into the diner that night feeling a little cold and bothered, even though I had my jacket on and spring was in the air. I dropped by the house to smell a little better while my dad slept and my mom babbled things to herself in the kitchen. I hoped my mom had some stability within her, but I still had to wonder.

The glass door swung closed as the bell above me rang and I saw Chief Ramzorin, sitting in the same spot we always chose. Some Frank Sinatra song played softly in the background as I stepped past the front podium made of a light wood and made my way left to the usual booth. There was so much red around the restaurant: red carpet, red wallpaper, and red everything. The lights were dimmed after 5:30 and the windows facing the streets were tinted so the restaurant made me feel safe, and hidden from the ugliness outside.

The Chief drank a hot cup of coffee and as soon as I started to slide into the booth he looked up.

"Ah, Victor, good to see you," he started with a small smile.

His short black hair and slightly bushy mustache made him look a little younger but his face showed experience. The small linear scar on the top of his right cheek stood predominant as the rest of his face contorted to a smile.

"Hello, Chief, same to you," I replied as I got comfortable in the booth.

Instantly, the waiter, Antonio (who always waited on us), walked up and asked, "What drink for you tonight, Victor, maybe a cream soda?"

"Just a Coke," I said plainly.

Antonio walked off and left me and the Chief in peace once more.

Now I knew what Chief Ramzorin was going to say next.

"How was school today?"

It was hard not to mouth the question with him for I knew it was coming. That was always his big opener.

"It was... I'm just glad it's almost over," I said.

"Yeah, I know I felt that way when I was your age. I was just ready to get out and go on to bigger and better things."

"Being the Chief of a ghetto is bigger and better?" I asked, not trying to be mean but it came off that way.

"Better than nothing."

Antonio walked up to us again with the Coke in a bulbous glass and set it on the table on a small napkin. The other two couples in the restaurant were extremely quiet and kept to themselves.

"All right gentlemen, should I pussy foot around a little more or are we just having the usual?" Antonio said boldly.

"Watch your tonio," Chief Ramzorin said in such a cheesy way. "I'll have Peterson come up and tow your car."

"Yeah yeah, I don't think he'd be able to. He can't even use his own 'lever' right."

Slightly ignoring their conversation, I said, "You're right Antonio, I'm just having the usual."

Antonio had his little receipt pad out, but he didn't even really need it. He probably just drew pictures in it while we ordered.

"Same here," Chief Ramzorin said.

The menus sat untouched at the end of the table and Antonio whipped them up as he walked away. Chief Ramzorin took another sip of coffee and I could tell the heat didn't even bother him.

"Still thinking about joining the force?" Chief Ramzorin asked with the mug in his hand.

I did contemplate it before he asked me, and I was excited about it before. But now, I just looked at it like an only option.

"Yeah, I'm hoping to after high school."

"That's coming up pretty soon, and then you'll miss it."

If only he knew...

Suddenly, my hand was shaking violently and I struggled to grab my glass right. Chief Ramzorin noticed and asked, "Are you really that cold? It's pretty toasty in here to me."

I decided to play it off and say, "You know I'm always cold..."

He gave me a look, a look that was filled to the brim with suspicion. He had asked before about the bruises, but I just said it was the kids at school playing tough. But that day, I think he knew what they were really from as I pulled my jacket down to cover the one on my right arm.

"How's your dad doing?" Chief Ramzorin started off.

"He's... not the same." I replied, not sure how I had avoided the question before.

Chief Ramzorin sighed and made himself a little more comfortable in the booth. When that happened, I knew he was going to say quite a bit.

"Man, Victor, it's sad, you know? I knew your dad back when his company first started up. He was a really nice guy and had that salesman aura about him. But, when your dad's and Mr. Hurston's company went under in '73, that was the end of that, for both of them. Mr. Hurston got out of here, and I mean that literally. I'm not sure you've ever heard the whole story but he just got in his car and drove. No one knows where he went, not even his wife and kids. Hell, I don't know where he went. He's never been found. At least your dad stuck with you guys and all, but I know he may not be the same anymore. In fact, I know he's not the same. I watched as he stumbled out of a liquor store and almost charged him with Public Intoxication, but I couldn't really tell if it was that or just pure misery."

With the last two cold words, Antonio walked up and handed us our food. I had the tortellini with alfredo and marinara sauce while the Chief had spaghetti and meatballs. Both plates were steaming and it caused a pseudo-wall to form between us, and before Chief Ramzorin could say anymore, my extreme hunger took over and I dove into my plate. About a minute or two later, I was done and Chief Ramzorin was still twirling his spaghetti on a fork and spoon.

"Jesus, Victor, did you even chew?" Chief Ramzorin asked.

Little did he know, this was the only meal I ever got each week.

"Sorry, you know what they say about teenage boys though, we're always hungry."

*****

After we ate and Chief Ramzorin paid as usual, I told him I preferred to just walk home.

"Are you sure? I don't mind driving you there," Chief Ramzorin explained.

"I'm sure… You know how my dad would be if he saw us."

Chief Ramzorin understood and didn't push it anymore. Plus, I wanted to walk home alone so I could do some personal reflecting.

*What am I going to do after high school?*

This is a question that I shouldn't really be asking myself right now. According to all the school counselors, I should already know. Chief Ramzorin was offering me a nice spot on the police force but… Is that really what I want? Or, do I even know what I want, if not that?

I was so lost mentally, but physically I could walk back to the apartment with my eyes closed. That wasn't really the best idea though, since this wasn't such a great town.

Turning left onto Easter I had four blocks to go. A few people stood outside and smoked or conversed and I was just alone with my shadow that moved under each orange streetlight, walking back with my first full stomach since last week.

I don't know why Chief Ramzorin always offered to drive me back. He knew, or at least I hope he knew, that it would end in a confrontation with my dad. But maybe he wanted that. Maybe he wanted to bring my dad in and try to talk some sense into him.

"Hey kid, you're not looking too well," some shady guy in a bandana against a brick wall started, "Want something that'll fix that?"

I didn't respond. Usually people like him only persisted if you did respond. I just walked on and minded my own business.

My only other hope with joining the police force was that I'd finally have more friends. Ramzorin had mentioned Peterson earlier at the restaurant, and I had actually met him once before. He seemed pretty cool, and I heard he usually trained people on their first day in the cruiser. Other than that, I didn't really know any of the other cops.

As I neared the apartment, I started to feel sick. My dad was usually passed out drunk with the TV blaring but what if he wasn't? He'd get mad about not being home on time... hell, he was mad no matter what happened. As long as there was some excuse to get mad and beat me, he used it.

Back at the old house though, when things were good, he never did anything like that. He asked me how school was, asked me what I learned, and if I needed help with homework, or if I had any new girlfriends...

Hah.

That brought a momentary smile to me, but as I ascended up the stairs to the door, I knew all my good feelings would rush away.

I opened the door and stepped into a small lobby area. To the left were all the other tenants' mailboxes and to the right was the indoor staircase that led to all the other apartments. Ours was the first one straight ahead after you walked in. The fading gold "1" was nailed in and a little crooked. I stepped up to the door. The news was blaring inside and I reached for the door handle slowly. If you opened it just right, it wouldn't squeak at all. That's what I was going for.

After turning the knob, I pushed it open as fast as I could. It caused the squeak to just be a quick and almost unnoticeable noise instead of painstakingly long and overbearing. But, as loud as the TV was, now that I had opened the door and stepped in, I didn't think anyone would hear it. So, when I closed it, I just pushed it closed and the click of me locking the deadbolt was hardly heard.

Right upon my entrance, I saw my mom.

She was on the couch with her head on the armrest. I could see the back of her head and her ratty hair as she snoozed away in her atrocious duck covered pajamas.

## The Platinum Briefcase

The TV was the only light in the house and it flashed bright white and then color and so on. The kitchen light just past the living room was on but dim. As I carefully walked forward, I saw that my parents' bedroom door was closed and it was dark in there. I hoped my dad was in there, asleep and peaceful in his own sick way. It was nearing eight o'clock and I knew he wouldn't be awake for another 14 hours.

I passed their door and saw the bathroom door to the left. It was just barely cracked open and no light was on in there. So just as I started to pass it to go to my room, which was the third door on the left, I had a sudden urge to pee.

Hoping it wouldn't make too much noise, I stepped back to the bathroom door and pushed it open.

"Victor!?"

I heard the grumble from inside the bathroom and there was my dad, waiting for me. He wore a faded white tank top with mustard, ketchup, and alcohol stains all over it and his pajama pants were plaid and torn. His face was fatter than before we moved and he wore his permanent five o'clock shadow with pride. His hair was long, like some of the Vietnam veterans you see moping around outside, but my dad had less honor than them.

My heart raced. I knew what was coming. A queasy feeling settled in and my dad was ready to do his worst.

First he pushed me, and it sent me flying to the wall on the other side of the hall. I crashed into some boxes that held pictures of all of the happier times we had together as a family.

"You talking to the Chief again, you miserable fuck?" he started.

Before I could answer, his fist slammed down into my face and I cowered. There was nothing else I could do.

"I already know the answer to that," he said in a drunken slur. "You were probably talking about how shitty I am, weren't you?"

Then came the kick. It hit my chest and there went all my air.

"I bet you had a gay ole time with him, didn't you?"

He kicked again, but this one hit near my groin at my upper thigh. I prayed he wouldn't kick my stomach, but praying had done nothing for me before, so why would it now?

"Fuck you and that… Chief. He's a hack and a liar. He doesn't know anything, and neither do you, you got that?"

I wasn't sure if he kicked me again because I couldn't answer, or because he found joy in it.

And just like I thought, he kicked me in the stomach not once, but three times as hard and as fast as he could, and finished off with a punch to my face. The sinister laugh presided as he walked off to the kitchen to get more booze, and I was left there in a tumultuous amount of pain. Suddenly, I felt the delicious meal I had just had rushing back up and I ran to the bathroom. The toilet was covered and so I threw my head in the half bath and let loose. Only after that moment could I breathe again, but only out of my mouth. My nose filled with vomit as I threw up once more, and I felt awful.

There goes a perfectly good meal – again.

# Chapter Three
## Thursday, March 4th, 1976

I cleaned myself up after the little incident as best as I could and then went to bed only to wake up the next morning with awful breath. I ate a bowl of stale cereal and brushed my teeth the best I could as my parents slept their lives away in their room. Afterwards, I headed on to school, or, my second hell.

I got looks from people as I walked in the front door. Even the secretaries at the front office looked at me funny and I knew why after I thought about it. My dad had given me a black eye when he was usually good about not leaving any extremely visible marks, and I saw it this morning as I brushed my teeth. I could also feel it, but it wasn't too bad.

None of my teachers liked me, and they didn't even care about the bruise. I sat through all my classes with them just giving me dirty looks, along with the other classmates. Sometimes they called on me so they could try and embarrass me if I didn't know the right answer. But, I'd always have it.

"Who was assassinated in relation to the beginning of World War I... Victor?"

I looked up at my American History teacher with my black eye and everyone else stared.

"Archduke Franz Ferdinand," I said, and then I continued scribbling in my notebook.

He moved on with the lesson and before I knew it, class was over and I was ready to go to the one class where, at least, I think the teacher cared about me.

English IV with Mrs. Huffman.

She was only twenty-three years old and got married when she was twenty-one. People made jokes that it was probably when she got drunk in Vegas and then just married the first guy she saw, but she explained it was more than that. They were high school sweethearts and he just knew how to charm her. I forgot what line of business he was in, but he was gone a lot and she missed him. Whenever there was free time in class and someone would listen, she would talk about him.

Most of the time, it was just me that listened.

She was so enchantingly beautiful with dark brown eyes that would stop any man dead in their tracks and blond hair that only waved in the wind; otherwise it stayed calm all the rest of the time. Maybe that's why I listened to her all the time. Also, she'd write little notes on my papers telling me I did well or she was glad I paid attention or something like that.

*It's so hard not to pay attention when you're so damn beautiful,* I'd always think, but of course, it was never said.

She was always in the classroom and greeted everyone as they walked in, unlike most teachers who stood out in the halls and talked. I didn't really hope that she would notice my black eye, but I felt like she would.

And she did, like anyone with two eyes would be able to.

"Victor...!"

I stopped in the doorway and looked at her, a little embarrassed. A few other kids looked over at me and she stepped up to me. I felt hot.

"Victor, what happened?" she started.

"Oh, this?" I said, acting like I didn't know. My head fell as I said, "Yeah, I tripped and fell, no big deal."

She carefully lifted my head and I let her. She made a face and I knew she didn't believe me, but then the bell rang and I said, "I guess I'll go to my seat now."

"See me after class, if you're not in too big of a hurry to go to lunch," she said, in a way that made me have bad thoughts. Hormones, what can I say?

We were finishing up *A Catcher in the Rye* and I really wasn't thrilled about it. I'm not even going to elaborate why, I just don't like it.

When class ended, I just sat in my desk and waited for every student to vacate the room. Once that happened, the lovely look from her eyes made me feel safe to tell her everything, but I knew I couldn't.

"What's going on, Victor? I know you didn't fall to get that black eye," Mrs. Huffman asked.

"It's uh... I..." I started.

"I know it's your eye," she said, and that made me smile.

"Look, Mrs. Huffman..."

"You can call me Ashley... just not in front of the other kids."

"Okay..." I said, feeling hotter. "Ashley, I just can't really talk about it. It's just..."

"Is it kids at school, or maybe your home life?" she asked.

"Uh..."

"Look, I know you had to move to Detroit three years ago because of your dad's company going under. Does he... take it out on you?"

I was feeling kind of mad and I almost went crazy on her for saying that, but instead I said, "It's kids at school, I guess... I gotta go to lunch, sorry."

And with that, I walked out of the room and didn't look back, but the whole time, I had a feeling that she was watching me.

## The Platinum Briefcase

*****

Lunch was about the same as usual; one of the lunch ladies likes me for some reason so she gives me a free peanut butter and jelly sandwich every day. Her name was Delores, and she had a nice smile, but I never really talked to her much. I just got my sandwich and sat down outside.

It was a pretty nice day outside even though it was getting a little warmer, but there was still a breeze to where I could still wear my jacket comfortably. When I sat down on the top step outside the front of my school, I felt a pain in my stomach from where my dad kicked me and I hesitated to eat. I didn't want to throw it all up again. That was the worst to me... Having that small sense of satisfaction after eating just to lose it all afterwards. I had heard of girls making themselves throw up, but I never understood that.

Just as I took a bite, I looked up to see the rulers of my second hell.

Johnny Fargo and his three friends were arriving to school, a little later than the rest of us. The only way he was able to skip was his dad basically paid for his education and Johnny didn't have to do shit.

He wore all the latest styles and he was kind of a hard-ass pretty boy. His hair was brown and kind of out there, and he wore jeans with a plaid button up shirt and a blazer. He sort of had a half smile and half disgusted face all the time, and opposite of what his appearance showed, he was pretty strong.

At least, I think he was. Or one of his other friends that hit me was strong.

But all of those thoughts ceased to exist when I saw him look up at me with the last puff of his cigarette.

"Hey, there's my punching bag," Johnny said with a sick smile.

I took my last bite of the sandwich and ran for the doors. They were still across the street and the traffic was moderate so I had a little headway on them.

I ran past the office and the secretaries saw me, and they knew what was going to happen, but they didn't care. In some ways, I feel like they cheer Johnny and his friends on. Maybe not out loud, but definitely in a mental sense. All because of how my father's company bankrupted hundreds of workers.

When I was halfway down the main hall, I turned left to the senior's hall and I heard them enter the front doors. Johnny called out, "There!" and I heard their feet coming toward me. I didn't even really have the strength to run but I tried the best I could to run away. The only way I could think of escaping them was the window in the bathroom. I had squeezed out of there before and it led out to the courtyard, and from there...

My right foot slipped on a milk carton and I came crashing down. The bruise on my thigh felt like it was on fire as I rolled over and tried to get up, but there they were, closing in on me in the middle of the hallway.

I was just inches from the bathroom door, and I knew they'd drag me in there and have their fun until the end of lunch.

"A milk carton, eh? Surprised it wasn't a banana peel," Johnny said, and he howled with laughter.

That's when he noticed my black eye and the expression on his face changed to something more sinister.

"Oh, daddy already got to you, didn't he?"

I really hated Johnny Fargo. Why his family moved from Jersey to Detroit, I have no idea.

"Oh well, I'll just have the leftovers then," Johnny said.

Just as he was about to pick me up, the men's bathroom door swung open and my hero came walking out.

It was Danny Ponchello, the most infamous kid at our school. He always wore a suit or something with a blazer and it was rumored that he was armed with a pistol every day, even at school. Crazy enough, they said he was armed because his dad was the Don of a small mafia right here in Detroit. Of course, I didn't really know any of that for sure. But that's what everyone said, so why not go with the flow?

Today he wore a polo shirt with black slacks and a black trench coat that went about halfway to his knees. He had a firm stance, and his messy black hair with the boyish face made all the girls crazy for him, but they never dared approach him for who he may be.

He stopped in the doorway and looked down at me, and then looked to Johnny Fargo.

"Who's the victim today, Johnny?" Danny asked, trying to act cool.

"Walk away, Daniel," Johnny said, and I could tell his ambition of beating me up was rapidly declining, "this isn't your business."

"It's slowly becoming my business," Danny replied in a light-hearted way, taking the toothpick out of his mouth and throwing it aside. "And if it's my business, it's my dad's business too."

That's when Johnny knew there was no hope in beating me up, at least, not for right now. He and his friends looked at each other and one of the friends said, "Okay Johnny, I think we should go."

Johnny looked to see his friends walking off without him, and so he looked back at me and made the final threat.

"You won't be so lucky after school," Johnny said, and with that, his little gang rolled out.

Danny stepped up in front of me and put his hand out to me. I was nervous to take it, but I did anyway. He pulled me up with ease and I brushed myself off.

"You okay?" Danny started off. "They didn't give you that black eye, did they?"

"No, that was an accident," I replied, too timid to make eye contact with him.

"Hmm, that isn't an accident," Danny argued. "I've seen my fair share of black eyes and I know that isn't an accident."

I was nervous to even be in the same presence as him, but luckily the bell rang and I said, "Thanks but I guess I better go to class."

And for the first time ever, I turned my back to a man of the mob.

*****

The rest of the day droned on and I really couldn't wait to leave, which was a little surprising. It's not like my house was really any better, but I was tired of getting all these weird looks about my black eye. And now, I got even more weird looks because people heard that Danny Ponchello saved me from Johnny Fargo.

No one even cared to ask me about it though; they just talked about it right in front of me.

Finally when the last bell rang, I started putting all of my Economics supplies away and everyone else walked out, ready to go hang out elsewhere. I was the last person to walk out; even the teacher went to the teacher's lounge for the last swig of coffee.

As soon as I walked out, I turned right and I saw them.

Usually, Johnny would've given up for the day and just waited till tomorrow, but I guess he was just really itching to beat the shit out of me. It made me wish I had that gun instead of Danny supposedly having it... just to have the upper hand, not to kill him.

The smirk appeared on his face again and I saw the bathroom. It's the only way to get out without having to run by him. I'll even bust the window out just to escape.

Then, Johnny and his friends started running toward me and I burst through the bathroom door ahead. The window was before me, but it was too high up. I grabbed the trash can and shoved it toward the window so I could climb up on it. I stepped onto it and started messing with the window and I didn't hear them running anymore. I couldn't take any chances though. I kept my eyes on the window, focused on my escape.

The window was already cracked open from kids smoking during passing period, so all I needed to do was just give it a little...

That's when the trashcan was kicked out from under my feet and I slammed onto the ground, causing my bruises to burn once more. I heard Johnny Fargo's laugh and trash was everywhere around me. So much pain, and so little time to care about it.

"You think your bitch friend is going to come save you now?" Johnny started, kicking me in the stomach.

I usually kept my mouth shut, but this was getting to be too much for me.

"Fuck you," I replied the best I could.

"You fight back with your words and not your fists. I like it," Johnny said, and he and his friends started closing in on me.

"Leave me alone, Johnny."

"Mmm, maybe after we graduate, I will. And I'll let your dad have all the fun."

My mind started venturing off into dark thoughts of how I'd beat Johnny up and make him pay… but before I went too far off into the deep end, my only savior returned again.

They started in on me but I saw the bathroom door swing open silently and Danny walked in, but this time he wasn't alone. Two I knew were thugs from his dad's mafia were here too, and they were dressed in all black with black trench coats. I wondered how they were able to get into the school, but I didn't care. They were coming to save me.

"Remember what I said, Johnny?" Danny called out.

The bathroom door swung shut and Johnny and friends looked back to Danny. The anxiety in the room was higher than Jimi Hendrix at Monterey.

"I said it was none of your goddamn business…" Johnny said.

Danny stood in the middle of the two henchmen and the showdown was about to begin.

"It's my dad's business now," Danny said. "You guys know what to do."

Both henchmen stepped forward and one of Johnny's friends was dumb enough to try and strike first. The first henchman knocked his fist away like a fly and then swung his right hand into his rib cage. Johnny's friend dropped to the ground like a sack of potatoes and I noticed the brass knuckles in the henchman's hand.

The younger henchman decided to go the taunting route by saying, "You know what a steel toe boot feels like?"

Before the other friend could answer, the henchman kicked him in the shin and he fell to the ground, instantly crying. The third friend started whimpering and he tried to run out, but the first henchman tripped him and Danny kicked him in the face.

Now it was just Johnny, who had just been standing there in shock the whole time. His friends were done for, and I started feeling a strange sense of satisfaction flow over me.

"All right, you guys had your fun," Johnny stated, trying to save himself.

"Not all of it," the first henchman said, and then he looked to the second one.

"Jordan, hold that kid for me."

The second henchman, Jordan, stepped up to Johnny and Johnny tried to defend himself but it didn't work. Jordan swung around behind him and locked his arms behind him. Johnny started crying before the first henchman even started hitting him.

"Hey kid, don't cry yet. I haven't even started," the first henchman said. "Look, I'll take it easy on you and just have brass on one of my fists, okay?"

Johnny screamed and tried to break free, but the henchman started swinging and it was unlike anything I'd ever seen. He was either a boxer in the past life, or just recently retired. He went at him only for a few seconds and Johnny's legs went weak.

That's when Jordan turned to me and asked, "Do you want to finish this?"

I decided I should probably get myself off the ground at that time, and as I did, I replied, "No..."

I figured they had already done enough.

But then, Jordan nodded and said, "Okay then, I'll do it."

Jordan whipped his arms away and put Johnny in a headlock and began squeezing. Immediately, Johnny started trying to fight back and his face turned redder than a tomato. Gasping for air, he started spitting and squirming, but I really began to worry when he started to not fight back.

"Jesus Christ, you're going to kill him!" I shouted.

"Relax, kid, I'm just giving him a nap," Jordan said with a small laugh.

"No, actually, I think the kid is right, you should let him go," the first henchman said.

"Oh all right."

Jordan eased the grip up on Johnny and threw him to the side like nothing. Johnny slammed into a stall door and collided with the pee-stained tile floor. The other kids were moaning and groaning on the ground and I didn't really know what to make of the situation. In some ways, I actually felt bad for Johnny Fargo and his crew.

I didn't really want to make a big deal out of it though, so I just looked to Danny and said, "I better get going."

I rushed past them and out the door. As the door swung shut, I heard Danny call for me, but I kept walking and made my way home in the strangest mood.

# Chapter Four
## Friday, March 5th, 1976

Last night went surprisingly well after the craziness at school. My dad was watching TV and wasn't in an angry mood and my mom slept away in her room so I just went on to my room and stayed quiet. I always liked to write poetry in my free time, and draw pictures. I felt like I could do whatever I wanted to in those moments.

Also, I couldn't really fall to sleep that night without wondering what happened. Why was Danny so hell bent on helping me? He had never helped me beforehand... maybe he was just tired of being alone too. Nobody really talked to him, just about him. And he knew I was in the same situation too.

But bringing his dad's men with him to beat up a few high school bullies..?

Did that mean all the rumors were true? Danny's dad was a... Don? A crime boss? Someone who made money in practically every illegal way possible?

I couldn't really remember which thought I left off on before falling asleep, but I guess I could find it all out sooner or later. Maybe even Chief Ramzorin would know about it.

Anyway, I went to school on Friday feeling a little more confident. I really hoped Johnny wasn't dumb enough to try anything again, but he might be. When I saw him in the hallway, he was weak with a noticeable goose egg on his forehead where he hit the floor. Only two of his friends were with him today, and they were both bruised and pitiful. Johnny was telling some bullshit story about some black kids jumping them at the park or something like that, but no one really believed them. They knew the other side to it. How exactly? I don't know. I didn't boast around telling people about it, and I was surprised the principals didn't intervene or anything.

I still got some looks, but they were now more fearful than spiteful. I kind of liked it. There was no reason they should hate me. They just judged me on how I dressed and my lack of communication with everyone. I was the anti-social freak.

Oh well.

Even Mrs. Huffman gave me a look, but I couldn't really read what it meant.

At lunch, I started to head over to where I sat yesterday, but I wondered if Johnny would see me.

Surprisingly enough, he approached me.

"Victor."

I turned around, a little startled by Johnny's voice. It was now raspy and a little more threatening.

"Next time, Danny and his little goons won't know how to find us, you got that?" Johnny said.

With this new found confidence, I decided to talk back.

"I don't think you're in any position to make threats like that."

"He's right."

I turned around to see Danny walking up behind me, but he was all alone. I didn't think that really mattered though.

I saw a few eyes in the lunch room look over at us and Johnny felt the heat.

"Why don't you and your still able-bodied friends go take a hike?" Danny suggested.

Johnny sneered and started to turn away.

"Your dad's a crook."

He said it so quietly I almost didn't hear him, but Danny did.

"Don't be surprised if you come home to ashes, Johnny," Danny said, and he grabbed me to talk to me alone.

We stepped over by the water fountain on the other side of the cafeteria and I wondered what Danny was going to say. His final comment toward Johnny sort of made my day.

When we stopped, Danny looked at me with a faint smile and said, "I'm a little hurt, Victor. I expected at least a thank you after what I did for you yesterday."

I tried to figure out how to put all my thoughts together.

"I appreciate that you... saved me. But I thought it was a little too much."

"A little too much?" Danny asked. "They were asking for it. They deserved it. Johnny Fargo has been king of the playground for too long."

"I just, I don't know... I haven't seen anything like that before..."

"At least, not on other people," Danny said, finishing my thought. "But you get hit like that, Victor. I know you do. I know what your dad does. I know that black eye wasn't an accident."

I hated when people mentioned my dad.

"You don't know my dad," I said.

"My dad does."

That surprised me.

"Or, he used to. But that doesn't matter."

"What do you want from me?" I finally asked.

"Friendship. Trust. The usual," Danny said with a smile.

"This is some way to make a friend."

"Well, and maybe a job offer."

That's when my brain kicked in.

"No, I'm not working for your dad," I stated.

"Hey," Danny interrupted. "Whatever you've heard about my dad is bullshit. He's a businessman, that's all. You'd be working in a warehouse moving boxes and sweeping the floor, that's it. It's a legitimate business."

He seemed sincere, but I wasn't sure what to say.

"C'mon. All I ask is that you come over after school. I know you don't have anything better to do."

He said it with such confidence it hurt my feelings. But he was right. Besides, when was the last time I hung out with someone besides Ramzorin, someone my own age?

"Okay, where do I meet you?" I asked.

Danny smiled, knowing he had won me over.

"You know which car is mine, right?"

"Yeah, the '74 Stingray?" I asked, a little excited.

"That's the one. Just meet me there and we'll hang out."

I could feel there was nothing more to be said for now, and my feeling was reassured when Danny walked away.

But, I was worried to find out if what people said about Danny's dad was true or if Danny was telling the truth.

I guess I'd be the first to actually find out.

## Chapter Five

I had never been so excited about school being over in my life.

At first, I was very worried about hanging out with Danny after school. I mean, everyone said that Danny's dad was a Mobster and all this other bad stuff, but they never really talked to Danny or even went anywhere with him to find out if it was true. I was going to be the first one to actually go with Danny somewhere, and I felt kind of special, to say the least.

As I stepped out of the school and into the student parking lot, I saw kids standing by their cars and discussing where they'd go next. I was never a part of those crowds, and my presence seemed to make them all shiver. They had no idea why I was out there, but if they kept their eyes on me, they'd soon find out.

I browsed over the parking lot, trying to find Danny, and when I did, I was surprised I didn't see him earlier.

Danny was standing beside his prized possession: A 1974 hard top Chevy Stingray with a glossy red finish. Danny's trench coat flapped about in the wind and he wore black aviator sunglasses to shield out the sun that popped out from the clouds every once in a while. He stood alone, and no other cars parked near him. There was a story that one time, a little sophomore girl scratched her station wagon against Danny's car and Danny went ballistic. But thinking about it now, I never saw Danny get mad about it, or even shed a tear.

When I started to approach him, I felt peoples' eyes widen and a few comments thrown around, but I decided to ignore them, just like usual.

Danny looked up at me but I couldn't tell exactly where his eyes were from how thick the glasses were. I knew for sure when he said my name.

"Victor," he started out, throwing his toothpick to the side. "Are you ready to go?"

"Yeah," I said, with only half confidence.

"Well, get in," he said as he turned around to put the key into the door and open it up.

I stepped over to the passenger's seat door and squeezed in. I wasn't used to fitting into such a small car, but after I settled in it was rather comfy. As soon as Danny started up the car, "Trampled Underfoot" came on the radio and it was pretty loud. Danny rolled his window down manually and I reached over to roll mine down too.

"I love Zeppelin," Danny commented. "What about you?"

"Yeah, they're good," I replied.

Danny revved the engine a few times and then we pulled away, heading to... wherever.

"Excited for school to end?" Danny asked.

I could hardly hear him over the music.

"I'm excited," Danny said before I could answer. "I can't wait to start working full-time for my dad."

"And what exactly is this work you were talking to me about?" I asked.

Danny turned the music down a little as we cruised by every other car. It's like they were moving out of the way for Danny.

"Huh? Oh, the work. Yeah, it's nothing that big. Just moving boxes around and stuff. He pays four bucks an hour if you do a good job."

"That's a lot," I said, and a few fantasies ran through my head.

"You bet it is."

"But, what does your dad... do, exactly?"

"I told you," Danny started off, "he's a businessman. He owns different businesses and makes sure everything goes right. The warehouse you'd work at is just part of my dad's business. He owns little shops and stores around Detroit. Nothing too crazy."

"Then why does everyone say he's a mobster?" I asked.

Danny looked at me with a little bit of a disconcerting look. When he turned away, he explained.

"I won't lie to you, Victor, I know you're smarter than that. Yes, my dad runs somewhat of what you'd call a gang, but I promise you that one day, it will be legitimate as a business. The warehouse is nothing illegal, so if you're worried about falling into that crowd, don't. My father just has enemies, like yours."

I started to feel worry and regret as he kept driving out of town and farther north.

"What about you? Which side do you fall on?" I asked.

"I work at the warehouse. My dad doesn't let me work with... the other side."

"Are you wanting to?"

"It's a little more exciting. You get out more often and it's better than lifting twenty pound crates a hundred times a day," Danny explained.

When the silence came around again, I started to think about other rumors I could ask Danny. One came up, but I didn't want to ask about it. Rumor has it that Danny's mom was killed by Danny's dad because she knew everything about the gang and she was going to run off and tell the police. I didn't know how true that was either. But since I hated people mentioning my dad and everything that happened, I decided to not mention his mom.

We had been driving up toward Birmingham for about twenty minutes when Danny suddenly veered left and took a small secluded drive into the hills. Ventura Highway was playing on the radio and I knew Danny knew this route by heart. Trees loomed over us and I felt as though we were about to enter a fortress.

But when the trees subsided, I set my eyes upon the most massive house I had ever seen.

Up the drive just a little further was an iron clad gate that had two guards standing by it, both were standing still and I knew they had guns on them just by how they stood. Beyond the gate was a plain gray rock mansion that was longer than it was tall with a vast green empty courtyard before it. The roof was slated with stone and the windows were ovular and tall with balconies outside almost every one. To the east of the house was a garage that was built the same way, but the garage doors were shut and didn't look very penetrable at all.

It was a fortress, and it made me scared and excited to be able to go in.

"Wow," I went ahead and said.

"Thanks," Danny said. "My grandpa designed it and built it quite a few years ago, back when my dad was still young. He remembers building it alongside his dad. Then, my dad and I added on the garage when I was little."

"That must have been quite a project," I commented.

"It was. Our handprints are in the concrete on the slab right in front of the door."

But as we got closer to the gate, the two guards became a little more suspicious of us and I figured it was because of me. Danny slowed down since the gate wasn't being opened and one of the guards stepped up to Danny's window.

Danny stopped the car and the questioning began.

"Who's your friend?" the guard asked.

The other guard walked up to my door and put his hand into his coat. I felt queasy.

"This is Victor," Danny said.

"Oh, the one from school that Leo and Jordan saved?" the guard asked, a lot more light-hearted now than before.

Danny nodded and the guard stuck his head in. The guard by my window stepped away to go open the gate.

"Hi, Victor," the guard by Danny's window said. "My name's Scott, and welcome to the manor."

I nodded and he stepped back to let Danny drive through the now opened gate. As we drove over to the garage, I saw a few other men in black suits walking about and smoking. There were so many men already, I wondered how many would be inside.

"Am I already known around here?" I asked.

"To a certain degree, yes," Danny said, and he turned his radio completely off and put the Stingray in park. The engine didn't want to go to sleep just yet.

"Let me get the garage door and you just stay here," Danny said as he stepped out of the car.

I was scared to even try and go anywhere without Danny. It seemed like if I stepped out for just a second, I'd get shot.

Danny pulled up the garage door with ease and then ran back to the Stingray. When we pulled in to the brightly lit garage, I saw a ton of other vehicles and realized how big the garage was. There were about ten other vehicles in there, all in different designated parking spots and all ranging from the early 20s to today. Danny drove all the way to the other end of the garage and pulled into his spot, which was actually marked with his name. The car we parked by looked seriously reinforced and hard to mess with and I knew it must be the car that Danny's dad rode in.

When Danny finished parking, he turned off the car and stepped out. I stepped out with him and looked around. The garage was clean and bright. The other cars were waxed and polished to a fine point, and it almost hurt to look at them, but it was worth it.

That's when I realized we weren't alone.

The sound of a wrench hitting the concrete floor startled me and Danny motioned me to follow behind him.

"Goddammit!"

We approached a black and white 1954 Bel Air with the hood up and I almost drooled. The car was practically brand new, but the angry mechanic came rolling out from under it with grease all over his hands and a new red mark on his face.

"That's the second time today I've dropped that wrench!" the mechanic complained as he sat up and wiped his head.

"But it was the first time it hit your head?" Danny asked.

"First time today, but not the first time ever," the mechanic said, and then he looked at me.

"Oh, sorry Phil, this is Victor. Victor, this is Philip Masters, our mechanic."

What hair he had left was slicked back and grease stains were all over his hands, face, and blue-ish gray jumpsuit. The redness on his forehead increased but he still managed to keep a slight smile on his face.

Phil didn't care about the grease as he stuck out his hand and said, "Nice to meet you, Victor. I actually used to work for your dad back in the day."

It's a small world.

"I knew your name sounded a little familiar," I said as I went ahead and shook his hand.

He saw that my hand turned black after the handshake and he said, "Oh, I guess I should've wiped off my hands first. But you're a man that's not afraid of getting a little dirty, I like that."

He grabbed a rag off the ground and started to wipe off his hands and face. It mainly just smeared it around, but I wasn't going to complain to him.

"Coming to work for the family, kid?" Phil asked directly.

"Uh, it's possible," I replied, not sure what to say.

"I would highly recommend it. They take care of you here, might even offer you a room if you need it."

As much as I liked the idea of not spending another night in fear at my house, I wasn't sure that this place would make me much more comfortable. My father had said I needed to leave after graduation, but Chief Ramzorin had said he would be able to take me in at that time.

"Well, I'm going to go ahead and take Victor inside," Danny said as he started walking away.

I followed behind Danny and Phil said, "Okay, just close the garage door on the way out. It was nice meeting you, Victor."

I agreed with him and we stepped outside into the cloudy atmosphere. Danny pulled the garage door shut and then said, "Come this way," and we ran across the freshly mowed grass to the front door of the manor. To my surprise, the door wasn't locked as Danny pulled down on the door handle and pushed the great door forward with ease.

We stepped into a small resting area with a green hallway that extended just a little bit until it split east and west. The first door on the right was to a separate bathroom that stood alone, and then as we walked forward into the hallway, to the left there was an open double doorway that led to a living area with the back of a couch facing us and a staircase in the left corner. There were men in there with the TV on and they played cards. Smoke danced about as the A/C kicked on and Danny led me farther down the hallway.

"If you take the right hallway, you'll pass the kitchen, the dining room and the basement door on the way to the other staircase, and if you take this left hallway, which I wouldn't recommend, you'll go on to my dad's office, which is where he talks to you in private."

When he showed me the long stretch to his dad's office, he turned around and headed to the kitchen. The whole experience was a little breathtaking, considering I hadn't been in such an enormous house in so long. The family pictures on the walls showed such a great time span that I was surprised they could fit them all on the walls. One picture I noticed was a black and white grainy photo of a small ship leaving some dock. I wondered if Danny's family immigrated here, or at least, how long ago they did.

Danny led me into the kitchen and there was a petite woman in an apron walking around and cleaning. She had a darker tone of skin and I couldn't tell if she was just tan or maybe from somewhere else, but that question was answered when I heard her speak.

"Victor, this is Michelle. She keeps the house clean," Danny asked.

"As clean as I can," she said, and the Italian accent almost spewed out of her.

She left with an intoxicating smile and I was glad I got to see her.

Pots and pans hung above the stove in the middle of the kitchen and it made me wonder what all the cabinets were full of.

Danny showed me pretty soon after the thought passed.

"Are you hungry?"

Before I could answer, Danny opened the pantry door and my eyes lit up. There were all kinds of chips and snack foods and I couldn't believe my eyes. I thought the pantry was aisle seven at the grocery store. I felt my mouth start to salivate like crazy but I tried to just normally say, "A little, yeah."

He tossed me a bag of potato chips and then he grabbed himself a Twinkie. I waited for him to open the Twinkie before I ripped into the bag and devoured the chips. I think he watched me eat the chips in amazement, because I finished them before he finished the small Twinkie.

"You know, you could stay for dinner too if you'd like," Danny mentioned.

"Uh, maybe some other night," I said as I glanced at the clock above the doorway. I needed to be home within the next hour, but I didn't want to complain.

"We would love to have you," a new voice boomed from the entrance of the kitchen.

I jerked around to see who spoke and I was a little shocked to find out who it was when Danny spoke.

"Hi, Dad."

Danny's dad stood in a black suit with a silver tie and he looked like a model from a magazine. His hair was slicked back perfectly and there was a little bit of scarring on his face. Standing at six foot-one, he was lean and happy looking. He seemed wise and well-to-do, but I didn't want to buy into it so quickly.

"Hello Daniel, is this Victor?" he asked smoothly.

"Yes."

Danny's father seemed to smile as he waved his hand lightly and said, "Come on back to my office Victor, I'd like to have a word with you."

Danny's dad started to walk off and I was frozen in my place. But, Danny's semi-comforting voice said, "You better not keep him waiting," and just seconds later, I found myself locked inside the mobster's office.

## Chapter Six

At the time, I didn't know how rare it was for someone to go into Don Ponchello's office without being in trouble or having a high chance of coming out alive. The dimmed hallway on the way to his office made me feel a little more insecure again and I started to wonder if all of this was even a good idea. Sure, I liked Danny a lot already. He was the first person besides Chief Ramzorin and the lunch lady that fed me, and Danny was the only one who had protected me. But, maybe coming over here and accepting a job was too much. Phil seemed happy, sure, but what about me? Right now I wasn't very happy, I was full of anxiety.

More pictures hung from the green wallpaper with white diamond shapes riddled all about and I walked past without paying much attention to them. Danny seemed to think that his dad didn't like to wait, so I wasn't going to make him. I hurried down the hallway and saw a guard at the end by the office door. He was wearing a red button up shirt that was faded and his slacks had seen better days, along with his warping dress shoes. He looked like he was in his mid-fifties but he was built and stout, and only a little taller than me. His black hair was thinning out and it was starting to turn white. As I stepped up closer to him, trying to act like I wasn't intimidated, a small smile danced across his face and he spoke first.

"It's nice to see you again, Victor," the man said.

"I don't believe I know you," I replied.

"Well you should," he said, sort of in a joking way. "I helped Jordan beat up those punks for you at the school."

"Oh!" I said, and I remembered him as the boxer. "Yeah I remember you now. Thanks, by the way."

"Don't mention it," he said. "My name's Leonard, by the way, but most people just call me Leo."

"Nice to meet you," I said.

"Likewise," Leo replied in a deep and rough voice. "But, the boss is probably waiting for you to go on in, so I'll let you go ahead."

With that, Leo turned sideways to open the door and I stepped into the bright office.

The office was lavish and everything looked like it was worth a million dollars.

The chandelier hanging above his desk seemed out of place but I didn't even mention it. Behind the desk a majestic portrait of a man in an old suit hung on the wall a little farther up from everything else. A few oak chairs sat about for other people, but there were mainly two chairs in front of the desk for guests. The desk had papers neatly assorted in different stacks and a green attorney's lamp was there for extra light. A bookshelf full of fiction and non-fiction books was to the left and the right just had a mirror and a chest of drawers. The main color in there was red though, and it made me think of Christmas.

I think Don Ponchello noticed my admiration and he let me take it all in for a little bit more as Leo asked, "Do you need me in here, boss?"

"No, I think I'd like to just be alone with Victor," Danny's dad said as he slowly pushed in his chair and remained standing.

Leo nodded and closed the door softly. The light click made me look back at the door and then when Danny's dad spoke, I turned back around.

"My name is Mark Ponchello," he said as he stuck out his hand.

I stepped forward and shook his hand. He smiled as I did and then afterwards, he pointed to one of the empty chairs in front of his desk and said, "Please, sit down."

I didn't want to seem nervous or anything like that, so I glanced down at the chair and pulled it out to sit. Once I tried to make it look like I was comfortable, Don Ponchello began a little speech.

"You might be wondering who the man in the portrait is?" he asked. "That's my dad, and I still look up to him more than anyone else. He knew the importance of hard work and dedication to family and friends and I tried to keep those values when I took his place in power. Sometimes though, in this day and age, it seems like people are getting harder and harder to trust, and so it's not easy to keep that dedication with people who aren't loyal to me."

I felt like I knew where he was going with this, but then he took a hard left turn.

"I know you've probably heard rumors about me or about Danny's mom."

I didn't respond, but he stared me straight in the face and said, "All I can say is, I didn't kill Danny's mom or have her killed. She ran off when he was seven and never gave a reason why. I tried to find her, but I couldn't. She was long gone. We met in Chicago and I looked there first, but she wasn't there and her family didn't know where she was either."

That made me feel bad for Danny. I knew what it was like to have a parent who changed drastically and made me not like them anymore, but not what it would be like for them to just run off completely. But also, I wondered if Don Ponchello threatened Danny's mom, which then made her run away.

Who knows?

"I knew your father, and I'm sorry about how he is now," Don Ponchello moved on. "He was a nice man just a few years ago. It's a shame what money can do to someone."

"It's okay," I said, surprised that he even knew my dad. "How do you know what he's like now?"

"Oh everyone knows what he's like now... And I don't mean to sound nasty when I say that. When Mr. Hurston ran off, all the attention went to your father since he stuck around, and after your mom's article in the paper... Need I say more?"

I shook my head.

"Anyway, Danny knew that black eye wasn't from those bullies at your school. One of your neighbor's has complained about the cries from your apartment. I truly am sorry about all of it though."

"Don't worry about it..." I said, not wanting to talk about it anymore.

Don Ponchello stepped toward his desk and pulled out his chair to finally sit down. He pushed his tie closer to him as he sat down and looked at me.

"So, let's talk about these bullies you have at school," the Don started, and I saw him pull a cigarette from his jacket. "Do you mind if I smoke?"

"No, not at all," I replied.

"Good," he said as he struck the match on the side of the desk and covered the cigarette with one hand to light it. Afterwards, he waved the match around in the air to put it out, and after a long puff, he continued, "Victor, I don't like bullies. I never have and I never will. I used to get picked on as a kid because my English wasn't great. But that's when I decided to show them who was in charge, and my dad helped me with it. So, since I know your father doesn't care, I was going to offer you the chance to make those bullies disappear."

The way he said "disappear" made me automatically think he meant something else. That had to be what he meant.

"No," I said, and the demanding tone seemed to surprise him. "Why would you kill them? They're young and stupid, that's all. I don't need them dead."

Knowing this was all a bad idea, I started to stand up and walk out, but then I knew that was an even worse idea.

"Victor," the Don said calmly. I stopped getting up out of the chair and looked at him. "I'm sorry, that's not what I meant... I just meant, relocate them somewhere else. But I understand if you want to deal with this on your own."

"I don't think they're going to bother me after what Jordan and Leo did to them,"

I said.

A smile appeared on the Don's face and he said, "Good. Then the lesson was learned."

He flicked off some ashes into the ashtray and took another puff. The smoke came out of his nose and mouth and he said, "Now, let's move on to the real reason you're here. Danny said you might like a job."

I didn't want to try and specify a legal job, so I just said, "Yes."

"That's good. I could use someone like you. Young and not entirely hating life just yet," he said, and I could tell he decided to reword the rest of what he had to say. "I'd like you to work at the warehouse with Danny, but I have a little more of a pressing matter at the moment."

"Like what?"

"Well, today's the day we need to collect from the businesses I own and Danny's wingman is out of town right now, so I was wondering if you could go with him."

I waited for a second to see if he'd say more, and when he didn't, I asked, "Right now?"

"Well, yes, if that's okay with you," he replied.

"What do I do?"

"It's very simple. Just ride with Danny back into town and follow him to all the stores while he collects and keep an eye out for any suspicious activity. I'm sure he'll take you right home afterwards."

It seemed simple enough, but I hated to think about what his definition of "suspicious activity" was.

But, I really had nothing to lose, and I wasn't too worried about it. If he trusted two teenagers to get this done, it shouldn't be that bad.

"Yes, I'll do it," I said with confidence.

"Good, I'm glad," Don Ponchello said with a smile. He pushed a button on his phone and said, "Leo, you can come in here now."

Leo opened the door and stepped in.

"Leo, could you go get my son and tell him Victor is going with him on the 'bacon run'?"

"Sure boss, I'll catch him for ya," Leo answered.

Leo stepped out and Don Ponchello stood up and walked around his desk. I stood up as well and made sure the chair was pushed in as closely as I could get it to where it was before. He finished off his cigarette, pushed it to death in the ashtray and then stepped forward to me.

"You ever need anything that isn't too crazy, just ask," he said.

He reached out his hand again and we shook hands once more. A feeling of acceptance ran over me and I smiled at him. He returned the smile and said, "I'm glad you're with us, Victor."

And at that moment, I thought I was glad too.

# Chapter Seven

We hopped back onto the highway from the manor and headed back into town for the bacon run.

Danny was speeding most of the way there and the wind whipped around in the car. He kept his aviators on but I was surprised the wind didn't rip them off. The radio was on but I can't remember what song was playing, because eventually, Danny turned it down and started talking.

"How'd you like the house?" he asked.

"It was beautiful," I said, feeling like I was in some sort of trance of money and power.

That's all they had, besides each other I suppose.

"Thank you," Danny replied with a smile. "My dad's dad built it from the ground up with only a few other people. They slept outside in tents until it was done."

"That's a lot of dedication."

"You're telling me. I thought building that garage with my dad was bad."

I looked out off the highway to the trees and greenery that were around us. It was the most peace I had in a while.

Even though Danny and his family were marked as bad people, I was getting comfortable with them real fast. His dad, although he worried me when he mentioned the bullies, seemed like somewhat of a nice guy.

But what did he mean by… "glad you're with us"?

What exactly was I with, or in?

Looking back on the conversation that was just moments ago, I couldn't figure out what my role was in this gang. Also, some of the stuff Danny's dad said kind of rubbed me the wrong way, but there was nothing I could really do to retaliate against it. Not without getting my head blown off.

It seemed like Danny's dad really cared about me though, and it appeared as if Danny did too. But… why? Why me? What did I do?

"Jesus, I'm going a little too fast," Danny said as we slid towards the exit that would lead us back into the city.

"So… What is this bacon run exactly?" I asked.

"Eh, it's really simple stuff, Victor. My dad owns these businesses in town and we, once a month, collect his earnings."

"How many places does he own?"

"Oh… Seven or eight small shops in town… and then a few factories and stuff on the outside of town. But Leo takes care of the factories and such. We just go to the small businesses."

"Isn't that sort of a… monopoly?" I asked, feeling a little queasy again.

"Well… Depends on how you look at it. My dad has some tax guy who always makes sure everything he does isn't too… out of line, I guess you could say. But sometimes, my dad does things that…"

Danny stopped there and I knew why. There was no way that most of the stuff they did was legal.

"I don't think it's bad though," Danny started again. "My dad offers these businesses protection and makes sure that no one hurts, damages or robs them. It's almost like he doesn't own them, he just secures them and makes them safe. You know how much crime there is around here."

I almost said, "I wonder how much of that crime is caused by your dad," but I decided that statement wasn't a wise one to be spoken.

Just off of Fifth, I saw our first business: Jack's Convenient Gas and Snacks.

I had stopped in there before and personally, I thought it was a little dirty and unkempt. Maybe Danny's dad was working on making it better.

"My dad just recently invested in this one," Danny said as he pulled up to a gas pump. "Sometimes the owner, Jack, let's us get free gas. So, why not?"

I wondered if Jack did it out of fear or kindness.

Before I could even answer the question myself, Danny stepped out of the car and headed up to the front.

"Just stay there, Victor. Keep an eye out, will ya?"

I hesitated to nod, and then he gave me a smile and went on inside the gas station. The red paint on the building was peeling off and the windows that stretched from the ground to the ceiling were dirty and grimy. The glass cover over the meter on the pump I sat by was cracked and dirty.

Was this really a smart investment?

I guess for free gas it was.

I saw Jack inside and Danny walked up to the counter to chat with him. Jack had white hair and a gray jumpsuit on with some grease stains scattered about. He looked frail and worried when Danny came in, but after a little discussion, a brown doggy bag was handed over and Danny nodded in an appreciative way. When Danny walked back out, he looked around to check what I hadn't been checking and walked around to his door.

He stepped into the car and tossed the bag at me. Surprisingly, I caught it and held it in the air for a second.

"You're not too active, are you?" Danny asked as he started to shift his car into drive.

"I used to be."

"Well hey, I know you're smart and this doesn't take a lotta brains so can you count that for me?"

"Uh…" I said, bringing the bag down to my lap. "Sure."

Danny idled for a while with his foot easing on the brake as I rustled open the bag and reached in to find ten twenties and a fifty dollar bill.

"It's two hundred-fifty dollars," I said, sort of in shock that I hadn't seen this kind of money in ages.

"Okay… That's about what my dad projected," Danny said.

With that, we drove off and onto the next stop: Laura's Laundromat.

Danny did the same thing. He made sure to park where no one was obstructing my view so I could watch for anyone, he went up to Laura and talked to her for a bit, and she seemed upset as she handed over the doggy bag of money. Danny came out, had me count it, and tell him the amount.

"It's one hundred-thirty dollars," I said, not sure how to react.

"Eh, Laura isn't getting much business since she charges extra for fabric softener and detergent if you don't bring your own. But she's a family friend and we cut her some slack."

"How much should she have given us?" I asked.

"About one-eighty. But, like I said, family friend."

Danny drove off and we headed to the next place: StrikeZone.

The bowling alley had seen better days, and this time, Danny parked so I was able to face the street. I wasn't able to see him when he was inside or anything, but I figured it was the exact same scenario playing out.

When he walked out with the doggy bag, I counted the money.

"Two hundred-ninety," I announced.

"Hey, hey!" Danny exclaimed. "That's good. He put in a little extra so that should cover for Laura."

Now the fourth place: The Family Diner.

I was able to see Danny this time and it was the exact same thing as Jack's and Laura's. Danny walks in, seemingly harmless, but the people have faces that don't make it seem very harmless. They're all disappointed about their money going, but

I guess…

"How much is this?" Danny asked as he climbed in and tossed the bag.

I flipped through the money in a trance of greed and said, "It's three hundred-forty."

"Seriously?" Danny asked in a surprised way. "You sure?"

"I'm sure, unless you want me to count it again," I suggested.

"No, it's fine, I trust you. Not sure if I should trust Bob, though."

Fifth stop: Magnificent Cakes.

I had heard about this place before. Most people getting married in this area trusted this place to make the most magnificent cake for the "best day of their life". I think my parents even got their wedding cake there. But, the overweight baker, Giovanni, also had melt-in-your-mouth cookies and breads.

"Do you want a cookie or something while I'm in there?" Danny asked.

"Oh, uh… I guess a snicker doodle would be nice," I said, still uneasy.

"Okay… Just relax, Victor, nothing bad ever happens on these, you're just a precautionary measure."

Danny stepped out and headed for the shop. Immediately, I saw Giovanni rise like yeast and he started out friendly but ended on somewhat of a disappointed note.

The doggy bag was finally handed over to Danny, and I saw him get two cookies from Giovanni after only a little conversation. Giovanni, unlike the others, actually waved goodbye as Danny walked out and took a bite of a sugar cookie that looked like it was straight from heaven.

After Danny stepped in his car and the crumbs spilled about, he handed over two bags and said, "Here's the money, and here's your cookie. Giovanni worries that he might be a little short this month. He says that the money for the spring/summer weddings will be massive next month."

"Thanks, Danny," I said for the cookie.

He nodded with a smile and then anticipated me counting the money. After I counted it, I announced, "Five hundred dollars."

"Ooo," Danny said with some hurt. "Yeah, he's about one-fifty short. Oh well, it can slide this time."

Sixth shop: Dave's Mechanical.

It was a little farther out on the edge of town but still technically in the city. Broken down semis and even some forklifts were all around in the parking lot and it seemed like Dave was a little short-handed.

I felt even worse about my wording when I saw he only had one hand.

But, he was a very punctual guy. He ran out from his office to meet Danny half way and he handed the money over like it was nothing. And, he did it with a smile on his face, which was also rare. Danny shook Dave's hand and got back in the car. It was the quickest transaction of all of them.

"Dave's a good guy," Danny said as he gently handed me the doggy bag so I had time to put my cookie away. "I think he's just afraid we're going to take his other hand and that's why he runs out to us."

"Did you take his first hand?" I asked in a surprisingly nonchalant way as I started to open the bag and count it.

"No... Lost it in Vietnam. He actually served with one of my dad's men, Roy. Did you meet him yet?"

"No, I haven't seen him."

"He's sort of an odd ball," Danny started. "He still wears a bandana that's faded green and his brown hair is getting longer and curlier every day. But, he's a good man. The war didn't make him too crazy."

When I was done counting the money, I said, "Seven hundred-fifty."

"That's good. Dave's done a lot of repairs I assume," Danny said.

Seventh shop: The Tailor.

Now this man had class written all over him. Not only did he make sure every person fit their clothes perfectly, but he fit his perfectly, too. He was old, but still able to be very precise. After the bride and groom bought their cake over at Magnificent Cakes, the groom would come over here to make sure his tux fit him well.

Mr. Dainov was his name, and Danny told me he used to be a hit man.

"I'm serious, Victor," Danny said as we pulled up and saw the old man adjust his glasses and reach down for something on the ground of his shop, "he used to work with my dad's dad and they were inseparable. Mr. Dainov was, and is probably the best out there."

Before I could comment more, Danny stepped out and went into the tailor shop. From what Danny told me, it sounded like he didn't need any protection.

Mr. Dainov greeted Danny with a hug and had the money behind his register at the front. The old man kept talking to Danny in a nice way and wishing him luck in school. Then, he made some hand gestures and I guessed he was saying that Danny keeps getting taller. That's what most adults talk about anyway. It was long and drawn out, but finally he let Danny go and Danny came out to me.

"Man, that grip he has," Danny said as he handed over the bag and then rubbed his hand.

"Why does he need protection if he's so good?" I asked as I opened the bag.

"He's still old, mind you. He's sharp as a tack but slower than a turtle. Plus, my dad feels an obligation to watch after him."

"By taking his money?" I asked.

Danny didn't seem too crazy with my tone and I decided to hold it back a little.

"I'm sorry, I didn't mean it like that."

"No, I know you did mean it like that, and all I have to say is, my dad is a good man and he's just trying to protect these businesses, Victor. My dad helps these people out more than the cops would ever do. Hell, my dad even helps them get business."

I didn't argue anymore and I just counted the money.

"Eight hundred-fifty," I said, almost unable to catch my breath from the amount.

"Mr. Dainov is a nice man," Danny said with a smile as he pressed on the gas.

Now the eighth and last shop: Mickey's Bar and Grill.

I wasn't able to see in, but I got the idea. My only question was, did Danny's dad really protect and help these places that much or was it all just extortion? I was thinking it was the latter, but Danny was really trying to convince me otherwise, and I was on the verge of believing him.

Danny came out and handed me the bag.

"That place is so damn smoky I couldn't even find the owner," Danny complained as he coughed.

I took the doggy bag from him and opened it up. As I counted the money yet again, the sun started to set.

"Four-eighty," I said simply.

"That's not very good. Leo is going to have to have a talk with him," Danny said. "That's the second time he's shorted us."

"What happens the third time?" I asked, partially not wanting to know the answer.

"We switch out the owner," Danny said.

I didn't want to explore that any more.

Danny drove off away from the bar and as he did, he said, "Well, that's it for the bacon run. How'd you like it?"

"It was relaxing at times," I said.

"Well good. I mean, I'm guessing the cookie was the best part," Danny said. "So… Think you wanna hang out or go to a party or something? I mean, it is a Friday night."

"Uh…" I started, only slightly tempted. "No, I need to go on back home. My dad will be mad if I'm out any later and he catches me."

"Okay, I understand. Some other time, then?" Danny asked.

"Yeah, of course," I said with a smile.

I liked Danny, he was a cool guy. But, his family and all this money…

It actually didn't seem like enough to run an "operation" of any kind, especially with the amount of people I saw walking around the manor.

But Danny did mention there were factories and other businesses that they gained revenue from. So, it's not just tailors who used to be hit men or one-armed mechanics.

Soon enough, Danny pulled up to my apartment complex after I told him the way and we lingered outside in his car.

"Well, thanks for the cookie and everything," I said as I started to get out.

"Wait, you need to get paid for your work."

Danny took each doggy bag and took a twenty out of each one.

"Eight stores... twenty bucks each... so how about one-sixty for keeping an eye out?"

"Oh," I said, feeling bad. "I mean, I don't know. That seems like a lot..."

"No, c'mon Victor," Danny said as he flapped the money at me. "Take it, you deserve it."

I stared at the money intently and didn't know what to do. Danny waited patiently and I felt like he knew I was going to end up taking it.

*But if I take the money, did that mean I agreed to every activity that they partook in?*

"Okay, if you say so. Thank you."

"No, thank you, Victor. I'm glad you want to work with us. I'll give you more details on the warehouse job soon, okay? I guess next week when I see you at school or something like that, all right? You have a good weekend."

"Thanks, Danny, you too."

I closed the door and tucked the money away in my jacket pocket. Danny peeled off and made someone honk at him and I just laughed.

It was the first involuntary laugh I had experienced in a while.

Now, I had to hope my dad was passed out or asleep.

Luckily, when I entered the house, the TV was blaring really loudly and I faintly heard snoring. I snuck past my parents' room to my room and locked myself in. Then, I looked around for something to hide the money in.

There was no way I was going to just hold that much money on me all the time.

That's when I spotted the box my grandfather made a long time ago and passed down to my dad, who then passed it down to me. I never put anything in it, so why not the money?

After I put the money in the small lock box, I tucked it away in my dresser and took my shoes off. I sprawled out onto my bed and smiled to myself.

That's when I realized I finally had a practical friend.

# Chapter Eight

## Monday, March 8th, 1976

My weekends are never all that exciting. For the most part, I try to stay in my room and read and draw when I can. Early in the morning, I try to go and fill up a jar of water with ice cubes and just stay in my room as much as I can. I would love to escape and go somewhere, but I know that would make my dad angry, if angry is even a good word for it.

That's why I was never sure which one I hated more: Home or school. At home, I was under the constant feeling that my dad would burst in at any moment and beat me into the next world, but at school, I felt like everyone was watching me and praying that I would explode and make a show for them. Teachers and students would just pry away at me with their eyes.

Luckily, after the incident with Johnny and Danny, Johnny Fargo stayed far away from me. If I would accidentally look his way, he would occasionally flip me off or flex, but it didn't scare me anymore.

On that Monday at lunch, Danny sat alone at a lunch table with not much hope in his eyes for a lunch buddy, so I decided to be his.

I saw everyone look over at us when I approached Danny. We were the two outcasts that everyone was afraid of.

"Hey, Danny, can I sit here?" I asked as I walked up with my questionable egg salad sandwich.

"Are you kidding?" Danny asked as he pushed out a chair with his foot, "Of course you can sit here, Victor."

I smiled at his comment and he returned a grin. I sat down beside him and everyone moved on with their lives.

"So…" Danny started out, "Spring Break starts right after school tomorrow. You excited?"

"I'm not really going anywhere or doing anything, so not really," I replied.

"Well hey, speaking of that. I talked to my dad over the weekend about you working at the warehouse and he said he'd love for you to, if you still want to."

"Oh, yeah," I said, glad it was the legal side of things. "Of course I want to."

"Cool," Danny said as he took another bite of mashed potatoes. "My dad really likes you, Victor. He says you remind him of… him."

"Oh?" I said as I decided that taking it as a compliment was the best option I had.

"Yeah. But hey, you wanna hang out tomorrow after school? I have a few little things to do today so that's why I can't today."

"You mean, just 'hang out'?" I asked cautiously.

"Yeah man, just go cruisin' or something," Danny replied. "Actually, if you want specifics, there's a really good diner that just opened up not too far from here. It's right in town, actually. They have the best milkshakes, I promise."

"Oh, uh…" I started, and I almost used the excuse that I didn't have any money, but then I remembered what Danny gave me from the bacon run. "Yeah, we can do that."

"Sweet," Danny replied with a smile.

"How long are the shifts at the warehouse?" I asked, taking the first courageous bite out of my sandwich and feeling relieved that it was good.

"We go in at about eight or nine and get off at five or six. Is that all right?"

"Yeah, that'll work. I just have something to do Wednesday night, if that's okay."

"Sure, Victor, of course it's okay. It's not like we own you now or something, you just have a job."

"It seems like my dad's job owned him…"

Realizing I said that out loud, I made a face at Danny and he looked at me with concerned eyes.

"Victor… You don't have to live there anymore. You're eighteen, right?"

"Yeah I am, but my dad said I have to stay until after I graduate so… I guess I'll just have to wait till then. Otherwise…"

Danny decided to let me stray away from the topic and we finished our lunch in peace and quiet, for the most part.

Danny was really starting to feel like a friend to me, and he seemed to feel the same way.

"Y'know Victor," Danny started, "I think this is the first time I've had someone sit by me at lunch since elementary school when they made us sit together."

"Yeah…" I said, and as I looked back on it, I replied, "I think it's the same for me too."

## Chapter Nine
### Tuesday, March 9th, 1976

School was out for the rest of the week and Danny and I walked out of school triumphantly to go to the diner he raved about the day before.

People still gave us looks as we walked out to his car to drive off, but I finally didn't care. Danny was a good guy in my opinion and I didn't think he took much interest in doing bad stuff for his dad. For the most part, he seemed like an errand boy, which I was fine with. In fact, that's all I really wanted to be if it ever came down to it.

Danny unlocked his car and we climbed in. He exclaimed something as he shut his door and started the engine.

"Woo! Aren't you excited that we don't have to come back to this shit hole for almost a full week?"

"Yeah, it's exciting," I said.

Danny didn't quite understand my living situation yet. Actually, I don't think anyone understood it.

Pretty soon, we arrived at the diner just a little ways away from Michelangelo's. Like most diners, it was built in the fifties and still tried to keep that look with it. All of the waiters wore classic diner outfits with little white hats on. Unlike the last diner I went to when I was a kid, this one was very calm and collected. Not very many people showed up there after school and I figured that's why Danny liked it. That made me like it too.

Danny headed straight for the counter after the ringing above the door stopped and the glass door closed behind us. I followed behind him, even though the sign at the front said, "Please wait to be seated". After a few more steps, I saw an older man in his late fifties give Danny a smile and open his arms to the empty seats at the counter.

"Danny, my boy, come on in, sit wherever you'd like," the husky man said as he graciously gestured to the open seats, not seeming to mind his dirtied clothing.

"You know I can't resist sitting at the counter," Danny said.

Immediately, the man wiped it down and Danny sat on a sparkly red bar stool. I pulled out the one next to him and sat down.

"Oh, you got a friend," the man said. His hair was graying and his teeth were a little bent out of shape, but other than that he looked harmless.

"Yes I do, we go to school together," Danny said. "This is Victor."

"Hi, Victor," the man said, and when I wasn't sure what to say back as we shook hands, he added, "the name's Sid."

"Hello, Sid," I replied with a smile.

"Nice to meet you," Sid said as he threw the towel over his left shoulder. "Now, I know you want the banana milkshake, Danny, but what about your friend?"

"Uh…" I said, not even knowing what they had.

I looked up at the chalkboard with all their specials and ice cream flavors. They even had ones I had never even heard of.

"I'll just go with chocolate, if you recommend it," I said jokingly.

"Of course I do, otherwise, how would I get business?" Sid asked as he leaned in and then backed away for a laugh. "Yes, the chocolate is good. One banana and one chocolate shake coming up, boys."

Sid turned his back to us to make the shakes and Danny cut in to talk to me.

"Sid is a nice guy. He's been in business here for about seven years and I've been going here ever since. My dad used to come here with me a lot too, but then…"

Danny wasn't sure how to sugarcoat it, so he just came out and said it.

"A man like my father can't really roam around in public anymore. If he does, the police follow him and threats are made. It's a complicated life."

Before I could say anything, Sid walked back over to us and one of his bus boys continued making our shakes. I never understood how those things worked, with the silver cup and the long metal rod that comes down and… shakes it, I guess. But I soon found out that the making of shakes was the least of my worries.

"You guys got a couple of lookers," Sid said with a silly grin on his face.

Danny reacted a little stronger than I did.

"No shit?" Danny exclaimed as he started to turn around to look.

Sid's eyes pointed out the two girls at the booth toward the corner of the diner. They were drinking sodas and occasionally glancing over at us. One girl was a brunette with an AC/DC shirt on and she instantly caught my eye. Her jeans looked punishingly tight and dark blue and I was in a daze. The other girl was a blonde with a loose blouse on and jeans that were similar to the brunette's. If they had a redhead with them, I guess I could make a joke.

"No, I'm serious," Sid said as he eyed them down. "You guys should go over there and say hi. I'll bring your shakes over to you."

I started to object but Danny said, "Yeah, Victor, let's go!"

Danny's eyes lit up and he jumped out of his seat to approach them. I didn't want to let him go alone, so I followed steadily behind him. As we walked over to them, I saw the blond blush and lean in to tell her friend that we were walking over to them. I was pretty sure that Danny would go for the blond, and he did.

"Hi," he started off, "is anyone else sitting here?"

"You can," the blond perked up and said with a long smile.

"Cool," Danny said as he slid into the booth beside her.

I remained standing for a second until the brunette said, "Is your friend shy or something?"

Danny scowled at me for still standing and said, "No, he's not shy, he's very personable actually," but the look in his eyes said, "Sit down right now".

I sat beside the brunette and she took another sip from her straw as she looked me up and down. I felt extremely nervous and hot, but Danny made it seem so easy.

"So, I guess we'll start out with names," Danny said in a suave way. "I'm Danny, and that's Victor, and you two are...?"

"I'm Jessica," the blond said, and then she looked to the brunette, "and that's Kassidy."

"As in, Butch Cassidy?" I asked.

"Well, it's spelled with a K instead of a C," Kassidy explained to me.

Instantly after that remark, Danny and Jessica broke off into their own conversation and left me and Kassidy to speak alone.

"You guys go to school around here?" Kassidy asked.

"Yeah, it's uh... Mavis High," I said, and pointed faintly in the direction of where it was.

"That's fun. Jessica and I are attending Ghost School," Kassidy said with a weird smile, but it seemed to intrigue me anyway.

"Huh?"

"Here you go, boys," Sid jumped in to hand us our milkshakes and then let us be.

Jessica turned to me and Kassidy while I took a sip of my smooth and creamy chocolate milkshake.

"Kassidy and I dropped out at the beginning of this year," Jessica explained.

"Oh," Danny said. "Why?"

"Our parents don't care, and I worked enough over the past few summers to get us an apartment together," Kassidy added on.

"That sounds cool," I said, referencing their freedom from their parents.

"It is," Kassidy said, and we moved back into our own conversations.

I stirred in the whipped cream and cherry and continued sipping as Kassidy kept talking.

"Do you still live with your parents?" Kassidy asked.

"Sadly," I replied.

"Wait, how old are you?" she suddenly asked, seeming a little worried.

"I'm eighteen," I answered.

"Oh, good, I just didn't want to be doing anything illegal right now."

"We're just talking, isn't that legal?"

"Talking is fine under the first amendment, but some of my thoughts aren't protected under the Constitution."

"Oh."

My face ran hot and my legs shuffled around a little.

"Are you okay?" Kassidy asked. "You seem nervous. Never talked to a girl before besides your mom?"

That's when Danny shot me a look that said "Don't ruin this for us" and so I swallowed my fear and said, "No, I've talked to girls."

I knew if I said "Plenty of girls" that she might find me as a player, so I took the route I thought was the best. And it worked.

After I saved us (well, mainly myself), we broke off into our separate conversations again and kept talking forever. We talked about everything: Music, family, books, movies. Of course, I hadn't seen any new movies lately and Kassidy was happy to suggest that I see one with her sometime in the future. She really seemed to take an interest in me, but she definitely took my breath away. In the end, my shake began to just be pure liquid chocolate and I sucked it down real quick. Danny took that as a signal, but I didn't mean it to be.

"Hey, so uh, listen," Danny said, and included me and Kassidy in the conversation. "This Friday, I'm having a party at my house."

"A party?" Kassidy asked, "Like, a birthday party?"

"Or a surprise party?" Jessica threw in.

"Oh there'll be surprises all right," Danny said as he grabbed at Jessica pretty forwardly and she giggled.

"Well, sure, we usually have Fridays off. We work at Guadalupe's downtown as servers."

"Speaking of that," Kassidy said as she looked up at the clock above the bar. "We gotta get going. We're going to be late for work."

"Hey, wait, lemme write down some directions for you," Danny said as he scrambled for a pen in his pocket.

"Here's our number, just call me and explain it," Jessica said with a smile and poppy red lips.

She had written it down before we even came over to them.

Danny took the number and then hesitated as Jessica tried to get out of the booth. I moved to let Kassidy leave and she slid out like butter on a hot pan.

"You can call us and just give us the directions. We get off at ten," Kassidy said, and she leaned in to give me a hug.

It was my first embrace in a long time and I accidentally squeezed a little harder than I meant to, but she seemed to like it. With a final smile from both girls, Danny and I were left in our imaginations.

Then, my brain clicked in.

"Wait, a party at the manor?" I asked incredulously.

"Yeah, why not?" Danny said with a smile as he left a pretty big tip on the table. "Live a little, Victor. I know you didn't even want to go talk to those girls earlier and now look, we got dates."

"But what about your dad?" I asked as I followed him out of the diner and to his car.

Sid gave us a distant wave as we stepped out into the piercing sun and Danny put his hand behind his head to wave back as we walked out.

"My dad will be out of town, Victor. Now the only problem we have is convincing the guards that stay behind that the party will be fine. It'll be contained and not too crazy, you know?"

"Already sounds like it'll be crazy if they come along," I said, hinting at the girls as we climbed into Danny's car.

"Look, Leo is going with my dad, so convincing Roy, Scott, and Jordan shouldn't be that hard. They're pretty cool guys."

Danny started up the car and I didn't want to argue anymore. I now knew I had to go to the party Friday night, otherwise, it'd piss Kassidy off, and I didn't want to do that. She was... wow.

We kept idling for a little while longer and I finally said, "Okay, where are we going now?"

"Well I'm kinda hungry... and Michelle makes the best tortellini."

I had a feeling I knew where this was going, but I didn't.

"How about you just come stay the night at the house and then we'll go to work tomorrow, bright and early?"

"Oh, uh..." I said, not sure what to say.

"I know your dad is... different, but trust me. If he does anything to you I'll have some of my dad's guys straighten him out, whaddya say?"

He jokingly elbowed my arm and I gave him a look that told him it wasn't funny to me.

"Yeah, and then you'll never see me again," I said gravely.

"Well I wouldn't want that," Danny said with a gleeful smile.

I laughed a little and tried to shake it off. Danny's charm didn't just work on Jessica. Sadly, I was falling for it too.

I thought it over in my head, and I remembered one time when I came home really late but my dad didn't even know the time of day, so he thought I just got back from school. That's how intoxicated he was… and that's how intoxicated I hope he'd be when I got back.

"Plus, you have a job now. What's so bad about that? He'll be proud of you."

Danny should have been a salesperson and not a soon-to-be mobster.

"Okay, Danny," I said, and I flailed my arms up. "Let's go eat Michelle's creamy tortellini."

Danny started to laugh as he put the car in reverse and said, "That's gross, Victor."

*****

When we arrived to the manor, the house was filled with different aromas and each one smelled better than the last. Steam rose from a huge pot as Michelle boiled the cheese-filled noodles and danced a little. At one point, Jordan came up behind her and tried to guide her into a new dance. She was all for it at first, but then he said something in her ear and she pushed him away. He laughed and so did the other guys in the kitchen. It was a madhouse. Everyone was being loud and telling stories and Danny and I were somewhere in the middle of it all.

"Jordan messes with Michelle all the time," Danny explained to me as I took a sip of root beer straight from the bottle. "I'm pretty sure they had a thing at one time, or a thing is about to happen."

Leo stood against the wall and observed the crowd as Scott and some other man approached him. The other man wore a green military jacket and a green bandana with a dark purple peace sign sewn in. His black hair looked frayed and weak like a broken up bale of hay and his posture was a little slouched.

"You see that guy right there?" Danny asked as he pointed to the man in the green jacket. "His name is Roy Harrison. He served in the Vietnam War and just got back a few years ago. No one cared about him so my dad brought him in and now he works for us."

I heard stories of Vietnam veterans not being very psychologically stable, so I asked, "Is he okay though?"

"As okay as he can be," Danny said. "You wanna go over and talk to him?"

"Sure."

We walked through the thick crowd and stepped up to Leo and the others as everyone else acted like hungry wolves waiting for their prey to fall in front of them on the fine china.

"Hello, gentlemen," Danny said in a silly sort of way.

"Hey, Danny," Leo said, which made Roy and Scott turn around.

"Oh, is this your new friend?" Roy said immediately. His mustache moved around as he talked and the rest of his facial hair stayed put.

"Yeah, this is Victor."

Roy extended his slightly dirty hand to me and I shook it.

"What's the news?" Roy asked as we finished shaking hands.

"Nothing, just, hungry," I said.

"How was the bacon run?" Roy asked.

"It was fun," I replied.

"Yeah, fun," Roy said with a scoff. "Maybe it's fun the first time but it gets really old after a while. Before you came along, I used to have to do it every single month."

"Hey, wait a minute," Scott argued. "I used to always do the bacon run."

"Bullshit," Roy said firmly, "I used to drive that piece of shit station wagon to do it while you stood by the gate."

"We've all done the bacon run," Leo said, cutting out there pointless arguing. "Besides, I'm the one who has to knock some heads together if they don't pay up."

"Or switch out the owner?" I asked innocently.

They all seemed to sort of look at me, but mainly Leo gave me the most attention.

"Yeah, or that."

For a moment, I thought back to when the Don proposed for me to go on the bacon run with Danny. He said Danny had a partner before that would do it with him, but no one had mentioned who that partner was. Was it a lie? Or had I just not met that person yet?

Finally, the roaring of the hungry crowd seemed to fall as Don Ponchello walked into the kitchen in one of his perfectly fitted suits and he got everyone's attention.

"As most of you know or you now know because you didn't pay attention before, I will be leaving tonight for business in Las Vegas."

"Pfft, no one does business in Vegas," Jordan said.

There was a small laugh about the crowd and it was obvious to me that only Jordan could get away with a comment like that.

"Okay, Jordan, you'll get your plate last," Don Ponchello said as the crowd woo-ed. "Anyway, in the event of my absence, I have decided to make you all my infamous garlic bread, but I guess Jordan will just have to eat the end pieces."

There was a more powerful laugh as Don Ponchello took off his suit jacket and threw an apron on. He looked a lot less threatening now, and a lot more jovial. As he slipped on the huge plaid oven mitt, he opened the large French oven and started to pull out the loaves of bread.

"C'mon guys, get a plate and have at it."

It was by far the best home cooked meal I had ever had.

The tortellini was smothered in a green pesto cream sauce that was to die for and the noodles were perfectly boiled and just right. The cheese inside was a little strong with pepper but the cream sauce made it less harsh. Don Ponchello's garlic bread was so good that I now knew why he made four loaves. Everyone had two slices to eat: one with butter and then one to wipe around on their plates to get the rest of the sauce. It was crazy how much food was made but not a single bite was left over. I was stuffed to no end and we all ate at the massive dining table that could seat about thirty people. Of course, Don Ponchello sat at one end and nobody sat at the other. For some reason, Leo was the only one who ate standing up against the wall diagonal to the Don like a body guard. I was only two seats away from the Don with Danny separating us. Don Ponchello got mad while Michelle kept walking around to give everyone seconds.

"Please, Michelle, sit down and eat. I'm surprised you haven't passed out from all the heat."

"Okay Mr. Ponchello, I'll take a seat soon," Michelle said.

She was the only one who called him Mr. Ponchello. Everyone else was ordered to call him Don or Don Ponchello, Leo called him boss, and only his past wife was allowed to call him Mark.

"So, what's going on in Vegas, Don?" one of the men asked.

Everyone's eyes went to Don Ponchello and he was caught off guard. With a little bit of sauce on his face, he reached for his napkin, wiped it away, and cleared his throat.

"Danny, are you and Victor finished with your meals?" Don Ponchello asked.

The question chilled me for some reason. I knew whatever was going on in Vegas was probably bad news, or part of the illegal activity that I knew happened with these people but I wasn't supposed to know about just yet.

But for a moment, I was actually interested in what was going on too. I felt like, *maybe*, maybe I was becoming a little too invested in all of this.

"Victor, are you done?" Danny asked.

I looked at him straight in the eye and said, "Yes, I'm done. It was very tasty though."

"I'm glad you thought so, and I'm sure Michelle will be glad to hear that too," Don Ponchello said with a smile.

"I'm done too, Dad. I'll just take Victor up to my room and show him where he can sleep, and tomorrow we're going to work at the warehouse."

"That sounds good, son. I'm glad to hear it."

I almost picked up my plate but the guy next to me said, "No, don't worry about it. That's what Michelle is paid for."

Danny left his plate and started to run off to his room so I ran off with him. A few of the guys laughed and then the Don began discussing his trip but I couldn't hear any of it. Danny went into the living room and walked straight across to the staircase. The TV was blaring still but Danny didn't do anything about it so I went ahead and followed him.

"C'mon Victor, I got some pretty cool stuff to show you," Danny said as he bolted up the stairs.

I followed behind him and the upstairs area was very confusing. There were tons of doors everywhere and I wondered how anyone would ever remember where their room was. At the top of the stairs, Danny turned around and followed the railing beside the stairs that was now to our side and below us. He headed straight down the hall and said, "There's my room, just straight down the hall."

I almost asked where Don Ponchello's room was, but when we stepped up to his door, I could tell that the Don's room was just to the left of Danny's room at the end of the hall. The door was out and at an angle and it was two large doors with lavish door handles.

I wondered what it looked like in there, but I could only wonder for now.

Danny's room door creaked open and he flicked on his light.

The room was about four hundred square feet with little decorations and knick-knacks all over his bookshelf, along with books of course. The red plush comforter puffed up from the mattress and the red pillows looked softer than clouds. He had two nightstands; one had an alarm clock with a lamp. A chest of drawers was on the right side of the room with another door next to it.

"That's my bed, the bookshelf… I don't mind if you read any of the comics just put them back… and that door leads to the bathroom. It's nothing special, I'm sure you had a better looking room."

A massive framed picture of *The Persistence of Memory* hung from the only open space on the wall and Danny kicked off his shoes toward his opened walk-in closet on the left. He plopped onto his bed and said, "Man, I didn't realize how tired I was.

I guess this happens when I talk to the ladies."

"Yeah, I guess so."

Danny let out a long sigh and kicked his feet around. Then, he looked at me and said, "Hey, you can take your shoes off."

"Oh, okay."

I started to kick off my shoes but then Danny jumped up and said, "Oh yeah, you wanna see something cool?"

I nodded and Danny jumped out of bed to show me. He stepped up to his bookshelf in excitement and reached behind it. He now presented to me a movie poster of *The Wizard of Oz* and there were signatures next to the casts' names. Danny looked over it, and then looked at me for my reaction.

"Wow that's... cool," I said.

Danny seemed to frown as he said, "Well, I mean I could've shown you my grandpa's pistol from WWI, but... my mom left this behind when she left... and I bet it'll be worth a fortune one day."

I wasn't sure how to take Danny opening up about his mom. I knew it was a sensitive topic, to say the least. But his happy look seemed to fade the more he thought about it, and he finally tucked the poster back behind the bookshelf again.

"I don't want to hang it on the wall because my dad would be furious," Danny said.

"I bet..." I said.

"Okay Victor, hint taken. I'll just show you the pistol next time."

*****

Danny let me shower as we headed to bed at about 10:30, and then I climbed into the same bed as him. It was big enough that we didn't have to touch each other but I thought it was strange. I hadn't slept in a bed with someone else in a very long time. The last time was probably when I was young and I would have a nightmare so I had to sleep with my mom and dad for the night.

Luckily, I didn't stay up thinking about that. The shower relaxed me enough to start to fall asleep, but at about one in the morning, I heard the first laughs in the hallway.

"... yeah, yeah. Haha! No, you remember that guy... and you busted his fuckin' head open?"

At first I thought they were the final words from the bad dream I was waking up from, but instead, it was a real life conversation that was happening outside Danny's door.

"Well, he didn't pay up. And he had a signed baseball bat hanging from his wall, so…"

I could tell the defensive voice was Leo's. The other voice… I could only guess it was Jordan's.

Then, some other voice came in and said, "That's not the time I remember. I remember when old Leo here came up behind that barber and started choking him to death, and then when Leo let go and tried to ask him if he was okay, he puked all over Leo's newly shined shoes!"

"I remember those times, but man, they weren't as bad as the war times," I heard Roy's voice say.

"Say, what happened over there, Roy? How many gooks did you kill?"

"Fuck… That's not a question you ask, man. But I killed so many, I thought I could win the war by myself. Y'see, unlike other wars, this one is solely based on body count. It's not territories you take over or whatever. It's how many of those bastards you kill by the end of the day, and that was it."

"I just hope this deal goes down good in Vegas," Jordan commented after a small silence to respect Roy. "If not, I fear we'll all be thrown into a different kind of war."

"Yeah, and this war will be at home," Leo said.

After that, I only heard the sound of doors opening and closing and they said goodnight to each other.

I tried to shake the images out of my head before going back to sleep, but I don't remember when I finally got them to go away. Because before I knew it, I was awake and ready to work at the warehouse.

# Chapter Ten
## Wednesday, March 10th, 1976

Whatever was discussed last night between Leo and the others now seemed like a bad dream as Danny and I headed to the warehouse bright and early that Wednesday morning. The clouds were scattered about in a unique fashion and my head felt light from how soft the pillows at Danny's house were. Danny and I hadn't talked much. Danny wasn't much of a morning person, but I liked mornings. The earlier I woke up, the longer my day could be. That was something my dad used to mention... or I guess I should say, my "old dad".

Michelle made breakfast this morning. Ah, breakfast... It was wonderful. Scrambled eggs with peppers and cheese, crisp bacon, waffles... I felt like I was at a resort hotel.

Danny turned on the radio and we started listening to "Badfinger". I sort of nodded my head to the song "No Matter What" but it looked like Danny only nodded his head to stay awake. I decided to talk to him to show him what I knew about the band.

"That's too bad about Ham's suicide."

Danny looked over at me and said, "No, yeah, that's really terrible... What a terrible way to go. I'd rather someone kill me than having to kill myself."

"I think they are really underrated," I added, after I thought about what Danny said.

"They are," Danny ended.

A small moment of silence, and then I asked, "So what exactly do we do here?"

Danny smiled, and I realized I had already asked him a few times before. He smiled because he knew I was still worried.

"We just move boxes, all day long until about... six or so?"

"So a nine hour day?"

"Yeah, but we'll get an hour break. Today is pizza day at lunch time."

"Fun," I said.

*****

The work wasn't that bad. It was more lifting than when I moved houses, but I needed the exercise. Most of the men were a lot bigger and older than me and

Danny. It looked like they did this for a living.

The only thing strange about the work was that Danny told me that I didn't need to punch in. I would just get paid weekly, directly from his father. I didn't know if that was an honor, or something being pushed under the rug and out of sight. Maybe I was just doing this for a little bit so I didn't have to go through all the paperwork or prove I was legal.

The lunch break was interesting. It was a full hour of just eating pizza and hearing dirty jokes from the other workers. Joe and Pete were two jokers who kept at it the whole hour. I don't even know when they stopped to eat their pizza. It was hard for me to eat since I was laughing so hard. Mainly, it was weird to laugh again. It seemed like the days of laughing and having fun were far away in the past, but at this moment they seemed alive and well.

Toward the end of our shift, Danny and I were grabbing some boxes out of the back of a semi and I heard glass shatter.

I almost dropped the box, frightened by the sound, but Danny carefully lowered his box and ran up to mine to hold it steady.

"Whoa, whoa, whoa, easy Victor. Don't drop the whole box."

We carefully lowered in to the ground and Danny looked it over. After a small observation, a grin appeared on his face.

"What?" I asked.

"Oh, Victor, remember the party coming up in two days?"

"Somewhat," I replied, just to be distant.

"Well, to put it in code," Danny said, "you can't have spaghetti without any sauce."

That's when I looked down to see what glass had broken... and it was a big bottle of vodka. The box must've had ten more in it.

"I don't... I don't drink though," I said, thinking about my dad.

"Oh, right, I'm sorry Victor," Danny replied after reading my mind. I was glad that he seemed to care so much about me. He lifted the box and covered the hole as he stood up. "See, we can't ship this to my dad's liquor stores, they'll think we tampered with it somehow, so this will just be for the other people at the party, you know? Like, the girls and maybe some other people that come."

"Who else is going?" I asked.

"Even though people at school don't like us, they still want to party."

Danny started walking out of the warehouse and I followed behind him, a little mad.

"You invited people from school!?" I practically shouted as we walked across the parking lot to Danny's car.

"Don't worry, Johnny Fag-o isn't going to come, and neither are his other little monkey goons."

Danny rested the box against his car and dug out his car keys. After he unlocked his car, he opened the door and tossed the box in his back seat.

"Victor, I know you're probably not very happy with me, but I promise, no one is going to bother you at the party, okay? Do you even remember who my father is and how much the people we go to school with fear him? Even though my dad won't be there, there's no way that anyone is going to try anything at the party. They just wanna drink and do stupid shit. But if they break anything or mess with you or anything like that, ZIP! They're out. Okay? I give you my word."

I shook my head, still irritated. My heart tried to look for some way to forgive Danny and move on.

"How do you even know those girls are going to come?"

"I called them while you were taking a shower. They are excited to come to the party, and I heard Kassidy is trying really hard to hold out for you."

Danny's silly voice toward the end of that statement made me laugh. Sure she was holding out for me…

Before Danny closed his car door, I glanced at the analog clock in his car and my heart dropped.

"Is that the real time?"

Danny glanced over and said, "Oh, yeah, neither fast nor slow. 6:25, on the dot. Are you mad that we're not off right at 6?"

I was supposed to be at Michelangelo's by 6:30…

"I need to go… if that's okay."

"I didn't scare you off, did I?" Danny checked.

"No, I just, I have to meet a family friend for dinner. We eat every Wednesday night around 6:30."

"Oh, right! I remember you saying you had something to do. Yeah, lemme just run in and tell Bradley that we're splitting and then I'll rush you there, okay?"

*****

Danny did rush me there, a little more than I thought he was going to.

What should've been a fifteen-minute drive was shortened to eight. When we arrived, Danny pulled me next to the curb a little ways out of Chief Ramzorin's vision, which was lucky enough.

I started to get out of the car but Danny asked, "Is there a time I should get you, or…"

"I'm going to stay at my house tonight, if that's okay? Could you pick me up in the morning from there?"

"Hey, of course, Victor, I understand. I'll get you at 8:50 tomorrow morning and we'll do some more exciting box lifting, okay?"

"Sounds good, thank you, Danny," I said as I stepped out.

Danny waved as I closed his door and rushed into the restaurant. Chief Ramzorin was in the normal booth and he looked up from his watch to see me at the entrance. I didn't wait for him to say anything. Instead, I headed on over to him and sat down.

"I'm sorry, Chief," I started, "I was working and lost track of time…"

"Hey, no worries bud… I just didn't know where you were," Chief Ramzorin said as he signaled Antonio, the waiter. "So, a job?"

"Oh, yeah, a warehouse job just a bit south of Grosse Pointe."

Antonio came up to me and I told him I wanted water as my drink, and the same meal I usually got.

"That's good, Victor! Who got you the job?"

"A friend of mine," I said at first.

"Oh yeah? What's his name?"

Now, this is where things could get tricky. I couldn't say his last name because that might cause sparks to fly when he found out who I'd been hanging out with. But, Danny wasn't really involved with the illegal activity, unless you counted the bacon run…

Trying to play it safe, I said, "His name is Daniel, I go to school with him. He invited me over for dinner with his family and then he said the warehouse he works at needs more people, so they hired me this morning."

"Well," Chief Ramzorin said with a big smile, "I'm glad Daniel is being a good friend to you."

I hated to lie to Chief Ramzorin, but it was the only way this was going to go. If I had told him the truth, I didn't think I'd have any friends for a very long time.

# Chapter Eleven

Chief Ramzorin drove me to my apartment, because this time, I didn't insist. Something was coming over me... sort of a new feeling. I didn't feel scared anymore. Well, I take that back. I had a few fears, but in the back of my mind, I knew Danny could be there for me at any second if I called him. I never felt that way about the Chief. Mainly since one time, maybe a year ago, I called the Chief about my dad. Sadly, he wasn't available at the station, and I implored for the secretary not to tell him I called.

For some reason, I still held that against him. But now, Danny could come to my rescue if I needed him to. I felt like I could finally rely on someone, and talk to them like a normal human being. Sometimes my relationship with Chief Ramzorin just felt like he was that stepparent who tried too hard and stepped over the line, and I was that kid that could never impress him. I didn't like that; I didn't like it at all.

I still appreciated him though, and the fact that he's never had to cancel on a Wednesday, or ever ditched me. That was a good quality in Chief Ramzorin.

"Okay, I'll stop here so your dad doesn't see me dropping you off," Chief Ramzorin said as he pulled next to the curb.

"Thank you."

I opened the door and started to step out.

"Victor, let me know how the job goes," Chief Ramzorin requested, "and if any problems arise, just give me a call, okay?"

"Sure, thanks," I said briefly as I closed the door to his sedan.

The door clicked in place and he waved as he turned his signal on to back onto the blackening street. The only thing that would flip the street's downfall to darkness was the street lights that just started to flicker on with that neutral orange color.

After sleeping at the manor, I wasn't sure I could sleep tonight at my house, especially with the monorail passing not too far in the distance.

Not feeling much fear, I sauntered into the "lobby" and made my way to my home.

I hated to call it that.

As I turned open the door, I heard the news anchor going on and on about something and a faint snoring from my father. He wasn't in his room though; he was out in the living room. I saw him sprawled out on the recliner wearing the same clothes he had on months ago. He was asleep enough that I could move freely without too much worry.

But then, something strange happened.

"Victor, is that you?"

The soft voice came from the living room, and I could barely recognize it. It made me sad when I saw it was my mom, leaning out from the wall and calling my name.

I only nodded to her, being the first time she had addressed me by name... maybe in a year.

She waved for me to come in the living room, and I was worried about my father waking up. She knew why I was hesitating though, and she kept waving. Somehow, I guess she knew that my dad wasn't going to wake up, so I made my way over to her quietly.

I felt like her old self was long gone as she stared at me with empty eyes and an open smile.

"Come, sit," she said as she patted the couch.

I sat down on the couch, adjacent to my father, but at a good point where I could run to my room if need be.

My mom stared at me for a long time, just making notes in her head. After staring, she started feeling my rough face and looking into my eyes.

"Victor..." she said. "What... what's been going on?"

"Oh, just school... You know, the usual."

She nodded in such a brain dead manner it almost made me cry. She was gone. I didn't know where she was, but she was gone.

"Do you have any friends?"

I was happy to answer this question.

"Yes, I have a friend named Daniel. He let me stay the night at his house last night, if that's okay."

Her face changed to a worried look, and then back to a happy look.

"Oh, no honey that's wonderful... You should get out more often."

"Well, he also has me working."

"A job?"

"Yes, at a warehouse. We lift boxes all day. It's simple, really."

"Oh, darling..."

She kept rubbing my face and I saw a tear start to roll down her cheek.

"Victor... you're still..."

I waited for her to finish, but she couldn't.

"Mom?"

"Victor, honey, you're still too young for a job… your birthday is still a few months away."

I thought my mom was half sober, but now, I didn't know what was wrong with her. My birthday was in January.

"Mom…" I said, trying to really get her attention, and maybe snap her out of whatever state of mind she was in, "How old do you think I am?"

"Oh Victor, you know how old you are. It's all the fingers on your right hand, and then the two on your left. You just came inside from playing with Tommy Elway out in the front yard, how was that?"

I was creeped out and hurt. My mom… what the hell had happened to her memory? She was talking to me like I was an adult, but thinking I was seven…

I didn't have to hear anymore. My dad started to stir in his recliner and my mom seemed to snap back into reality once again.

"Go, go to your room…"

I stood up and hurried to my room. Just as I closed my door, I heard my father wake up and ask my mom something. I heard her respond, "Victor's down for his nap… Miss Prylee didn't let them have a nap in Kindergarten today."

My dad yelled for her to stop being hysterical, but before he could do anything to her, the phone rang and it caught his drunk self off guard.

This wasn't a home to me anymore.

It was Hell.

# Chapter Twelve
## Friday, March 12th, 1976

I called Danny late last night from the phone in my apartment to ask him if we had to work. I had to wait until eleven for my parents to go to their room and sleep.

"No man, tomorrow is just a party day."

He sounded kind of sleepy, so I felt bad for calling.

"Don't feel bad, I understand. I don't think I told you that I don't work Fridays."

"Sorry that I don't have a car... are you going to pick me up tomorrow?"

"Don't be sorry that you don't have a car," Danny said as he sighed. "Soon, maybe you'll have enough to buy a car."

That was an interesting thought. I mean, I had my license from when I turned sixteen, so why not?

"I'll pick you up at Marlin's Grocer at about 5:45, okay?"

And, as usual, he was right.

I got to Marlin's Grocer at about 5:43, just in case he decided to drive a little faster than usual, but I ended up waiting that extra two minutes.

Danny rolled up, and the roar of his engine startled me. Honestly, I was worried about how the party would go. Liquor and teenagers never really seemed like a good combination. Sober teenagers were bad enough as it is.

After I hopped in his car and he drove off toward the highway, I felt that my palms were really sweaty.

"Victor, are you okay?" Danny asked. "You seem kind of... tense."

"I've just, never been to a party before," I answered with no way to sound cool or experienced.

"Oh, well it's really nothing. Be yourself, and I'm sure everyone will be fine. Like I said, nobody is going to care that you and I are there. They care about having a good time."

"But..."

"But what?"

I hesitated to say the next part, even though I knew that he knew it already.

"I've never had to... entertain a girl before."

Danny started laughing. I hated it.

"Victor, you're not going to have to entertain her, you just have to talk to her.

Kassidy's interested in you already, trust me. All you have to do is show that you're a nice guy."

Although Danny was extremely reassuring, a part of me wasn't falling for it. I felt like there was something more to all of this, and yet, that something was missing.

His back seat no longer held the box of vodka.

"Where's the liquor?" I asked.

"It's at the house, where people can enjoy it. I let some of my dad's henchmen take a few drinks."

When we arrived at the manor, cars were scattered all over the place. Some of them I recognized from school, others weren't as recognizable.

As soon as Danny pulled in, Jordan stepped up to the car, and I realized it was going to take a lot more than a few drinks to make him happy about this party.

"What's going on, Jordan!?" Danny exclaimed with a smile.

Jordan scowled and said, "Danny, I don't like this, not one bit."

"What are you talking about? It's a party, parties are fun."

"Not when you're security," Jordan argued. "Your dad will hang you by your shoelaces if he finds out about this. I've already had to send quite a few 'young men' home because of their wise guy attitudes and nonstop jabbering."

"You didn't make Michael Einsfeld leave though, did you?"

For some reason, I entered some sort of dazed state that someone would enter if they almost met a superstar. Michael Einsfeld was considered one of the coolest guys in my graduating class. He could play guitar almost as good as Clapton and he got any girl in school that he wanted; sometimes even two at a time.

"No, I don't think so."

"Good," Danny said before Jordan could say anymore. "Go ahead and close the gates. Only let people leave, no more can enter. If they come up now, just tell them they're late."

Danny drove off and toward the house and Jordan nodded as he closed the gate behind us.

"Really? Michael Einsfeld? How did you get him to come?"

"I asked him," Danny replied slyly.

I started to argue, but Danny said, "Look, Victor, it's just like I told you. Nobody cares about who we are. They hear the word 'party', and they become slightly interested. Throw in the word 'booze', and you have a sure thing."

Danny parked in the garage where no one else was and I didn't see the mechanic, Phil. So, I asked where he was.

"Phil usually hangs out with some other car connoisseurs on Friday nights,"

Danny said as he turned off his headlights and stepped out of the car.

As we walked to the mansion, I saw a few people already drunk on the front porch steps. They were talking in gibberish or just standing in amazement with their own inebriation.

Danny walked past them though, and they didn't even notice who we were or what we were doing. I guess Danny was right. No one cared that I was here, except for…

As soon as Danny opened the doors, I spotted Kassidy and Jessica standing outside of the living room drinking punch in the hallway. It looked like they were avoiding the main crowd, which I would come to meet soon enough.

Danny led me to the living room through the sea of people, all kinds of people, really. Kids that graduated the year before us, freshmen, sophomores, juniors, seniors, graduates… It was a mix of people, and I was right in the center of it all.

By the time we reached the living room, Jessica and Kassidy had moved to the kitchen. I felt like it was a race.

Also, rock music was blaring from the record player in the living room. Danny smiled as he waved to some people that recognized him.

"Go ahead, Victor, don't be so stiff. Drink some punch," Danny offered.

"Oh, I'm not really thirsty yet," I replied.

"Oh, okay. Well, how about you stay here and I'll go grab our ladies?"

Before I could object, Danny ran off.

Kids were everywhere, drinking punch and talking. There was a couple against the far wall making out to the music. Others were getting closer and closer and the room would go from extremely dense and crowded to empty and back every few seconds. It was havoc, to me.

At one point when the room cleared, I saw Michael Einsfeld, and he was actually the one playing the loud music. His sunburst guitar gleamed in the light and his dark amplifier roared. I had no idea how he was able to afford any of his equipment, but he did.

He was playing above the record player, showing off his moves to the girls in the room. They all stared, just watching and waiting for him to bend down and kiss one of them. He was already a rock star.

His style of playing ranged from Black Sabbath to Eric Clapton. He shook his long hair around as he played guitar solos and rocked the room.

I watched him play for a while and I was impressed. But then, trouble came quickly.

Michael looked up from his guitar and saw me staring just like the girls. I didn't realize he was staring me down until he said, "What are you looking at?"

Part of me was happy that he was talking to me, but the other part of me felt threatened.

"Oh, I just haven't watched anyone play guitar before," I replied calmly.

I saw a few empty cups on top of his amplifier. I figured he had been drinking. All of the math wasn't adding up good.

"Oh yeah? Well did you get a good look at how to play, faggot?"

The girls wooed and I stood there, feeling defeated.

That's when Danny came to my rescue.

"Hey, what did you call him?" Danny's voice called out from behind me.

Kassidy and Jessica were now here to see the spectacle too. I really didn't know how it was going to end now.

"I called your boyfriend there a faggot, is that okay?"

Danny scoffed.

"No, that's not okay. This is my house, Michael, and I don't appreciate how you're treating my friend."

"Eh, fuck off."

Michael was about to start playing his guitar again, but Danny looked at me with a full glass of punch in his hand and said, "You can't reason with people like this, Victor. I'll teach you what you need to do!"

At that, he threw his glass of punch at the amplifier and sparks went everywhere. Michael jumped and the girls scattered away. Then came the death glare from Michael as he set his guitar down in its case.

"I'm gonna kill you, Danny boy."

Right as Michael started to charge at Danny, a henchman came running down the stairs and tackled Michael to the ground. Jordan came into the living room to catch the end of it.

"Danny, what the hell is going on here?" Jordan scolded.

"Oh, nothing that Georgie here couldn't handle, isn't that right?" Danny said as he patronized Michael. The henchman (Georgie) pulled Michael up to his feet and Danny said, "Okay, he can be the first one escorted out. Let him take his guitar with him, but the amplifier stays here. I'll send you a check in the mail soon, but it won't cover the entire cost of the amplifier, just enough for you parents to go in on it halfway like they did with this one, sound reasonable?"

Now Michael was the loser getting escorted out of the party in shame. I felt awesome. I felt like no one could touch me. I felt like... how Michael did just moments ago.

Kassidy turned me around and hugged me.

"Are you okay, Vic?"

I hadn't been called that name for a long time.

"Yeah, I'm great," I replied with a gleaming smile.

Jordan gave me a look and then shook his head as he walked out with Georgie and Michael.

Danny had his arm around Jessica and said, "Well, now I'm going to need a new glass of punch. Are you thirsty now, Victor?"

I did feel a little hot after thinking I was about to be pounded by Michael.

"Yeah, some punch would be great," I said, and then I noticed Kassidy didn't have any punch. "Would you like some too?"

"Oh, I can get it for you, you and Danny can just sit down over there," Kassidy said as she pointed to the couch.

I smiled as Danny pulled me to the couch and the ladies departed to the punch bowl.

"Man, these girls are ready," Danny said.

I didn't understand what he meant, so I asked him.

"Oh, I mean that they're... looking for a lot of fun," Danny explained.

I nodded, acting like I knew what he meant. I had a feeling I knew, but, if it was that, then I wasn't sure how the night would go.

Jessica and Kassidy were staring at us as they gathered the punch. Kassidy looked irresistible, like a forbidden fruit. Her jeans were tight and her T-shirt stretched enticingly across her breasts. I was lustful, but I hid it as Kassidy and Jessica came back to us with drinks.

"Here you go, fellas," Jessica said in a silly way.

"Thanks, ladies," Danny played along.

Kassidy sat by me on one end of the couch while Jessica sat with Danny on the other side. She handed me the punch and stared deep into my eyes. I felt like something was wrong with her, or maybe, it was right.

"The punch has a little kick to it, I hope you don't mind," Kassidy explained as I started to take a drink.

I looked over at the punch bowl and saw the empty bottle of vodka sitting next to it. An image of my father flashed through my mind; the miserable drunk. I didn't want to end up like him. I didn't want to become an alcoholic loser. But, I'd heard that women make you do crazy things. The more I thought about it, my dad was a whiskey man, not a vodka consumer.

With that logic in mind, I replied, "Don't mind if I do."

This was a side of me no one had ever seen. Hell, I hadn't even seen it before. I had a new found confidence, and I was striving to be successful. I felt rich and powerful, just because a girl liked me.

I drank all the punch in one gulp, and I felt the burn in the back of my throat. I started to cough, but I covered it by clearing my throat. Kassidy giggled, but I didn't feel any shame.

"So, did you like it? Do you want some more?" Kassidy asked.

"Yeah, sure."

"Well, c'mon then."

She dragged me to the kitchen where we found an even bigger punch bowl, which probably contained two or more bottles of vodka in it. I didn't care though. The logic of my father being a whiskey man, and the fact that Kassidy was letting me stand really close to her made me not care anymore. Even in the huge crowd of people, I felt like it was just me and her.

She took the ladle and I held the glass up. She sloshed the punch into the cup and some splashed out and onto my face. After we laughed, she took her thumb and wiped some off only to then lick it off. The id of my brain, the part Sigmund Freud had warned us all about, decided to take its course.

"Hey, I think you missed a spot," I said as I pointed to my cheek.

This was actually something I had seen in my favorite movie as a kid, and I felt like she had seen the same one.

"Oh yeah? I think I actually see another spot too…"

Without being 100 percent ready, she swooped in and planted a kiss right on my lips. My heart flew through the ceiling and back as I put my cup down on the closest table and brought her in for more. It was a borderline make out session, but she slowed it down before it progressed anymore and talked to me.

"Wow, you're a really good kisser," Kassidy said as we parted away from our intimacy and I grabbed my cup of punch again.

"Really?" I asked, and then I drank more punch.

The burn was worse this time. The drink was probably thirty percent punch and seventy percent liquor.

"Yeah, really good. Do you wanna give me another dose, doctor?"

She had me hooked… in the kitchen of a crime family's house.

I don't remember much of the rest of the night because Kassidy and I just stayed by the punch bowl and drank and danced and kissed and… whatever else we wanted to do. All I remember is, we ended up going to an empty room upstairs, undressing each other, and the next morning, I woke up naked next to Kassidy.

But instead of the sound of rock music still playing, the sound of the Don yelling at Danny downstairs was filling the manor.

# Chapter Thirteen
## Saturday, March 13th, 1976

"What the hell were you thinking, Daniel!?"

Although I didn't want to run downstairs, I knew it was the best thing to do. Kassidy was up and getting dressed, seemingly scared for her life. I got the covers unstuck from me and I got up to get dressed too. Kassidy didn't really look at me now, and I felt a disconnect from her as I tried to remember what even happened.

After we got dressed, we headed downstairs together and I saw Don Ponchello with Leo and Scott, and then Jordan and Roy stood with Danny as he got scolded. Jessica sat alone on the couch with ruffled clothing. The living room was trashed.

"Victor," the Don said, visibly upset. Then he looked to Kassidy. "Jordan, take those girls home."

"Yes, Don."

Kassidy gave me a pathetic smile as she walked away from me and she left with Jordan and Jessica. Danny was on the verge of crying, and now I felt the same.

There goes my baby... and here comes the pain.

"I can't believe you boys threw a party while I was gone!" the Don yelled at Danny, and then looked to me. "This house is sacred, and it isn't for stupid parties with fake friends from school. I am extremely disappointed, in both of you."

That hurt me for some reason. At one point, my only feeling toward the Don was fear, even before I met him, but now I started to feel respect.

"But, at least it showed who is trustworthy out of my henchmen. Georgie ran off with some seventeen-year-old last night and made Roy come up here to take his spot."

The Don started to walk toward the couch, but something was wrong. As he started to pause, I saw a dark red stain form quickly under his white dress shirt and he collapsed to the ground.

"Dad!" Danny called out.

Leo reached out to grab him and I ran down the stairs to be next to Danny.

"Back up, Danny, he needs some air," Roy said as he pulled me and Danny away.

"No, he needs to go to a hospital," I said.

Leo smirked at me and laughed quietly.

"We're not going to a hospital, kid. Scott, call The Doctor and see if he can come in, pronto."

"Right away," Scott said as he ran off to the phone in the kitchen.

Leo helped the Don to his feet and started taking him up the stairs.

"C'mon Don, you're going to be okay, we just need to get you in bed. I told you I should've bandaged you," Leo said.

Danny and I stood in silence as Roy said, "Okay Victor, time to go home."

"No…"

I didn't mean to blatantly object and Roy seemed offended by it, until Danny was also shaking his head no.

"I'm sorry, I don't want to leave though. I want to make sure the Don is okay," I said, trying to save myself.

"Oh, okay Victor. Well, how about you come with me? The Don wanted me to discuss some things with you. Danny, how about you go get your father some water and bring it up to him? I'm sure he'd appreciate it."

Danny nodded and ran away to the kitchen as Roy escorted me outside to his maroon Ford Granada. I did have a feeling of worry as we walked out, and I thought about what he said. What needed to be discussed? Was I in more trouble than I thought?

Roy started up the automobile and we headed to the highway.

"Where are we going?" I asked nervously.

"Magnificent Cakes. The Don loves to eat some petit fours when he's feeling down, so we'll surprise him."

"Oh, okay," I said, feeling a little more secure now that I knew where we were headed.

"The Don likes you, kid. He sees something in you."

"Really?"

"Yeah, he thinks you could be a good business man, like your father was."

Too bad I didn't want to be anything like my father.

"Roy, or…"

"Yeah, you can call me Roy."

"Okay, Roy, what happened in Vegas? Is that where he was hurt?"

Roy cringed as he went over the details in his mind.

"Leo only talked to me about it briefly on the phone and then just a little more right when they got to the manor… I guess business went bad. The idea of the trip was to try and get a man named Vincent Tandelli to do business with us. He and the Don have been friends for a long time, but I guess the Don interfered with some of Vincent's business back in the California days and some business here in Detroit, so he wasn't too happy about the Don's offer to buy one of his casinos. Long story short, some security man at the airport went turncoat and killed one of the Don's bodyguards and shot the Don once. They stopped the bleeding in the Don's plane on the way here, but I guess they didn't have it looked at yet. Then the Don comes home to see it's a mess... Well you can only imagine how he feels."

Now I felt worse, but I wasn't sure if it was all the alcohol from the night before or how things happened in Las Vegas. A part of me felt sorry for the Don, another part worried about what was going to come.

"There's gonna be a lot of changes soon, Victor, I can tell you that. I know you didn't want to be a part of this, but it's too late. The second they see you with any of us, even Danny, they might use you to take us down."

"Who's 'they'?" I asked.

"Vincent Tandelli and his men. From what I gathered, they're not done with the Don. They'll be coming here soon and try to take us down once and for all. We're all at risk."

My stomach felt queasy, but this time I knew it wasn't the alcohol. Did this mean I was now involved with everything, no matter what?

Since Roy was being so open though, I decided to check the Don's credibility. I asked, "What about Danny's mom?"

"Oh... Adrianna..." Roy said, as if she was a haunted beauty. "She was a great woman, and very sweet. She swore to be by the Don's side in sickness and in health, till death do they part. But one morning, she just ran out on them. No one really knows why. Word on the street is that the Don had her killed, but I know that isn't true. Leo was on that kind of detail and he's trusted with pretty much every job the Don assigns. If the Don had her killed, Leo would have been the one to do it, and I'm sure he would have told someone by now. But Leo and the Don tell me the same thing I'm telling you, kid. She ran off, just like that."

It was slightly reassuring to hear that, but I hated it at the same time. Poor Danny... if she really was a great woman, she would have stuck around. Right?

I didn't have the real answer for that, and I doubted that Roy did either. All I knew was, we were all in danger, and the Don likes petit fours.

## Chapter Fourteen

I decided to stay around that weekend to make sure the Don got better. There wasn't much to do around the house, except for play board games and cards with the other henchmen who really didn't have anything to do except occupy the house.

And boy, did they occupy the house.

Roy explained to me that the Don still owned a few businesses in California but it's just too dangerous for him there so they moved out here to Detroit to try and recover the city after the race riots. Not the best idea in my opinion, but anyway... Several men were flown in from California to be on security detail around the house. There were so many men, it was really impossible for me to catch all of their names. The only one that seemed the most important was a man named David Weston.

"Who's that?" I asked Danny.

"David Weston, one of the best shooters in North America," Danny said as he "hit me" with a card. "My dad decided to make some changes to some people's positions and David is now going to be my dad's personal bodyguard. It used to be Leo... sort of. But now Leo is going full surveillance."

"Surveillance?" I asked.

"Yeah. Spying and making sure other people don't make advances on my dad or that anyone here rats anyone out."

David Weston wore a sharp black Armani suit and square sunglasses. His goatee made him look more deadly as he smoked his cigarette on the way up the stairs with Leo. He looked cool and dangerous, but he was supposed to.

After they passed by, The Doctor came down the stairs in his white lab uniform and made an announcement.

"It looks as though the Don will be fine. All of his vitals are normal and the bleeding has stopped for good. He just needs plenty of rest and relaxation, so if he tries to go anywhere, stop him, even if he is your boss."

With that, The Doctor took his glasses off to wipe his face with a handkerchief and then he made his way to his car outside. The news was relieving to the massive crowd.

That was all that really happened on Saturday, and then Sunday it was a little calmer. Not as many people loafed around the house but Danny and I played Battleship for the millionth time. It was around six PM when Roy came up to me.

"Hey, I forgot to say that the Don really appreciated those petit fours we got for him," Roy said.

"Why didn't I get any?" Danny complained in a joking way.

"They were for your dad, that's why."

"Well, it was your idea, Roy, I didn't think of it. I just rode along," I said.

"True, but he'd still like to see you for staying here this weekend. He really appreciates it and wants to have a word with you."

For a brief second, I thought that maybe Roy was just sugarcoating the whole thing and the Don really wanted to yell at me some more about the party. But, when Danny seemed glad for me, I stood and followed Roy upstairs.

We walked to Danny's room and made a left to where I had seen the lavish doors once before. My excitement was ridiculous as we stepped up to the doors and Roy opened them without giving me another second to breathe.

At first, it looked like it was just a study, with bookshelves and a roll top desk in the corner and another normal desk to the right of the room with a telephone and lamp. There were lots of paintings hanging about and a glass chandelier illuminating it all. Leo was griping at someone on the phone as Jordan and some other henchman played cards and smoked. Roy led me in and they all simply glanced at me and then continued what they were doing. I felt like I was one of them... but in an innocent way.

Eventually, we made it to the skinnier doors that would lead us into the Don's room.

When Roy knocked, David's voice called out, "Who is it?"

"It's Roy and Victor. The Don wanted to see us."

After the Don softly gave David validation, David instructed us to come on in and Roy opened the doors.

The room was dimly lit with just a hint of sunshine trying to come through the shaded windows. I couldn't really see what was in his room, except for some shelves with model cars, airplanes, and trains that were already highly collectable. His bed was the biggest bed I had ever seen, with four posts sticking up taller than me and almost hitting the ceiling. It was a ridiculous bed, but it looked really comfortable.

David stood at the Don's bedside and Roy and I walked up to see him. His body was propped up against his headboard and he smiled as he saw me come in.

"Oh, Victor, it's good to see you. Roy, could you please leave me, Victor and David in privacy?"

"Certainly, Don, I'll just wait out here in the study," Roy said as he turned and left, closing the doors behind him.

Now the room was darker as David sat down in the chair by the bed and I remained standing alone. David's sunglasses were off now and he stared me down. His short, black hair looked like a ton of needles stacked on each other and ready to shoot out at me. Only the tie on his suit had changed color, the rest looked virtually the same.

He wasn't smoking this time, but after he sat down, I saw him take a small case from the nightstand and set it in his lap.

"Hi, Don Ponchello..." I started, "Are you feeling any better?"

"Yes, much better, thanks for asking. I really enjoyed my petit fours. Giovanni makes the best pastries... have you had one?"

"No, I haven't. Well, I take that back," I said as I felt nervous to ever lie to the Don, "Danny gave me one of his cookies once before, on the bacon run."

"That's good, and I bet you enjoyed it."

"Yes, it was great."

The Don smiled for a second more, and then his face turned grim and I knew business was about to be discussed.

"Look Victor, by now, you probably know the story of what happened in Vegas. I would love to tell you there's nothing to worry about, and that everything will be okay, but... I don't want to lie to you, because I have more respect for you than that. I hate that it's come to this, but I can't reverse anything. As redundant as this may sound, what's done is done, and what will happen will now happen. I wish you weren't involved in this, but you are. It's not your fault, though, and I hope you can forgive me for letting it happen. But here's the bottom line, Victor. I care about you. Danny cares about you. Even some of the guys around here think you're a good guy, especially Jordan and Roy. Because we all care about you, I want you to be safe, and I want you to be able to protect yourself when the time may come that you need to. So..."

David opened the little case and a handgun was revealed to me.

"It's a Smith and Wesson Model 39, takes nine millimeter rounds and each magazine holds eight rounds. The serial number has been removed, and it's loaded and ready to go. You also have a second magazine loaded and ready to go here too when you need it," David explained coldly.

I was in shock and amazement at the same time, and judging from my face, the Don finally said, "You've never handled a gun before, have you?"

I shook my head no and David sighed.

"Very well. David will have to take you to the basement in a second and show you how to use one. All I can say Victor, is that I'm sorry and I didn't want you to be a part of this, but we're all at risk and I want everyone to be able to protect themselves if danger comes. Do you understand?"

My brain stopped working as I spoke, "Yes, I understand, Don Ponchello. I will protect you, me, and Danny if need be."

The Don's smile after my statement really made me wonder what prompted me to say that.

*I think all of this power is going to my head...*

"Good, Victor, but I have David here to protect me and Danny can take care of himself. I appreciate your concern, but I just want to make sure you are safe, even when you're not here."

I knew it was disrespectful to not accept or appreciate something that was offered to you by a mobster, so I said, "Thank you, Don Ponchello, I will use this only when I'm in danger."

"Yes, I don't think I have to tell you that it isn't a toy," the Don said with a laugh. "But I even want you to carry it when you're in school, okay? Carry it on you at all times."

David closed the box and said, "Okay, Victor, let's teach you to be only half as good as me."

*****

When we went downstairs to the basement, I saw just how lethal this gang could be. Military firearms and other random handguns hung from the wall behind a simple wooden counter that was full of different kinds of ammunition and magazines, all labeled and organized. Past all of that was a simple shooting range with bullet shells littered all over the ground. Someone had been practicing quite a bit recently and didn't care to clean up their mess.

"Alright, grab a target," David said as he pointed to a plain box on the side of the booth.

David yanked the wire overhead to bring the target clip up to us. The target choices were Richard Nixon, a normal target, or a human silhouette holding a gun. I guessed the Nixon ones were for Roy as I picked the silhouette.

"Okay, Victor, now when you use that gun, you'll probably have to hold it with both hands at first, but eventually it'll be better for you to know how to shoot with one hand."

I handed him the target and he clipped it up to the wire and slid it down the line.

"We'll start at ten yards, okay?" David said, and I nodded.

David then set the case on the table and opened it up. He took hold of the light brown handle and held the gun in both hands.

"This is how you wanna start off holding it, okay? And hold it tight 'cause this gun has a little kick to it."

I nodded as he handed it over to me and I held it at the same stance he did.

"Okay, this side has what's called the slide release, and that thing at the back is the safety. If you have that down, the safety will be on. When you cock this gun back with a new magazine, the slide release needs to be pulled down before you can start firing, okay? Like so."

He took the gun back into his hands and slowly demonstrated how to unload the pistol and reload it. He handed it to me and I tried.

"Good, you're a quick learner," David said. "Now, go back to the firing stance and I'll tell you how to aim. You want that red circle to fill up the middle of the iron sight; you see what I'm talking about?"

"Yes, I see it."

David handed me some big headphones to cover my ears and then he put some on too.

"Okay, now just aim it where you wanna shoot and slowly squeeze the trigger."

There wasn't much fear building in me as I stared down range with the handgun ready to fire. I thought I was squeezing it slowly, but before I knew it, a bullet zipped out the end of the barrel and hit bull's-eye on the target.

"Right in the head! You're a natural," David said in amazement.

A rush of excitement flowed over me and I started to take another shot. They weren't as good, but after mindlessly firing a hundred rounds with David, he said, "Okay, Victor, I think if anyone messes with you, you'll be able to take 'em down pretty damn easily. Just always try to hit what you're shooting at."

## Chapter Fifteen
### Wednesday, March 17th, 1976

I went to school Monday and Tuesday with Danny and stayed at the mansion the rest of the time. Danny was serious when he said they wouldn't mind me being there. Everyone there at the mansion treated me like family, even Michelle, the maid.

Everyone at school now thought Danny and I were pretty cool, throwing a party and tossing out the coolest guest and all. Michael gave us dirty looks all the time but he knew he couldn't touch us. Plus, my jacket concealed my pistol tucked away between my jeans and back. I felt powerful and in control. People seemed to respect me now, and Danny and I felt like kings at school.

The only thing I felt like I was missing was Kassidy. I really thought she and I had hit it off, but she wouldn't answer my calls.

"Don't worry," Danny said one day at lunch. "I haven't been able to get ahold of Jessica either."

"Why do you think that is?" I asked.

Danny sighed and took a bite out of his sandwich while we were at lunch.

"Girls are weird sometimes."

"The only thing that really sucks is... I can't remember any of what happened except for us kissing and drinking. We woke up naked next to each other the next morning, so I guess we... But I just hope I didn't do anything to offend her or hurt her feelings."

"They might have been scared off when my dad came in and started yelling," Danny explained. "I passed out in the living room with Jessica next to me. We were in our underwear, so that was kind of awkward, to say the least."

That's probably what it was. Danny's dad probably scared them off and now they would never want to come back to the manor. I mean, he was pretty mad that morning. But why couldn't they just meet us at the diner again?

"Hey, I meant to say, sorry that the punch was spiked. I know you didn't want to drink or anything and I feel bad that someone spiked it. It wasn't me, just so you know."

"Oh, don't worry about it. I figured that my dad is a whiskey man, so as long as I don't drink that, I'll be okay."

Danny laughed and patted my shoulder.

Wednesday after school, Danny dropped me off by my house so I could get cleaned up and eat with Chief Ramzorin.

"I'm not sure if we'll be able to work at the warehouse anytime soon, but I can let you work there on the weekend if you want to," Danny offered.

"Yeah, that sounds good. I'll call you or talk to you at school about it," I responded as I got out of his car.

Danny saluted me as he drove off and I waved.

From all of my new found confidence, I didn't really think about it as I waltzed into my house and entered the hell that I had almost forgotten about. When I slammed the door, I heard the roar of the beast.

"Victor!?"

The fear I once felt 24/7 arrived quickly as I saw my father get out of his recliner and make his way toward me. My mom followed slowly behind him, crouching in fear.

I knew what was coming, but for some reason, I still let him do it.

He swiped a punch across my face and I fell to the floor. Sweat dripped off of him as he yelled from above me, "Where the hell have you been!?"

"Far away from you," I said as I wiped my mouth in disgust.

This was a shock to my father. I had never back talked him, except when I was a little baby and didn't know any better. It was the first time since then, and I felt powerful, and angry. It had been a week since I had been home, and I didn't miss it at all.

He kicked me once, right in the stomach.

"You're a piece of shit, you know that? Your mother tells me you went off and got a job, and I want my rent money."

"What the fuck are you talking about!?" I yelled, finally letting my oppressed anger flow as I struggled to stand up. "I don't owe you anything."

My dad started to punch me again, but I reached behind me for the pistol. When my dad noticed I was reaching for something, his hand lowered and he smiled.

"Whatcha got there, Vic? Have a random change in mind to pay me? I already got your little stash that was hidden away in your room. I'm about to use that to pay for the A/C to come back on, if you don't mind."

Now I was even more furious than before. He used my money, my hard earned money… he probably already used it for more booze.

No, I wasn't going to let him take my life away anymore.

I pulled the pistol on him and pointed it at him. My mom flinched but my dad just lifted his hands in the air and laughed.

"Is that what this is coming to, Vic? You probably don't even know how to handle one of those things, you stupid shit. It's probably just a cap gun."

Right when he finished his sentence, I aimed the pistol right next to his foot and fired off a shot. The gunshot rang out and I heard the upstairs neighbor scream. My ears started to ring uncontrollably and the pain from my headache joined forces with my anger. He hopped back and cried out, even though I didn't hit him. I didn't want to shoot my dad, I just wanted to show him who was now in charge of my life.

After he did a little dance that was almost comical, he roared, "Get out of this house, *right now!* And never come back! Don't even go to your room, you just walk right out that front door!"

My mom was sobbing behind my father and I hated to see her like that. Honestly, I hated to see any of us like this, but that's just the way it is.

"You ruined us, Dad. Just remember that," I said coldly.

With that, I turned my back on my only family and tucked my pistol back behind me once again.

*****

I walked around aimlessly for hours after that. I would have called Danny, but he would probably want to hang out and talk everything over. I was pretty sure I could just tell him later after I ate with Chief Ramzorin. But right then, I just needed some alone time to really digest everything that happened. I had several conflicting thoughts about what had just happened. But deep down, I felt like it was the right thing to do.

Eventually, I made my way to Michelangelo's. Right as I was stepping up to the door, Chief Ramzorin was actually just down the street locking his car.

"Hey, Victor, wait up!"

Chief Ramzorin seemed a little more jolly than usual as he ran up to meet me at the door and direct us both in. He made sure his hair was okay as we walked in and the front hostess pointed to our booth.

"Victor, you look a little out of it, is that job wearing you out?" Chief Ramzorin asked.

"Oh, no I was just taking a walk before I got here."

"Oh okay," Chief Ramzorin said.

As we sat down and sort of leaned in to be seated in the booth, Chief Ramzorin started sniffing loudly.

"Is that gunpowder I smell on your shirt?" Chief Ramzorin asked.

I froze for a second, trying to put together some kind of lie, and fast.

"Oh, Daniel and I went shooting the other day at a range out in the country," I said, only hoping that Chief Ramzorin would believe me.

He did believe me without further questioning, and that hurt me. I hated to lie to him, but I couldn't tell him the truth. In fact, I could probably never tell him the full truth ever again.

## Chapter Sixteen

After the meal, Chief Ramzorin took me back to the street my apartment was on and I really didn't care to tell him what happened, even though he started pressing me about it.

"So, is everything going better at home?" Chief Ramzorin asked, but I felt like his voice was lacking any sort of hope. It was just a routine question by now.

"No," I said, not able to tell him much else. "But they're not getting any worse, so I guess that works."

"Yeah, that's… a positive way of looking at it," Chief Ramzorin replied.

The car started to slow down to a stop and I thanked him for the meal.

"Hey, Victor, I just want you to know, you can talk to me and tell me anything you want to get off your chest, okay? Talk to me or Daniel and we'll be there to help you."

"Thanks Chief," I said as I smiled for him, "I will remember that."

I closed the door to his car and he drove off into the sunset. I hoped to one day be able to do that. It always appeared so happy and peaceful.

After mentally reminding myself how I couldn't go back into the apartment, I walked over to the payphone near the drugstore on the corner and dug some change out of my pocket. I dialed in Danny's number and Leo answered with a gruff, "Yeah?"

"Oh, hi Leo, this is Victor."

"You wanna talk to Danny?" Leo asked, not wanting to waste any time.

"That would be good, thanks."

They put me on a silent hold for a second and Danny answered.

"Hey, Victor, what's up?"

"Uh, not sure how to say this but I kind of got kicked out of my house… I was wondering if we could…"

"Say no more, Victor," Danny interrupted. "In the time it takes you to walk to Marlin's Grocer, I could pick you up from there so then you don't have to sit on the curb and wait."

"Yeah, that sounds good, I'll head that way," I said, happy to have a good friend. "Thank you so much, Danny."

"Hey, don't mention it, man. I'll be there in a jiffy."

Walking to Marlin's Grocer in the cooling night was fun. The stars were just about to pop out with the moon for the night shift, and let the sun have some rest. It really made me relax and forget about all the ugliness I left behind at my home… or my "used-to-be" home.

I didn't know what to say to Danny. I mean, he and his dad seemed to be okay with me staying there, so maybe they want me to stay permanently. I just didn't know yet.

All I could really think about was Kassidy. Why would she not call me back? What happened with her? Jordan did take them home, right? That wasn't some sort of code for anything, was it?

I doubted it. The girls posed just as much of a threat as an ant to a mantis. Don Ponchello wouldn't have them killed. He seemed like a more reasonable person than that.

Also, to have Jordan kill them, who I take to be a funny and not so serious guy, it wouldn't make any sense.

After my thoughts passed, I noticed a black sedan with two men had been following me pretty closely for the last block or so. I looked over to them, and they stared right back at me.

Was it the Don's men watching after me, or…

Luckily, as I got to Marlin's, they drove off as they saw Danny drive up to pick me up.

"Hop in, Victor," Danny said enthusiastically.

I didn't hesitate. I worried those men were up to no good.

I climbed into Danny's car and he sped away.

"So, do you wanna talk about what happened at your house?" Danny immediately asked.

"I mean, only if you want to listen," I said as I checked his side view mirror.

Danny looked over at me and said, "Hey, is there something else that's wrong? You're not mad at me or something, are you?"

"Of course not, you didn't do anything wrong," I said, feeling a little queasy. "I think we're being followed."

"What? By who?" Danny asked, not entirely worried yet.

"When I was walking to Marlin's, about half way there, I saw those men in that black sedan behind us and they were driving next to me. I didn't say anything immediately because I thought they might be your dad's men, but…"

Danny looked in his rear view mirror and saw who I was talking about. By the expression he made, I knew they weren't friends.

"No, those aren't my dad's guys, they would have told me if they had a look out for you and me. And they're not cops, either," Danny said as he started to seem nervous too. "Thanks for saying something before we got to the manor, Victor. I have an idea on how to lose them."

Without discussing his plan, he headed toward downtown Detroit and they followed us all the way there. The street lights were flickering on and people were out and about in the city.

"Geez, they're still following us," Danny said.

"What should we do?" I asked.

"We'll go into a nightclub that my dad owns. They'll be dumb to follow us in there."

Danny accelerated at a yellow light to try and lose them and then he parked in the side alley of a place called "The Tease". The sign was made with bright pink fluorescents and it was hard not to see it, but it kind of looked like a place for a sleaze.

"C'mon, Victor," Danny said as he turned off his car and we headed to the front door.

Just as we were about to enter, I saw the black sedan screech to a halt and park on the curb just across the street. Danny and I both ran past the nightclub guard at the front door and ran inside to safety.

The place was a mess. Smoke filled the room and you could hardly see the scantily clad women dancing against poles to the music of the Bee Gees. The women were very attractive though, and it made me stop thinking about Kassidy for a while. But then, after being like a deer in the headlights, Danny grabbed me and took me farther into the nightclub.

"What the hell," Danny said after surveying the night club. "None of my dad's men are here."

Then, just by the bar was an African American pimp in all fur attire: A white fur coat with soft red pants and lifted shoes that looked impossible to walk in. He sat with his back to the bar and more scantily clad women were standing around him.

I thought Danny was just staring at his ridiculous clothes, but then Danny started to approach him and I followed.

"But Daddy, that's all I got to pay you," one of the women complained.

He held a black cane with his right hand, which was in possession of a ridiculously diamond studded ring. The pimp didn't seem very happy, but Danny interrupted their business.

"Hey, where's Mickey? And the others?" Danny asked the pimp.

The pimp seemed to be offended by Danny's intrusion, and I really didn't know how to feel. The smoke was making me want to cough up a lung.

"What the hell are you talkin' 'bout, kid? Did the daycare let you out early? What are you even doing in here? I don't know you and I don't know no Mickey," the pimp said as his head jerked around with each statement. He was a very passionate man.

His hair looked like a wig as it fell back into place without any combing or anything. Danny looked to me in confusion as he looked around the club once more.

But then, we were out of time.

"Ballz, what are you doing talking to these kids?"

Danny and I turned around to see the two men from the black sedan standing before us. They both wore nice suits and had ugly teeth.

"Sheeeeit, I don't know. They come bustin' up to me sayin' this and that and who knows what. Lookin' for some cat named Mickey."

"Mickey doesn't work here anymore, kids. Tandelli owns this joint now, and The Ballz here is the new pimp."

My gut twisted. It was two of Tandelli's men, the guys who shot the Don. They were already here in Detroit and taking over businesses. I didn't know how everything in the mob worked yet, but I knew this wasn't good.

"What are you doing following us across town?" Danny asked with a harsh tone.

One of the guys smiled maliciously, displaying a set of crooked and yellow teeth.

"We just wanna talk to you kids, that's all. Get to know you. We're new to the neighborhood and wanna know a good place to get some laundry done. We were looking into Laura's Laundromat, would you recommend that?"

The guy talked fast and I knew what he was hinting at. They were here to wreak havoc on the Don's operation.

Before I had time to breathe, Danny ripped his pistol out from behind him and fired once at the fast talker. He toppled backwards to the ground and the other man jumped behind a table. The sluts and pervs that suffocated the club started screaming and running out the front door. The Ballz covered his ears and cowered at the bar while Danny quickly looked around for an exit.

"Victor, c'mon!"

I pulled out my pistol and ran toward the bathroom at the back of the club with Danny. Just as we entered, the man behind the table fired at us. I didn't care to shoot back.

Danny locked the bathroom door behind us and we stumbled upon a few people playing with needles and spoons. At the time, I was ignorant to what was going on, but they were high as kites.

"Whoa, dudes, I'll have your money next week, I promise…" one of them said as a smile disappeared and then reappeared to his face.

Danny scoffed as he ran past them to the window that was out of reach. It reminded me of the one back at the high school that I had climbed out so many times.

"I know you can climb out of that alone, but could you give me a boost?" Danny said frantically.

There was pounding on the door and I nodded. I kneeled down on one knee like they taught us in P.E. and put my pistol on the ground to lock my hands for his foot. Luckily, the window was already open to let the smell leave the bathroom, and I hoisted Danny up and out of the window. Then, just as the second man fired at the door to open it, I climbed up and out the window with my pistol. Picking myself up out of the muck of the alley, I saw an ember glow coming from ahead. Danny was frozen stiff.

His car was being cooked.

In any other moment, I think Danny would've cried about the loss of his prized possession, but at that moment, our lives were more important.

All of a sudden, we heard the window for the girl's bathroom open and The Ballz, in all of his ridiculousness, climbed out of the window and fell. Danny and I had our pistols aimed at him and he put his hands up.

"Look kids, I don't know what the hell is going on, but I can help you if you let me live. I see your car's blazing, I can drive us somewhere safe."

"No more time for talk, just take us to your car and I'll tell you where to drive," Danny ordered.

The Ballz nodded as we lowered our guns and he ran out of the alley to find his car. I had a feeling I knew which car was his as soon as I spotted it.

The car was a Cadillac with pink carpeting all over it and very tinted windows, along with fuzzy dice and other little knick knacks hanging from his rear view mirror.

"It's unlocked, jump in," The Ballz ordered as we ran up to his car.

Just as we all got in and The Ballz started it up, one of the two men ran out and fired at the car. Danny and I fired from the backseat and ruined his back windshield. The glass shattered and the man took several hits to the chest and his legs. He would spend the rest of his night bleeding out on the curb. The Ballz cursed loudly and burned out of his parking spot.

"Nice shot, Victor, I think you finished him," Danny said as he reloaded.

I didn't really want that on my conscience, but something inside told me that what I did wasn't wrong. At this point, it was just survival. Kill or be killed, and I chose to kill to stay alive. I didn't even think when I fired back at him, I just did it. He wanted to kill us; otherwise, I wouldn't have done it. I never would have done it.

Danny directed The Ballz to the manor without The Ballz knowing we were going there. As soon as we started approaching the gate, I saw guns come out and they were all pointed at our car.

Danny called out, "Wait!" as he stepped out of the car and had his empty hands up in the air. "It's me and Victor, open the gate, we were just attacked!"

"Were you followed?" someone's voice yelled out.

"No!" Danny exclaimed back.

With that, the gates creaked open and Danny got back in the car and led The Ballz up to the front of the manor. When I got out of the car and heard the stillness of the night, I knew we were safe…

For now.

## Chapter Seventeen

"So," the Don started as me, Danny, The Ballz, Leo, Roy, and Jordan, along with David and a few other henchmen all piled into the dining room across from the kitchen, "who wants to tell me *what the fuck* happened?"

The anger that was seething from the Don was one of the scariest things I had ever experienced. I knew he couldn't be mad at us though, could he? We did what he asked. He warned me that this day would come, and although it was a lot sooner than I thought it would be, we had reacted pretty reasonably in my opinion.

But, the only person who mattered at this point was the Don.

"Dad, it's not what you think, okay? I know you said I couldn't leave the house, but Victor's dad kicked him out and he had nowhere else to go, and after I picked him up, he told me he saw some guys following him but he thought they were your guys. So, I told him they weren't and we couldn't get them off our tail so I thought we could lose them in your club. Then when I get in there, none of your guys are there and Little Mickey is gone too. I panicked and decided to ask this pimp where Mickey was, then the guys came in and said they were Tandelli's men, and they wanted to talk to us, but I knew they wanted more than that, so I shot one of them and then we escaped out the bathroom window and my car was in flames, so the pimp here drove us out of there after we took out one of the guys and then I told him to come here and… now we're here."

Danny needed a breath of fresh air after that drawn-out explanation, but he wasn't the only one. It was a lot for the Don to take in. He let out a large sigh, which was always preferable in a bad situation. Then, he looked to me.

"Is all of that true, Victor?" the Don asked in a calmed voice.

"Yes, yes Don, it's all true. I didn't mean to have them follow me, I swear. I thought they were your guys or something."

"No, Victor, it's okay. It's not your fault," the Don said, and I felt relieved. "I'm glad you guys are safe."

"Dad, you should have seen how Victor took out the last guy. He's a marksman, I tell ya," Danny said, almost like an excited little kid.

"Good, I'm glad David taught him well," the Don said with a slight smile. Then, he turned his attention to the pimp. "What's your name?"

The Ballz seemed nervous ever since he had come into the manor. Mainly because Leo escorted him in at gunpoint to make sure he didn't do anything shady.

"My name is Michael 'The Ballz' Ball, but you can just call me 'The Ballz'."

"I'm not going to call you that," the Don said in disgust. "What happened to Little Mickey?"

"Dude, I don't even know who the fuck that is, honest."

"Why were you pimping at my club?"

"Tandelli told me to. Said it was his club."

"His club?" the Don exclaimed with a newfound anger.

"Actually, boss, that makes sense," Leo said. The Don turned to Leo and we all paid attention to what he had to say. "For the past few days, I've been trying to call The Tease and get someone to answer but they never would. I thought it might be occupied by Tandelli's men, so I knew it was too dangerous to go in and check it out."

"So you let my son check it out and almost get killed instead!?" the Don fumed.

Leo shook his head out of embarrassment and said, "No, boss, that's not what was meant to happen."

"Why wasn't I told any of this? Why didn't anyone tell me anything!?"

"In all fairness," Jordan piped in, "The Doctor said to leave you be if you were resting."

"I don't give a shit what that quack doctor says. I didn't need three days of rest with no information!"

The room fell silent as everyone realized their mistakes. This was all getting out of hand faster than I could even grasp.

"So, what now?" I asked.

Everyone seemed perturbed by the question, but I thought it was an appropriate one.

"Well," Leo started, "if this piece of shit pimp isn't going to tell us anything, I guess we should just take him out."

Leo started to expose his pistol and shoot The Ballz right there in front of all of us, but after The Ballz started crying out and yelling something about having information, the Don said, "Leo, stop it! Not in my house."

Leo let the pistol fall at his side as we all waited for The Ballz to speak.

"What is it, Michael?" the Don asked.

"Well, y'see, some of Tandelli's men are going to meet with me tomorrow morning for a collection. Maybe you guys could follow me to it, or whatever. Just don't kill me, please! I didn't know about any of this shit. Tandelli just flew me in from Cali and I had no idea it was your club, I swear! I can help you guys! I even saved your kids from those men at the club!"

The Don nodded as he thought over everything.

"So, we're going to ambush them? Try to get more information on Tandelli's whereabouts?" Roy suggested.

"Yes, that sounds like an excellent plan," the Don said, and then he looked at The Ballz. "You're going to stay here tonight, but you're not allowed any phone calls, you understand? Jordan, you're on watch with the pimp. What time is the collection?"

"Ten thirty in the morning," The Ballz answered.

The Don glanced at his watch and said, "Well, we need to plan out this ambush and then hit the hay. Tomorrow's going to be a big day, like it or not."

I started to leave, but the Don asked, "Victor, where are you going?"

I stopped and turned around.

"Oh, I just thought you had business to discuss so I thought I'd get out of the way."

"No Victor, stay right there in that seat. You're going to be a part of this ambush, too. You and Danny."

## Chapter Eighteen
### Thursday, March 18th, 1976

Basically, school was not a main concern anymore.

Danny told me that when he was younger, if something went bad and they thought he might be in danger, they would keep Danny home from school for weeks on end. As a kid, staying home that long would be paradise, but as a high school student, it meant a lot of homework.

The plan we made up the night before was pretty simple: The Ballz was going to meet up with Tandelli's men inside a warehouse by the pier and we were going to hide out and ambush them. The goal was to keep one man standing so we could further question him, and find out where Tandelli was hiding out.

Because Danny's car was torched, we ended up riding in a cargo van with Leo driving and Roy in the passenger's seat. The Don basically owned the docks, and there was no one to be found working them today, because he ordered them not to come this morning.

Jordan, Scott, and Roy all held M-16 assault rifles while Danny and I only had our pistols. The Don claimed that we would have enough fire power and to not worry, but I really didn't know how many guys we were going to be up against. Two? Five? Twenty?

It made the trip there a little exciting, but not in a good way. I still didn't feel good about any of this, not the ensuing ambush, and not yesterday's shootout. But the Don made it clear that it was kill or be killed at this point. To me, it was all about survival. There was no way I was going to let these guys kill me.

I looked at Danny and asked, "Why didn't your dad come?"

Danny shook his head and laughed, almost as if I was stupid.

"Victor, it's not safe for my dad — a crime boss — to come to this. He might get shot. Even if David is a great shot, he still couldn't protect my dad from a group of ten guys at once. Besides, my dad doesn't need to see this. We'll just take care of business, and then report back to him," Danny answered as he cocked his pistol.

In the back of my mind, I noticed Danny wasn't sugar coating anything anymore. He wasn't calling his dad a businessman… now he called him what he was: A crime boss.

In some ways, I cared about how my future would end up, and worried about how deep into all of this I was going to get. But another part of me just thought of the fortunes and glory that had already been bestowed upon me.

Finally, the van started to come to a stop as Jordan opened the side door of the van and jumped out. Danny, Scott, Roy, and I all followed suit. Leo stayed in the van and left it running as Jordan did the talking with The Ballz.

"Everything good? Are they coming?" Jordan asked as we stood outside the warehouse.

"Yeah, we straight. Just don't hit me in the crossfire, would 'ya?" The Ballz argued.

"No, we wouldn't dream of doing that," Roy said as he cocked his M-16.

For some reason, I didn't pay much attention to the conversation and I looked out on the water instead. The water was shining brightly into my eyes, but then, something shined into my eyes from above.

When I looked up and across the water, I noticed a crane up high in the sky and not being used and I thought I saw a figure move in the control area.

"Victor, are you paying attention?" Leo called out from the van.

Everyone's eyes were on me and I snapped out of it and said, "No, sorry... I thought I saw something move in the crane."

Danny was the only one who seemed to believe me as Roy said, "You're probably just daydreaming, kid. We said we're going to fire down on them from the office building up in the warehouse. It gives us a clear view of where they'll meet. Leo's going to go park the van around back. The most important part is, don't shoot the guy closest to... The Ballz."

"Damn right you better not shoot him or me. He'll be able to tell you the most information. If there's anyone else here, they're just extra goons."

"Yeah, yeah, yeah, Michael, we've got it," Leo said as he put the van in drive. "I'm gonna park this and I'll meet you guys in the office."

Jordan glanced at his watch and said, "Better hurry, Leo, they'll be here soon."

"Don't you worry too much Jordan, it'll mess up your aim," Leo said with an evil smile as he pulled away.

After comprehending all the instructions, I glanced back at the crane to see if there was any more movement. When I didn't see any, Danny said, "Victor, c'mon."

We all ran to the warehouse and up the clunky stairs to the all-seeing office. The plush orange office had windows on all sides, but I saw how we were going to look out over The Ballz and the other gangsters. We ran up to the windows we'd be firing out of and watched as The Ballz comically tried to run to his car in those ridiculous lifted shoes. Jordan laughed first, and I laughed with him to ease the tension I felt. All of this was scary and exciting at the same time.

"Okay, as soon as we see those cars come in, we need to duck down and stay out of sight. We have the office door opened to hear what they're saying. As soon as The Ballz says something about handing over the money, we're going to fire down on them, okay?"

"But don't hit the guy that talks or The Ballz?" I asked.

"Yeah, kid, you never want to hit The Ballz if you get what I'm saying," Roy said as he started laughing.

"Very funny, guys."

We all jumped and turned around to see Leo standing there behind us. From then on, I knew why he was seen as the surveillance man.

"Jesus, Leo, we all have loaded weapons ready to go and you decide it's a good idea to scare us?" Jordan yelled.

"Don't bitch too much, Jordan," Leo said roughly. "Just pay attention and... get down!"

Leo's commands never got any back talk. We all dropped to the ground as three black sedans rolled into the warehouse. Leo got really close to the windows and looked out over the scene.

"Okay, they're all piling out. It looks like... shit, about nine guys."

The way Leo said that made me worry, until he looked back and said, "Don't worry, kids, we got this."

Danny seemed to be annoyed that we were always called the kids, but I understood it. It would take time for me to get enough respect that they'd call me by my first name.

When the car doors closed and The Ballz stepped out, the talking began.

"Michael 'The Ballz' Ball, man it's been a while since I've seen you," the main man said.

We all looked out to see a man in a finely tailored navy blue suit. He shook hands with The Ballz and The Ballz responded, "Yes, it has been a while, Nicholas."

"That's our guy," Leo commented.

We all shook our heads and continued to watch as the men conversed.

Nicholas looked over The Ballz' car and made sure his black hair wasn't messed up. He slicked it back and said, "My oh my, what happened to your car?"

Nicholas was referring to the bullet holes and he examined them closely, meeting each hole face-to-face.

"I ran into some of Ponchello's dudes, you know," The Ballz replied.

"Oh, the same ones that took out my soldiers at the club?"

"Yeeyuh," The Ballz replied, and I noticed he was trying to think of a good cover story before replying. "Will and that other guy were checking on business and when they were about to leave, those Ponchello suckahs started shooting the place up! When I ran out, they fired at my car and complained about someone named 'Little Mickey'?"

Nicholas met eye-to-eye with The Ballz and said, "That's the pimp that used to be there under Ponchello's control. Don't worry, we took him out."

Jordan and Roy seemed distraught as the news was brought to them in such a terrible way.

"Oh, yeeyuh I understand. Hey, y'know, I was wondering when I might be able to see Don Tandelli, y'know? I haven't seen him since I got here. Last time I saw him, he was sucking one of those fat cigars back in Vegas."

The Ballz laughed but Nicholas started to worry.

"Michael," Nicholas started as his men tensed up with their guns in hand, "You're not wearing a wire, are you?"

Danny and I looked at each other and feared the worst was about to happen.

"What? Are you kidding, fool? I ain't wearin' no wires up in here. I'm doing illegal shit just like you guys. I got twenty pounds of weed in the back of my ride, you know I don't work for cops."

"Okay, Michael, just checking."

"See, I even got your money from pimpin', right here!"

That's when Leo gave us all the big nod and we stood to fire.

The sound of the gunfire and glass shattering was enormous as we all fired down upon Tandelli's men. I was firing but I didn't really aim at anyone in particular. I just fired around the same area where Danny was firing. For some reason, I didn't like the idea of just gunning these people down. Mainly since they didn't fire on us first.

Before I could change my mind and try to shoot at someone else, it was all over. All of the men were down, even Nicholas...

"Shit, I said don't shoot him!" Leo yelled as he ran out of the office to check on him.

We all followed behind Leo and Jordan shouted, "I didn't mean to hit him, it was a ricochet, honest!"

As The Ballz got out of his crouch and back on his feet, we all ran down to see the destruction we had caused. The eight men around us were bleeding all over the warehouse floor. Their faces were blank and lifeless.

I didn't like to look, but I felt like I had to. I wondered who they were, what their names were, why they'd ever want to do anything like this. I wondered if they even knew what was about to happen to them. We ended their lives… but were they ready for their lives to end in this made up war?

Nicholas coughed as the blood stain on his chest got worse and worse. The sight bothered me, but I couldn't help staring. Leo slung the M-16 on his back and looked over Nicholas for a brief second before asking questions.

"All right, Nicholas Ortiz, you tell us where Tandelli is and I might try to save your life," Leo ordered.

Nicholas looked over to us and then back to Leo.

"Fuck you and your Don," Nicholas spat.

Danny got mad and actually kicked Nicholas in the chest where he was shot. Nicholas shouted in pain and Roy pulled Danny back. He was angry.

"Danny, you must have misheard Nicholas," Leo started as he grabbed his collar. "He just wants a little fresh air, right?"

Before Nicholas could answer, Leo started dragging him all the way across the warehouse and to the outside doors where we first met up. The Ballz followed us out there and he leaned over Nicholas.

"C'mon man, just tell them what they wanna know! I'm tired of all this killin' man," The Ballz said in an emotional way.

Nicholas seemed to sympathize with The Ballz, but then he turned and said, "You betraying son of a-"

A shot was heard from afar and a stray bullet hit Nicholas in the head and blood sprayed up in The Ballz' face. The Ballz shouted as he jumped up and started spitting. Everyone tensed up and started to move for cover, but we knew the sniper only had one target. Immediately, I looked to the crane and saw a man stand up and start his way to the ladder.

"See?" I yelled out, trying to oppress what just happened out of my memory. "There he goes!"

"Jesus, kid, good eye," Leo said as we all stood in amazement. "Doesn't matter though. I feel like if we chase him, he'll lead us into a trap. Let's just scram back to the manor. We'll regroup there. Michael… you better follow behind us."

*****

We were now all in the meeting room, telling the Don that everything went south. It was never how we wanted to explain things.

"A sniper?" the Don asked.

"Yeah, he picked off Nicholas Ortiz right as we were questioning him," Jordan explained.

"So, you're telling me that Victor saw this sniper, but no one cared to check it out?" the Don asked.

Danny elbowed me in a congratulatory way and I smiled as the Don seemed upset with the older men.

"Look, Don, the only reason that sniper was there is because this prick sold us out!" Roy exclaimed as he pointed to The Ballz.

Before The Ballz could retort, Leo said, "No, Roy, The Ballz didn't sell us out. Tandelli is just smarter than we're giving him credit for. He knew we were going to use Michael to lure them out and get information. I noticed that Nicholas was guarded by some of their lowest paid men."

Leo really did do a bunch of spying. He seemed to know everything. I still worried if he spied on me, but I knew the moment I asked him, he'd be on to me about something.

"That's quite a few men to cover one guy," the Don commented.

"Which is exactly my point. They were going to try to fight back our ambush but they didn't know where we were. They thought the cops got Michael to drag them out of their hole. Some of the men still had their safeties on their guns. Look, before today, Michael hasn't talked to anyone since Danny and Victor ran into him at the club."

The Don looked around the room and gave everyone a look. Unbeknownst to me, it was a cry for help.

"So, what do you think we should do now?" the Don asked.

"Uh," Jordan said, and we all knew he was going to say something non-serious, "I dunno Don, you're supposed to call the shots."

"And I will!" the Don said fiercely. "Men, we are going to war, as if this wasn't enough of a war already. I don't know where Tandelli is, and neither do any of you... Leo, that's your job. Find out where Tandelli is, and fast. Talk to our cop on the inside and do whatever you have to do to find him. Jordan, find someone who can torch down The Tease. That'll send a message to Tandelli, trying to take over my businesses. Scott, call the other businesses and make sure we have people watching them at all times, I don't want any more take-overs. Danny and Victor..."

The Don stared at us for a second and I think he could see the worry and fear in my eyes.

"You two, take the rest of the day off, but don't leave the manor. Today was probably a little too much for you guys, but it'll grow to not bother you one day. I'll have new orders for you in the morning, okay?"

"Thanks, Dad," Danny said as he got up to hug the Don.

"I love you, Daniel," the Don said before he kissed Danny's head and messed up his hair.

Danny and I left the meeting room and headed up to his room.

"C'mon Victor, I'm going to teach you some card games," Danny said as we headed up the stairs.

"Danny," I said, trying to call after him.

Danny stopped mid-stairway and looked at me.

"Yeah?"

"Didn't killing those men bother you?" I asked without hesitation.

Danny made a face that said "more or less" but he said, "Victor, in a way, it does bother me a little. But those men want my dad dead, they want you dead, and they want me dead, no matter what. So I'm going to protect myself, my father, and you, because I care about all of us. Now, the worst way to deal with this situation is to dwell on it for too long. C'mon, let's go play cards. I know what they're going to have us do tomorrow, and trust me, you'll be glad I taught you some games."

## Chapter Nineteen
### Mid-March, 1976

Danny was right about teaching me those card games, because the next day (and the next few weeks to follow), he and I were part of a security team for a bar the Don owned. Danny and I were always there, and then the other two guys would swap with us at the end of the day. The extra security was to ensure that Tandelli didn't take over or attack another business of the Don's, which was said to happen. Surprisingly, the whole time we were on security detail, I never heard of anything else happening.

Both sides were relatively quiet as this real life chess game played out.

But, like my experience with chess, it could be extremely boring.

Finally one day, instead of being stuck inside the smoky bar, Jordan and Roy said it was okay for us to go outside and play cards out on the concrete. We all started playing a friendly game of Blackjack with Jordan as the dealer.

"Ha! I win again," Jordan said as he took our pennies.

I shook my head and sighed loudly. Danny followed suit.

"How do dealers always win?" Roy asked as he shook his head and took a puff from his cigarette.

Jordan ignored Roy as he looked over to me and Danny and said, "You kids tired or something? You wanna run on home and take a nap?"

"Can we?" Danny asked eagerly.

"Pshhh..." Jordan said as he waved his hand. "No. You know what, you guys should actually be glad right now."

"Why's that?" I asked.

"Well," Jordan said as he shuffled the cards. "It used to be that when war was announced, a blood bath ensued pretty quickly afterwards. But, you kids are lucky. Hell, we even get to sit outside today from the lack of activity these past few weeks."

"Will things pick up?" I asked.

"Fuck if I know. Hopefully not."

"How long have you been in the gang, Jordan?"

Danny looked at me like it wasn't a good question to ask, but Jordan acted proud of his answer.

"Well let's see, I'm thirty-six now, and I was pretty much a runt back in the day... I think it's been about twelve years or so. Danny was only six when I came bouncing into town."

"Yeah, that's right," Danny clarified.

"But," Jordan said as he handed out the cards, "back in those days, the Don… was like a violent king. Like Macbeth, but not as crazy."

"You can read?" Danny asked with a sly grin.

"Eh, shut up," Jordan said. I asked to hit on my cards and I got nineteen. After I said stay, Jordan looked to Danny. "So, hit or stand? Stand? Okay… anyway, back when anyone posed as a threat to us… hit or stand, Roy?… we used to hunt them down and fish them out. I remember one showdown was almost like how the British used to fight us in the Revolutionary War. They were all in a line, and advanced on us… ah, I bust. Guess you guys win."

I wasn't sure how to feel about that, but the card game kept me distracted enough to not think about it too much.

"Hey, Jordan," Danny asked as Jordan shuffled. "What about you and Michelle? How's that working out for you?"

"What?" Jordan said, surprised. "How do you know about that?"

"Everyone knows about that," Roy replied.

"Oh, well in that case," Jordan said as a cheesy smile went over his face. "Let's just say when your party was going on, Michelle and I were having our own private party."

"Are you saying…?" Roy started, but then he laughed too hard to finish. Finally, he regained his composure and said, "Are you saying the party was private or it was a party with your privates?"

Roy started to laugh harder and harder and Danny and I joined him. Jordan seemed a little embarrassed at first, but he finally started laughing too and said, "All right, yeah, yeah, yeah, you got me."

We played a few more games, and then Danny asked, "What about you, Roy? How are you liking it here?"

"What? As opposed to fighting a made up war in a hot tropical shithole? Yeah, this is a lot better. The Don is a good man in my eyes. He wants what's best for me, and for you guys, too. He offers you a job and he wants you to make yourself a worthy person to be around. I feel like without him… Gosh, I don't even want to think about what I would have done. Probably the same thing some of my comrades did."

"What'd they do?" Danny asked.

"Oh, you don't wanna know… and I wish I didn't."

"Fellas?"

We all looked up to see Scott approaching us with a doggy bag in one hand and a soda in the other. Another henchman that I didn't recognize was standing behind him.

"Oh, are you taking our spots?" Danny asked.

"Yup, time for you to report back and say what all you've observed today," Scott said as he sat on the curb with Jordan and Roy.

"A whole lot of nothing," Jordan said as he started a new game of cards.

"Really? We actually saw some guy snooping around at Giovanni's. Thought he might be a problem. Turns out, it was some queer food critic."

"Hey, how are we supposed to get home?" Danny asked.

"Oh yeah, your car went up in flames, didn't it?" Scott said.

Danny almost got mad, until Scott threw the keys to his Mustang to Danny.

"I'll just hitch a ride back with Jordan and Roy," Scott said. "Just don't scratch it."

"Wow, thanks Scott!" Danny shouted.

"Actually, wait a second," Scott said as he ripped open his doggy bag and pulled out a greasy cheeseburger. "How about you let Victor drive?"

"Yeah, Victor, you should!" Danny said as he handed me the keys.

"Geez, I don't know, Scott, that would be really cool, but…"

"Hey, as long as you know how to drive a stick-shift… I can't stand how they make all cars automatic nowadays."

I looked at the keys and felt an overwhelming feeling of excitement.

"Yes, I know how to drive a manual without riding the clutch," I answered.

Roy and Jordan laughed as Scott said, "Okay, well, have fun."

I opened the door and climbed into the red 1967 convertible Mustang. The top was already down, so Danny hopped over the door and got in with a huge smile.

"All right, Victor, bring that thing to life!"

I started the engine and we pulled away from the curb. Scott probably had immediate regrets as we headed onto the highway with Danny screaming with excitement. I laughed at Danny as we sped along the highway.

"Hey, Victor!" Danny called out as we were driving. "I started thinking about it and noticed you didn't go eat with your family friend these past few Wednesdays?"

My heart sort of dropped as Danny mentioned that to me. Sadly, because of the idea that Leo might keep surveillance on me, I didn't go eat with Chief Ramzorin at all the past two weeks. I did call him though, and told him I wouldn't be able to for a few weeks due to my new work schedule, but it still made me feel bad.

"Well, he went out of town so it actually kind of worked out for the better," I lied to Danny.

***** 

After pulling into the garage and tossing the keys to Phil, Danny and I headed towards the Don's office to report on the non-existent events of the day.

Danny knocked four times on the door and we heard the muffled voice of the Don say "Come on in".

Danny opened the door and the Don and Leo continued their conversation as we entered.

"So you haven't been able to find Tandelli?" the Don asked Leo.

"No. Ever since we killed his men at the warehouse and torched The Tease, I haven't been able to find any of his other men in these parts. Even our cop on the inside can't find anyone."

"And you said you have a theory of sorts?" the Don asked.

Leo nodded.

"Yes, boss, I believe that no matter what, Tandelli's plan was to kill you in Vegas and make sure you didn't come back. I have reason to believe that as soon as you left, his men took over The Tease and they were going to have us for breakfast the morning after you were killed in Vegas, but it didn't work out that way for them. Instead, you came back to life and their plan failed so now they're trying something else. I don't think Tandelli has arrived yet, if he is coming here."

"Well, we're not going to take the fight to him. I bet he has the airport there in Vegas ready to shoot down my jet if they see it."

"Do you have the airport here ready to take him out?" Leo asked.

"No. They're just supposed to call me if he flies in. We'll handle the rest from there. I'm not going to waste any of my good men dicking off at the airport."

Finally, the Don ended his conversation with Leo to pay attention to me and Danny.

"Hello, anything of interest happen today?" the Don asked.

"No, sir," Danny responded.

"Hmph," the Don responded as he leaned back in his leather rolling chair. "All right, well you two have done enough today. Thanks for staying vigilant."

Danny and I nodded as we left his office and headed to the living room to watch TV.

"Man, I mean," Danny said as he pulled up the remote and turned the TV on, "I'm kind of glad nothing has happened, but maybe all of this has no point, you know? Maybe Tandelli doesn't even want any more trouble."

"You think so?" I asked.

"I'm pretty confident. Just like Jordan was saying, it used to be a bloodbath. I remember I had to stay home from school most of the time so I wouldn't get kidnapped and used as bait. But now? Nothing is happening. I think they fled."

"You kids better be careful what you say."

Leo's voice echoed as he walked up behind us. We both turned around in a shocked way and looked over the couch at him. He had a red apple in one hand and he tossed it up in the air a few times before he made his point.

"Tandelli is like a snake. Right when you think he's not going to bite, he does. But don't worry; we're going to bite first."

# **Chapter Twenty**
## Early April

I don't think I've mentioned it before, but owning a gun makes me feel... Cool, I guess. I'm not really sure what to make of it. At first, I felt really powerful. I would see someone walking in the streets and I felt safe, even if they posed as a threat. Then other days, well, I feel like a threat. I feel like other people know I have a gun on me, and so they stay away. I keep them away. Not sure how I feel about it yet...

Anyway, Danny and I still had to watch the bar for a few more weeks. The only "interesting" thing that happened was, I guess no one cared to mention that the bartender was a racist.

An African American man had asked for a drink, and an outburst soon followed.

"Hah! Like I'd serve some nigger. Get the fuck outta here."

The bartender started to reach for a baseball bat, so Danny and I intervened. It appeared that the bartender had participated in some quality control with his liquor supply earlier in the day.

The African American man was big and strong; taller than anyone else in the bar. But, Danny and I were the only two who could take care of the situation without any bloodshed, since Roy was in the john and Jordan was out getting some lunch.

"Hey, Jimmy, take it easy, will ya?" Danny said with a mocking accent as he took one of the African American's arms. "This way, buddy."

I hesitated to grab the man's other arm. He had a long gash over his left eye. It looked like a knife had jaggedly cut down from his forehead to his cheekbone. He looked distraught, and upset.

The man jerked lightly and Danny held tighter.

"Uh, Victor, a little help here?"

I finally swooped in and grabbed the other man's arm, but he peacefully walked out. After the escort, the man looked to us and said, "So, are you kids some kind of soldiers or something?"

"Look," Danny started, "we don't want any trouble. We're just trying to keep the peace, and our bartender has the right to decline any customer of service that he chooses. Okay? There's a bar a few blocks down the road if you're really thirsty."

"Heh..." the African American man started, "Sure, kids... I get what's going on here. Maybe I'll see you guys again."

With that, the African American man strolled off and Danny looked at me.

"Hmm, what a strange guy," Danny commented with an estranged look.

"I'll say."

Finally, the message came through. The one that, I guess, we had been waiting for.

"Guys, we're all supposed to meet at the manor right now. It's urgent," Jordan said as he stepped out of the bar into the sunlight.

We all piled into Roy's station wagon and we headed toward the manor. When we arrived, several men with guns stood around outside and inside. This didn't look good to me at all.

Scott led us into the meeting/dining room and Leo was standing to the right of the seated Don and David stood to the left. We took our seats wherever we could and the meeting started.

"There's good news, and then there's better news," the Don said with a grim smile. "Leo has finally located where Don Tandelli resides. But, he's there with his family, so it's out of the question to attack him there. Luckily, Leo figured a different plan."

Leo took over talking.

"Tandelli is opening a spa here, and its first private opening is tomorrow. He's going to meet with some people who have betrayed us and this will give us a perfect opportunity. The plan is: I'm going to plant some chlorine gas in the vents and have it start to leak after I get out. They'll start choking to death and get all kinds of fucked up. The steam will make it all even worse. So when they do try and escape, the back door will be the only one unlocked and we'll be waiting for them so we can gun them down."

"Y'see, we can't just kill Tandelli," the Don explained. "The other men that will be in there are traitors to our organization. They must be eliminated too, are we clear?"

I noticed The Ballz was also in the meeting room, so I guessed he had worked out a deal to stay alive.

"When are we attacking?" Danny asked, with a slight sense of hesitation in his voice.

"Tomorrow morning, 9 AM. That's when we'll get there with the guns."

"What am I supposed to do?" I asked.

The Don smiled and said, "Victor, I thought you were a part of us now?"

All eyes were on me as they anticipated my response.

"I am," I said, not sure what else to say.

"Then you'll be part of the firing squad. David says you're a good shot, and you spotted the sniper who killed Nicholas. We'll need you out there, Victor."

"Damn, I never got this much moral support," Jordan argued in a joking way.

"Well maybe David here should train you some more in the range," the Don said, and everyone fell into laughter, even the Don. But when the Don clenched where he was shot, everyone fell silent.

"The main objective is," the Don started in a dark voice, "make him pay."

## Chapter Twenty One
### The Next Day

Everyone was awakened at 6:50 to start getting ready for the "big day". It was safe to say I didn't get much sleep that night. The thought of killing several people haunted me each time I started drifting. Plus, even though I could barely hear the muffled sound of gunfire down in the range, it still kept me up. When a man knocked on Danny's door and told us to wake up, I was already there, but Danny was a little less ready.

"Mmm, just give me another minute or six," Danny muttered as I shook him.

"Danny, c'mon dude."

At this point, I thought I should be paid to wake up Danny.

After we got dressed and went downstairs, the kitchen was filled more with guns than breakfast.

David met us down there and he looked to have a clean shaven face for once. He drank some hot coffee and got my attention.

"Victor, I wanna show you something."

Danny, still half asleep, walked over with me as we ate some cereal.

"Now, this here is an M16 assault rifle. We're going to give you and Danny these to use instead of your pistols."

David proceeded to tell us how to use them and that they might have quite a kick to them compared to the pistols. I started to feel a little more excited, but also very nervous.

"What about the police?" I asked after David explained.

"What about them?" David asked.

"Well, aren't they going to show up right after we start shooting up the place?" I asked.

Eerily, the Don walked up behind me and said, "No, we won't have to worry about the police until later. Our man on the force is patrolling that area and he's going to let it slide."

I jumped after he said that but I didn't turn around. Afterwards, he patted my shoulder and said, "It'll be fine, Victor. But I'm glad you're so observant, unlike my son here, who seems to still be asleep."

"No, I'm awake," Danny argued.

"Good. I don't want you asleep behind the trigger."

When our bowls were empty and our stomachs were half full, we walked outside with our M16s and piled into one of the two vans that were going to the attack. Roy checked his watch and said, "All right, it's 8:30. Leo should be just about there and get the ball rolling for us."

Scott and Jordan started to walk past and Danny stopped them.

"Hey, what are you guys doing? Aren't you getting in the van?"

They shook their heads and Jordan explained, "The Don asked us to do something else. We'll see you after you're done, though."

Now, Danny and I were stuck in a van and we only knew Roy. The rest of the people held assault rifles too, and they talked to each other like this was nothing. It seemed that Danny and I were the only nervous ones.

Fortunately, Roy also expressed his concern.

"Jesus, I haven't held one of these in my hands since the war," Roy said as he indicated the M16.

I would have carried on the conversation, but I remember late that one night when he and Leo were chatting about it with Jordan. The thought made me shiver, on top of the whole situation making me queasy.

The vans were puttering, waiting to drive off. It was a waste of gas that didn't make anyone bat an eye except for me. Finally, the Don walked out of the manor with his M16 held high and he said, "All right, we're moving out!"

The Don ran up to the back doors of the van and looked at me and Danny.

"You boys shoot whoever comes out of that spa, okay? All of them."

I nodded with Danny and the Don smiled. Then, he made sure our feet were out of the way and he closed our doors. Danny and I looked at each other; all Danny could say was, "Here we go."

*****

Because it was a bumpy ride, it was hard to hear all of the instructions that were yelled by one of the unknown men, but Danny repeated them to me.

"Okay, when the van stops, we're all jumping out and fanning out and you better get into position quick. When they start spilling out of the back and the Don says to fire, we fire. Afterwards, we'll climb back in the vans and move to the next location. Everyone ready?"

I nodded and checked my M16. It was fully loaded and ready to go.

My heart raced and my palms were sweaty as I heard the "shotgun" passenger say, "We're almost there!"

"Man, fuck this guy Tandelli," one unnamed man said. "He shoots the Don, we shoot him to bits."

Danny seemed to grimace and I followed suit. This almost didn't seem right, but the way the guy explained it made me feel more compelled to do it.

"Okay, this is going to be a little rough!" the driver yelled as he swung the van around and put it in reverse.

"Just like your mother likes it!" some other guy yelled.

"Up yours, Ray!"

When the van screeched to a stop, Roy grabbed the handle to the back door and pulled it down. The doors flew open and we all spread out in a single file line. All of the feet stomping into position was a thrilling sound that made my adrenaline soar. Our weapons were all aimed toward two foggy glass doors at the back of the decrepit building and we all waited. Danny was on my left, and then everyone from the other van was on his left. The Don was close to Danny's side, but we all just waited in a dirty, empty alleyway, waiting for the first victims to walk out.

First, we heard blood curdling screams.

"Everyone ready?" the Don asked.

I started to feel sick. All of this pressure was starting to just be too much.

Then, we saw the first blurry figure walking toward the foggy glass door.

"Get set," the Don said.

"C'mon, you pieces of shit," one of the armed men said.

Finally, the disturbing scene began.

A man with a sizzling afro walked out and steam was lifting off of him. But then, when the steam persisted, I realized it wasn't steam. It appeared that his flesh was being burned off by whatever Leo made. I paid attention in Chemistry sophomore year, but I never saw anything like this happen. The smell was horrible, but luckily it was faint. The afro man, only in swimming trunks, was about 10 yards away when the Don finally gave the order.

"Fire."

The Don fired first and the man cried out, but several more men walked out of the glassy doors with the same thing happening to them. Their flesh was burning red and their eyes were melting away. The only reason I started to fire was to put them out of their misery. The screams and cries were terrifying, and the only thing muffling them was the tremendous amount of gunfire. They were defenseless. They never saw it coming. I thought what we did to the people at the warehouse was bad, but this was just plain murder.

About fifteen men ended up walking out, and against a firing squad of sixteen men who all had at least thirty bullets each, they were all dead meat in the end. When the final man walked out, I could tell it was Tandelli. He was still wearing part of his suit and it was being burned away by the steam. He must've just walked into the front of the sauna when the chlorine gas started to form. He panted while he stumbled out and we all paused for a second to let the Don have the honor of putting him down.

"No, we all fire," the Don said, heartlessly.

So, with only a few bullets left, we all fired our last rounds into Don Tandelli. As the gunshots echoed out, Tandelli's final shout was heard all over Detroit.

Everything fell silent and the sizzling pile of bodies laid there in murky blood that filled up the alleyway. Gun smoke joined the steam as it ascended, and I knew we had won when the Don said, "Okay, let's get moving."

I felt sick as I stared at the bodies. It was disgusting to look at, but it was impossible to look away. Danny finally grabbed my arm and said, "C'mon Victor, we gotta go."

We left the corpses behind and moved on to the stronghold where Don Tandelli was living. It was on the south side of town in a little Victorian hotel that was so run down, I thought it was a joke. But, after we met up with Scott and Jordan, who were escorting the rest of Don Tandelli's weeping family out of there peacefully, Danny seemed to try and look on the bright side of things as we entered.

"Damn, Victor, look at this pad! Can you imagine the kind of parties we could throw in this place?"

I wanted to scold Danny, and ask him how he could even think about parties at a time like this, but I decided not to as the Don overheard him and said, "No, no parties. As soon as his family is moved out, we burn it down. This business has betrayed us."

Danny seemed disappointed, but as soon as he saw the look of disgust on my face, he started to sympathize with me.

Don Ponchello seemed happy as this whole thing came to an end, and so did the rest of the henchmen. But as for me? I couldn't feel worse about the whole thing. It was disgusting to me, and I resented the Don, especially after the newly widowed wife and her two young children wept as they passed me.

"Victor, you look a little pale," the Don commented.

"I've just never seen anything like that before," I said with emptiness, trying to collect my thoughts.

"Well, we came down on him a lot harder than we usually do with people who double cross me. Next time, which I hate to say there will be a next time, it won't be this bad. Trust me."

With the thought of there being a next time, I bolted away from everyone and threw up against a wall. Danny ran up behind me and patted my back. I gagged as more felt like it was going to come up. Sadly and surprisingly, the Don came up behind me too and started to pat my back.

"Everyone else get to the vans, we'll catch up," the Don ordered.

As I started to stand up straight and wipe my mouth, I looked up at the painting A Sunday Afternoon on the Island of La Grande Jatte, and for the first time in forever, I felt a sense of comfort.

# Chapter Twenty Two
## Monday, April 12th, 1976

Instead of being stuck watching over the bar or the Ponchello manor, Danny and I were finally allowed to go back to school. Although I once felt uncomfortable always carrying my pistol, it felt more empowering than ever before. The look that people gave me now was quite different than before. It's as if I intrigued people. They looked to me in a sort of awe, rather than fear or disgust like before. The rumors had circulated as to why Danny and I were gone for so long, but none of them were the truth. In fact, I was glad that no one else would ever know what happened.

But, I guess during my English class, I sort of dazed off and started to think way too much on my own. At one point, I was stuck in a psychotic state in my mind, not able to connect with anyone in the outside world. I was staring intensely out the window and Mrs. Huffman's words finally broke through.

"... everyone else get to work. Victor, Victor?"

Finally, she broke me out of whatever was happening.

"Yes, Mrs. Huffman?" I asked after one awkward laugh filled the silence.

"Could I have a word with you out in the hallway?"

In some ways, I had always had a fantasy about this moment. I always had feelings for my English teacher but I never knew how to address them. Well, it's not that I didn't know how to, it's that I knew better than to address them with her. Even though she was young, she was married and I knew I never had a chance.

But, the fantasy was further ruined by the idea that everything in my life had changed over the past few weeks.

I followed her out in the hallway and I heard some whispers among the other students. After Mrs. Huffman closed the door, the uncomfortable conversation began.

"Victor..." Mrs. Huffman started after a sigh. "I don't know why you were gone for so long, but I know that whatever it was changed you."

I didn't respond. It was best to let her do all the talking.

"I know kids have picked on you over the years and I'm sorry about that. But, I can't help you unless you let me know what happened. Why were you gone for so long? Some kids are saying you and Danny went and committed some terrible crimes, and after that shooting at the spa..."

That got my attention. No one had ever put that together. They just thought that Danny and I robbed some bank and had to lay low.

"Now I don't believe that theory, but you need to help me help you."

Her soft lips formulated her words perfectly and I started feeling a lot more uncomfortable than before.

"Mrs. Huffman," I said, trying to pull something out of my ass, "my parents just hoped that I would stay home for a few days and help them move some things around... it's a family thing, really. It's personal..."

"Victor, I know that's not true," Mrs. Huffman said bluntly. "Chief Ramzorin called and he's been looking for you. He didn't even know where you were. It wasn't until this weekend that the school was informed by some agency that you were not to be given any homework and that you were returning soon so none of your absences should count."

"Chief Ramzorin called?" I asked, feeling a little mad.

My anger then changed to fear as I questioned if Chief Ramzorin knew where I really was, and who Daniel really was.

"Yes. He was concerned about your safety and so was I. We were told not to bring this up to you, but I'm really worried, Victor. Now, just let me know what happened, okay? I can help you."

"Mrs. Huffman," I said, struggling to lie. "I just... I have a headache. Can I go see the nurse?"

"What is it, Victor? Are you afraid?" Mrs. Huffman asked.

"No," I said sternly. "I just need some medicine, that's all."

My face was red hot and I felt embarrassed for the outburst, but Mrs. Huffman seemed to understand as she said, "Okay Victor, but I'm not letting you go to the nurse. I'll grab some Tylenol out of my purse and you can go get a drink from the fountain at the end of the hallway."

When she brought the pill back to me, I looked into her beautiful eyes and said, "Thank you, Mrs. Huffman. I really do appreciate it. I wish I could tell you what happened, but don't worry about it. It'll all be better soon."

## **Chapter Twenty Three**
### End of April

After school on one Friday, Danny and I returned to the manor to find everyone having a discussion in the meeting room. Leo walked up to us and said, "Hey, where have you guys been? You need to get in there."

"Well, we were learning, Leo, at a place called 'school'," Danny said sarcastically.

"Just get in there," Leo said with a smug look on his face that seemed more directed toward me.

As Danny and I walked in, the Don made it obvious.

"Ah, there they are. Our two newest men."

The Don started to clap for us and the other men joined in. The appreciation almost made me forget the horrendous thing we had done.

"Sit down, kids. We're discussing some future plans."

Danny and I took our seats quietly and the Don continued talking.

"Well, now that Tandelli is taken care of, we can focus on some new things. I have a few men out in Vegas now trying to take control of the hotels he ran. That will help us financially, and I've also gathered some intel that Tandelli ran quite a few businesses in New York. Now, if we play our cards right, I think we can make some money there and possibly recruit some people from out there to join our gang."

It was the first time Don Ponchello admitted that this was a gang, but for some reason it passed by without fazing me.

"Who are we sending over to New York?" Scott asked.

"Me and Victor?" Danny said with excitement.

One day at the bar, Danny was drawing and I saw how good he was at it. He said his dream would be to one day go to NYC and participate in an art show, or even just go to one. I felt that he could do really well if he did.

But, the Don said, "No, Danny. You and Victor need to stay here. You guys are too important. You've both made your mark here."

That made me feel good. I was actually accepted and wanted.

"Thank you," I said to the Don, even though Danny was disappointed.

The Don smiled at my appreciation and he continued to say, "Leo is going to New York for a few weeks, maybe even a month. We already have a small operation there but we hope to try and expand, as long as the Italians don't get too perturbed."

"So I'm going alone?" Leo asked.

"Well, who do you want to take with you? You're taking the jet into JFK and then meeting with Eric there. There shouldn't be any problems, but if you want, you can take Scott."

"But then, who's going to open the gate for everyone?" Jordan asked.

Michelle walked in with a pitcher of water to help replenish the Don. As she did, the Don took the moment to degrade Jordan in front of his "woman".

"You'll open it for us, Jordan. Scott's been on that duty long enough."

A few people laughed and Jordan seemed embarrassed. Even Michelle laughed lightly to herself.

"Anyway, I think that's all we needed to discuss for now. If anything else comes up, I will let everyone know, okay? Meeting is adjourned."

Everyone started to stand up and talk amongst themselves and Danny looked to me.

"Well, you wanna go play some basketball outside?" Danny asked.

"Actually, Daniel, could I speak to Victor?" the Don asked as he approached us.

"Uh, yeah, sure," Danny said as he started to walk off.

"Daniel, give me a hug," the Don requested before Danny exited the room.

Danny came back in to give his father a hug and then I said, "I'll catch up with you, Danny."

Once Danny left, I looked around to see everyone else talking to each other, which made me feel as if the Don and I were alone. As usual, David eventually joined the Don's side. It was at that moment the Don started in on me.

"Victor, I know that what happened last week was probably a big challenge to your morality, and I know that what we did was terrible, but those men were going to kill us, do you understand?" the Don said coolly.

"Yes, I understand."

"And I admire your courage, and how you still came through for me. That shows dedication, and I want you to know that I don't let that go unnoticed."

The Don started to reach into his inner coat pocket and he pulled out a fat envelope.

"Take this, Victor. You deserve it. I want you to know that I'm proud of you, and that I'm glad Danny has you as such a good friend."

"I'm happy to be his friend," I said sincerely.

The envelope was right in front of me and the Don wagged it.

"Take it, Victor. Go on."

I took the envelope carefully and started to peek to see what was inside.

Right away, I was astonished.

Tons of hundred dollar bills were stacked side by side and I felt uncomfortable. It was the most money that I had ever seen.

"It's five grand, just to save you from counting," the Don said with a smile.

"Wow..." I started, "I... I don't know what to say."

"You deserve it, Victor. You're loyal and kind, and you do what needs to be done. Hell, if I just had ten of you on my team, I think we could work wonders."

The Don opened his arms for a hug and I embraced it. Yet again, I was feeling comfort, even if it was from the wrong side of the law. But I was now a part of it too, and I felt like there wouldn't be an easy way to get out if I ever wanted to.

"Well, we won't keep Daniel waiting. I suggest you put that in a safe place and make sure no one tries to look for it."

"Yes, yes Don, I will."

The Don started to walk off and David stopped to say, "You're a good kid, Victor. And a pretty good shot too."

I feel like my past self would have associated the phrase "good shot" with basketball, but now, the new Victor Carez knew that it meant something completely different.

## Chapter Twenty Four
### End of May
### Graduation Night

Well, I did it. Actually, Danny and I did it. We graduated from high school with A's and the ceremony was spectacular. Our valedictorian gave a ridiculously long speech and then, we received our diplomas. Don Ponchello made a very brief appearance toward the end of the ceremony, and he congratulated us both on a job well done.

I thought my parents would come to graduation, but unfortunately, they didn't.

Honestly, I didn't care. For a split second, I did, but the Don was there for me, and that's all I cared about.

"Now, I have to run, but here's some money for you guys. Go out and have some fun, okay?" the Don said as he handed us each a hundred bucks.

"Thank you, Dad," Danny said as he hugged his father.

"Thank you, Mr. Ponchello," I called him by his civilian name as I hugged him afterwards.

"Just don't cause any trouble, okay?"

Danny and I nodded and we were on the loose.

Danny's new car was a 1970 orange Dodge Challenger with black racing stripes on the front hood. It was a little more comfortable than the Stingray, but I knew Danny still missed that car. If he didn't, I missed it for him.

We cruised around for a long time in the city and then finally paid a visit to The Ballz at the new club, Studio 9.

"Hey kids, what are you doin' here? You know what happened last time you fellas paid me a visit!" the Ballz said emphatically.

We all had a nervous chuckle about that and Danny said, "Ballz, we need some girls, y'know what I'm sayin'?"

"Hey, you don't gotta talk like that for me to understand, playa. You gotta celebrate for graduation, right?"

For some reason, the conversation made me think of something.

"Hey, Victor," The Ballz said, "something tuggin' at yo thoughts?"

"Yeah, actually, I just thought of something," I said.

"What? Do you have a date with Mrs. Huffman?" Danny asked.

I lightly pushed Danny and said, "No... I forgot that my parents said I could move out after I graduated, and all of my clothes and stuff are there."

"Well shit, man!" Danny yelled enthusiastically, "We need to go get your stuff! That is, if you want to stay at the manor?"

"Of course I do."

With that, we left Studio 9 and headed toward my parents' apartment. On the drive over, Danny asked, "Hey, Victor, I hope I didn't offend you about the Mrs. Huffman joke."

"No, you didn't," I replied. "But I told you how she was all over me about us being gone for so long, didn't I?"

"Yeah, you did. Did I tell you about when she pulled me aside and asked questions?" Danny asked.

"Oh, no I don't think you did tell me that."

"Yeah, I'm pretty sure she has the hots for you, Victor."

But at that moment, Danny's choice of words couldn't have been any worse.

When we pulled around the block, dark black smoke was billowing up into the sky from the massive fire that was raging on the apartment complex.

The one I used to live in with my parents...

Who I felt were probably still inside.

Danny had stopped the car out of amazement and lights were flashing all up and down the street. Sirens blared as more police cars and fire trucks arrived on the scene. It all looked like a nightmare, except it was one I had never had. If it wasn't for the tremendous fire and emergency lights, I wouldn't have even seen the smoke.

In the huge blocked off area, a few of the other tenants were outside talking to the police. As soon as Danny stopped the car and started to say something, I jumped out and ran toward the building.

"Whoa, kid," a police officer said as he held me back. "You can't go in there, it's too dangerous."

"My parents are in there!" I screamed.

Danny came running up behind me, cursing softly to himself.

Out of the huge crowd, one man who I wasn't crazy about seeing in that moment appeared.

Chief Ramzorin spotted me and started to make his way over. He looked frustrated and confused.

"Jesus Christ, Victor! There you are... You know how long I've been looking for you? Why didn't you call me or anything?"

"Chief, it's a long story..." I started, "My parents kicked me out after our last meal together and then I've been working with Danny at the warehouse in the meantime."

"What about..." Chief Ramzorin was about to scold me about school, but a small explosion happened on one of the top floors of the building. It shook everyone there and Chief Ramzorin came in for a hug. "Victor, I thought you were a goner."

I tried hugging him back, but I was still confused.

"What happened?" I asked the best I could through a choked up voice.

"I have no idea... I thought maybe you'd know."

"Chief," I started as I parted from his embrace, "I've been staying with Danny ever since they kicked me out. Tonight was graduation and they said after I graduated, I could come get my stuff, and then we get here and..."

My arm fell from gesturing at the building and I felt defeated. The embers rising from the flames seemed everlasting. There was no way the fire department could put the fire out. Not even a hurricane could put it out.

"One time, my dad dropped some alcohol on the ground and then he later dropped a cigarette on it. I was there to put that fire out, but..."

Chief Ramzorin's face showed deep concern as we all started putting the pieces together. I didn't know what to say or how to feel.

"Victor, I don't know how to say this, but your parents didn't make it out, and everyone here seems to think the same thing you do. The other tenants smelled the burning from inside their room and they evacuated. Once the fire department came here... Well, they just can't put it out."

"Victor," Danny said as he came up behind me. I knew this wasn't good for him to see me with Chief Ramzorin, but Danny didn't seem bothered. "I'm sorry, man... This is... terrible."

But I didn't cry. Instead, I swallowed my feelings deep down, knowing this was inevitable and asked, "What now...?"

"Victor, you can come with me. I can lend you a place to stay," Chief Ramzorin said.

I looked back at Danny, who was also lending out a helping hand.

"Or if you want, you can come back with me to the manor. Maybe when they put this out, we can try to find some of your possessions," Danny offered.

Suddenly, Chief Ramzorin pulled me in really close and said, "Victor, come with me. I know who that is and I don't want you hanging around him. Do you know who that is?"

"Do you even know who I really am?" I retorted.

Chief Ramzorin fell quiet and I stepped back toward Danny. With all of the anger and confusion, I only had one clear thought.

"C'mon Danny, let's go. I can't stand to see this anymore," I said.

In the end, Chief Ramzorin seemed hurt as I walked away with Danny, but I felt it was the right decision. Danny had been there for me more than Chief Ramzorin ever had. Chief Ramzorin took one measly day a week out for me, and it was only for an hour or so. Danny was there for me all the time. Danny befriended me, he took me in… he and his father took care of me, and that was a lot more than Chief Ramzorin had ever done.

But now that I look back on it, I almost regret my decision.

Almost.

# Part Two:

## The Adjustment to Change

## Chapter Twenty Five
### One Year Later...

    A lot can change in one year, and a lot did change over the course of this one year in particular:

    Summer of 1976 to summer of 1977 was quite a crazy time, and here's why.

    My involvement with the Ponchello Crime Syndicate grew immensely and Danny and I were handed more and more responsibilities by the Don. While Leo was away in New York recruiting members to our ever-growing group, Danny and I started to lead a group called "The Kids", which was basically a bunch of guys around my age who were all interested in being a part of the gang. There was now Roger (had long messy dark hair, kind of quiet, tall and lanky, got along with Danny right from the start); Al (a tough guy from Brooklyn, tried to be a wise ass at times, medium build, didn't take no for an answer); Blake (another wise ass from Brooklyn, slightly more muscular than Al, darker skin but not black); Charlie (German immigrant, left his family behind at the age of twelve, strong as hell, calm, one of the most liked); Jacob (quiet, respectful, shy, had shadowy eyes, skinny but strong); Nick (annoying, attempted to be a tough guy, had to learn respect as soon as he was initiated, still had mild acne) and an actual Sicilian named Modellini (cunning, daring, didn't care about authority). All of these "Kids" were runaways and orphans living on the streets of NYC. Leo tested their loyalty, and made sure they were up for the gang life.

    When they came over about a year ago, the Don brought us all in for a talk.

    "To prove your loyalty to me," the Don said with a glass of brandy in his hand, "Danny and Victor will split you guys up and you'll start hitting up the businesses that deny that they need my protection. The idea is to show them that they do need protection."

    There was a small laugh among us, and then we headed out. As I think of the memory of hopping out of the car, pulling the ski mask over my face and pulling a pistol, the song "Pick Up the Pieces" by the Average White Band plays through my head. They were fun times… especially the Chinese fire drills that Blake and Al would announce. And by the end of the summer, we had almost tripled the revenue that would be collected during the bacon runs.

    Then fall came, and everything seemed to slow down. The stick-ups weren't really deemed necessary anymore and we were all able to cool down, especially with

Don Tandelli out of the picture. I was told the lack of backlash from taking him out was quite surprising. We had let his wife and two kids go, and at one point, the Don acted like it may have been a bad idea, in case the kids grew up to seek vengeance. But, I was glad we didn't kill them.

As it turned out, Leo going to NYC and recruiting new members didn't really bother the distinguished Italian Mob all that much. While in NYC, Leo was informed that Don Tandelli had been turning on all of his allies and tried to make his own empire that as we know, eventually failed due to our intervention. The lack of upset from our actions pleased the Don even more, and more allies were gained.

I was glad Leo was gone for so long. I felt like he didn't like me that much. Never knowing what I did to cause his disgust towards me was bothersome at times, but I felt like he would eventually get over it.

Any time the Kids or Danny were busy with something else, I would get more training from David, Roy, Scott, Jordan, or even the Don himself. They would teach me about street smarts, finances, how to run the gang, and how to keep a level head when things went bad.

I knew how to keep a level head though, mainly because The Ballz was always happy to supply us with women at the rebuilt club, Studio 9.

Also, Danny ended up convincing his father to buy out the diner we always went to. Sid was able to keep his job, and they even started hiring nearby black men and women to work there. And after we cleaned up the jukebox, the place became a hit.

"Great investment, Daniel," the Don said as the place stayed packed all day and night during its grand re-opening.

We all had to dress nicer as well, which was expected with our new pay. And after my parents' apartment burned down, the Don reimbursed me in a monetary way since my father took the money from my lockbox. I remember he said, "I know it won't replace any family photos or anything like that, but it's a start."

A part of me felt like that incident was a long time ago, especially since I was a part of a new world; One that didn't involve Chief Ramzorin. And it wasn't until I got in contact with Chief Ramzorin again on Christmas Eve that I realized it wasn't so long ago when the incident occurred.

I showed up at the department and a lot of eyes turned to me and seemed very surprised. I walked over to the Chief's office, and he seemed happy and sad to see me at the same time.

"Victor, this is quite a surprise," Chief Ramzorin said as a cup of coffee descended from his lips.

He was happy to see me because it had been a long time. He was sad to see me because the last time I talked to Antonio at Michelangelo's, he claimed that Chief Ramzorin still went to eat there every Wednesday in hopes of seeing me. I felt bad for not going, and I knew Christmas Eve was the time to reconcile.

We embraced and I watched the snow fall outside his window. The box, crappily wrapped in yesterday's newspaper, was held against his back until our hug ended.

He looked into my eyes and there was a disconnect. Since last time we had met up, I had changed a lot. A lot more than I ever wanted to or thought I would. I felt like his eyes scanned mine and he knew I had killed men.

"So, what brings you here?" Chief Ramzorin asked, ignoring the box in my hand. He sat down and motioned for me to sit. I did.

"Well, Christmas is tomorrow, so I brought you a present."

Chief Ramzorin sort of chuckled and smiled.

"Oh! Aw, Victor, you didn't have to go and do that," he said as he patted his breast pocket, trying to think of something to give back to me.

"Well, I feel bad because I've just been so busy lately… I went by Michelangelo's and Antonio told me that you still go on Wednesdays and I felt bad for never telling you that I couldn't make it."

"So you didn't even have time for a simple phone call?" Chief Ramzorin asked in a condescending voice. I felt bad until he laughed and said, "It's all right, Victor. Y'know, I even went there before your… before you lived here. They've been open almost fifty years and I used to go there with my parents until they passed away."

"Really?" I asked in amazement.

"Yeah, I love their food. Haven't gotten tired of it yet. But anyway, what do you have there for me?"

I handed it over to him and said, "I'll let you find out."

Happiness filled the room as Chief Ramzorin unwrapped my present like a little kid. He had full intent of ripping it apart until the box was revealed and he saw that it was a "state of the art" Remington Electric Razor.

"Victor, if this is your idea of subtlety dropping a message, I'll cut the mustache off."

"No! Hah!" I laughed. "No, I just, it's supposed to be the best electric razor out there right now, without even going to the barber and having him knick you with the straight razor."

"Well, Victor, I don't know what to say. But I will at least say thank you," Chief Ramzorin said as he smiled at me. "My barber was kind of getting on my nerves, so this will be a nice alternative."

We made eye contact and I checked my watch. The Don asked me to be back to the manor by 7:15. I'd have to catch a cab.

"Well, I have to head out now," I said as I stood up.

"Really? Have plans, tonight?" Chief Ramzorin asked.

"You could say that," I said as I shook his hand and headed for the door.

He was about to let me loose, but then he stopped me halfway through the doorway and said, "Victor."

I turned around and held the door with one hand.

Chief Ramzorin gave me a long stare and said, "Be careful."

"You can count on that," I said, reflecting on the new lifestyle I was a part of. "I'll call you in advance and let you know when I can start coming back to Michelangelo's."

"I'd like that," Chief Ramzorin said.

The next day, I realized it was the first time I had been with anyone besides my family on Christmas day. Don't get me wrong, it was still a joyous occasion. Leo had flown in a few days before and he seemed impressed about how Danny and I were handling the Kids. I thought maybe I'd be able to make amends with Leo. Maybe he would finally respect me.

Everyone gathered in the living room the best they could and the Don was actually in his pajamas rather than a suit. It was kind of a strange sight, it seemed to make him look more... vulnerable. But it was good to see he wasn't completely heartless.

He gave all of the Kids little bonuses on their pay, along with the other associates. The associates would come and go so they could spend time with their own families. As for me, Danny, and the other Kids, this was our family.

Later that day, the Don said, "You guys keep this game of Risk going, I have something to show Victor."

They all agreed and I put some house shoes on so I could step out into the cold snow with the Don.

"What is it, Don?" I asked.

"Victor, I can't just tell you, it would ruin the surprise," Don Ponchello said as we started walking to the garage.

As we headed for the garage and he said it was a surprise, only one thing came to mind.

And I was right.

Don Ponchello pulled up the door to the garage and said, "You know how I asked you what kind of car you wouldn't feel embarrassed being caught dead in?"

"Oh... Oh no, no way..."

The door came open and there she was... a jet black 1952 Bel Air.

The Don had asked me the question back in September and I didn't think anything of it. In fact, the question made me sick back then because I didn't want to think about dying, but now I knew why he asked.

"Pretty sure this is the one you were talking about… and now, she's all yours. Runs perfectly, and there's reinforced plates and windshields, you know, just in case."

"Don, this is too much…" I said as I went over to touch it.

It was so shiny and clean… it looked like it was straight out of the factory with a bubble protecting it all the way here to me.

"Phil does a good job, doesn't he?"

"I'll say," I said as I smelled the interior. It was fresh and creamy looking. I almost drooled. But, before I completely accepted it, I turned to him as I hunched next to the driver's side window that was cracked open and I asked, "Are you sure?"

He jingled the keys from his hand and said, "I'm sure."

I went over to him and we embraced before he handed over the keys. I was ecstatic. It was by far the best Christmas I had ever had, and I had no regrets in saying that.

After winter, spring came and went. Before I knew it, the summer of '77 was underway and I started to get back in touch with Chief Ramzorin.

Everything seemed to be going good as usual, until the Don called the Kids in for an unscheduled meeting.

I was at the diner with Danny when Sid came up and said, "Danny, your dad wants to talk to you."

After Danny's brief conversation on the phone with his father, we stepped out into the blazing sun and made our way to the manor.

About halfway to the manor I asked, "Does it sound bad?"

The last time anything "bad" had happened with the gang was back in November when one of the Don's close friends got shot in a drunken rage over in Vegas.

"I don't know, something to do with the Kids," Danny said as he took the last puff of his cigarette.

"Are sales down?"

The Kids were also in charge of distributing drugs to lowlifes downtown. Danny and I were supposed to only oversee it, and no one from the gang was allowed to partake in any use of the drugs. We sold grass and the best crack cocaine on the market in Detroit. In the beginning, we had to run out a few of the other dealers before establishing ourselves in the territory. Some of them were even turned into our men.

"No," Danny said. "I think they caught a user among us."

Danny and I lived by the code to never use the drugs we sold. We just smoked cigarettes, like most of the people in the gang, and of course we drank when we could. But some of the other Kids were now being brought into questioning.

"Who do you think would be using?" I asked.

"I don't know," Danny said as we exited off the highway, "but we're going to find out."

When we arrived to the Ponchello manor, which was being overrun with ivy that was slowly dying, we walked into a living room that was cleared out except for the Don and the Kids.

"It's good of you two to finally join us," the Don said.

"Sorry Dad, we were downtown eating lunch when we got the call," Danny said.

"I know. Sit."

He motioned toward the couch and Danny and I tried to find an open spot. I sat next to Modellini and Charlie while Danny sat on the other side with Nick and the others (Jacob, Blake, Al, and Roger).

"How is the diner doing, Danny?" the Don asked to begin the awkward meeting.

"Business is great, Dad. I've never seen it so busy on a Thursday at lunch time."

"Great," the Don said with a smile, and then his grave look took over. "Well, you all are probably wondering why I called this meeting. I will let you all know that when a meeting is called in such a random fashion like this, you should be worried."

I swallowed air and waited for the next part. I knew I hadn't done anything wrong, but I still worried. The Kids that surrounded me were ones I liked. I didn't want to see anything bad happen to any of them.

"Y'see, I never really wanted to start dealing in drugs because I knew about the backlashes with selling them and manufacturing them. Luckily, we have other outside sources manufacturing them, but there can still be problems with selling them and dealing them in general, and one problem has been brought to my attention."

The Don remained standing as he walked around the room to give us all the look over. I instantly thought it might be Roger. The other day, we called him down to the kitchen at about 3 PM and his eyes were blood red. He said he was tired, but…

"My father always told me that one bad leaf on a tree before the fall would start to prompt more bad leaves. The only way to stop that from happening is to pluck one of the bad leaves out."

As he stopped his observation of us, he faced us all and said, "Now, I'm not going to have all of you whip it out and pee in a cup for me. I want to do this as peacefully as we possibly can and without any problems. So, Modellini…"

There was a sort of silent gasp among everyone and all of our eyes darted to

Modellini, who started shaking and turning red.

"Moe!" Danny said in disgust.

"Daniel," the Don said sternly. Danny sat back in the couch and Modellini wasn't able to speak out of pure embarrassment and disgrace.

"We've already packed everything up for you that was in your room, including the marijuana that you were cutting from your sales and keeping to yourself. There's a car with Scott waiting for you outside. He'll drive you to the nearest bus station in town and you're on your own. I never want to see you in my town again, understand?"

It seemed like Modellini (only the Kids called him Moe for short) should feel grateful that the Don was letting him go so easy. I never knew what the punishment would be if we dabbled into the drugs, but I always feared and figured it was punishable by death.

Modellini didn't even say a word. He kept his composure except for the blood red face, and he shook his head as he walked out.

We all watched in awe as he walked, but after he did, the Don said, "The same will happen to any of the rest of you who do what Modellini did. This is the final warning. I know I can trust you guys, but I want to make that one hundred percent clear."

When the tension seemed to move out of the room with the A/C coming on, Danny said, "Y'know, I thought when you said one of us was doing drugs, it was going to be Roger."

We all started laughing to lighten the mood and Roger said, "Fuck off, Danny. I don't do that shit. I know better."

The medium-sized Al from Brooklyn said, "Well, you need to start waking up earlier than 3 PM, then."

"I can't sleep," Roger said as he pushed back his long hair. "Something about the sheets or something."

"Those are eight hundred thread count sheets from Egypt," the Don said, slightly insulted.

"Don, don't tell me you fell for the sales pitch at the mall," Charlie said with his deep booming voice.

"Chuck, you better watch yourself..." the Don said, and then he slapped his own forehead. "Are you serious? Those aren't real? The guy swore to me up and down they were."

"I didn't want to say anything but I've had the same problem," Jacob said quietly. "The sheets make my dick itch."

"No, that might just be from that girl The Ballz set you up with the other night," Blake said. He always knew what to say at the right time, but sometimes it was annoying.

There was another collective laugh from the group and the Don said, "All right, new assignment. Whoever can bring me that camel jockey's gold tooth gets a bonus next month."

The laughing continued, but something told me that the Don wasn't kidding about the assignment.

# Chapter Twenty Six
## Monday, August 8th, 1977

Usually when we did the bacon run, Danny would do all the driving. But when I got the car for Christmas, we said we could trade-off on who drove. This time, it was my turn.

The 1952 jet black Bel Air that I now had in my possession also had a cassette player and we listened to Jefferson Airplane as we drove around.

When we started getting paid by more and more businesses for protection, the bacon runs became a little easier. We divided the city into four sections, and whatever section their business fell under, they all went to the same drop off point. The drop off points were similar and different at the same time. Each point had a lockbox that only had a way to put the envelopes in and not take them out. Danny and I, and probably the Don just in case, were the only ones who held the keys required to unlock the boxes.

The first one, on the northeast side of town, was chained down in a random pipe that stuck out of the opening to the sewer like a sore thumb. It required one small key to open up the cap on the pipe, and then the other universal key to open the lockbox. That was the only part that may seem stupid, that all the lockboxes used the same key, but there was somewhat of a guarantee only three of us would have keys, and all the locksmiths in the area were told that if they got a mold of this strange key, they were not allowed to make a new one without the Don's permission.

After I pulled the money from the lockbox, I ran back up the slanted concrete to my car and handed Danny the wad of envelopes.

"All twelve of them were there?" Danny asked.

"Yes," I replied simply.

Danny still took the time to finger through them, just in case I was dazed from the long day. We only worked at the warehouse about once or twice a week now, and today was a bruising.

"Okay," Danny said as he grabbed the manila envelope and shoved the smaller envelopes into it. "Now for the cemetery."

*****

The cemetery hiding spot on the southeast was debated for a long time. It seemed rude and crass to hide money in a cemetery, but we were all fans of The Good, the Bad and the Ugly so it just seemed cool to do it. Plus, we made sure that the gravestone we used as the hiding spot wasn't near anyone else's real grave.

It was pretty easy to lift the gravestone up out of the dirt, but no one could get into the lockbox without the key. This time, Danny ran over to get the money and I waited in the car.

When Danny got back, he reached for the manila envelope and started to shove the smaller envelopes in.

"Were all fifteen in there?" I asked him as he asked me before.

"Yes," Danny said, and he started to shove them back in again until I reached over and tried to grab them from him. Danny acted mad as he said, "Hey, what the hell?"

I gave him a long look and felt bad for making him mad. "Geez, I was just going to make sure they were all there like you did with me."

"Dude, I know they're there... No need to check me."

I wasn't sure what was bothering Danny. He acted this way at the sewer, too. Usually, one of the other Kids would tag along with us, but this time, it was just me and Danny for the first time in a long while.

I felt like there was maybe something he wanted to say, but I didn't press at him about it yet.

Next was the southwest spot, which was an abandoned warehouse. The Don owned the property, but nothing was to be done with it. Instead, it just sat in limbo as some blueprints for a new building sat idly by back at the manor.

The lockbox was pretty obviously placed here against the side of the building, but the area was closed off to only us and the business owners who made the drops. The tall grass next to the warehouse also helped.

Danny started to get out of the car again and I said, "Isn't it my turn to get it?"

Danny didn't even turn to look at me as he got out. He replied, "Does it really matter?"

I hated his tone and how he was acting, but I also felt deep concern. I hadn't seen him act this way, ever. Just a few days ago, he was doing fine. But it seemed like over the last few days, he started getting a little more confined in himself rather than being himself for everyone to see.

Finally, when we reached the last box at the southwest corner of the city in a park dug down next to a tree, I followed Danny to the lockbox, and I noticed he just stopped when he faced the tree.

He didn't look back to see me, rather, he kept staring at the tree and said, "I'm sorry, Victor... I can't hold this back anymore."

"C'mon, dude," I said in the most comforting way possible. "What's going on?"

Danny turned around and gave a sad smile to me. I saw his eyes were starting to water.

"Well, I picked this spot for a reason as one of the drop locations. This is the tree my mom used to sit under and read while I played at the park over there," Danny said as he pointed off in the distance to the park.

He then motioned me over and showed me a small etching in the tree that was slowly fading away. It said, "DP and Mommy are happy to be". It was corny, but it was also one of the only things Danny had left that reminded him of his mom.

"She did that when I was about five... and today would've been her forty-seventh birthday."

"Danny, I'm sorry, man..."

"Why did she leave?" Danny asked aloud after he started messing with the lockbox. "I'm sorry to bring this all up, but as it got closer and closer to her birthday, I realized this was a stupid drop point."

"Don't be sorry, Danny," I started off. I hated to compare my life to his, but I felt it was the only way to get through to him. "I don't know why your mom left... It's the same reason I don't know why my mom and dad started drinking and became losers when they lost their jobs. They should've been able to find happiness some other way, but they were so caught up in money."

"I know the rumors say that my dad had her killed, but that's not true... is it?"

"No, not at all," I said as I patted his back. "The first time I sat with your dad in his office, he told me to make sure everyone knew that the rumor wasn't true. Your dad is a good man. He would never do that to you."

Danny seemed to smile again as he stood up and wiped his eyes.

"Victor, I'm glad you're my friend."

"Same to you," I said, and I checked my watch. "Hey, we still got some time before we have to go back to the manor. How about I buy you a float?"

"Sure, Victor, thanks," Danny said, and his tone began to shift back to its normal pitch. "I'll stop being a sissy and we can go pay Sid a visit."

I didn't think Danny was a sissy for nearly crying about missing his mom. It only made me wonder why I never got emotional about my parents anymore.

## Chapter Twenty Seven

Danny and I arrived at Sid's Diner and made our way to the bar. Sid greeted us like usual but another younger girl came by to take our order.

"Hi, Danny," she said with a smile covered in metal. She only looked to be about sixteen or so, but I had a feeling that hadn't mattered to Danny at some point.

"Hi, Rene," Danny said with a faint smile. Her long brown hair was tied up tight in a bun and she waved to me too. I waved back. Danny actually co-interviewed most of the people that now worked there. I felt like he might've done a little more than interviewed her though.

"What will you boys be having?" she asked in her ditzy voice.

"Well, toots, I think we'll both be having root beer floats, unless my man Victor here wants something else."

Sadly, my attention was being taken by three punk teenagers who looked to be harassing one of the young black waiters employed at the diner. Danny didn't realize it just yet when he elbowed me and said, "Right, Victor? Two root beer floats?"

"Oh, yeah, sure," I replied as I turned back around to face the bar.

"Okay, coming right up!"

She hummed some stupid song to herself as she walked off and Danny glanced over where I was looking before.

"What, Victor, you know those cats?"

"No, not really, but I'm glad I don't."

"What were they doing?" Danny asked as he gave them the stink eye. The punks were keeping themselves entertained though, and had no idea of our presence.

"Eh, it's not important," I said, as I thought they might have been friends with the waiter and just gave him a hard time for laughs.

"All right, Victor, if you say so," Danny said as he turned back around and faced the bar.

We didn't look over there again until I saw the black waiter walking the drinks over to the teenagers. Right as they were about to get their drinks, one man at the edge of the booth put his foot out and tripped the waiter to the ground. The glasses shattered and the soda went all over the floor. The waiter was on the ground in the pool of carbonation and sugar while the punks howled and laughed. The waiter started to stand up with his now stained and untucked uniform, but one punk kicked the waiter back down and said, "Now you stay there, nigger. There's no need in you getting up. I like you right there."

Danny and I didn't even have to say anything. We both stood up and headed over to the booth.

As soon as we made our way there, Danny demanded, "Get your foot off of him."

The first punk moved his foot away after laughing and looking at his friends. I bent down to help the waiter up and to make sure he was okay. His big nostrils were bleeding and he looked scared.

After I lifted him up and handed him a napkin, I stepped next to Danny again, who said, "Now what the hell do you think you're doing to my employee?"

I thought it was bold of Danny to call the waiter his employee, but the punk laughed and said, "Oh, sorry, I didn't know he was your nigger."

"He's not!" Danny yelled at the punk. The punk started to stand up to face Danny head on, but one of the other guys said, "Dude, Josh, that's Don Ponchello's son."

"You think I give a shit who that is?" the punk in questioning, Josh, replied.

I started getting pissed off as Danny let this guy have his moment.

"It's a free country, I can do whatever I want."

"Yeah, I guess you can do whatever you want. But that means I can too," Danny said.

Danny's fist launched out from his side and hit Josh in the gut, which sent him back into the booth. When Danny and I stepped back, Josh stood up again and reached for his knife.

Danny, without hesitation, pulled out his pistol and waved it in Josh's face.

"You think I'm scared of you with your puny knife?" Danny said in a threatening voice. "Ever had a bullet in your head, or do you just have that tiny brain of yours in there?"

"Jesus Christ, Josh, I think that's real," the third punk said.

"You wanna find out if it's real?" Danny said as he pulled back the hammer. "Cause if you don't, then you and your friends need to scram and never come back."

Josh and the others looked like they were wetting their pants as they ran out of the diner. Danny put the hammer back down and put his pistol away. I was never worried that he would use it, but it was still weird to see him just bring it out like that.

"Fuck those guys, Victor. What's wrong with people?" Danny said as he shook his head.

We both looked to the waiter, who started to walk off.

"Hey, where are you going?" Danny asked.

"I don't want any more trouble," the waiter said as he headed for the bathroom.

"Hey, no, stay right here, man," Danny said as he grabbed the waiter gently by the shoulder and pulled out a chair for him. "Sit right here and don't move. I'm gonna get you a wet washcloth and some water and we'll get you all fixed up. What's your name?"

The waiter looked at Danny and the fear started escaping from his eyes.

"It's Emmitt," he told us.

"All right, Emmitt, just hold tight like I said and Victor will stay here with you. Sid, we need a mop and a broom," Danny said as he started walking back to the kitchen.

I stood there, looking at Emmitt. We had learned about the riots and such that took place a decade ago, but I had never seen full blown racism first hand like that. When I was a kid, I didn't understand or even remember anything like this. I felt sorry for him, but I figured it probably wasn't his first time with an encounter like that.

"So, you're all right?" I asked again.

"Yeah, man, I'm fine. I just hit my nose when I fell but I don't think it's broken."

"Well uh..." I said, not quite sure what to say. "I'm Victor, and the guy back there struggling with the mop is Danny."

Danny jerked the mop around trying to get the wheels to roll and he cussed at it.

"Nice to meet you both. I've heard a lot about you guys."

"Really?" I asked, "Anything good?"

Emmitt laughed as he said, "Yeah, some good things, some not so good. But I'll push the bad things aside for now."

I smiled.

"You live near here?" I asked him.

"No, not really. I live down at the southern edge of town. I take a bus to work every day, and luckily when I was out looking for a job, this diner hired me right away."

"That's good," I said. "Did you know those guys?"

"No," Emmitt said, "never seen them in my life."

"That's messed up."

Danny finally pulled the mop over to the mess and Sid walked behind him with the broom and dustpan. As soon as Danny got to us with the wet rag and the mop, he said, "Jesus, finally. After all that sloshing, I need to pee. Rene, do you think you could help clean this up?"

"Sure, Danny," she said dreamily.

"Thanks, babe," Danny said with a grin as he walked over to the bathroom.

I sort of rolled my eyes as I continued talking with Emmitt.

"Do you work quite a bit?" I asked him.

"Well, not really. Some weeks I work four days and some I only work three. I'm trying to save up to go to art school."

"Really?" I asked him.

"Yeah. My father says I really know how to draw."

"Well, good luck to you. Are there any art schools here in the city?"

Emmitt nodded, then added, "But I was hoping to go to Chicago and go to school there."

"Huh, that's quite a bit of diner-ing that you would have to do," I said with a smile.

"There's also some money in a savings account for me, I just can't touch it yet," Emmitt explained.

"Ah, okay."

I was starting to like Emmitt. Talking to him made me remember what it was like before I was in a gang. Sometimes, I wondered what it would be like to get out, but...

"Hey, Emmitt, if you don't mind me asking, would you want to hang out sometime?"

"What?" Emmitt said as he pulled the wet rag away. "You want to roll with me?"

"Yeah, if that means hang out," I said with an embarrassed grin.

"Well, sure, man... You free Wednesday?"

"Yeah, are you?"

"I sure am," Emmitt said, and he started to reach for a pen. "Lemme write down my number and you can call me Wednesday. We'll try to set something up."

"Sounds cool, dude," I replied.

Emmitt wrote his number down on the back of a receipt and handed it over to me. Danny came out of the bathroom just as I tucked the number away in my pocket. I wasn't sure how Danny would feel if I told him about hanging out with someone else besides him, but he probably wouldn't care too much.

Danny stepped up to us and said, "Victor, where has the time gone? Looks like we need to split."

Danny dug down into his wallet and pulled out a fifty dollar bill.

"Here, take the rest of the day off, Emmitt, and get yourself cleaned up when you get home."

Danny and I headed toward the door and I waved to Emmitt as we headed out.

I was excited to hang out with him in the future.

And as we got in my car and drove off, our root beer floats sat untouched on the counter and slowly melted away.

# Chapter Twenty Eight

The next day, I woke up and made my way downstairs for breakfast around nine AM. This was around the time when most of the traffic was going on in the manor. People were either coming in from being out all night, some were just starting their day, like me, or others woke up around seven and stayed around the house, like the Don.

This morning in particular, as I poured myself a bowl of Kix, the Don sat at the kitchen table with Danny, Roy, and Jordan. The Don had a steaming mug of coffee next to his face as Roy and Jordan talked over things. Danny still looked half asleep, even though he had woken up an hour or so before me.

Once I heard the cereal cling and clang around in my bowl, it kept me awake.

Next I poured a little too much milk into the bowl, grabbed a spoon and sat next to Danny.

"Morning, Victor," the Don said to me with a blank face.

"Good morning, Don," I replied as I took my first bite of cereal.

"How's everyone today?"

"Ehh," Jordan said to start us off, "had too many cocktails last night if you get what I mean."

Roy was the next to retort, "Doesn't that just mean you drank too much?"

"Or is there some innuendo there?" Danny asked. Maybe he was more awake than I thought.

"No, if I was to make an innuendo about last night, I'd say…"

"Jordan," the Don said to cut him off. "I don't want to hear it. As long as I know that whatever it was, you slept it off and you're ready to work today."

Jordan knew when it was time to cut it out.

"Okay, Don, yes, I slept it off and I'm ready."

"Same here," Roy said.

Danny and I nodded in agreement as the Don looked over at us. The Don shed his first smile of the day and said, "Victor and Daniel, although they are good, still need a little more training in the field. Victor, you're going to be with Roy. Roy, you're going to show him how to deal with that problem we were talking about earlier. Daniel, you're going to be with Jordan. Try to not let his jackass attitude rub off on you much more, eh?"

Jordan laughed while Danny seemed happy to have Jordan as a partner. I was pleased to have Roy as a partner. He was very thorough in his teachings, but not in a way that made you feel threatened.

At about ten o'clock when the businesses would definitely be open and not too busy, Roy finally said it was time for us to leave the house. As Roy and I headed down the highway to the city in his early 70s maroon station wagon, Roy said, "Now, you boys have been doing a good job on the bacon runs, especially since they're handled a little differently now."

"Oh, thanks," I said.

Roy nodded a "You're welcome" back to me, and then continued, "But, we still have to muscle in on the people every once in a while, especially these new shops."

"Are they not paying enough?" I asked, not quite sure what the right amount would be.

"Sometimes they don't pay enough. They think we can't do math or something. Well, I have news for them. Twenty percent of five grand is one grand, not eight-fifty."

"We take twenty percent of what they earn?" I asked Roy.

"Yeah," Roy said in sort of a "duh" way. "That's quite a deal if you ask me, Victor. Some people take about sixty or seventy-five percent from businesses. They have to do that because they don't get to own as many businesses over in LA or NYC. They have to share it with the other gangs around town, whereas, we're the only ones here."

"But, there's a reason for that," I said as I reflected on the news saying this city was becoming poorer and poorer.

"Hey, the Don had a good idea if you ask me. We're actually making more of a profit here than they did when they were in Chicago. Part of it is thanks to you Kids, too. We run a good gang, even though most people thought we never would. They said, 'You can't have some hybrid mixed gang bullshit. Gangs and mobs are supposed to be all family, or all Sicilians, all Italians, all Irish…' It's bullshit, really, that they thought we couldn't do it. I'm proud to work for the Don, and I hope you are too."

"Yeah, I am," I said, without a doubt. "Who didn't pay enough?"

"Well, we have quite a few stops to make besides just who didn't pay. Some of them didn't put their earnings for the month, and we need that to make sure they did pay us enough," Roy said. "So, first stop, right here."

It was StrikeZone, one of the spots of the original bacon run. As Roy started to step out of the car, I stayed inside and lit up a cigarette. When Roy turned around and gave me a look, he said, "Oh, I guess I'm supposed to be teaching you. When you're going to go muscle in on people, make sure two men go inside. Makes the owners cooperate better."

"Oh, sorry," I said as I stepped out and flicked the ash off my cigarette. The flow of nicotine into my veins started to pump me up for whatever was going to happen inside.

When Roy and I stepped in, the place was dead. Only one younger couple was enjoying their last week of summer bowling as Roy and I headed up to the front counter. Standing there, as usual, was Rupert, the old fart that owned the place. I really didn't want Roy to "muscle in" on Rupert, but I knew it was better to stay on Roy's side, which was ultimately the Don's side.

"Oh, hello there," Rupert said with a placid smile, and then he noticed I was there as well. "Victor, good to see you."

"You too, sir," I said plainly.

"Do you know why we're here, Rupert?" Roy asked.

I started feeling queasy from the idea of Roy beating up on Rupert. It just didn't seem fair.

Rupert's smile seemed to fall as he said, "Well, no… I mean, it is a little early to bowl, and I sent my nephew to the drop point just like I always do. He's a good kid, he'd never do anything wrong."

"No, Rupert, we received the payment, don't worry about that," Roy started. "You just forgot the earnings sheet."

I felt overwhelming relief as Rupert sort of laughed and said, "Oh, well golly, I'm sorry. You know, I'm getting up there in age and sometimes I just forget things… I'm sorry, fellas. I'll make a really obvious note for me to see next time. It won't happen again."

Toward the end of his apology speech, he started shuffling back to his office so he could grab the sheet for us.

"It's all right, Rupert, we don't mind seeing you," Roy said, and then he looked to me and shook his head. "This might be the second or third time we've had to do this since the new drop method started, but eh, I can't blame the guy. He is getting a little older."

"I thought he didn't pay his amount… I was worried," I said.

"He always does, and sometimes extra, but policy is policy. We still need that sheet. Also, Victor, I was going to say that, if they give up pretty easily and give in to your demands, make sure to show them respect so they don't feel too threatened. Only threaten the people who need to feel threatened."

I nodded as Rupert came back from his cash office with the thin paper being flailed around in his right hand. He walked in a funny way and hunched his back over until he saw us. One time, I remember him saying he pulled his back pretty bad several years back from working on the railroad.

"Okay fellas, here you go, and again, sorry for making you have to come all the way out here," Rupert said as he handed the paper to Roy.

"It's not a problem, Rupert, just try to remember next time," Roy said with a smile.

"You fellas take care now," Rupert said as he smiled and waved, realizing his face wouldn't be bashed in today.

"Goodbye, Rupert," I said as I finished my cigarette and put it out in the closest ash tray.

Roy and I stepped into his station wagon and the sun started to beat down and heat up the city. I looked at my watch and noticed it was almost eleven.

"Okay, next order of business, we gotta stop by the cleaners over on the southwest side and get the Don's tux."

We rode over there in silence since Roy's radio didn't work. I once asked him why he didn't get it fixed, and he said something about radios reminding him too much of the war. He didn't like them. The radio had failed on him back in Vietnam, so he didn't even want to mess with them here.

When we arrived at the cleaners, Roy and I stepped out and headed up to the door. For a second, I thought I had left my gun at home and I patted the back of my pants for it, and found out I did have it. I was so used to carrying it around all the time now; I didn't even feel it back there. It was just part of my daily attire.

When Roy and I walked in, the Asian man looked to us and said, "Oh, hello. Pick up?"

"Yes, for Mark Ponchello," Roy said.

"Oh, just one minute please, it'll be right out, promise," the Asian man said in a somewhat frightened voice.

Everyone in town knew who the Don was, and everyone feared him for the most part. It was always either respect or fear, or both.

The Asian man came back and handed us the tux all covered in plastic.

"Here you go, no charge," the Asian man said as he handed it off.

"No, Hong, we'll pay for it, don't worry," Roy said as he handed him the money.

"No, no, I insist, it's a gift!" Hong replied with a smile.

"Okay Hong, the Don appreciates your kindness," Roy said as he tucked the bill back into his pocket and I grabbed the tux.

"Thank you, come back," Hong said as we walked out.

"Just set that down flat in my backseat," Roy said as we walked over to the station wagon.

I placed the tux carefully in the backseat and then made my way to the passenger's seat. Roy and I drove off and Roy said, "Victor, you hungry for lunch yet?"

I didn't even console my stomach. I just looked to my watch and saw it was about 11:30.

"Eh, why not?" I said.

"Good, cause this next guy we have to see… I don't want to hustle him on an empty stomach."

*****

Roy and I ate at one of the best pizza places in Detroit known as Slices. It was right smack dab in the middle of the city. You could buy it by the slice, or you could order a whole pizza to yourself. Roy and I shared a large supreme pizza with extra cheese. I picked out the onion as we devoured it, and then we sat there and talked for a while before heading over to the last stop, the one Roy had been dreading.

Magnificent Cakes: Giovanni's euphoric masterpiece.

When we arrived, it surprised me. Giovanni was a good guy, and always treated the Don and everyone else with respect. He even made the Don some petit fours when he was recovering.

*So, why did we need to come here?* I wondered.

Instead of just wondering about it, I asked, "So, Roy, why are we here?"

"Well, this is a rare case of plain disrespect to the Don," Roy said as he punched his fists into his hands. "Now, I don't expect you or Danny to open the envelopes and search the contents, but Giovanni here only put Monopoly money in his."

"What!?" I asked incredulously. "Why the hell would he do that? He's loyal, isn't he?"

"There are only two possible explanations. Either A: He thought it'd be funny and we wouldn't notice or B: He was bought out by someone else and is refusing payments."

"Has he done that before?" I asked.

"No, which is why I feel like this might just be a misunderstanding. But hey, don't let personal feelings get in the way of business. We're still going to have to go in there and bust him up a little bit, because either way, he fucked up."

Roy seemed to leap out of the car and I followed behind him. When Roy opened the door, Giovanni turned around behind the counter and his jaw dropped to the center of the earth.

"Oh no, oh please, no."

Giovanni tried to run but he was too fat from eating all the leftover sweets day in and day out. Roy grabbed him and threw him against a wooden cupboard that seemed to serve no purpose except for decoration.

Giovanni fell to the floor and Roy started yelling, "You didn't think we'd notice, Giovanni? You think we're stupid?"

Giovanni coughed and I just watched.

"No, no please," Giovanni pleaded.

"Victor," Roy ordered, "find something heavy that you can break that display case with, unless you wanna hand over the money."

I started to search for some kind of object while Giovanni kept pleading, "No, I can explain, just let me explain. Help me up, and I'll explain."

"Eh, you can pick yourself up, fatty," Roy said in a harsh tone.

Roy could be a lot meaner than I ever thought. Every time I was around him he was pretty calm, but now the uglier side was grossly apparent.

Giovanni struggled to pick himself up, so Roy finally lifted him up and set him up against the cupboard. I found a rolling pin, but I waited to break the display case until after Giovanni explained.

"It's not my fault, honest," Giovanni said as he put his right hand over his heart with hardly any breath left to use. "When I was leaving the other day, these people attacked me…"

"Who were these people?" Roy asked.

"I don't know, they didn't use any names, had rough voices. They took my envelope, took all the money I put in, and replaced it with Monopoly money, and then they pulled a gun on me and said I still had to deliver it, and that they'd be watching me."

Roy stood there for a second and all that came to my mind were profanities. Why would anyone cross the Don so blatantly?

"Giovanni, I believe you, but you gotta learn to protect yourself, and especially the money. Didn't you check before you walked out to your car?"

"Well, I had to lock up the shop and I fumbled with my keys for a while, so… maybe I didn't see them."

"Jesus Christ," Roy said as he pushed back his long hippie hair. "All right, c'mon Victor, put that rolling pin back and let's go. We gotta go see Leo now."

Giovanni began to cry as I put the rolling pin behind the counter and headed out to the car with Roy.

"Shit, so much for a learning experience," Roy said as he changed course to the phone booth.

"Who would steal from us, Roy?" I asked as I stepped beside Roy and we left Giovanni crying in his display window.

"I have no idea. That's why we're going to make a phone call and see Leo."

"Isn't Leo out of town?"

"We'll find out soon enough."

*****

When we arrived at Studio 9, we walked around the side alley to a ground door that led us down to a gambling ring that I wasn't usually allowed in. Tons of men already sat around even though it was still early afternoon and played Blackjack, Roulette, and Poker. Smoke filled the room but I only liked to smoke a cigarette every three or so hours.

Leo sat there playing Blackjack, and it looked like he was losing all of his money. Roy and I approached him cautiously as he sat there in a daze and said, "Hit me."

"Leo? We have a problem," Roy half whispered into Leo's ear.

Leo slowly turned around and faced us as the dealer dropped another card and said, "Nineteen."

"I'll stay," Leo said without looking back. "What is it, Roy? Hey, kid."

"Hi, Leo," I said back.

"Leo, we have jackers who are hitting up Giovanni for his money."

Leo said to the dealer, "I know you probably have twenty so just give me a second and I'll be right back."

Leo stood up and made his way over to the small bar where we could talk without as many people listening in.

"All right, tell me about it, Roy," Leo said as he smoked a cigar.

"So, we went to see Giovanni, and," Roy stopped himself and then looked to me, "How about you tell him, Victor? It'll be good for you to learn."

"Okay..?" I said awkwardly. "Well, I guess Giovanni had dropped his envelope at the drop point but it was full of Monopoly money instead of real money 'cause some thugs attacked him when he was locking up his shop and they took the money, and then replaced it with the Monopoly money. He says he doesn't know who they were though."

Leo scratched his head and then said, "Did he leave the earnings slip in there, though?"

"Yeah," Roy answered for me since I didn't know.

"Hmm, this isn't good news at all. Right when I thought things were gonna run smoothly."

"Well, they did for a few months, but it looks like we have new enemies," Roy explained. "The Don wants you to stay in town until this is all cleared up."

"Yeah, I'm on it. I'll call my New York associates and tell them to take care of things."

And with that, Roy and I left so we could deliver the tux to the Don and I worried about a future battle with a new enemy.

# Chapter Twenty Nine

I had called Emmitt the night before to make sure we were good to hang out on Wednesday. He agreed to it, but asked that I come out to his part of town to pick him up.

This worried me. Not because of there mainly being black people in that area, but a lot of crime happened in that side of town. He was taking me out of my territory to go into his. The idea just worried me.

And when I arrived to his side of town, I quickly discovered my worry was justified.

There was a tall fence that covered the basketball court where several blacks were playing, mainly younger kids though. On the outside of the fence facing me, a line of strong black men stood there and smoked cigarettes. As I slowly drove by and I noticed I was nearing the entrance to the apartment complex, they all stared me down and made sure I didn't do anything I wasn't supposed to.

At the end of the fence where the sidewalk went into the apartment complex, I saw Emmitt standing with three other older black men.

I pulled up next to the curb where they stood and parked my car. When I stepped out, Emmitt ran around to my door to greet me.

"Hey, man," Emmitt said with a smile as he extended one hand.

I was going to shake it, but he grabbed by the fingers and made a fist with our hands, then slid his hand back.

I started to explain that I didn't know what had just happened, but Emmitt said, "Don't worry, you'll get better at it. C'mon, you have to meet my brothers and my dad."

I closed my car door and locked it before heading over to his brothers and father.

"Okay, so this is Marcus, my oldest brother," Emmitt said as he pointed to the tallest man with thin hair like Emmitt's. They were all physically strong and fit, which also made me worry. All those jokes my father said in his drunken days would definitely not be accepted here.

"And then, here's TJ, the middle brother," Emmitt pointed to the second tallest man standing there. TJ's afro seemed to bob as he leaned over to me with a smile and shook my hand. Marcus was the only one who had given me a mean look.

## The Platinum Briefcase

"And finally, here's my father, Jackson Burose."

I started to shake his hand, but then his face hit my memory bank like a thunderbolt and nine million warnings went off in my head.

It seemed like it was yesterday that I had seen this man, even though it had been a little over a year.

Jackson Burose was the man from the bar, the one Danny and I had escorted out. His last words ran in my memory like it was yesterday…

*"Sure, kids… I get what's going on here. Maybe I'll see you guys again."*

He sported a jagged scar that started on his left eyebrow and then went down to his jaw bone. It was a gruesome scar that puffed out just a little bit from the cut marks. The rest of his face looked like it had been burned before at one point or another.

But, I pushed that all aside from my mind as I brought myself to shake his hand normally. He didn't seem to recognize me… yet.

"Nice to meet you, Victor," Jackson said in a booming voice. "I appreciate what you and your friend did for my son the other day at the diner."

"Don't mention it, they were pricks," I said as we shook hands.

Jackson shared a small laugh with me and then said, "So, what are you boys going to do? Beat up some more pricks?"

"No, Father," Emmitt said, "Victor and I were going to go bowling, right? Didn't we talk about that?"

"Yeah," I said as I wasn't sure who to look at. The only ones giving me nice looks were TJ and Emmitt. "A friend of mine owns the bowling alley StrikeZone in town. We were going to bowl a few games there."

"A friend of yours, you say?" Jackson asked in a questionable way. "This friend of yours would have to be quite the businessman at your age."

I could see what was happening. Jackson didn't appear to be ignorant to my line of work.

"Well, it's a friend of a friend… of a friend, you know?"

Jackson's smile faded but his tone changed for the better.

"Okay, well you boys have fun. I'd like my son home by eight at the latest. If you've watched the news lately, you've seen this area gets a little risky the later it gets."

I felt like it was more of a threat than a warning, but I nodded anyway in acknowledgement.

While I was driving to StrikeZone, Emmitt started asking me some questions, which really seemed inevitable.

"So… I mean, I know you work for Don Ponchello…"

"How's that, though? How do people just know that?" I asked. It was hard being on the inside and understanding everyone's perspective on the outside.

"I don't know, man, people talk. We went to different schools, but sometimes, Johnny Fargo would come over to our school and talk to a bully I went to school with named Chad Berger."

"That's really his name? Berger?"

"Yeah, probably why he had to start pounding people. But anyway, man, when Johnny came by one time he talked about Danny's dad's goons coming to your rescue, and how toward the end of the year you missed like… three weeks of school or something and still graduated."

"Yeah, that's true."

"Well, why?"

I sighed and started, "Look, Danny and I were both outcasts at school. I'd rather not get all into it, but Danny wanted to be my friend since we shared a common problem. No one liked us at school, so we eventually became friends and I started working at the warehouse his father owns, that's it. They took me out of school because the whole gang was in trouble, even those not completely associated in it, and until that was over, I had to hide."

"Victor, you don't have to lie to me. I know that you're in the gang just as much as Danny is," Emmitt said firmly. "But I respect you guys after what you did for me. You didn't have to do that. Shit, most people wouldn't. They would've either not intervened or only intervened just to make those guys leave. But you guys actually cared about me too, or that's what it seemed like."

I wasn't quite sure what to say back. I was glad he appreciated our help, but as for my actual line of work… I didn't want to lie to Emmitt, but there were some things that were better for him to not know.

And as the drive became awkwardly silent, Emmitt finally said, "So, Victor, what do you guys do, exactly?"

He sounded like a curious kid and it almost made me laugh. When I answered, I started out by saying, "Why, do you want to be a part of it?"

"Hah!" Emmitt cried out. "No, my dad would kill me before any of the gangsters did. I'm just wanting to know what you guys do, y'know? You make a lot of money?"

"Yeah, I make about two hundred or so a week, depending on my 'job performance' and how I'm seen by the gang. And the stuff we do… well, some of it is classified and the rest is just providing protection for the businesses we have share in."

"Wow, that's a lot, man. Now I see why you have this car."

I was going to start talking about how it was a Christmas present from the Don, but I didn't want to ruin Emmitt's imagination. I was just going to let him think what he wanted to, unless it was something contradictory to the wants and needs of the gang.

## Chapter Thirty

Poor Rupert almost crapped himself when I walked in with Emmitt. He swore up and down that he had paid his dues and I finally had to reach over the counter to pat him and calm him down. Afterwards, Rupert felt relieved and let us bowl for free.

I was never all that good at bowling, and right when I'd start to get good, my wrist would hurt. It seemed like there'd never be a way for me to get any better. One hundred sixty was my top score and I never went over.

Emmitt was tearing up the alley though. He was bowling better than anyone I had ever seen. He got in the mid-200s and didn't even break a sweat.

When the third game was over, I felt my wrist start to hurt and I said, "I think I'm done for today."

"Yeah, me too," Emmitt said as he munched on some cheese fries that were now cold. His face didn't change to show they tasted bad, but I knew they couldn't have tasted good.

When we left, it was about 4:30. The games lasted so long because we would talk about our dislikes and likes between each throw. We both seemed to like the same music for the most part, except I was more for Elvis and Led Zeppelin and he was more for Chuck Berry and Little Richard.

As we started to leave the bowling alley, I stopped before I started my car and said, "Well, want me to take you back home or would you want to come eat with me and a friend of mine?"

"Is it one of your mobster friends?" Emmitt asked harshly.

After I thought about Chief Ramzorin, I said, "No, quite the opposite."

Emmitt gave me a confused look before he answered, "Well Victor, I would go with you but... I know my dad said I could be back any time before eight, but really, the earlier the better. He likes me to be home for dinner."

"Oh, yeah I understand," I replied as I started my car.

The drive back to his side of town was a little quiet. We just let the radio fill the silence on a low volume.

When I got him back to his house, he said, "Victorman, I had a lot of fun. We should definitely hang out again soon if you're not too busy dumping bodies in the nearest river."

"Hah," I said, not really sure how to take Emmitt's jokes. "Yeah, I think we should too. But we should play a sport I'm actually good at next time."

"Oh yeah? Like what? Tennis?" Emmitt said with a smirk.

"Dude, whatever. I can outshoot you in basketball, trust me."

"Better watch what you say about that, Victor, I'll be accepting your challenge."

As I started to think that he was probably good from living right next to a basketball court, I said, "Or, y'know, we could catch some girls next time if you want."

Emmitt was already outside of my car and about to close the door.

"Yeah, that'd be cool too. See you, Victor."

He shut the passenger door and I started to pull away. After checking my watch, I saw it was five-ten.

I went ahead and made my way to Michelangelo's. When I got there early, I didn't really care. I started talking to Antonio at the front and then ordered some fried mozzarella with marinara sauce. When Chief Ramzorin came in at five till six, he seemed really surprised to see me sitting at our booth. He was always the early one, not me. And the last time I had met him for dinner was the beginning of June.

Chief Ramzorin scooted into the booth and looked to me with a surprised face.

"Victor, you're here, and you're early."

"I wanted to make sure I didn't miss it," I said with a smile back.

Antonio walked our fried mozzarella over and the restaurant seemed to be just as quiet as usual.

"Oh, we're not getting our usual items?" Chief Ramzorin asked.

After the Don had fixed his tortellini with pesto cream sauce, I swore I'd stop ordering it at Michelangelo's.

"Chief, it's just an appetizer, calm down."

The Chief seemed happy that I was more jovial than usual, or maybe he was just happy I was there. It had been a while, and I felt bad for not coming more often. But, things were different now.

After I convinced myself in my mind that I wasn't followed, Antonio handed me a Coke and Chief Ramzorin a black mug of coffee.

"So gentlemen, are we getting the usual or not?" Antonio asked.

"Eh…" I said as I picked up the menu. Chief Ramzorin had just started to say yes, but I interrupted him.

"Y'know, that pepperoni and chicken calzone looks pretty good," I said as I placed the menu back over behind the napkins.

Chief Ramzorin shook his head at me as he took a sip of coffee and asked, "Well, hell, does that have onions or mushrooms?"

"Yeah, it has both," Antonio replied.

"Okay, well take out the mushrooms and put some more onions in there and I'll have that," Chief Ramzorin said as he made a face to me and put his menu away.

Chief Ramzorin and I laughed at one another and took some sips of our drinks. Then, he decided to take our conversation to a different topic, one I had a hard time talking about.

"So, are you still working for Don Ponchello?" Chief Ramzorin asked boldly as he softly blew on his hot coffee.

"Yes, I work for Mark Ponchello," I said, trying to make him sound like a better man. He was a better man to me, but maybe not to him.

"Oh yeah... and tell me," Chief Ramzorin said as he set down his coffee and interlocked his fingers, "what exactly do you do for him?"

"I thought I told you before," I said, a little irritated at Chief Ramzorin's tone. "I work at the warehouse he owns moving boxes and crates all day."

"Okay, Victor, I just want to make sure it's nothing illegal."

"It's not illegal," I said, lying straight to his face. I hated to disrespect the man, but it was either disrespect Chief Ramzorin or disrespect the Don, and the Don scared me more.

"Well, good," Chief Ramzorin said.

The rest of the time, we sat in silence, and when our calzones came, I ripped into mine and started eating. The food at StrikeZone wasn't very filling, so I started feeling hungry as soon as I dropped Emmitt off. The calzone was filling, and I finished before Chief Ramzorin.

When Antonio brought the check over, I dropped a twenty on the table and said, "Look, Chief, sorry to eat and run but I gotta go. It was good seeing you again."

Frankly, I was just leaving because of his tone earlier, but the Chief acted surprised as he said, "Wait, Victor, you don't have to pay."

"It's all right, Chief," I said as I stood up. "I have a job and it's time for me to pay for once."

Chief Ramzorin gave me a hardened look as he said, "I hope you're still being careful, Victor, and I hope to see you next week."

"Same," I said, and I headed out the front to my car.

# Chapter Thirty One

The sun started to fall behind the massive buildings downtown as I made my way over to Studio 9 with my windows down and my music rocking. I was mad about Chief Ramzorin's tone, but I knew where he was coming from. He was probably upset that I never mentioned joining the force anymore. But, how could I now? The Don would have me killed if I did, I know he would. Even if I was Danny's friend, there are some things that just can't save you. I wasn't bulletproof from pissing off the Don, and I knew that. No one was bulletproof from that, especially his own son.

I really wished that Chief Ramzorin could talk to me normally and not grill me like he had before. I wanted to talk to him like we used to, but back then, I was still in school and had never fired a gun before.

Now there was no common ground. We just knew each other, but our present lifestyles didn't connect anymore. I was a thief and a killer, and he was an enforcer of the laws I had broken. That's the way it had to be now.

I still wanted to be his friend, but there was no way it could be as casual as it was before. Never again.

When I pulled up to Studio 9, the pink neon lights bounced off my car and made me visible. I thought back to when Danny and I got in the shootout with Tandelli's men. It was nice to roll up without any fear, but maybe I was going around not being cautious enough.

Pushing some bad thoughts aside, I headed in to see The Ballz and have a little chat with him.

When I walked past the front two guards, they nodded to me and I went right on in. It was like I co-owned the city with the Don. It was crazy how much shit I could get away with if I wanted to, but I tried to only take actions that would help the business.

This little trip, however, was personal.

After walking through the valley of smoke and past all of the loose women, I saw The Ballz sitting at a round table with women on his left and on his right. When I approached him, he seemed happy.

"Victor, man! Feels like it's been a while since I've seen you up in here! C'mon over here, man, have a drink or something."

"I'm good," I said as a few of his girls looked me over.

As soon as The Ballz realized he was losing their attention, he said, "Y'know what, get these bitches off of me, man. Go on, bitches! I don't need you here."

They seemed offended as they walked away and I was now left alone with The Ballz with the music blaring in the background.

"So, what's up, Victor? Trying to score some tail tonight?"

"No," I replied as I looked around the club.

I wasn't really sure how to make the request to The Ballz, so I sort of stood awkwardly and glanced at him every once in a while.

Eventually, The Ballz said, "Ay man, you know I be paying my dues just like I'm supposed to. I'm not taking any shit out or underpaying."

"No, that's not why I'm here, Ballz," I said awkwardly.

"Oh. I just assumed because I heard about that baker."

"The baker didn't do anything wrong, he just needs to be more careful," I said as I lit up a cigarette. "He got jumped by a couple of punks."

"Hah, cowards, messing with the Don. They must got shit for brains!" The Ballz said with an uproarious laughter.

I nodded and took another puff from my cigarette. I was trying to calm down so I could ask him my favor, but... I just didn't know how to.

"So, if you don't want a bitch, and you don't wanna beat my ass, I know you didn't just come here for a friendly conversation."

The Ballz was right. I just needed to spit it out.

"Okay, I was wondering if you might be able to find someone for me."

"Find someone for you?" The Ballz repeated, a little crazily. "What do you mean by that? I know the rats live in the sewers, the Don lives in his big ass mansion, and the bitches are here!"

"No... this isn't a bitch," I said as I reached into my pocket to pull out the picture of the girl I was missing.

The picture was of Kassidy, the one I was only able to spend one night with. I missed her from day to day, but I didn't like to show it. Recently, it had really started eating away at me. The Ballz saw everyone in town, even if he didn't mean to, and he had an impeccable memory of seeing those people.

As I handed him the picture that she left for me the night we made love, The Ballz looked at it for a second and said, "Oh, is this the girl we talked about before?"

I nodded and The Ballz looked over the picture. He tsk-ed to himself and shook his head. His pity for me practically filled the room.

"Do you think you can find her, or let me know if you see her?" I asked as he handed back the photo.

And with a simple reply, he said, "For you, Victor, anything."

# Chapter Thirty Two

My dreams were troubling that night. I didn't sleep well, and when I woke up the next morning on Thursday, everything got a lot worse.

Just as I sat up from my bed and scratched my back, Leo burst into my room and charged at me.

"Hey, hey, hey!" I yelled as I started to reach for a weapon.

Leo just grabbed me by the collar and started dragging me downstairs. His grip was strong and I didn't want to fight back. Instead, I let him drag me downstairs and past all the other men into the Don's office. Even Danny gave me a distressing look.

When I was thrown into a chair in the Don's office, I rubbed my neck to try and ease the pain. Leo slammed the door behind us and I was presented to the Don in my pajamas. Not really the way I wanted the day to start.

As I sat there and tried to catch my breath, the Don pulled his cigar away and said, "I'm upset, Victor. Leo! Don't hit him just yet."

My head jerked around as I saw Leo putting on a pair of brass knuckles. I felt like soon, it was going to be lights out.

"We know who you've been hanging out with," the Don said darkly.

"What? He's just a friend from the diner!" I yelled, not completely awake yet.

"I'm not talking about that black kid," the Don seethed as he pulled out an enlarged photograph and threw it across the table at me.

The black and white photo showed me and Chief Ramzorin eating at Michelangelo's. It looked like it was taken yesterday. I tried to fumble something together after I saw it. Fortunately, I didn't have to lie my way out of anything.

"No, no Don, Don Ponchello I swear to you, it's not what it looks like. I'm not some rat."

"Really now?" the Don said in an incredulous way. He leaned in towards me like a threatening snake. "Victor, do you know what this could mean for the gang, if you've been telling him about our operation?"

"I haven't told him anything! Can't I just explain myself?" I pleaded. I didn't wait for the Don to give me a clear answer. "Look, he's a family friend. He was there for me when my father started being a jerk to me and my mom. We meet there once a week on Wednesdays at six. I'll admit that. I have not told him anything about *anything*. He's a friend to me, Don, and that's it. He's not my boss, I'm not his informant. We just eat there once a week, and yesterday was the first time I had gone in a long while. I swear to you, I promise!"

I almost started crying because I knew that if they didn't believe me, I was going to be thrown into a river, but the water wouldn't have to make me cold.

The Don sat back and Leo sighed as he said, "As much as I don't want to believe him, the audio I took from their conversation proves almost everything he's said. The Chief was trying to muscle in on him and get him to talk about our operation, but he only talked about working at the warehouse."

"See, Don?" I said, exacerbated. "My loyalty is to you, not some pig. He's just a friend that was there for me before Danny. I would never turn my back on you, Don."

I hated to call Chief Ramzorin a pig in one sentence and then a friend in the other.

But, the Don believed me as he leaned in and said, "Victor, calm down, okay? I believe you. I knew you'd be smarter than that, Victor. I knew there was a better explanation for all of this."

He smiled and I started to calm down. For the first time in a long time, it felt creepy to be in his office.

"Quite a few of our men have been brought in by the police lately. We wondered if maybe you were telling the Chief who to nab next. Don't worry, Victor. Right when Leo brought this to me, I had my doubts of you being a traitor."

"Why was Leo spying on me anyway?" I asked.

Leo walked around to face me as he put his brass knuckles away.

"Because, kid, when I'm told I need to find who took the money from the baker, that means everyone is a suspect," Leo said sternly.

"Oh, okay…" I replied softly.

"Speaking of that, any other leads besides this one that just went down the drain?"

Leo shook his head.

"Whoever did this either never wants to do it again and realizes their mistake, or knows our pattern and is going to strike at the next bacon run."

"Well, we're not going to change the scheduling. We'll just have to wait and see," the Don said without any way of changing his mind.

I thought it was funny that they thought I took the money. I would've asked more about it, but I didn't want to raise any more alarms.

"Don't worry, boss. We're asking everyone in town and making sure this doesn't happen again. They won't strike at the next bacon run. They're probably just some scared punks trying to make some extra dough."

"Well, let's make sure it doesn't happen again," the Don said with a faint and evil smile.

Leo and I nodded and the Don said, "Victor, you're dismissed. Hope there aren't any hard feelings."

"No, there aren't, don't worry," I said as I walked out of the office, just happy to be alive.

# Chapter Thirty Three
## Friday, August 12th, 1977

Yesterday, after the intense talk with the Don, I went to work at the warehouse all day and didn't get to talk to Danny until Friday morning as we told each other we were off work. As soon as we started talking, I knew Danny never believed a word that came out of anyone's mouths about me being a rat.

"Dude, when my dad and Leo came in to talk to me, asking if I had ever heard of you eating with the Chief, I had no idea what was going on," Danny said as we grabbed breakfast at a drive-in downtown. "I thought they had gone nuts for a second."

"So, you never thought that I was a traitor at any point in time?" I asked him, to make sure we were on good terms.

"No, man, I mean, maybe for a split second I wondered, but I knew better than that. You guys are just friends; that's cool with me."

I finished off my orange juice and felt way too full from the egg sandwich and French toast sticks. Danny and I threw our trash away in the nearest receptacle and then Danny asked, "Well, what did you do all day on Wednesday? I know you didn't stay with that cop all day, did you?"

"Hah, no I didn't stay with him all day," I replied as I wiped my face and got back into Danny's car. "I actually hung out with, you know that black guy that you saved at the diner?"

"Oh, you mean uh... Emmitt? Is that his name?" Danny asked and I nodded. "Really? Was that fun?"

"Yeah, he's a cool guy."

"Well, you wanna see what he's doing?"

"What, you mean right now?" I asked.

"Yeah, I mean, did you have something else planned today? We're both off."

I thought for a second even though I already knew the answer.

"No, I don't have anything to do. Let's go see what he's doing. I'll show you the way."

Danny cruised down to the black side of town in his 1970s orange Dodge Challenger. His car was the brightest one around and we stuck out like a sore thumb. Passing by all the other people around, we got quite a few strange looks, and then one guy gave us a thumbs up on the car. Danny waved back and said, "Y'know, my dad always told to not come down this way but hey, it's the middle of the day, what's the worst that could happen?"

I shrugged and we pulled up to the high gates next to Emmitt's apartment complex. As Danny and I looked over, I pointed out Emmitt playing basketball.

"Okay, so there's Emmitt, and then that one right there that just looks like a taller and more muscular version of him is his oldest brother, Marcus, and then the middle brother is the one there with the afro, his name is TJ."

"All right, got it," Danny said as he stepped out of the car and started walking over to them like nothing could stop him.

I jumped out of the car and followed behind him. I didn't want to interrupt their game, but Danny didn't seem to care.

"Hey, Emmitt, how's it going?" Danny asked as he walked through the open gate.

They stopped playing basketball and stared Danny down. There were seven of them, all towering over me and Danny. Once TJ saw who was there, he smiled and gave me a high five.

"Hey, Victorman!" TJ said with a smile.

I returned his enthusiasm and Emmitt recalled Danny. Marcus maintained a hardened look on us.

"You guys just cruising?" Emmitt asked as he greeted me and Danny.

"Something like that," Danny said. "Victor and I are off today, and he was telling me about how much fun you guys had on Wednesday so I felt a little jealous."

"Oh, well I would hang with you guys but my cousin, Tyrel here, just came in from out of town."

Tyrel was the most buff and stout of the group. He stood at just under six foot tall, but he didn't look like someone to mess with at all. He was in about his mid-twenties, and he hadn't broken a smile the entire time we were there.

"Oh, well that's cool, welcome to Detroit," Danny said happily as he tried to shake Tyrel's hand.

Tyrel gave Danny a look that would make a lion step back. Danny eventually took the hint and retracted his arm.

"Well, we can get out of your hair if you want," I said as I only saw two of the men there accepting our presence.

"Nah, Victor," Emmitt said, which irritated his family and other friends. "After what you said Wednesday, I gotta see if you're all talk or not."

I thought back to Wednesday and remembered that I might've hyped up my basketball skills.

"Oh, did Victor flaunt his dexterity?" Danny asked in a sarcastic way.

A few of the guys in Emmitt's group actually cracked somewhat of a smile and Tyrel said, "White boy in jeans thinks he can out play us, huh cuz?"

"Maybe if I had a team," I said back.

There were a few smirk-filled gasps in the crowd and a few other black men, women, and children started watching us talk.

"Yeah, Victor, lemme call some of the Kids and we'll get a team going," Danny said as he ran to the nearest pay phone.

A few minutes later, Danny had called upon Roger, Al, Charlie and Blake to come play ball with us.

"But Danny," I argued. "They got seven and that only makes us have six. What about Jacob or Nick?"

"Jacob's working and Nick is annoying," Danny said, but he did see my point as he cursed at himself. Then, his face lit up with hope.

"What are you thinking?" I asked as Danny pulled out another dime and started making a phone call.

Later, I found out that Danny had called Spencer Mangello, one of the best basketball players that had graduated with us. He was just as tall as Marcus and more agile than all of my team combined. When he arrived in his little beat up Honda, he somehow got out of the car and he was all decked out in sports gear. High socks, basketball shorts, his old jersey, his old sneakers, and a water bottle.

The Kids had arrived just before him, and when we revealed our secret weapon to Emmitt's team, a small feeling of doubt swept over their team about their chances of winning.

I watched as Danny welcomed Spencer to the group and we all shook hands.

"All right, you guys ready to do this?" Tyrel asked.

"Fuck yeah," Spencer said in his goofy voice.

The game started right at 11:30 and the sun was beating down like no other. I usually played in jeans and a T-shirt, but this was too much. Spencer had the right idea by bringing a bottle of water, but luckily, there was a semi-clean water fountain nearby that ended up hydrating us all.

We were only down by about four points in the beginning, then we were up by one, and then they grabbed the lead again. Spencer and I seemed to be the best players on our team, but every once in a while, Danny or Charlie would make a good shot. My best shot of the day was a fade away three-pointer that even seemed to impress Emmitt's oldest brother, Marcus.

And of course, there was a little bit of trash talk that was expected to take place during street ball, but Spencer Mangello decided to take it a little too far.

As Spencer and Tyrel checked the ball to each other, a flare of anger came out of nowhere as Tyrel checked the ball to Spencer, and then Marcus came by and stole the ball from the now tired Spencer.

It was around one o'clock when the bomb was dropped.

"You niggers," Spencer spat.

Tyrel, who hadn't gotten along with Spencer the entire game, yelled out "What!?" and headed up to Spencer. When Spencer started to repeat himself, Tyrel threw out a tremendous punch that seemed to rock the entire court. The sound of Tyrel's fist establishing contact on Spencer's jawbone was unsettling.

Danny and I had stepped aside for a second to cool down when the punch was thrown. Marcus threw down the ball and started to fight Spencer as well, along with the rest of them. Danny and I glanced at each other and Danny said, "Oh, shit!"

Surprisingly, Danny jumped into the group that was trying to fight Spencer and pulled Spencer out of it. Emmitt and TJ tried their best to hold back their angry group as Danny walked Spencer over to his Honda.

"Emmitt, I'm sorry, I didn't think he'd say that," I said as I tried to explain to Emmitt and his brothers.

"Victor, just get that piece of shit out of here and don't let him come here again," Emmitt said as TJ tried to calm everyone down.

I nodded as the Kids and I walked over to get Spencer into his car and get him out of there.

Spencer's mouth was bleeding and his face was already starting to bruise. He muttered and mumbled as Danny walked him over to his Honda.

"Get out of here, Spencer," Danny said as he placed him in the driver's seat of his hot car.

"Fuck those guys," Spencer said as he slammed his door and started up his car.

I forgot that Spencer's temper got the best of him during pretty much every game he played, especially if the other team was winning.

"Don't come back," I said just before Spencer pulled away.

He hastily sped off and Danny looked to me and the Kids.

"Eh, we better get out of here before they decide to rip us apart too," Danny said.

And with that, we all agreed on a place to sit down, cool down and eat, and decided it had to be far away from here.

# Chapter Thirty Four
## Monday, September 5th, 1977

Emmitt and I didn't talk for a while after the basketball incident. I started to just hang out with Danny like usual or some of the other Kids for a while.

On this day, Danny and I had worked all day at the warehouse and now we had to do the bacon run. We had not found the group that stole from the baker, and after the baker made his drop, he called the Don personally and said there weren't any mishaps. After calling all of the droppers, the Don had found out that nothing was stolen.

Leo eventually said that it was some punks who learned that they got lucky and decided to never do it again. The Don hoped that was the case, and so did everyone else.

When Danny and I left the warehouse, Danny looked to me and said, "Victor, are you nervous at all?"

"Not really," I replied. "Are you?"

"I don't know," Danny replied. "I kind of have a bad feeling. Maybe those guys who stole before are going to steal from the actual boxes this time."

"Well in that case, we'll pop them," I said coldly as I pointed to my holster under my jacket. The colder weather made it easier and more comfortable to conceal carry, I just had to make sure I didn't take my jacket off in public.

Danny nodded and we were off for the bacon run.

The first spot was normal and there wasn't any activity. Danny and I both went down to the sewer and grabbed the envelopes. When they were all accounted for, we headed back to the car.

"Okay, first drop zone was good," Danny told himself as he started his car up again.

"Look, Danny, we're not going to seem like a bunch of girls if we call in for some backup," I said.

"No, Victor, it's all right. Those punks aren't going to steal again."

At the cemetery drop point, Danny and I climbed out together again and grabbed the envelopes.

"All of 'em there?" Danny asked me.

"Yup, all of them," I replied as I tossed them to him.

"Hah, good deal," Danny said as we walked back to his car.

The warehouse was the third drop point. As Danny pulled into the vacant lot, he said, "Maybe we should just drive around to check."

"It's up to you, man," I said as I sat back in the passenger's seat, not too worried.

When Danny looked to me and saw how calm I was, he said, "Nah, we're good."

Danny pulled his car into the narrow alleyway where the next box was. Right as we were pulling up, I saw something next to the box.

It was a brand new pair of long wire cutters.

"Danny, look at that," I said as I pointed to the wire cutters.

"Let's check it out," Danny said as he got out of his car.

We both stepped out of the car and slowly stepped toward the box. When we were about halfway to it, a group of men stepped out from the abandoned warehouse and everything started to make sense.

"Modellini!" I exclaimed.

Modellini and his crew held guns up at us as we stood our ground. He wasn't the only backstabbing son of a bitch there, though. As I looked over his crew, Johnny Fargo, the punk Josh from the diner, and one other kid that I assumed was Chad Berger, the one Emmitt had talked about, stood before us. I hesitated to grab my gun and so did Danny. It was the smartest thing to do at this point.

Modellini held a small pistol in his hand and said, "Well now, you caught us during our heist."

"You're the ones who stole from the baker," Danny said angrily and obviously.

"Giovanni can't defend himself, what with all of that fat he carries around from day to day," Modellini said.

Johnny Fargo sneered and said, "Hey, Victor, it's been a long time since I've kicked your ass."

"We should leave," Danny said quietly.

"No, don't leave," Modellini said with an evil grin. "Not until you hand over your key, Danny. It would save us a lot of time instead of prying it open. And while you're at it, you could hand over the other envelopes you've picked up. That'd save us a lot of trouble."

Modellini waved around his gun like it wasn't a dangerous object. I looked at Danny as he continued to stare forward with dead silence.

"Man, Victor, after all the good grades you got in high school, you turned out to be a no good, two-timing crook with Danny boy."

"Shut up, Fargo," I said strongly. "Not like you turned out any better."

"Shut it, both of you," Modellini said as he waved his gun at Danny once again. "Daniel, my old friend, hand over the key or I'll take it from your dead body."

The wind was the only sound heard by everyone for a while, until Danny said, "No."

Modellini didn't hesitate to fire his first bullet right into Danny's left shoulder. I quickly reacted and pulled my pistol out and had it aimed in Modellini's direction. When I fired, the bullet scraped his arm and then I turned to fire at Johnny Fargo. I put a bullet right into Johnny's leg just so he could feel around the same amount of pain he put me through in school.

I glanced to Danny and saw him writhing in pain as he headed for his car. I followed behind him as the rest of Modellini's men took cover from my incoming fire.

"Danny, climb into the back if you can and I'll climb over into the driver's seat!" I yelled over the gunfire.

I used his reinforced car door as a shield to the incoming fire. Besides the one shot Modellini made, their guns were incredibly inaccurate, which helped us out a lot. I wanted to kill all of them, but they outnumbered me and their bullets were hitting way too close for me to stay and try to pick them off.

Danny climbed into the back painfully and blood smeared over his driver's seat. I slammed the passenger door behind me and reached for the keys in the ignition. As I climbed over into the driver's seat, the bullets barely cracked the bulletproof windshield. Their impact made me flinch as I locked the doors and started Danny's car. It was time to go.

I jerked the car into reverse and backed out as fast as I could, then swerved the car around and headed for the nearest on ramp to the highway, not giving a shit about anyone else in the road.

My best friend was bleeding in the backseat and I needed to get him back home to see The Doctor.

"Victor?" Danny asked through his clenched teeth.

The car screeched onto the highway and I looked back at him.

"Yeah, Danny?"

"Did you," Danny started to say, but the pain took over and he groaned. When the pain passed temporarily, he asked, "Did you kill any of them?"

As my blood boiled in my veins and I raced along the highway to the manor, I dangerously replied, "Not yet."

# Chapter Thirty Five

As soon as Scott saw us flying up to the manor gates in Danny's bullet riddled car, he pressed red button in the pillbox to alert the Don of an emergency. Scott then pushed the other button to open the gates for us and I had to wait just a second before rushing in. I couldn't see straight; I didn't know what I was going to tell the Don. He was going to hate me for letting his son get shot.

The Don, Roy, Leo, and a few other men ran out to the car as soon as I pulled up and I began to help Danny out of the back. The Don seemed afraid as I pulled his son out of the car. I saw another bullet had hit Danny in the back of the leg and caused him to now limp.

"Jesus Christ, what the fuck happened?" Roy called out as he looked over the bloodied interior of the car.

"Roy, call The Doctor, now!" the Don ordered sternly as he took Danny from me. "Where'd they hit you, Son?"

"One in my shoulder, one in the back of my leg," Danny cringed.

"Let's get him inside and on a good bed," the Don ordered as he carried his son into the manor.

I hesitated to go inside as David Weston, the Don's bodyguard, stared me down.

"Did you get hit, kid?" David asked.

I shook my head silently and stood frozen in a state of mild shock.

"Modellini," was all I managed to say through my daze.

Thinking of how the Don had given me a hardened look before, David said, "Look, kid, you did the right thing. Danny looks like he's going to be all right, okay? Don't sweat it. Now lemme ask you again, are you hit?"

"No," I replied. "They attacked at the warehouse. We didn't check the perimeter. Danny wanted to, but I said…"

"Stop, Victor," David said sternly. "Don't blame yourself. That'll only make things worse. The Doctor should be here soon and then everything will be okay."

It was the most compassion I had ever seen David have towards me or anyone else. I guess he knew all too well what it was like to be on the other end of a forty-five.

"Thanks, David, I appreciate it," I said as I started to snap out of my confusion.

# The Platinum Briefcase

David patted my back and led me into the manor slowly.

The Doctor arrived about seven minutes later. In the meantime, Leo had stopped Danny's bleeding and made sure he was comfortable before The Doctor got there. Neither of the bullets passed through Danny, and The Doctor seemed perturbed as he went in to extract them.

The Don had locked himself in his office with Leo and Roy. Jordan was on his way from picking up the money from the fourth spot, which he had been told to do after David told the Don we only made it to the third drop.

The manor was busy and people were entering and exiting all parts of it. The Don wanted Modellini and his gang's heads on a platter and served to the dogs.

I sat in the living room and waited for The Doctor to come down the stairs and tell us what had happened. David, Scott, and even the car mechanic Phil and I all waited in the living room for the results of the at-home surgery.

When The Doctor came walking down the steps at around seven o'clock, he looked around the room and said, "He's going to be all right."

"Can I see him?" I asked eagerly.

"He's knocked out on morphine, so if you want to watch him sleep, sure."

I believed The Doctor and all, but I wanted to see with my very own eyes that Danny was okay. When I made it up to his room, the door was slightly cracked open and I slowly went in.

Danny was propped up on his bed with a sling on and some bandaging on his chest. He was shirtless, but covered by the sheets on his bed. All that was exposed was the top of his chest and his head.

I didn't say a word; I just stared at him in the dim light of his room as dust danced in the sun beams. I watched him as he breathed slowly in a deep sleep. I shook my head, glad that he was alive. We had both come close to death just an hour ago, but now, we were both safe.

Oddly enough, I hated that I didn't get shot or injured at all. I felt like the Don had even more anger toward me just because I didn't get hit in the crossfire. But, Modellini wasn't really trying to shoot me; he was trying to kill Danny. Why? Just because his father kicked him out of the gang? Modellini should be happy that the Don even let him live.

*Greedy fuck*, I thought in my head.

I felt guilty for not letting Danny check the other side of the warehouse... but I tried taking David's advice to not blame myself.

Suddenly, a dark voice from behind me said, "Victor, the Don wants to see you."

## Chapter Thirty Six

Leo led me down to the Don's office, but this time was more civil than the last. He walked behind me as I led the way. We didn't speak to each other, and I really didn't care to speak to him. He probably didn't think too highly of me and honestly, I didn't know what to think at all. David told me I did the right thing in the shootout, and that the Don would obviously be upset because it was his son.

I took all of that with a grain of salt as Leo stepped in front of me to open the office door.

The Don turned away from the huge portrait of his father that hung behind his desk and faced me.

"Victor, have a seat," the Don said neutrally.

I took the seat and waited for the Don to lay it on me like usual, not leaving out any details. To my surprise, he cut straight to the main points.

"Who were these cowards?" the Don asked me with gritted teeth.

I swallowed before I began explaining.

"It was Modellini and some other thugs that were with him: Johnny Fargo from school, another one that caused trouble at the diner, and some other punk. They had some cheap foreign pistols that can't shoot worth a crap, and they were trying to open the drop box with some wire cutters."

Instead of silence, the Don, to everyone's surprise, laughed. Eventually, we all shared an awkward chuckle, and the Don finally explained.

"I knew Moe was dumb, but I didn't think he was this dumb. They never could have opened that box without the key."

The Don took another drink from his glass of alcohol and cringed.

"Victor, I know I was upset earlier, and I want to apologize for not even checking on you. I am upset that they hurt my boy, but I'm glad you weren't injured too. If that had happened, I would've had to get someone else to watch over the Kids, and that's not a job that anyone really wants, or would be any good at."

"Thank you, and I understand," I replied.

"Good," the Don said with a faint smile. "Now, you're sure it was just those kids there and not anyone of a higher power? Not another gang or anything, just some punks led by Modellini?"

"I'm positive," I started off. "Modellini went with us on a few bacon runs. He was the only one who would've known where the boxes were, or even just the one. And, he's dumb enough to admit he stole from the baker."

The Don nodded and said, "Good. I was worried we might have another war on our hands, but in this case, it's just a minor bug problem."

The Don then turned to Leo and said, "Your job is to take care of Modellini, as soon as possible."

When Leo nodded, I spoke up and said, "Actually, Don Ponchello, if I may make a request."

The Don, Leo, Roy, and David all looked to me as the Don gave me a signal to go ahead and speak.

"I was uh, wondering if you could let me and the Kids take care of it."

"Kid, you're not ready for this kind of work," Leo said harshly.

"The hell I'm not," I snapped back at Leo. "Look, I know what they look like, and they seem to want something. Maybe I can work out a deal with them, or lure them to where they think it will be a deal or a meeting. Modellini is not the only one we should worry about."

"You don't talk to me like that, kid," Leo started.

"No, Leo, he's right. Besides, I believe it was you who searched for them for a month and still couldn't find them," the Don said harshly, which made Leo shut up. "All right, Victor, if you want the responsibility of taking care of this, I will leave it all on you. Just make sure that in the end they will no longer be a problem to us. That's all I ask."

I glanced at Leo, who gave me a mean look, and I said, "It will be done."

"Good, Victor. All I have for you is one warning: If my men have to intervene and end up taking care of this due to incompetence, you will face consequences."

"I understand. I will make sure I take care of it," I said.

With that, the Don dismissed me and I left feeling a power that I never had felt before.

I was in control.

# Chapter Thirty Seven

Everything changed after Danny was shot. I became a full soldier rather than just a footman. This meant I could be called upon at any moment to do what needed to be done.

I was the sole leader of the Kids now. Even the day after Danny was shot, everyone looked at me differently. They thought if it wasn't for me reacting so quickly and firing back, Danny would be a goner.

In some ways, I had gained a lot more respect among the gang as well. Prior to this incident, Danny, the Kids, and I were literally just seen as kids. No one expected for us to be into it this deep, but now we were.

Modellini and his men could strike again at any time. It wasn't necessary for me to work at the warehouse. All I needed to do was keep a tab on my men.

And boy, did they need direction.

"Victor," Blake said as he came up behind me.

"Yes, Blake?"

"When are we gonna go pop those bastards that shot up Danny?"

Blake's enthusiasm was good, but not needed just yet.

"Well, Blake, we'll have to establish contact of some sort before we do that, whether that's seeing them on the streets or actually talking to them. Then, we'll make our move."

Charlie came up to me next with a different question.

"So, some guy short changed me on a deal the other day. What do you think I should do?"

"Uh," I said, a little surprised at the question. "Beat him up a little."

"I would, but he had some other guys with him."

"Okay, then take some other guys with you. If you can't get that money or he pulls a knife, you pull a gun. Then he'll know who's in charge."

All of these questions getting asked on a Tuesday morning right after Danny was shot was one thing, but what made it even weirder was when Jacob, the quiet one, came up to me.

"Victor," Jacob said with his deep voice. His eyes bounced about the room. "Is Danny gonna be all right?"

"Of course he will be," I said confidently.

It didn't seem like much, but it was starting to stress me out. I tried to go out back on the lush green lawn that was slowly dying and smoke a cigarette, but it was making me sick to even try, so I gave up and threw the cigarettes aside.

Later in the morning, I was finally able to talk to Danny.

"It's crazy, Danny," I said after our conversation had gone on a while and he claimed to be okay, "these kids keep asking me tons of questions. Do they usually ask you?"

"I thought they asked us both?" Danny asked in a slight daze from the drugs.

"No, I've never really been asked any questions."

"Well, you're the leader type, Victor, you just gotta let it show."

The Doctor walked in and told me to leave so Danny could get more rest. I said farewell to Danny, and decided to make my way to the diner.

The budding friendship between Emmitt and I had come to a screeching halt about a month ago and I hadn't seen him since the incident on the basketball court. I thought maybe it'd be good to see him, and try to make amends.

I stepped into the diner and saw the destruction around the place from the lunch crowd. It seemed like everyone in Detroit had stopped by. Now, as the only sounds were the jukebox and the sound of sweeping and dishes clattering, I walked over to Emmitt as he bused a table.

"Hey," I said softly.

Emmitt glanced up from the table and didn't recognize my voice. After a semi-comical double-take, he went, "Oh, hello, Victor."

He placed the bus tub down on the table and stood up straight.

"So, I know it's been a while, but I just wanted to make sure you're all right, and that we're cool."

Emmitt sighed and said, "Yeah man, we're cool. It's not like you said it or anything. Tyrel really hates that Spencer cat though. Actually, we all do."

"Well, good. I'm not even friends with him, Danny just thought it was a good idea to call him because we were about to get our asses beat in the game."

Emmitt actually smiled and laughed. As his laughter subsided, he started nodding. "Yeah, that's true. Y'all had to bring out your secret weapon."

I felt a driving motivation to prove myself as I felt Emmitt's confidence in me as a friend diminishing.

"You know I'd never call any of you guys that, right?"

Emmitt looked weirdly at me and said, "What? You mean, the n-word?"

"Yeah, I would never say that to you guys. I don't think it's a good word. My dad used to use it though."

Knowing I had left myself open without any defenders, Emmitt asked, "What made him stop? A brother gave him a piece of his mind?"

"No," I started off, and it never got easier to say, "My father's dead."

"Oh," Emmitt said, a little surprised. "Now I remember I had heard about that… and your mom too, right? I'm sorry, Victor, I didn't mean to bring it up."

"It's okay, man, time has passed since then."

Emmitt looked around and said, "Well, were you going to order something? I bet you I'm better at mixing the shakes than Rene is."

"Man, I would but I gotta get back home. Just thought I'd check in on you," I said, and I started to turn and walk away.

"Let Danny know that we're thinking about him," Emmitt said.

I opened the front door and heard the ding from the bell above. I turned to face Emmitt and said, "I will, thanks."

# Chapter Thirty Eight
## Wednesday, September 7th, 1977

Today was my day off, but I didn't really feel like going around and having fun or stirring up any kinds of trouble. For the most part, the Don just wanted me to hang around the house and not stick my neck out too much. He worried that Modellini would hunt me down and kill me. At the time, Modellini seemed more interested in killing Danny at the warehouse. I guess that was to try and get payback on being fired. But, his best bet would've been killing me and holding Danny for ransom. The drugs really must've gone to his head, and I had a feeling he wasn't just smoking pot.

As I sat around the house watching TV, a flurry of activity surrounded me. The henchmen in black coats were scurrying around, and even the Kids were part of the hustle.

"Heya, Victor," Al said as he walked up to me. "I know it's your day off and all, but can I still ask something?"

At that time, I was reading over the sports section in the newspaper.

"Yeah, sure Al, what is it?"

"Well, I mean, you don't think Modellini is going to come after us, do you?" Al asked.

A little surprised at Al's question, I replied, "C'mon Mr. Macho Brooklyn man, don't be so scared. What are you doing today, warehouse work?"

"Yeah, the Don thought it'd be best."

"And he knows best, so I'd just follow his orders if I were you, and don't worry about it," I said. "Modellini's already made a big enough mistake."

Al smiled as he started to walk away with Nick and Jacob.

"Okay, Victor, we'll catch you later."

Later on in the day, after I ate lunch, there was a heated discussion between Jordan and Scott on who would take guard duty.

"Seriously, guard duty again?" Scott said in disgrace.

"Huh, that's weird," Jordan said as he turned and made a face to me.

I laughed to myself, knowing that Jordan was doing anything for the Don so he wouldn't have guard duty again. He even let the Don keep more of his paycheck so he could avoid it entirely. Scott had no idea, though, and his complaints made it all the more enjoyable.

"Don't worry, Scott," Jordan said as he patted Scott's back. "Maybe one of the Kids will take your spot soon. I mean, hell, we could just set Danny out there in his bed and have him push the button."

Jordan's joke wasn't humorous to me. I almost said something, but they were already gone. I'd have to get Jordan later.

I went back to eating an apple and feeling bored, until David came up to me.

"Victor, the Don would like to see you."

"Sure thing," I said as I placed the green apple on top of the newspaper.

I followed behind David as we headed to the Don's office, but oddly enough, the door was actually cracked open. I could see Leo pacing around in the office, and as we got closer, I could hear his voice.

"… but Boss, I think leaving this matter in the hands of the Kids is a bad idea. They don't know how to handle situations like this. They're gonna try to settle it in a game Pong or some shit like that."

David and I entered the office as Leo finished his thought. When I looked to the Don, the Don was still giving Leo a hardened glare. I joined in on the glare to Leo, but I knew he didn't regret what he had said.

"That'll be all, Leo," the Don said, which really meant "Get out".

Leo stepped past me to exit the office and I heard him murmur, "I hope you know what you're doing".

I nodded and David started to exit the room.

"Yes, David, you can go on, and close the door this time," the Don said sternly.

As David closed the door, the Don signaled to the chair before him and said, "You can sit."

I sat down in the soft leather on the oak chair and the Don stood up with a cigarette burning. The smoke danced around as he stepped over to the window and said, "You've been at the manor all day today?"

I nodded.

"It's pretty hectic, isn't it?"

"Yes, it is."

"Now you see why I can get irritated easily," the Don said with a slight smile.

I returned the smile as the Don sighed.

"Oh, today's your day off, isn't it?"

"Yeah."

"Well, I hope you don't mind me talking about business matters."

I shook my head.

"Good," the Don said as he pushed his cigarette to smithereens in the ashtray and sat back down. "The bacon runs are going to have to be changed, unless the

Modellini problem is fixed soon. Extra security has been placed on the warehouse, and I have two of your men, Blake and Charlie, scouting the town right now trying to find Modellini."

"And then Al, Jacob and Nick are doing warehouse work?"

"I actually made them part of the security at the warehouse. They didn't know until I told them last minute," the Don said with harsh honesty. "Those three are wimps, Victor. They're acting scared and anytime I mention something to them about the situation at hand, they shiver."

"They just haven't really been accustomed to the violent part of things. They're used to the highway robberies or the stick-ups."

"Well, toughen them up. Or else when the shit hits the fan, they're going down with it."

"Yes, Don," I said, not crazy about how he was talking. But I knew he was right, and he was right to send Blake and Charlie to scout out. They were two of the toughest Kids on here, besides me and Danny. One of the first jobs Charlie got was transporting a body to one of our construction companies that helped hide the bodies in the foundation of new buildings. If the buildings were torn down later, it'd be too late to charge anyone. Blake, on the other hand, he came from a rough background in the first place.

"Speaking of Modellini," the Don said as he put out one, then two fingers. "It's been two days since the attack. Have you come up with how you're going to take him out?"

I hesitated to answer, but I finally had to fumble through. "I'm not even sure if Modellini is still in town. He might have bolted."

"No, he wants something," the Don said, and then chuckled. "And whatever that something is, he's not getting it. You need to decide now what you're going to do, before it's too late."

I thought about it for a moment to myself. What was I going to do? Of course Modellini was a bastard, and I wanted him dead. But at one point, he was my friend. To see him in this new way hurt me, and I wondered if killing him would really be the right thing to do. A part of me knew there was a possibility of peace, but the only peace that the Don would accept is Modellini and his men resting in peace.

Finally, I said, "I was going to discuss it with Danny. See what he would prefer."

The Don looked me over, and then said, "Good, go ahead and speak to him. He said he was feeling better this morning, but I still want him to rest as much as he can. He lost a lot of blood."

"Okay, I will talk to him."

## Chapter Thirty Nine

I left the Don's office with a bit of a headache. The Don's commands and insults really took me down. What did he expect, Modellini's head on a platter within twenty-four hours? How was I supposed to do that when the Don was telling all my men what to do?

Leo's insults pissed me off too. Why did he hate me so much? My only conclusion was that the party Danny and I threw at the manor was strike one; strike two was him being sent to NYC to be a recruiter; and strike three seemed to be me asking to take control of taking out Modellini. Why did that not make sense to Leo, though? Modellini didn't attack Leo, he attacked Danny. Danny is part of the Kids, not a part of the actual mob that the Don runs. Maybe Leo just had some kind of blood lust or something. And when I got in the way of it, his temper flared. In my opinion, Leo needed to calm down.

By the time all these thoughts passed through my head, I was already almost to Danny's door. When I stepped up to his door, I pushed on it barely so that it would swing into the dimly lit room. Danny now left his door cracked most of the time, just in case Michelle came up with a steaming platter of food for him.

"Danny?" I called softly as I started opening the door.

"Victor, come in," Danny said, sounding like himself for the first time since the incident.

I entered the room with a smile and Danny could see it even in the dim light. He sat upright in his bed with a sling on his right arm and a book now lying on his lap. The lamp on his nightstand was the brightest light in the room, second was the light coming from the hallway, and third was the light trying to come through his blinds.

"Doing better?" I asked.

"Heh, the only thing I'm about to die of is boredom, lemme tell ya," Danny said. "This book... it's not so great. And neither was the last one."

"Can you move your arm?"

"Just barely. There's always a lingering pain but if I'm gentle, I can... Ow!"

Danny attempted to show me his mobility but it only caused him more pain than he wanted to deal with.

"What about your leg?"

"Yeah, I can walk without too much pain. I lost my balance at one point, but luckily I caught myself."

I got the small talk out of the way. That was always the easy part. And now, I needed to start the tough conversation: The one discussing how to deal with Modellini.

The problem was, even though I wasn't too against the idea of killing Modellini, I knew Danny might be. He was actually better friends with Modellini than I was, but Modellini was more hurt by Danny since his father kicked him out.

"So... Danny, we need to discuss something," I said.

"Yeah, go ahead," Danny said as he grew more serious.

We both understood the newfound tone of our conversation.

"It's about Modellini. Your father isn't happy with my progress so far on trying to find him, even though it's only been two days, and Leo is up my ass farther than Sears Tower. I have a feeling I know what to do, it's just... I don't know what to do, does that make sense? Like, do we kill him or try to work out a deal?"

With a strange glee, Danny replied, "Yeah, that's a good idea, Victor! You should kill him!"

Danny wasn't going to let the guilt fall on him as to why Modellini would be killed. He made it seem like it was my idea to kill him, which I guess it was in some ways... But...

Danny broke the previous mood and asked, "So, have you been to the diner lately?"

"Yeah, I was actually just there yesterday," I said blankly, until I remembered, "I saw Emmitt, and he said he's thinking of you."

"Really?" Danny asked. "So, does that mean he's not mad anymore?"

"I guess not... he was never mad at us, just Spencer."

Danny nodded and said, "Hey, by the way, now that you mentioned the diner, that's making me really miss my banana milkshake."

I knew where this was going, so I said, "Tell you what, I'll go get you the milkshake."

"Wow, Victor, you read my mind," Danny said sarcastically.

"Screw you," I said with a smile as I started walking out of his room.

*****

When I got to the diner, Emmitt was gone, but Sid was happy to help me.

"You know what? I'll make this shake extra free for Danny since he's hurt and all," Sid said with a wink as he told one of his bus boys to start the shake.

"Thanks, Sid. I know he'll appreciate it."

As the shake was made, I thought about the other times that Danny and I had come to the diner. One memory in particular seemed to dominate all the others. I almost felt like asking Sid if he had seen Kassidy, but that was neither here nor there. Last time I brought up Kassidy to… I don't remember who it was, but they told me to get over her, and I knew they were right. There was no reason for me to keep droning on about her. She had left my life, so I needed to forget about her.

Sid interrupted my thoughts as he handed the shake over to me and said, "Here you go, sailor. Tell Danny we made that one extra tasty for him."

I rattled my brain and said, "Yeah, I will, thanks."

I stepped out of the diner with Danny's shake in my hands. I had parked a little ways away from the entrance next to the curb and I opened the door so I could put his shake away. That's when Modellini decided to come up behind me with his goons.

"Step back from the car and close the door."

I felt the hard metal of Modellini's pistol pressing up against my back. If he fired now, I knew it would shatter my spine. After I placed the shake in the cup holder of my Bel Air, I did what Modellini asked.

"Good. Now, turn around slowly so I can see your hands."

When I turned to face Modellini and his gang, I felt no fear, even though there were two new members. The emotion I felt was hate, and regret that I couldn't rip my gun out and shove it in his mouth.

"Hi, Victor," Modellini said with a smile as he kept his gun low but still pointed towards me. "Out for a malt?"

"It's a shake, for Danny," I said, even though it was a pointless correction.

"That's nice of you, Victor. You always seemed like you'd be a good friend, but you were never that good to me."

"C'mon, Modellini, what are you waiting for?" Johnny Fargo said, and I noticed his pistol was out too. "Let's pop him."

"And let Danny's shake melt in the nice car? Tsk, tsk," Modellini said with a condescending tone. "Besides, then how would we get our money, Johnny?"

"What money?" I asked.

"You know, the Don's money. All I'm asking for is one million of it."

"A million dollars, really?" I asked, "I can tell you haven't been laying off the drugs."

That struck a chord in Modellini, and it wasn't a good one.

"Look Victor, here's the thing. If you don't do as I'm about to ask, my gang will continue to grow and we will be able to take down Don Ponchello's deteriorating mob."

Trying to reason with a madman, "Okay, what do you ask for, Modellini?"

"One million dollars, cash, tomorrow. You know that burnt down bar of Tandelli's that Nick got scolded for sneaking into? We'll meet there, around back. Bring your friends if you want to, but I understand if Danny can't come. You, or one of your pals, need to bring the money in a briefcase and be able to present it tomorrow afternoon at twelve. No tricks."

That's when I saw Modellini's eyes light up and I saw some headlights coming behind me. I turned to see Roy's station wagon speeding up to me.

"You agree to those terms?" Modellini asked as he and his men started running off into the darkness.

"We'll be there," I said firmly.

Modellini and his men ran off like the cowards they were as Roy jumped out of his car and ran up to me with a sawed-off shotgun. I wasn't sure he even put his car in Park.

"Victor! Is everything alright?"

"Yeah, Roy, I'm okay."

Roy looked off in the distance at Modellini and his cowardice clan.

"What the hell are you talking to them for, Victor!?"

"Roy, calm down!" I exclaimed. "They approached me, but we have an exchange planned."

Roy's excitement fell, and then rose again as he said, "Well, c'mon then, Victor, we'll have a meeting at the manor."

And as I stepped into my car and started it up, I said, "I'll see you there."

# Chapter Forty

The meeting was called and placed in a casual fashion. Instead of having everyone (me, Jordan, the Kids, Leo, the Don, David, and Roy) pile into the Don's office, or have everyone spread out in the dining room, we all assembled in Danny's room and I gave him his shake. Danny was worried that it took me longer than expected, but then I explained everything.

"Modellini snuck up on me as I was putting your shake in my car," I explained to Danny. "He wants to have a meeting tomorrow."

"About what?" the Don asked.

I sighed before I said, "He wants us to give him one million dollars in cash by tomorrow at noon."

"Hah!" the Don exclaimed. "Did you tell him we accepted?"

"I accepted to meet him, but he won't be getting that money," I said.

The Don nodded with a smile and Leo asked, "Where are you meeting him?"

"Tandelli's bar that went up in flames, the one that Nick went to once."

Nick kinda smiled and said, "You only caught me once… and well, they still have booze in there that wasn't touched."

We ignored Nick's comments and I added, "We have to meet him around the back, but when we're inside out of the public's view, we'll kill him."

"Wait, what!?" Al exclaimed.

"We gotta take them down, Al," Roger argued, which wasn't really like him to interject.

"That's right," I said darkly, "all of them."

After my statement settled in among the crowd, Danny asked, "I'm going too, right?"

"Absolutely not!" the Don practically shouted. When the excitement left Danny's face, the Don explained, "Not in the condition you're in. It's too dangerous. You can't even walk without cringing. All you can do is be a part of the planning process for the attack. Victor, you make sure they're all dead by noon tomorrow, that's all I request. How you strike, that can all be up to you Kids. I will not be a part of this; I believe in you men to handle it. But, if anyone comes up to me asking for the million dollars, you can find a new place to live."

The silence from me and the Kids was enough of a sign of understanding. The Don nodded and then made his way out of Danny's room. Roy followed him out, but Leo stayed for a moment to ask, "Do you want some help? I mean, with the planning?"

Roger, unlike his usual self yet again, said, "No, Leo, I think we can figure it out."

Leo's scowl was childish, and he left the room without saying any more. Closing the door behind him, I turned to face my crew and go over our options.

"The plan is, we'll meet him in the back, follow him into the bar, let him get his guard down, and then we'll take them all down."

"Victor," Jacob started, "how do we know this isn't just some trap?"

"Because they want that money, and we're going to hold on to it as long as we can."

"What money?" Nick asked. "You heard the Don, he ain't payin'."

"He doesn't have to."

"Hold up, how are we going to pay them when we don't even have the money?" Al asked.

"You're not making any sense, Victor," Nick argued.

"I agree," Blake said.

"How about you guys shut the fuck up and let me talk, eh?" I urged.

It was the first time any of them had really seen me get upset, besides Danny. Danny sighed and said, "Victor's right, guys. Listen to him, he knows what he's talking about."

I looked into Danny's sore and tired eyes and said, "Thank you." Then, I turned to my crew, and this time they looked as if they had hope. "I need one of you to find a briefcase that's not being used; one with a combination. Because when they realize it's locked, they won't kill us. They'll need that code."

"What about when we give it to them?" Roger asked.

I thought for a moment and then said, "We're going to rig it. Maybe with explosives. Wait, no. We'd be too close... Maybe..."

Nick and Blake chuckled to themselves and I stared them down.

"What's so funny?"

They stopped laughing but their smiles remained visible. Blake simply said, "A flour bomb."

"Flour bomb?" I asked.

"Yeah, you know: all-purpose baking flour with a little bomb."

"Not like, an aggressive bomb though," Nick said. "See, if we make a flour bomb, it'll cause a distraction after they open the briefcase, and then we can strike."

"Do you know how to make one?" I asked.

"Yes, Victor, don't you remember?" Blake asked in a condescending tone.

Suddenly, I saw Danny start laughing and a little of his shake spilled out of his mouth.

"Yeah, yeah! Victor, don't you remember? When it was Giovanni's birthday, we set up a flour bomb for him as a package in the mail and we waited out in the car while he opened it? Fat bastard got flour all over himself!" Danny laughed.

I smiled as I remembered. Giovanni had gotten the flour all in his eyes and mouth, all over his already white apron and chef's uniform. I didn't laugh though, because this time, we were using the bomb for a more sinister purpose.

"Okay, I like that idea. But what about the money?" Roger asked.

I didn't have to think too hard about that one, and Danny seemed to have read my mind as he said, "Well, they gave us Monopoly money, so why don't we give it back?"

# Chapter Forty One
## The Strike on Modellini
### Thursday, September 8th, 1977

The night before and the morning of, we all practiced shooting targets down in the basement. Some of my men weren't as good as I would have liked them to be, but I got them to the point of mediocrity. I doubted that Modellini's men were any better at shooting, especially considering that Modellini was the only one that was able to shoot Danny.

Modellini's men had cheap and unkempt guns. It was obvious when the shootout at the warehouse happened. To me, this was going to be a piece of cake. I worried about the other Kids, but they'd do fine.

First on the hit list was Modellini. He'd have to go first, and I was to have the pleasure of doing so. He was the biggest threat of them all, and we figured that he would be the one doing most of the talking. This was all going to be settled between me and Modellini. I instructed the other Kids to not smart off or make any other stupid comments. I told them, "Keep to yourselves; stay composed; be the threat."

I drew my pistol... I don't know how many times. Enough to where I had it down as a memorized reflex. I was able to rip out my pistol from my underarm sling and have it ready in a split second. I practiced forever, almost to a point where I made no mistakes, because this time, there wasn't any room for them.

All of us wore long coats and were armed with pistols, except for Blake. He insisted he needed to use a sawed-off double-barrel twelve-gauge shotgun, and eventually I let him. He set up the shotgun to where he could tear it away from inside his coat, and he actually made it not very noticeable that he had it.

Nick had set up the flour bomb while Danny watched. When Nick finished setting it up, he placed Monopoly money all over the bomb to cover it up. Then, he set up the switch so whoever opened the briefcase would not see it coming. The retired brown briefcase was perfect for the job. It had a locking mechanism that needed six numbers to unlock. All of us knew the combination, but we weren't going to let Modellini know that.

After the millionth time drawing my pistol, I walked upstairs to the kitchen, looked over my men, and said, "Let's go."

This late September morning had a rigid chill to it, and the sky was dark and gray.

The wind would gust every once in a while as we piled into one of the cargo vans we used when we took down Tandelli. Al was the designated driver while I sat in the passenger seat. Roger was in charge of the briefcase. Even with his long almost girlish hair, I could still see the fear in his eyes.

The silent ride to the decrepit bar was just as frigid as the air outside. When we were about midway to the bar, my blood was set on a slow simmer as I turned and said, "Now, you all remember what Modellini and Johnny Fargo look like, right?"

I was referencing to the night before when I showed them Danny's unsigned yearbook. The photo of Johnny Fargo in his graduation gown was burned into everyone's mind.

The six Kids nodded.

"I'll take them out first as soon as that flour bomb goes off. But, you guys will need to pull your weapons after I start shooting, okay?"

Everyone nodded. It was the darkest I had ever seen everyone's attitude. It made me disregard Leo's comments about not being ready. We told no jokes, we played no games; this was the real thing.

I turned to the front of the van again and looked out the front windshield. The street looked dead and I saw the burnt bar standing alone down the street on the right side. I pointed it out to Al and he nodded.

The bar stood alone on the outskirts of town. The only other thing nearby was a run down park with a twelve-foot fence surrounding it. Trash blew around in the streets as we came to a halt twenty meters from the bar.

Al placed the van in park next to the curb and I said, "Make sure you lock it."

"Sure thing," Al replied.

Everyone followed my lead. I stepped out of the car first as Al killed the engine and the Kids piled out of the back. When they slid the door closed, I made sure that our black entourage was ready to move forward.

The collar of my coat kept flapping up at my reddened cheeks in the wind, but I ignored it. I kept my hands buried in my pockets to keep them warm, and I felt my pistol sway under my left arm with each step. My heartbeat started to pound in my head as I stepped closer and closer to the meeting spot.

The bar was as charred as a piece of chicken that was left too long on the grill. There was still sort of a sweet, smoky smell coming off of the building as we stepped up to it. The underlying wood had gone dry, and the sign was impossible to read as it slanted in front of the bar, making the front doors inaccessible. I heard that kids used to dare each other to stand under it because they thought it was going to fall at any given moment. I saw why they thought that would happen as I heard the sign creak weakly in the gusts of wind.

Standing to the side of the bar was a guard, Johnny Fargo, and Modellini himself. As my men and I stepped up to him, Johnny Fargo gave me a death glare, but Modellini smiled at the sight of the briefcase and said, "Welcome to our home."

I didn't say anything back, and Modellini seemed upset.

"You're supposed to be a little nicer when you're the guest to someone's home, Victor. I thought you'd know that from when you lost yours," Modellini said with a smile. "Now, if your men are armed, we're going to need them to hand over the weapons."

The Kids seemed a little jarred but I said, "That wasn't part of the agreement. All you need to know is that we have them, and that we will use them if necessary. Just like how your men have guns."

Modellini gave me a long hard stare, but it wasn't going to work. If he wanted this to end right now in front of the bar as a shootout, so be it.

Finally, he gave in and said, "Very well then, follow me."

With my heart beating faster and faster, we followed Modellini to the bar and Johnny Fargo was limping at the very back, making sure we were all locked in. At the back doorway, the screen door was jagged and already open with two more men with guns. One had a submachine gun, but I put my mind to rest as I saw it was rusty and old.

"Come on in, there's a chair waiting for you on the other side of the dance floor, Victor. You and your men can have that area."

I nodded and stepped into the dim bar. The lighting was terrible at first, but I saw Chad Berger and Josh raise the blinds next to them. Modellini's crew had grown by about three more men overnight, but I knew we could take them.

We stepped down to the lowered dance floor as we passed the bar on our left. Like Nick had said before, all of the booze was still intact even after the fire. When I stepped down to the dance floor, I saw a plain square aluminum table with a chair on the front and one on the back. I made my way to the one that would allow me to look at the back door where we entered and I sat down. My men stepped behind me and stood at the upper level next to the burnt pool tables. Eventually, Modellini made his way in with Johnny Fargo and the two men outside. Altogether, I counted seven men, including Modellini. Including me, there were seven on my team. It was all fair.

Johnny Fargo stood by the bar with one of the men from outside who had a submachine gun. Modellini made his way over to me and sat down. As soon as he did, the meeting began.

"Well, thank you all for showing up. You weren't a minute early or a minute late,

I like that."

I didn't say anything. I tried following my own advice from earlier.

Modellini sighed and said, "You know, the Don really isn't as great as you might think he is. Living on the streets made me learn a lot of things, Victor. One of the main things is, the Don is weak. Everything was given to him on a silver platter from his father. Mark Ponchello does not deserve the title of Don but on the other hand, his father did. He gained the respect of everyone here in town, even public officials and cops. All of Mark's father's glory was just passed down to Mark in a measly manner. And people are starting to realize that, Victor. There will be an uprising against the Don due to his weak nature, and I'd really hate to see you guys get killed in the process. Especially since the Don did kill Danny's mom, but he just can't bring himself to tell Danny the truth."

"Get to the point, Modellini," I demanded.

Modellini seemed surprised by my tone as he said, "I'm offering a truce, of sorts. Or I guess you'd call it a merger, but I tried to avoid that word due to how terribly your father's company went down after their merger. Anyway, it's a business proposition. The money in that briefcase that you brought for me today, we can all share it, and you are all welcome to join my team."

"No way!" Johnny Fargo shouted. "We're not letting Victor and his pussies join our group."

"Eh, you're right, Johnny, but keep your mouth shut," Modellini argued. "How about just Victor, Charlie and Al? You're all welcome to join us. The rest of you, we'll deal with that later."

"No," I said firmly. "We're not joining your two-bit operation. The Don is a powerful man and he is becoming more powerful because of us. I don't know what uprising you're talking about, but I know you're full of shit. You're going to take the money we have in the briefcase and then get out of here for good."

"Hmm," Modellini said as he tried to not phased by my words. "Well, I knew that this would not be able to end peacefully. The money will just have to be pried from Roger's cold dead hands."

As I noticed Modellini reach into his jacket, I yelled, "Wait!"

Modellini stopped and gave me a look over. I wasn't even worried about them trying to gun us down, because my look said everything.

"The briefcase needs a combination to open it," I informed him.

"Really now?" Modellini asked sarcastically. "And uh, which one of you fine gentlemen know the password? Otherwise, I don't really need the rest of you alive."

I lied as I said, "The password was split up between my six men here, the Don's orders. They were each instructed with a number that they need to say at a certain time. Otherwise, you won't know the full passcode, and the briefcase will self-destruct."

"Bullshit," Johnny said incredulously, but Modellini didn't agree with Johnny.

"Roger, take the briefcase over to Johnny and we'll get this all sorted out," Modellini ordered.

I turned to look at Roger and gave him a solid nod of approval. I hated for Roger to be put into the line of fire, but it was necessary at this point. Everyone was on full alert after Modellini's threat of killing us, so we weren't able to strike just yet.

Roger confidently stepped over to the bar where Johnny Fargo awaited. As Roger carefully placed the briefcase up on the bar, Modellini said, "All right, which one of you has the first number?"

Roger's voice boomed first as he said, "Six."

Johnny started messing with the combination. The inputs clicked as they were rotated to the correct number. My heart was racing now more than it ever had before.

Next was Jacob, "Eight."

Click, click.

Charlie, "Seven."

Click, click, click.

Blake, "Three."

Click.

Nick, "Three."

Click, click, click.

Al, "Seven."

Johnny Fargo finished putting in the code and he started fiddled with the briefcase to get it opened.

"Well," Modellini said, "if that's what the code is, then I guess we really don't need you here any...-"

I watched in horror as Johnny Fargo's face changed from super excited to ridiculously distraught as he lifted the briefcase and saw the Monopoly money. The flour bomb did not go off immediately as planned. But as soon as Johnny opened his mouth to call out that the money wasn't there, the flour bomb did go off, and it sent flour into Johnny's mouth, eyes, and face. It was time.

I ripped my pistol out with ease and leaned my chair sideways so I could fall to the ground. Halfway to the hard concrete floor, I aimed at Modellini's head and fired. From my angle, the bullet went through his chin and exploded red out of the top of his skull. Modellini fell back with such force that his legs hit the table and rattled the entire room. As soon as I fell on my right side, I aimed toward the blinded and confused Johnny Fargo and fired three times. Two bullets hit his chest and one hit his Adam's apple. Each hit made blood and flour dance up from his body and he fell against the bar. Roger jumped back and started to pull his pistol, but the other man at the bar with the submachine gun was too quick for him. The man sprayed bullets toward Roger and Roger was down within seconds.

Blake yanked the sawed-off out from under his coat and ran forward to shoot diagonally toward the submachine gunner. The first shot hit him right in the gut. We all heard him cry out in agony and Blake fired again at his face. The buckshot hit his head and the liquor in the cabinet behind him. Booze started flowing out and I watched as Al started firing his pistol toward Chad and Josh. Josh was gunned down quickly, but Chad didn't go down so easily. Luckily, Jacob noticed as he turned his gun on Josh and fired upon him. The last three men were holed up at the back entrance and Charlie gunned them down with slick precision.

The whole thing lasted less than ten seconds, but it seemed like an eternity. After I stood up, the gun smoke rose to the ceiling and the sound of bullet shells clattered against the hardened ground. Then, I looked over to see Blake, Nick and Jacob all standing over Roger's body. As soon as I stepped up to his body, I knew he was long gone.

"C'mon, we gotta torch this place again and scram," I said as I started knocking down all the booze and made it shatter on the ground.

"What?" Nick asked, surprised. "What about Roger?"

"What about him? He's dead," Al said as confidently as he could. "Victor's right. There's nothing we can do, and we can't really walk out with a dead body. We don't have time for that."

I was glad that Al was willing to explain that, because I sure as hell didn't want to. The police knew there was always something going on over here. It'd only be a matter of time before they barged in to put us all away.

After the Kids were done saying their goodbyes, we threw liquor all over the bar and over the bodies. Then, Charlie took out a Zippo from Roger's pocket.

"Rest in Peace, Roger, and the hell with the rest of you," Charlie said before he threw the Zippo out to the bar.

The flames flickered up instantly and we all walked out, leaving Roger and all bad feelings toward Modellini and his men behind.

As we headed toward the van, we saw one of Modellini's men trying to break in. The kid only looked about seventeen years old, and his bowl hair cut kept hopping around in the wind as he tried to bust the door open.

Suddenly, I saw Blake pull out a pistol and kick the kid off of the van and onto the pavement. As soon as the kid started pleading for his life, Blake fired one deafening shot into his face, leaving a disturbing red portrait on the pavement.

"That'll show people to not *fuck* with us," Blake said.

I didn't scold him for the killing. But before anyone could argue, we piled into the van and left the bar that was now engulfed in flames. As the van pulled away, we could all feel the absence of Roger.

## Chapter Forty Two

There's a time where leaving a body behind seems like a necessary thing. In the life of The Ponchello gang, it happens all the time.

When the Kids group started, the Don instructed for Danny and I to leave any of them behind if they were killed.

"The police will just think they're roamers or deserters," the Don had explained before.

That was the reason we had to leave Roger behind. That, and the fact that the police would be there just a few minutes later, which is definitely something I was happy we avoided.

After we arrived at the house, we climbed out of the van and tried to make it into the manor as quickly as possible. We were all happy to see the fireplace was lit in the living room; the Don, David, Leo, Roy, and even Danny were sitting down there waiting for us to return. When we all gathered the living room, the Don and Danny seemed to smile, but I could tell that Leo knew what had happened.

I started to say, "It's done, but…"

"Roger?" Leo asked coolly.

Danny's face seemed to fall into sadness as the Kids and I bowed our heads.

"One of Modellini's men got him," Blake explained.

The Don paused after Blake's comment before he said, "Well, Roger was a good kid and he'll be missed. Just let this day remind you all that you're not immune to death… none of us are. On that note, Modellini is done for, correct?"

"Yes, Don," I replied.

"Good. I'm glad to hear that, despite the other misfortune that has been bestowed on us today," the Don said with real sincerity.

Next, we all seemed to look over at Danny all at the same time. His face seemed ghostly and pale, and he started babbling, "He shouldn't have gone… I should have gone… It was my issue, not his…"

"Danny, you couldn't have gone," I argued. "Not with your arm in that shape."

"Yeah, man," Jacob spoke up to explain. "You, heh, you couldn't have made it any farther than him… He just got caught in the crossfire, you know? He was forced to be in a spot that none of us would've wanted to be in, so we should celebrate him, not pity his death."

"It's not your fault, Danny," I emphasized.

Before we could make sure Danny was okay, Leo cut in to say, "I'm actually surprised you guys didn't lose more people than Roger. I'm impressed."

"I told you to give these 'Kids' more respect. They did all the planning and everything, so they should be rewarded."

The Don paused before he unveiled how he would reward us.

"Did anyone see you?" the Don asked.

"Anyone that did is dead," Al stated.

"In any case, you boys should probably lay low for the weekend. I'll grant you the weekend off, but you're not to resurface until Monday, got it?"

All of us smiled faintly and appreciated the Don's gift, but it was still not enough to replace Roger. Nothing would be.

I could tell when I looked at Danny that he had the pained face of losing two friends. Sure, Modellini was a terrible person who tried to kill him, but before that, they were good friends. The betrayal was what hurt Danny the most, and I understood that.

We all took turns shaking the Don's hand and went our separate ways. I went over to Danny and helped him up from the couch to take him up to his room.

As we left the warmth of the living room and headed upstairs, Danny asked, "So, what exactly happened? How did he die?"

I shook my head in sorrow as I replied, "Modellini instructed him to bring up the briefcase and... after it went off, one of the men by the bar fired upon Roger with a machine gun. He didn't really have a chance."

"No one tried to save him?" Danny asked.

I couldn't believe how ignorant Danny was being in that moment. It made me mad, and I unintentionally snapped at him.

"We tried, Danny, we tried. I was busy shooting the asshole who tried to kill you, and the fucker who ruined my school life every day. Besides, Blake killed the fucker that killed Roger, what else do you want?"

My anger, even though it was controlled, still scared me. And I could tell that Danny was afraid too when he responded, "I just didn't want one of ours to die... I don't give a shit about them, and I don't blame you for what happened, I just didn't want to lose anyone."

With my anger taking a step back for a moment, I said, "I'm sorry, Danny. I know what you mean. I also wish we didn't lose Roger."

Danny and I seemed to now be on the same level as he nodded and I finished taking him to his room. When we entered his room, I started to turn some lights on but Danny said, "No, leave them off, please. I think I might just take another rest."

I did as Danny commanded and I walked him over to his bed. He climbed in perfectly fine by himself, and I watched out of the blinds for a moment as he got situated.

"I'm glad they're gone, though," Danny said plainly.

"Yeah, it's quite a relief."

"I think Leo was about to have to intervene, and I know we wouldn't want that. Then, all of our asses would've been chewed."

"That's what the Don said, too. But, why does Leo hate me so much? Have you noticed that?"

Danny laughed for a moment and I figured he had the golden answer for me.

"Well, the Don, or my father, kind of had Leo picked as his favorite for the longest time… and now, I think you're taking that spot, Victor."

"What about you?" I asked Danny as my feeling of surprise still lingered.

"I'm his son, that's a given. Of course he's going to like me. But, of his made-men, you're his favorite."

This was odd to me, and somewhat fitting. I felt like the last time I was someone's favorite was back in English with Mrs. Huffman; just thinking about her brought warmth to my heart. I wondered for a second what she was doing; what she was wearing. I knew she wouldn't approve of my new life, but I didn't have to tell her, if we ever saw each other again.

"That's… good then," I said, and I said it for two different reasons. I wanted the Don to respect me, but I also didn't want to live in constant fear of maybe being thrown out on the streets if I didn't do a good enough job.

As usual, it seemed as though Danny read my mind as he said, "You have nothing to worry about, Victor. The odds are forever in your favor."

With a smile, I talked with Danny for a little while longer, until he started to grow weary and I noticed it was about five o'clock. Michelle brought up some dinner for Danny and when she noticed I was in there too, she said, "Oh, let me go back and I'll bring you a plate too, Victor."

Danny drowned his meatloaf in ketchup and started mixing his corn and mashed potatoes together. A few moments later, Michelle brought me a plate too and I thanked her. And for the first time since the incident with Modellini at the warehouse, Danny and I ate and talked together for a very long time.

# Chapter Forty Three
## The Weekend on the Down Low
## September 9th-11th, 1977
## The Ponchello Manor

With the weekend off to make sure there was no outstanding evidence found at the bar against any of us, all the Kids and I mainly just sat around the living room and talked. Sometimes, we'd bust out games like Monopoly or Risk, and the Don kept ordering pizzas and Chinese takeout for us. The weather outside was atrocious that whole weekend, with rain and sleet coming down almost non-stop. The fireplace roared in the living room and we all joked around and laughed, and Danny was able to come down and sit with us too. It was fun to lounge around on Friday and Saturday, but about halfway through Sunday, things started getting dull.

"And I win, again," Al said with a grin.

The Risk board was covered with the little green men that Al had chosen in the beginning, and an accusation started to fly.

"How are you winning so much!?" Nick argued as he cleaned up his men from the board. "Let me check those dice!"

"You accusing me of cheating?" Al argued.

Danny and I smiled as they kept arguing and debating who would win in a real fight. All of the Kids had their scuffles before, but they didn't dare mess with me or Danny, and with good reason.

Even though I wasn't necessarily scared of them, Al and Charlie did seem to be the only ones who posed as threats to me. I wasn't as strong as Al, but I was faster, and Charlie was the opposite. Hopefully, it would never come down to that. At this point in our age group, it seemed like disputes were handled with a more dangerous selection of items than our fists.

Eventually, Leo dropped by the living room to update us.

"Well, our cop on the inside is telling us not to worry too much about what happened at Tandelli's old bar," Leo started off. "The detective investigating the whole thing is saying it's just a mass homicide with no other parties involved."

"Good," Nick commented.

Jacob seemed a little more cautious though.

"Can we trust this cop knows what he's talking about? I mean, we don't have a detective on the inside, just some run-of-the-mill cop who overhears things?"

Leo studied Jacob for a long time before he said, "Look, Jacob, I appreciate your concern, but in this case, you really don't know what the fuck you're talking about. Our man on the inside has been there for seven years. Everyone likes him, everyone respects him, and no one suspects him. If we need information, we go to him. There's no need to bribe anyone else, so quit your worrying."

Jacob was usually the quiet one, and I could tell with the look on his face that he wished he would have stayed that way. He started to lower his head and nod as Blake popped him on the arm with his fist and said, "Oh Leo, you know that's our Jacob. Just wants to make sure all the cracks are sealed."

Leo painted on a demeaning smile as he said, "Yes, of course."

Blake knew how to make people feel better, even when they had just been put down. In seconds flat, Jacob had a smile again as he resumed his card game with Charlie and Blake.

"Does that mean it looks good for us to be out in the open tomorrow?" I asked.

"I'd say it looks more than good. Honestly, Kids, with something like this that happened and we got away with it, even if the detective suspects something, first they're going to feel fear in the department. They're going to realize how slick and powerful we are. You guys got in, took care of things, and only left one man behind. No trails of blood, no nothing. They've realized that the last kid you guys shot was killed after the ones in the bar at some point, but that makes them worry even more. As long as we keep the cops in fear, we'll be okay. Now, we just need to be careful not to cross that line of fear and accidentally put them into anger. That's when we'll have problems, and that's when they'll really start cracking down and wanting us in cuffs, or dead."

Leo was a very knowledgeable man, and I respected him for that. I took everything he said as extremely important, but I can't say the same for the others.

"So, as long as we don't make fun of Chief Ramzorin's dick size, we'll be fine!" Blake said.

Everyone started laughing for the most part, except for me and Leo. I felt like Leo watched me for a reaction, but I didn't give him one.

Eventually, Roy stepped in and said, "Man, I really must've missed a good joke."

Al replied, "Eh, it was alright."

Al received a punch from Blake as Roy said, "Well, I know something that may pique your interest."

Everyone, except for Leo and Danny seemed to be interested in what Roy had to say. I was worried at first, even though Roy said it in such a calm tone.

"I'm sure none of you, except for Danny, has heard of the Platinum Briefcase?"

*The Platinum Briefcase? That sounds extremely impractical... and a burden to carry around,* I thought.

I wasn't the only one with confusion filling my mind.

"Roy, are you high again?" Blake asked.

"Shit, no. I'm being serious. Have you guys ever heard of the Platinum Briefcase?"

"Yeah, actually," Charlie said, "I think some guy at the warehouse talked about it one time on a lunch break. Said it was full of money, and platinum isn't all that cheap either of course."

"Yes, exactly," Roy said with a smile. "Some speculate that it's full of money, or divine power, or a book that can alter the future. Some say it's not real, some say it definitely is. Hell, some people say they've seen it."

"Have you seen it, Roy? And if so, where is it?" Nick asked.

"No, I have no idea where it is. It's rumored to be here in the manor somewhere. But no, I haven't seen it before."

"No one has," Leo commented sternly, as if this was all made up.

"That's really cool, though! Especially if there is a book that could alter the future," Nick said.

"Yeah, maybe you could make things go your way for once," Blake said.

"Shut up, asshole."

After a few seconds, Danny said, "I was told about the Briefcase as a bedtime story, guys. I was told by my mother that the Ponchello family, when they first made this place, hid a Platinum Briefcase here in the manor for someone to find one day. For all I know, that day may never come. No one has ever really tried to look for it, and I don't really see the point."

I was interested in finding it. Money and power always seem to be interesting things to everyone, but the idea of a *divine* power being inside tempted me as well. If I had the Platinum Briefcase.... Well, I didn't know what was in it so I'm not sure what I would or could do with it. Finally, I looked at Roy and said, "Are you saying we should go look for it?"

Before Roy could answer, Don Ponchello entered the living room and said, "No. There's no need to look for it. Danny's mother just made it up as a bedtime story, that's all."

That seemed to ruin everyone's interest in it, except for mine. I planned to one day find it. Not sure how or when, but one day...

## Monday, October 10th, 1977

No one found any evidence against us after wiping out Modellini and his men. We were free after that weekend in September when we stayed crammed in the house, and it was nice to not have any more threats around. The Don praised me over and over, saying that I did a great job leading the Kids. And when I tried to say that we lost Roger and it was my fault, the Don made sure I knew that he didn't die in vain.

But things slowed down for about a month. And on Monday, after a long day at the warehouse and making sure everyone was doing what needed to be done, I stopped by the diner and saw Emmitt cleaning up a table. I was just going to walk on by the diner, but I felt compelled to go and talk to him.

As I entered, Sid waved me in and I waved back. Emmitt did a double-take as he looked at the main door. The second time, he kept looking and said, "Victor Carez."

I walked over to him and said, "Emmitt Burose."

Emmitt finished wiping off his hands and then came in for a hug. I was taken off guard at first, but I let the hug happen, and as soon as it started, it was over.

"What's goin' on, man?" Emmitt asked. He started wiping down the table more and said, "Still don't have any bullet holes I see."

"No, I sure don't, but you have plenty of ketchup and mustard stains," I joked.

"Hah, you got me there."

"You working a lot?" I asked.

"Why do you ask?"

"Just curious."

"You know, Victor, you're a cool cat, and I don't want to see curiosity kill you."

Emmitt seemed different; he was a little more loose and relaxed. I hoped that the days of him being bullied in the diner were over. In fact, a few men of the Don's had been sent out here the past few weeks to make sure of that.

"I was wondering if we could maybe hang out again soon, like we talked about before."

Emmitt finished wiping the table off and he looked at me.

"Yeah, of course. I think we can work out something here soon. Check back with me tomorrow if you could."

I thought it was an odd request, but I agreed to it.

"Good. I'll catch you later, Victor. Sid hates when we have to stay late cleaning and shit."

I nodded and decided to leave him alone. Sid offered me a to-go drink as I stepped out, but I declined.

My foot hit the concrete outside and I was cut off by three men. My eyes darted to the one I thought was in charge, and I saw it was Jackson Burose.

Jackson's burned and scarred face moved awkwardly as he smiled and said, "Hello, Victor, nice to see you again."

They were trying to intimidate me, and sadly, it was working. But I tried to play it off and say, "You too, Mr. Burose."

"Oh please, that's not necessary," Jackson said as he took a puff from his cigarette. I noticed that he and the other two men were wearing black berets, but in the lighting I couldn't tell what the symbol was on them. "You can call me Jackson."

"Okay, Jackson," I said as calmly as I could, "What can I help you with?"

His fine leather jacket crinkled as he put his arm up on my shoulder and said, "Victor, there's no need to be afraid. I wanted to ask if maybe you'd come eat with us, at my house. Alone, if you don't mind. I would ask your friend Danny to come too but I know he's not feeling too great lately."

I remained cautious as I asked, "You'd like me to come eat dinner with you at your apartment, alone?"

"Well, Emmitt, TJ, and Marcus will be there too of course. I just want you to come alone. It'd be nice to get to know more about you."

"Sure, Jackson, I'm honored that you'd ask me," I said, not giving away my fear. "What time would you like me to arrive?"

"That's a good question. How about... hmm... I should have the meat and vegetables grilled by 6:30, so let's say... 6:45 or seven?"

"Sounds good, I'll be there."

Jackson smiled and he stepped back with his men.

"Good, we'll see you tomorrow then."

The trinity of fear walked away from me and I took a deep breath. What the hell was all of that about? Jackson was just trying to get a rise out of me. *Well, it's not that easy anymore, Jackson.*

I stepped back into my car and started heading back toward the manor. The more I thought about the dinner tomorrow, I decided it was best not to tell anyone about it. If I told anyone about it or my worries, suspicion of Emmitt's family would go through the roof, and eventually, that would mean something would happen to Emmitt, or an entire war would be discussed, which I did not want.

*Dear God... will this ever end?*

## Chapter Forty Four
### A Dinner with the Burose's
### Tuesday, October 11th, 1977

I kept the promise I made to myself as I left the Ponchello manor in secret. I still told Danny right before I left that I was heading out, but I didn't say where to.

"Oh, are you finally getting with a girl?" Danny asked with a smile.

"Something like that," I replied to Danny as I slipped my coat on.

"You still have your gun on you? I guess you *are* getting with a girl."

"Haha."

After I left the manor, I headed toward the Burose residence in the chilly night. I looked at my clock on the dash and saw it was nearing 6:40… Hopefully they wouldn't mind me being a little late.

As I arrived into the "black" part of town, I started getting all the funny looks again. It had been a while since they had seen my car roll up, and the last time didn't go over so well.

Luckily, I saw Emmitt standing outside in a leather jacket similar to his father's, but with no beret. When I pulled up to the curb, I parked the car and powered off the engine.

Stepping out of the car, Emmitt approached me and said, "Hey, Victor. Glad you could make it."

"So am I," I said as I closed my door and went up to shake his hand.

"Are you ready to feast? My father is a very good cook," Emmitt said as we headed into the apartment grounds.

"Yeah, I'm excited."

We started to walk into the apartment grounds, which I had felt like I had done before. The apartments had the same one opening on the west side and one on the east. All of the apartments were still enclosed in a square with a courtyard in the middle. The only difference was, a lot of men were standing outside, and all of them were wearing those berets I had seen before with Jackson. When I looked closer at the berets, I saw they had buttons on them, or they were stitched with a large black cat on them, and they read, "Black Panther, Black Power".

That's when it clicked. That's when I knew that things were not going to be the same between me and the Burose's anymore. I contemplated turning and running back to my car, but everyone had their eyes on me again, and I knew there was no way out.

Emmitt didn't give off a threatening vibe though. He talked with me like normal as we went up the stairs toward his apartment, and he also chatted with the other members briefly as he passed by them.

Finally, we arrived to his front door and Emmitt led me in.

"Oh hey, Dad, Victor's here!"

TJ finished what he was saying and smiled as he walked over to me with open arms. His afro bobbed a little as he approached and I opened my arms to him too. I hoped they wouldn't feel the gun I had on me, or if they did, I'd have to think of some stupid excuse.

After TJ and I embraced, the oldest brother, Marcus, also walked up to me and extended his hand. We shook hands with faint smiles on our faces, and I saw Jackson standing in the background, observing the confrontations.

Eventually, the space between me and Jackson broke and he was standing before me.

"Victor, thanks for coming. My famous spicy roast beef is just about done, along with the vegetables. Emmitt and TJ can show you the way to a plate and a glass though."

"Thank you," I responded.

"Would you like someone to take your coat?" Jackson asked.

"No, that's quite alright," I said. My gun was under my coat and I hoped it would stay there all night.

"Well, come on in here, Victor," TJ said as they led me into the kitchen.

The apartment was pretty big, a lot bigger than what it looked like on the outside. Right when you stepped in, there was a small coat closet on the left along with a living room straight ahead. The kitchen was walled off with its own little doorway: one doorway right as you walked into the apartment, and another doorway on the left side. Then, as I passed through the living room, I saw the bedrooms were back in a hallway behind the living room and to the left of the dining room. The wallpaper was a wavy dark orange and black color all around the living room, with plush orange carpet and fans with ovular wood.

But when we stepped in the kitchen, it was bright white and almost tacky. It was really blinding stepping from the dim orange living room to the bright white kitchen. If TJ wasn't there to lead the way, I probably would've fell over from the blinding contrast.

The dining room was the same color as the kitchen, which is what I saw as I stepped into the kitchen and looked to the left. The chairs in the dining room looked small and uncomfortable, but as big as Marcus was, he seemed to fix himself up a plate and plop down in one with no problem.

Emmitt handed me a plate and TJ said, "Hey, Victorman, I'll grab you a glass. What do you want? Lemonade, water, tea, Kool-Aid?"

"Lemonade sounds good, actually," I said.

"Oh, lemme make sure we have some, and then I'll pour you a glass."

"Yeah, we got some at the store last week, don't worry, TJ," Emmitt said to TJ as he pointed out the food.

Before I looked at the food, I noticed some art displayed on the refrigerator.

"Hey, are these some of your works?" I asked Emmitt.

Emmitt was messing around in one of the cabinets and he said, "Oh, yeah."

There was one of a woman writing in a journal in the highest branch of a tall green tree. She looked busy and distant, and that's the part I liked the most. She was at peace, doing what she loved.

"I like this one a lot," I said to Emmitt with a smile.

"Well, thank you, Victor. My dad likes that one, too."

Eventually, my plate was filled with corn, grilled peppers and squash, some sliced strawberries, and then the spicy roast beef, which had a slight red tint to it. Not because the meat wasn't done, but because of the spices.

I saw that Marcus was waiting for everyone to get over to the table, which also had some kind of bread on it. I supposed that we would say grace before eating, and I knew what I would pray for.

After our plates weighed five pounds apiece, we all sat at the table and waited for Jackson to sit down. Sadly, I was sitting across from Jackson at the circular table, and for now his beret sat there instead of his plate.

Jackson let out a sigh as he sat down and moved the beret.

"I think I outdid myself again, boys," Jackson said as he coughed into his fist.

"You always do," Marcus commented.

Jackson nodded, and then looked straight at me.

"Victor, I thank you for not eating right away... we do like to say grace before our meal, if that's okay with you."

I felt like everything Jackson said to me was a test in some way. My answer always determined if I passed or failed.

"Sure, I don't mind," I replied.

Jackson said a prayer that wasn't too long, but I could tell they were all itching to rip into the food. Surprisingly, I was able to keep my eyes closed without the worry of my life coming to an end.

Honestly, I didn't really listen to Jackson's prayer. I just started wondering about what the Black Panther Party stood for and everything. At one point, I felt like my father told me they were the opposite of the KKK... still stood for the same things, but instead of being for white power, it was for the spread of black power. Either way, I didn't stand for either one.

My thoughts were interrupted as Jackson said, "Amen," and we all repeated it afterwards. Marcus reached for the bread first and I started to take a bite of the spicy roast beef. As soon as I swallowed, the word spicy seemed like an understatement. Either that, or it was poisoned.

Jackson saw my face contort and said, "Ah, I was worried I might have added too much cumin and black pepper. Here, have some milk bread. It'll smooth it out."

I did as Jackson said and my tongue started to thank me. The bread was very soft and heavenly; I grabbed another piece.

About half way through the meal, I heard Jackson clear his throat and everyone's eyes were on him.

"So, Victor, what line of work are you in?" Jackson asked casually.

This was my cue to make sure nothing rash was revealed. My lines were already memorized from the previous performances I had with Chief Ramzorin.

"I work at a warehouse that Danny's father owns... We lift boxes and... oh, thanks Emmitt... and we make sure they get to the right trucks so they can be shipped out to stores."

"A warehouse job? That's it?"

Sadly, Jackson's tone made me realize that he wasn't convinced. It was true that I worked there, but that was only usually one day out of my five-day work week.

I decided to stay quiet, but the silence didn't last long.

"What about... Spencer, is that his name?" Jackson looked to his boys for confirmation. Marcus confirmed it. "Does he work at the warehouse?"

"No, he's just a friend... or, was a friend," I said.

Jackson seemed displeased as he continued eating and the dining room was only filled with the noise of forks clattering against the porcelain plates. Finally, I realized I needed to make some statement before I was taken out in a body bag.

"Look, Mr. Burose, or Jackson, as you prefer... I don't believe in people getting treated differently just because of their race. I know that what Spencer said was terrible, and I won't forgive him or stand up for him. I wish that there wasn't this separation between us. I also wish that Emmitt here wasn't picked on by whites as he's working. But I made sure to tell Mr. Ponchello about Emmitt being harassed and he's sent some guards to be there in the diner if need be. Isn't that right, Emmitt?"

It was weird to say "Mr. Ponchello", but I had to push through it. Emmitt nodded at what I said and Jackson seemed to smile lightly.

"And what about Mr. Ponchello... how does he feel about black people?"

I answered honestly, "I don't know for sure. He's never expressed any certain views on how he feels."

Jackson seemed to smile more as he said, "What you said before, Victor, was nice, but I just don't think I can trust you yet. I'm not going to go as far as to say you're a white devil, but that Don Ponchello is someone I am worried about. I know you're not telling me the whole truth, but I can understand why you're not able to. For if you did, it would give me even more reason to convince my son as to why he shouldn't hang around you."

I didn't know what else to say, but Emmitt gave me a look that said, "I'm sorry" and I raised my eyebrows at him.

Eventually, we were able to excuse ourselves from the table and I walked into their living room with Emmitt. He kept his voice low as he said, "I'm sorry, Victor, but you know why he feels a resentment towards you... you're in a gang."

"Yeah, but I'm not trying to bring that lifestyle to your doorstep, I just like hanging out with you."

Suddenly, without really resolving the conflict, I saw they had a turntable and had a Martha Reeves and the Vandellas album waiting to be played on it. I powered on the turntable and started to play "Dancing in the Streets", and as soon as it came on, Emmitt was a little frightened by the horns section at the beginning. Then the song hit the verse and I turned down the volume. Eventually, I saw Jackson peek out of the kitchen and saw him smiling.

"You like this song?" he asked me.

"Yeah!" I said. "My mom and dad used to dance to it at our old house..."

Jackson nodded his head as he dried off the plate in his hands with a dish rag. At that moment, I knew that I might be in his good graces after all... for now.

## Chapter Forty Five
### Friday, October 14th, 1977

Over the next few days, Danny was actually able to be by my side again as we worked. Phil had ridded the orange Dodge Challenger of all the bullet holes and everything was working as smooth as butter once again. Sadly, on Friday, we had to work at the warehouse all day. Danny tried to track down the person that talked about the Platinum Briefcase, but no one wanted to say a word.

Fortunately, Danny and I worked alongside Al and Blake. At one point, I told them they should be a comedy duo, but they declined the offer.

"If we told our jokes at the bar the Don owns, I don't know if the people would laugh because our jokes are funny or because they're drunk," Al said.

"Maybe both," Blake snickered.

At one point, Danny seemed to cringe as he lifted a box with me. It was very heavy, and I was sure to warn Danny before we tried.

"I'm all right, just not used to all the heavy lifting."

"Well," I said as I checked out the analog clock that everyone looked at on a minute-by-minute basis, "we'll be out of here soon enough, and then what do you wanna do?"

Danny started to make a grin and I realized what he was going to say.

"I want to kick back, relax, and have some chick all over me over at Studio 9."

"Sounds good," I said, for more than one reason.

The rest of work seemed to fly by, and off we went to Studio 9. Of course, since it was a Friday night, it was pretty busy. Men and women stood in line as they waited to enter, but Danny and I parked the car on the other side of the street and were able to walk right in.

"Hey, hey, Danny Ponchello, that's you ain't it?"

Danny and I stepped back out of Studio 9 and saw some guy dressed in a nice suit yelling at us as he stood in line.

"Hey, must be nice having your dad own the place so you can just waltz right in!"

He was yelling at us with a woman standing right next to him, who I assumed was his date. I felt sorry for her as she tried to calm him down.

Danny didn't even respond with words until he punched the guy right in the nose. The man fell like a sack of potatoes tumbling off of a flatbed as Danny replied,

"Yeah, it is nice."

The crowd seemed to find Danny and I cool as we walked in and let the doorman take care of the guy from there.

"What an asshole," Danny said.

"Yeah... But I guess you haven't lost your punch!" I said with a smile.

We both laughed softly as Danny brushed off his knuckles and we walked up to The Ballz, who was sitting there with two women.

"Hey, Vic and Dan, how you guys doin'?" The Ballz said with his gold tooth shining.

"Not much, we were wondering if you'd be able to hook us up?"

"Actually," I said, and Danny looked over to me. "I asked you about two months ago if you knew anything about Kassidy, and I still haven't heard back from you?"

"You're still interested in her?" Danny asked, a little peeved. "Why don't you just let her go? You deserve someone better, Victor, like... this girl, right here, what's your name?"

"Darcy," the blond said with a smile as her boobs spilled out of her lingerie.

"C'mon, Danny, I just want to ask if he has seen her or what."

The Ballz didn't seem to be very excited at all as he said, "Victor, the thing is... I found her a long time ago, but I just didn't have the heart to tell you... she's owned."

"Owned?" I asked. "You mean, some other pimp has her?"

The Ballz nodded and Danny said, "Who else is pimping around here? It should only be you."

"Down south, I guess there's another club that's opened up... primarily for people of color. There's a pimp there, but I don't know his name. He be banking though."

"Who owns the club?" Danny asked.

The Ballz didn't have the heart to tell us that either, but he still did in a sad voice. "Jackson Burose."

"What?" I asked as my heart dropped. Emmitt's father, Jackson, had Kassidy under his arm being used as a whore? My anger started to flow over me and I said to Danny, "I gotta get some air. I'll catch a ride back to the manor, don't worry about me."

Danny tried to plea for me to stay, but it was too late. I was out the door, and I wished there was someone there for me to punch.

# Chapter Forty Six

Now that I knew about Jackson's other business dealings, I couldn't get my mind off of it. He was using my girl... Kassidy... as a hooker. I couldn't believe it. Nothing could make me believe it.

A part of me tried to explain that he wouldn't know she was mine... How would he know that? He didn't do it on purpose, he's just trying to do business and she was... recruited, or whatever.

I wasn't quite sure how all of that business worked but it made me mad either way. I took it personally, and it made me hate Jackson Burose.

Danny only seemed interested because the new studio down south along with the new pimp probably had an impact on the Don's business. I knew that was also a concern that I should have, but it wasn't. I didn't care about the business; I cared about Kassidy. I wanted to be with her, but she did everything in her power to not have anything to do with me. What did I do wrong? Maybe I'm just...

"Victor, is that you?"

I stopped and started looking up ahead of me. When I saw the person who spoke, there was a moment of blissful silence. I was in the middle of the nicer part of downtown and I saw Mrs. Huffman walking with some bags and her purse. She had on a nice brown coat with a thin layer of fur on it, and as she got closer to me, I noticed the other bags were full of clothing as well.

"Mrs. Huffman?" I said, even though she had told me before to call her Ashley.

She walked up to me slowly and met me eye-to-eye. She smiled brightly, but her eyes looked dull and like they had lost some life.

"Victor, it's so good to see you... It feels like it has been forever."

"Yeah, it really does."

"How have you been?"

I kept smiling in her presence and all my worries of Kassidy flew away with a brisk gust of wind.

"I've been okay, how about you?"

"About the same," Mrs. Huffman said with a sad nod. "Could be better."

"Why do you say that, Mrs. Huffman?" I asked.

"Oh Victor, do you really want to know?"

"Of course, why else would I ask?"

She took a small pause before she struggled to say, "Well, I divorced my husband a few months ago. He was cheating all the time with multiple women. There was no way I could forgive him."

"Really?" I asked, shocked that anyone would ever do that to her. "I'm so sorry."

"Well, it's okay. I'd just prefer you to call me Ashley now though… Plus, I'm just glad we didn't have any kids. That would've been hard on them."

I agreed with her and we stood out in the cold like a couple of idiots. I looked at my watch and noticed it was nearing seven o'clock, and my stomach growled.

"So, we should get out of the wind here and go out for dinner somewhere, if you'd like."

Ashley seemed very thrown off as she said, "What? You want to take me out to dinner?"

"Well, yeah, if you're hungry. I'm pretty hungry… Sadly, I don't have my car, but if you have one I'll reimburse you."

"That's very nice, Victor, but don't you think that'd be weird? I mean, I was your teacher for crying out loud."

"It's only weird if you think it's weird. I'm just asking if you want to go eat with me and not be out in the cold. Now if you think that's weird, then…"

"Okay, Victor, no need to get smart with me," she said with a smile, and I saw the life glimmer in her eyes again.

So, we climbed into her tiny sedan and she piled the bags of clothing in her backseat. As she started up her car, she said, "Know of any good places?"

"Well… there's that one place up at the top of Star Tower. I've heard it's supposed to be really good."

"Yes, and very expensive," she said, not seeming too interested in it.

"Don't worry, I'm buying," I said with a smile.

After a little more convincing, she seemed giddy with excitement as we headed off to it. It wasn't too far from where we met up, but taking the car was a good idea.

I wasn't sure how bad of a guy her ex-husband was, but she made it seem like he didn't take her on many dates.

"Oh my gosh… this place is absolutely beautiful, Victor." Ashley said as we started walking in.

After we exited the elevator, the maître d at the front of the restaurant said, "Oh, the Misses is dressed nice enough, but I'm afraid you'll have to spiff yourself up a little more, sir."

I knew exactly what to say and how to say it.

"I was told by Mr. Ponchello that there wouldn't be an issue for me to eat here," I replied with a grin.

Ashley glanced at me for a second as the host almost pissed himself.

"Oh, yes, of course, you're one of Mr. Ponchello's friends... Come right in, we have a great window seat for you."

The maître d led us into the pristine white restaurant with random artwork placed on the walls and massive chandeliers. I smiled as I let Ashley follow first to our table. Nothing seemed weird to me right now... it seemed like it was a dream finally coming true. But I felt like my dreams of her from before had us both with less clothing on.

The maître d pulled a chair out for Ashley to sit in and I pulled out my own chair. The light fixture we sat under made us feel like royalty.

"May I take your coat, madam?" he asked nicely.

"Yes, sure," she said.

Ashley removed her coat to show off a slightly revealing dress underneath. It was more of her than I had ever seen.

"And you, sir?"

"Oh, no thanks, I'm always cold," I said.

"Very well, sir."

The menus were sitting on the table there in front of us and we started taking a look. As I opened mine, I got annoyed by the fact that they were in French and English. I didn't know of any people in Detroit who spoke a word of French.

"Would we like to start out with some drinks?" our waiter asked.

"I'll have..."

I was about to say a coke, but I knew I'd have to be fancy with Ashley here.

"Bring us a bottle of your finest red wine."

"That would be $125, is that okay?"

"Yes."

Ashley was totally thrown off as the waiter walked away and said, "Victor, are you sure you can afford this?"

"Yeah, I'm sure," I said with a smile.

We both browsed through our menus until the waiter brought the wine.

"Victor, are you sure? I mean, what do you even do for a living?"

I hated to lie to her, but I said, "I still work for Mr. Ponchello at the distribution warehouse. It's really good money, and I was promoted recently."

The waiter popped the bottle open and started to pour it into fine wine glasses with golden rims on them. Other well-dressed patrons seemed to be observing our luxurious meal.

"Victor, I still find it hard to believe that you make that good of money doing that. Now come on, what do you really do?"

"I thought you were an English teacher, not a math teacher," I said in a sly tone.

Ashley let it slide as the waiter finished pouring our glasses and said, "Are we ready to order?"

"I'll have the quiche Lorraine," Ashley answered after she sighed.

The waiter wrote down her choice and then said, "And for you, sir?"

"The beef bourguignon looks good," I said.

"Excellent choice, I commend you on it," the waiter said as he wrote it down.

I hated our waiter, but I'd ignore that for now because of Ashley. She seemed to be in love with the place as she kept looking around and taking a sip of wine. I tried drinking the wine, and it was actually pretty sweet rather than dry like the wine Don Ponchello had.

"So, Victor, did you ever have plans of going to college?" Ashley asked.

"Not exactly," I said, not ever giving it much thought.

"Why not? I think you'd be more than capable to go. Especially with all the money you're making."

I looked at Ashley and thought about what she had to say. It was true, I did well in school but I didn't have the time to go to college, plus it'd appear that I was betraying the gang if I just up and left like that. They'd resent me.

But, to keep everything as quiet as possible, I said, "I don't really have the time. The warehouse job keeps me really busy."

"Well, must be a miracle that I ran into you on the street then."

"Something like that."

"Why are you out on the town alone, Victor? Don't you have a girlfriend or something?"

"No, actually, I don't. Or if I do, I think I should consider the relationship over."

"Why's that?"

"I haven't talked to her in a year."

Ashley actually seemed to laugh as she set her wine glass down and pulled up her napkin to her mouth. When she saw I wasn't laughing, she stopped and said, "Oh, gosh I'm really sorry, Victor… the way you set that up made it seem funny rather than sad, so I just thought…"

"It's okay, Ashley, I know… I'm trying to get over it, so maybe I should just laugh with you."

"Exactly. Plus, you have a fine woman before you as well, so who cares about her?"

The hotness in my body that I hadn't felt since I'd seen Ashley in school started to make its way over my body once again. I felt embarrassed and out of touch, and I didn't know if she had maybe already had too much to drink. As I glanced at the bottle, I saw that she might have refilled her glass at least once already.

Before I could make a fool out of myself by saying something more, the waiter and another assistant began carrying our plates out. I cleared the way and they set down a salad for each of us first, and then our main courses. I didn't remember getting a choice before, but it worked.

"Enjoy," the waiter said before he walked away.

I started to dig into the beef before the salad, and it seemed to melt in my mouth after taking a bite. Ashley started to gently toss her salad around with her fork to make sure the dressing was distributed evenly.

Of course, I ended up finishing my meal way before Ashley did, and I took some more wine as she finished up her quiche.

"Was it good?" I asked her before I took another sip of wine.

She wiped her mouth delicately with her napkin and she said, "Yes, yes Victor it was all very good."

I saw the life leave her face as she seemed to become sad. I wondered if it was something I said, or did... but she decided to tell me before I could ask.

"Victor... Thank you, so much. This really has meant a lot to me."

She looked like she was on the verge of tears, but yet they were still being held back. I said to her, "Well, sure, I mean, I was happy to do it. Thank you for driving."

She had a faint smile that only lasted a second, and then she said something I never thought would be said.

"You know, Victor, a year ago... when I had you in class, I always liked you."

I decided not to jump on what I thought she obviously meant, and I waited for the waiter to drop the check by first before we continued the conversation.

"I wasn't that great of a student... I didn't really pay attention, I was always daydreaming."

"About what?" she asked with a seductive smile.

*This can't be happening right now.*

"Well... you."

The boldness made her just barely flinch. She gasped slightly and then regained her composure in a flash.

"Really? And what exactly would you think about that had to do with me?"

This seemed impossible, and wrong in a few states. But I didn't care. This was something I had thought about since day one of senior year, and it seemed to finally be coming together. Plus, she was only three or so years older than me.

I pulled out my wallet and started to count out the money and tip for the waiter as I said, "I mean, there is a hotel room a few blocks down that I have reserved at any moment. If you'd like, I could show you there."

If I hadn't of had any wine, none of these words would have been able to be formulated. I was acting like an arrogant king, knowing my limitless power over Ashley.

She quickly let out an anxious laugh and said, "Well, what are we waiting for?"

Needless to say, we both stood from the table and I left the enormous amount of cash there for the waiter. As we stepped by the host booth, she grabbed my hand and led me into the elevator. And as soon as those elevator doors closed, she was on me like a lion on a gazelle. Our mouths felt like they were sewn together as the elevator descended to the lobby. Our bodies pressed together like an iron on a new dress shirt. The elevator ride was maybe only thirty seconds, but it was thirty seconds of pure lust. It was the most satisfying make out session I had ever experienced.

We were far from done, though. When the doors opened, I smacked her butt and she cooed as we headed to her car. Once in the car, we made out some more and I was feeling hotter than ever. My heart and mind were racing. All this time, all this build up…

Long story short, we ended up practically running through the hotel the Don owned. I fidgeted with my keys to open the door, and our clothes were all over the place in a matter of minutes. And there we were, me and my former English teacher. A relationship that was once so innocent and non-existent had turned into a one-night love I'd never forget.

## Chapter Forty Seven
### Saturday, October 15th, 1977

The next morning, I woke up to Ashley naked and hanging onto me for dear life in her sleep. I hadn't forgotten a thing, but I didn't really know where it could go from here.

We stayed up till the wee hours of the morning with each other, and now, as I looked to the clock on the bedside table, it said it was almost noon.

I carefully freed myself from Ashley's grasp and made my way to the bathroom to take a long piss. Walking around naked was nice for a while, but as I went to the bathroom, I started to think of several things.

One was: should I even tell anybody about what happened between us? It seemed like a terrible idea, and honestly, with how everything happened, I felt like this was really a one-time thing.

Besides, the only two people I'd consider telling were Danny and Emmitt.

*Emmitt...*

That reminded me of the disturbing information I had found out the night before about Jackson having Kassidy as a hooker. My anger about the subject came back, but not in full swing. I needed to confront Emmitt about it and see if he even knew what was going on.

When that thought subsided, I heard the phone ring in the bathroom. I finished up peeing and I grabbed it.

"Yeah?"

Danny was on the other end, and I heard him laugh at how alert I was on the answer.

"Well, well, Victor. You ended up scoring after all, didn't you?"

"Big time," I said with a small grin.

I peeked out the bathroom door and Ashley rustled around in the covers that were totally ruined.

"Good for you, man. You needed it, and deserved it. Say, just for doing so well, and when I found out you ended up there, I had some of my father's men bring by your car. It's parked out front for you when you need it."

"Thank you, Danny. I can always count on you."

"Aw, shucks," he said through the crackling of the phone.

"Also, I have a lot of crazy things to tell you about later, if that's cool."

"Of course, Victor. Whatever you want to tell me. I understand you probably can't discuss it now because you have a guest to attend to."

"Yes, I do actually. I made certain with Mrs. Huffman that I could make it after school to talk with her."

The silence on Danny's end said everything, and then he exclaimed, "You didn't!"

And with one swift move, I said, "I did" and hung up the phone.

*So much for not saying anything...*

As I stepped out into the bedroom, Ashley rolled over and exposed her breasts to me as she sat up.

"Hello, Victor," she said softly with a smile.

"Hello, Ashley."

I started to pick up my clothes from the ground and put them back on. After a while, she asked, "Are you leaving?"

I shook my head and said, "Yes, sadly, I have something I have to attend to. You can order whatever room service you want though, and once you tell them the room number, they won't charge you a thing."

I finished getting dressed and holstered my pistol once more. Once I was finished, I saw Ashley staring at me with a half depressed look and half scared look.

With a cleared throat, she said, "You do work for the Ponchello Crime Syndicate, don't you?"

We stared at each other for a long time and I heard the hurt in her voice. Without saying another word, I decided it was time for me to leave. I kept a serious face before I turned around and made my way out the door, and I left there with the unambiguous answer floating in the silence.

When I reached the lobby floor, I walked up to the front desk and asked, "May I borrow your phone?"

"Of course, Victor," the front deskman said.

I called up Sid's Diner to see if Emmitt was working.

"Hello, Sid here."

"Hey, it's Victor. I was wondering if Emmitt is there."

There was a strange pause on Sid's end before he said, "Oh, no, Emmitt didn't come in today. You might wanna give him a holler on his house phone. Do you have the number?"

"Yes, I do. Thanks, Sid."

I hung up the phone and started to dial up Emmitt. The phone rang twice, and then it was answered.

"Hello? Burose House."

I couldn't tell if it was Emmitt or one of his brothers. They all had similar voices, only varying slightly in depth.

"Hey, this is Victor."

"... Oh, hi Victor."

It was Emmitt.

"Hey, man, I was wondering, if you're not doing anything, I could come pick you up... I have something I want to talk to you about."

"Yeah, same here, actually."

Emmitt's voice sounded full of anger and hurt and I wondered what was going on, but I thought it was best to confront the problems in person.

"Okay, I'll be there in ten."

"Alright, man."

*****

When I arrived near the apartment complex, Emmitt walked over to my car and the bright sun gleamed down upon us for the first time in quite a few days. Emmitt didn't seem all that excited when he got in my car, but honestly, I wasn't either.

I started to pull off and Emmitt asked, "So, Victor, what's on your mind? Can't be my friend anymore or something?"

"What? No, I never said that," I said, and then I started getting even more irritated. "I'm pissed that your father seems to think he can muscle in on Don Ponchello."

"What are you talking about?" Emmitt argued.

"You know what I'm talking about, Emmitt. Your dad is starting a gang here on south side and let me tell you, it's starting to affect the Don's business as well."

I wanted to slap myself. That's not what I was mad about, I was mad about him having Kassidy. Why did I say it was all about the business, then?

"Look Victor, I could give less of a shit about what my father is doing and what your 'Don' does. Or at least, that was the case until he fired all of us at the diner."

"What? Who is 'us'? Who fired you?"

"A few of the Don's men went in, and Spencer Mangello was there for some reason. All of the black people got fired, and were told that they were replacing all of us with white people. So now what, Victor? Is that why you met up with me? Are you going to fire me as a friend as well 'cause I ain't white like Danny?"

"No, that's not why I really came here. I'm mad because one of the girls that your dad's pimp is using was my first... love."

I didn't know a better way to say it but there it was and the message was received loud and clear by Emmitt. It looked like we were both screwed by our "leaders".

"I'm sorry, Victor, I didn't know that…"

"I'm sorry too, Emmitt. I didn't know that he was going to fire you. I have no idea what made him do that."

"It's aight… I just… I mean, I got several people in this community jobs through the diner. They loved me for it, and we weren't treated too badly after you instilled the guards but…"

Out of nowhere, Emmitt and I witnessed a fairly new Mustang fly past us and we both jerked our heads around to see who it was. I had no idea, so I looked to Emmitt and said, "Do you know who that was?"

"Yeah, that's Tyrel's car."

Suddenly, it clicked.

"And you said that Spencer is there at the diner…?"

*****

Spencer Mangello stood outside with some of the other mob men, including Leo Morton, who was his favorite of them all. They had just fired all of the Negroes working at the diner and Spencer was happy to help. He wasn't necessarily a made man in the mob, but he was considered an outside source for them. When the Don started pushing drugs more, he ordered Spencer to find some people who might want to distribute, and Spencer was happy to do so. After he did so well, the Don made a deal to give him 10 percent for life as long as the drugs kept selling in the districts he pushed them in.

Spencer was never all that bright, and always had a real bad temper, especially as a kid. Only time he really got mad now was due to anything involving competition.

Just moments ago, Leo and a few other made men were walking toward the diner when Spencer spotted them.

"Hey, Leo, how's it going man?"

Leo actually cracked a small smile to Spencer and said, "Oh, not too bad. Say, you wanna come help us with something?"

"Yes, of course!"

So, without asking any questions, since you're not supposed to ask too many to your superiors in a gang, Spencer tagged along like an idiot, clenching his fists and getting ready for something big. Sadly, that wasn't really the case.

"We're escorting out all the black people from the diner. All the black workers, that is. The Don wants them gone."

"I don't blame the Don, they're fucking disgusting," Spencer said harshly.

Leo didn't say anything back, and neither did any of the other men. They just continued forward and then into the diner.

After they pushed all the black kids out, who were previously working so hard for nothing, Leo and Spencer and the other men stood outside and just waited. About twenty minutes passed and then Spencer began to get curious.

"What are we waiting for, exactly?" Spencer asked.

"We're waiting for the replacement workers to get here," Leo explained.

"Ah, okay."

So, to pass the time, Spencer Mangello pulled out a cigarette and flipped open his Zippo. The cigarette lit up brighter as he took in the first puff. It was always his favorite part of smoking, that first puff. Cleared his mind, eased his worries.

Spencer was told some time ago that smoking would kill him one day. But until that one day, Spencer had never feared dying, even when the day finally came.

Which was today.

Spencer started to take a second puff of his cigarette and they all heard the Mustang screeching to a halt in front of the diner. Leo started to pull out his pistol, but it was too late. Tyrel stepped out at the ready with his handgun aimed outward. First, he fired one shot into Leo's arm, which made Leo drop the gun and fall to the ground. Then, Tyrel pointed the gun at Spencer with much delight and he pulled the trigger once.

The bullet sliced through the center of Spencer's chest and smoke seemed to rise, followed by the blood rushing out. Spencer sucked in as much air as he could out of shock, and then Tyrel fired a second shot that went straight through his head. Spencer tumbled back and violently crashed through the glass of the diner, which was weakened by the first two shots. It rained down on him, stabbing and cutting him up; it was a gruesome scene. Before any of the Don's other men could have their weapons ready, Tyrel had already jumped back into the car and they were off. Only one of the Don's men was able to fire a few shots at the car as it sped off, but no matter. Spencer Mangello was dead.

# Chapter Forty Eight

I arrived at the diner with Emmitt but it was obviously too late. Two police cars, a CSI van and an ambulance were all there trying to process the scene. I saw the glass of the diner was destroyed on the right side and I also saw Leo sitting on the edge of an ambulance.

"Jesus Christ," I said as I shoved the car into Park and jumped out.

Emmitt jumped out behind me and followed me to the scene. The yellow tape hadn't been distributed yet but the police seemed a little peeved when I tried to walk up.

"Hey, kid, you don't wanna see this," a cop said as he tried pushing me back.

"Victor?"

I turned around and saw someone that I was happy and unhappy to see at the same time.

Chief Ramzorin.

"Chief, what are you doing here?"

"I was actually on my way to get some lunch, and when I drove by I saw this… What about you?"

"I was supposed to meet up with a friend here named Spencer," I lied, and I felt Emmitt's eyes sear into the back of my head.

Chief Ramzorin knew I was lying, and just to test me further, he said, "Tim, you can let these two men pass. I know them."

The cop moved his arms away and we walked past the cop car that was up on the curb. After we walked past it, I knew why they set it up that way.

It was a bloody mess of glass and death. Spencer lay back with a shard of glass perpendicular to his legs and the upper half of his body was on the tile of the diner. He looked up lifelessly at the ceiling with an open mouth and his arms out. His kneecaps were bent over the still-intact glass and I saw blood on his shoelaces.

"What the fuck…"

"Victor!"

I turned to see Danny, Roy, and David Weston all run up to me and Emmitt. Chief Ramzorin gave me a disconcerting look as he realized what was going on. Danny stayed with me as Roy and David ran over to Leo on the back of the ambulance.

Danny scowled at the Chief and Emmitt before he grabbed my arm and said, "Dad says to come with me. Right now."

Danny would've addressed his father as Don, but with Chief Ramzorin and Emmitt standing there beside me, it was best not to.

As Danny started to pull me away, a final plea was made.

"Victor, you don't have to go," Chief Ramzorin said sternly with hopeless eyes.

"Yes, I do," was all I replied, not wanting to argue.

The oblong armored car that always sat untouched at the Ponchello manor was now out on the street. As Danny dragged me to it, I left Chief Ramzorin and Emmitt alone to share their mutual disappointment in me.

Danny opened the back door to the car and stepped in. I followed suit. The car stood still after I closed the door. Looking forward, I saw the Don was sitting with his back to the driver, and he did not seem pleased.

"Do you see what your friend has done?" the Don asked as he pointed to Emmitt.

There was no way anyone could see inside the car due to the ridiculously tinted windows, but we could see the mess outside just fine.

"It wasn't Emmitt that did this, though," I argued. "It was Tyrel."

"It doesn't matter. Whether it was Tyrel or one of Emmitt's older brothers, they're all causing trouble in Detroit that we didn't have to worry about until now. And they're all taking orders from Jackson Burose."

"But Emmitt isn't doing anything wrong! We were just going to hang out today and-"

"Quiet, Victor! That is enough," the Don shouted.

I sat there frozen in fear as the Don collected himself once more and said, "There is no more arguing to be done. I want you to hop in your car with Danny and make sure the ambulance gets to the hospital safely. Afterwards, head to the manor. There will be a meeting tonight to discuss what further actions must be taken. Understood?"

Sometimes, I acted more like a son to the Don than an employee, especially after what he said. I ended up storming out of the reinforced car and walked by David as he started to get back in the oblong vehicle. Roy climbed into the back of the ambulance with Leo as they started closing the back doors, and I got into my car and started it up. Danny knocked on the passenger side window and I leaned over to unlock it.

"Victor," Danny said as he climbed into my car. "C'mon, man, you know that was a bad idea to storm out on my dad like that."

"Your father is wrong."

Danny seemed a little worried as he said, "You better be glad that I'm your friend or else I wouldn't take that."

"Danny, I'm sorry. I'm taking this out on you and I shouldn't. But your dad is wrong about Emmitt. He's not associated with what his father and brothers are doing."

"So, it is true," Danny said. "They are bringing up the Black Panthers at the command of Jackson."

"Yeah, but I wish it wasn't," I said, and we followed the ambulance to the hospital in silence.

# Chapter Forty Nine

Late that Saturday night after we took Roy back to the manor with us, we were finally called into the dining room for the dreaded meeting.

"It's on," the intercom in Danny's room buzzed with Roy's voice.

Danny tried to make sure I was calm before we headed down for the meeting, but there was no way I was going to keep my cool. After what happened with Tandelli and Modellini, I knew the Don was just going to want bloodshed on the highest level. That would definitely include anyone even slightly involved with Jackson Burose. It pissed me off, to say the least. If the Don wanted Emmitt dead, I was going to argue until I had my way. But if it was just Tyrel and Jackson that he wanted dead…

Not quite sure what my rebuttal would be to the Don's commands, I stepped into the dining room behind Roy and some of the other henchmen that I did not know by name yet. The Don was standing behind the massive table with David Weston at his side. David's eyes were not covered by his usual sunglasses, and he looked exhausted.

It was silent as everyone took their seats. The Don waited for everyone to get settled and I ended up sitting quite a few seats back from the Don with Danny at my side.

"Gentlemen, it appears we have a new threat. Not only one in the way of economics, but it also poses as a violent threat."

David Weston reached inside his suit jacket and pulled out a photo to pass around to everyone.

"This is our new threat, Jackson Burose. He is trying to band together a new form of the Black Panther party. But this Black Panther party only wants one thing and one thing only: Complete control over a place that we already claim as ours. Roy, if you can share some other details, I'd appreciate it."

Roy seemed to twitch after the Don mentioned his name. When Roy stood up to talk, the Don sat down and David remained standing behind him.

"Leo was doing surveillance on Jackson Burose. Where he lives, who he talks to, etc., etc. Leo found that more and more people are joining this party and these people joining aren't just niggers. They're still less than half of our strength, but there are small things they are doing to hurt us. They opened up their own club south of

Studio 9 that is now getting more business. Everything there is cheaper, but it's also lesser quality. We've heard that people don't want to come to Studio 9 due to a hostile environment, but we're going to get that changed soon by showing how bad it can get at their club. They're also hurting us in the underground gambling rackets. They are offering smaller buy-ins and free drinks to anyone gambling. It's their way of getting people to play and play. Get them drunk and they just keep spending their dough. Leo was only able to find two of these rackets, but he believes there are more."

"Thank you, Roy," the Don said as he lit up a cigarette. Roy nodded nervously and took his seat again. I passed the photo of Jackson to Danny since I didn't need to see it. "Now, I do plan on having us kill every last one of them. I want to completely exterminate every last person that is affiliated with this party or Jackson Burose. However, if we do that, we will have to play it smart. Spencer was killed out of retaliation from us firing all of the black employees who were associated with Jackson's band. Leo was also shot and we know they intended to kill him too, but they did not. They meant to kill all of our members who were there, but luckily, Jordan was able to fire a few shots back at them and they fled."

I didn't even remember seeing Jordan there, but it didn't matter. Even though this was a one-way meeting, I decided to make it a debate.

"This was not a full retaliation from Jackson," I argued as I stood up from my chair. "This was Tyrel acting out of pure hate towards Spencer. He got a call that said Spencer was there, and so he went to take him out. Leo was just caught in the crossfire. It was an accident."

The shock in the room from my bold statement seemed to subside as one henchman argued, "Victor, I was there. Tyrel was the one firing from the car, but they had several other men in the back seat just in case it became too out of hand. This was not a petty revenge, it was an attack."

The Don took over calmly as he said, "I don't know why you're trying to argue this, Victor. I understand you are friends with Emmitt, but they did attack us. They meant to attack all of them, even Leo."

"No, that's not…"

"Look, like it or not, I am telling you all that we will take everyone out at the same time. If you see them on the street, do not attack. Only fire if they fire on you. Only fight if they pick a fight with you."

"Don, please," I said.

I was really pushing my luck, and I could tell by all the looks I was getting from everyone in the room. Even Danny had elbowed me at one point to cut it out. But, what Don Ponchello was saying to me was preposterous. Not everyone is involved with Jackson Burose's wrongdoings, especially not the other black people that worked at the diner. They were young teens, not criminals.

"Okay, Victor," the Don said, obviously irritated but wanting to give me a chance. "What do you suggest we do? I mean, you handled the Modellini situation quite flawlessly without any help, so maybe it's time you handle the current situation without my help or support?"

I froze once more. It wasn't my place to suggest action for Jackson Burose and his gang, but I wanted to make sure Emmitt would not be harmed.

"Well," I started off weakly, "I could try and meet up with Emmitt at some point to talk about making a peace agreement. I'll convince you that it's only Tyrel we have to worry about at that point, because I'll tell them to hand him over, and that his surrender will cease any further violence between us."

There was a scoff in the room, followed by some murmuring around the table. My proposal seemed too democratic for such a gruesome assembly of men.

To our surprise though, the Don gave me a small smile as he said, "Okay, Victor. If you can convince them and me, then I'll let your friend off the hook. Okay?"

I calmly nodded once as I sat back down and Danny stared me down for a long time.

"In the meantime, I will be going to see Leo in the hospital tomorrow where Jordan is watching over him. Anyone else who wants to go is welcome to join me."

"I'd like to join you, Dad," Danny said.

"So would I," I said, even though I wasn't too keen on it.

With a nod, the Don dismissed everyone from the room, and only Danny would talk to me for the rest of the night.

# Chapter Fifty
## Sunday, October 16th, 1977

I thought the trip to see Leo would be a bit more embarrassing (especially after yesterday's outburst), but it wasn't.

Around noon, the Don, David Weston at his side, Danny, and I all piled into the armored vehicle to drive to the hospital in the middle of downtown. The car was sleek and comfortable with leather seats and a sun roof that no one ever touched. Phil, the mechanic, decided to be our driver as we coasted on the highway to go see Leo. I knew he wouldn't be ecstatic to see me, but I had a feeling he would want to be in the know about my peace idea.

The whole thing was a big issue that was going back and forth in my mind. I hated Jackson Burose, and I hated Tyrel, but I didn't hate Emmitt or any of his brothers. All of the people employed at the diner were good people. They weren't all part of Jackson's radical gang. But the Don didn't understand that. He thought they all wanted to try to take down his operation. For all I knew, Jackson was just trying to take control of an area that was already in the blacks' control in the first place.

Danny and I talked it over the night before, and he agreed Emmitt didn't necessarily seem like a threat. Jackson definitely did, but it would be hard to keep Emmitt as a close friend if men that I'm affiliated with ended up killing his father.

With all of that rolling around in my mind, we pulled into a reserved parking spot for medical staff only, but I knew that the Don had already worked something out.

The parking spot kept us very close to the entrance, just in case there was an attack or anything. A childish part of me wanted something exciting to happen at the hospital, just so I could see David in action.

We all piled out of the car and Phil stood guard beside it. As we walked through the pristine lobby of the hospital, staff and others looked at us with worried expressions. The Don was still feared, and if we ended up exterminating the Burose's, worried looks would be replaced with people running scared.

We didn't check in, we didn't consult with anyone as to where Leo was, we just headed to the elevator and the Don pressed the Up arrow. Once we exited the elevator, we started stepping down the bright hallway and I saw Jordan standing outside of the room slouching against the wall.

"Jordan, you look as alert as ever," the Don said.

Jordan seemed to snap up for a second and inhale loudly through his nose. He patted his chest a few times and got himself out of the stir. Danny carried some smelly Chinese food we had picked up for Leo before getting to the hospital and Jordan eyed it.

"Wow, you guys were nice enough to bring me some food, even though I didn't get shot."

"Shut up, Jordan," Danny said jokingly. "If Leo doesn't eat the egg roll, I'm sure he'll let you have it."

David Weston turned around to the Don as we stepped up to the door and the Don gave him a nod. David Weston opened the door and we all started walking into the room.

Leo instantly let his newspaper fall to his lap as he sat up straight in the bed. He wore a patient's robe that was a darkened baby blue with little red flowers or something stitched all over it. His eyes looked weary and worn out as he turned his head toward us.

"Hello, boss," Leo started out, "and David, Danny, and Victor."

Leo's voice dropped off after saying my name and he began coughing into his fist. When the coughing subsided, the Don said, "We brought you General Tso's chicken, some fried bread and an egg roll."

"Thank you, boss," Leo said with a faint smile.

Danny handed over the bag of Chinese food after Leo pulled over an adjustable table from his side so he could eat on something. The mechanics of the table were very simple and they appeared to have seen better days. Leo started ripping into the bag.

"You don't like egg rolls, do you?" Danny asked casually.

Leo rolled his eyes and said, "Here, give it to Jordan. I know he wants it."

I smirked as Leo handed the egg roll over to Danny.

"Really, being here in this room is unnecessary. I could've patched up the wound myself, but hey, the morphine is nice," Leo said.

There was a pause in the room, until the Don turned to me and Danny.

"If you two don't mind, I'd like to speak with Leo alone," the Don said.

"Sure, Dad."

Danny and I stepped out of the room and closed the door behind us. Jordan stood at full alert as Danny reluctantly handed the egg roll over to Jordan.

"Twenty bucks," Danny said after the exchange was made.

"Hah! Bullshit. I need to get paid more to stand here all damn day," Jordan said as he ripped into the egg roll.

We shot the breeze with Jordan for a bit, until the murmuring inside the room came to a halt and the Don stepped out. David came out behind him and looked at me.

"Leo would like to speak with you alone, Victor."

Danny seemed a little worried for me but I just nodded and headed into the room. After I stepped in, David closed the door and left me and Leo alone.

Leo had already eaten about half of his Chinese food. His face seemed to be regaining its color again. As he lifted his plastic cup to his mouth and took a drink of water, he saw I had already entered the room. I stepped to his bedside and waited for him to speak. When he didn't say anything after setting down the cup, I decided to relieve the tension and ask, "How's the arm?"

"I probably can't throw a fastball anymore, but oh well," Leo said.

I laughed quietly and Leo joined in for a second.

The tension in the room seemed to die for just a second, but Leo's grave face made everything worrisome on my end.

"So, the Don tells me that you requested a peace trade of sorts," Leo said in a mildly condescending way.

"Yes," I said firmly. "The Don believes that anyone in association with Jackson Burose is considered a threat, even though Emmitt and his brothers never did anything wrong. Tyrel and Jackson are the problems, and maybe there are some others that we should worry about."

"Yes, there are others we should worry about. Some of them were mentioned in what you just said, though, which is why you and the Don don't meet eye-to-eye."

"Okay, so what do you think about the peace trade for Tyrel?"

"Honestly? I think it's stupid," Leo spat. "If you really think they're just going to hand over Tyrel, you have another thing coming. They meant to attack us, Victor. It was not just an act of vengeance against Spencer; this was an attack on all of us."

"Look, I know Emmitt is not a part of this, and neither are his brothers. We do not need to murder all of them."

"Yes we do, Victor," Leo seethed as he threw down his plastic ware. "Open your fucking eyes and look at everything from how I see it, and how the Don sees it. These men are not going to negotiate. They want full power and they want to take us out."

Leo's words were harsh and I felt like he was a vicious dog barking at me after entering his yard uninvited. I started feeling angry so I yelled, "Why do you hate me so much, huh? What the fuck is your problem with me, Leo? You don't like that the Don is giving me a chance? You think I'm just some burnout off of the streets?

Some rich kid who doesn't know what a hard life is?"

My face reddened... I was shaking. Leo seemed entertained and surprised by my retaliation. The room fell into an uncomfortable silence as Leo took a deep breath and asked, "Emmitt has two brothers, Marcus and TJ, right?"

I took a deep breath as well and nodded.

"Victor, they were in the backseat of the car that Tyrel was shooting from. I saw them holding guns as well, ready to kill everyone at the diner if they had to. Now, that doesn't include Emmitt, but I can guarantee that if his brothers are a part of it, Emmitt will soon be a part of it too. That's why we can't just kill Tyrel, we have to kill everyone."

"What?" I asked in disbelief. There's no way Emmitt's brothers were in the back seat. Why the hell would they do that? Was this just Leo and the Don trying to trick me?

"Now, I'll agree with you... it probably was just an attack on Spencer, but they know that they won that without any problems. That will make them haughty and look for new ways to hurt us. I commend you for trying to make peace, but... it's just not possible if you look at everything realistically."

*Is this how it's going to have to go down every time we have enemies?* I thought. But aloud, I said, "Are you sure Marcus and TJ were back there?"

Leo didn't wait at all to answer, and he didn't care that his food was getting cold. "Yes, Victor. I'm sure."

I sat back to try and soak it all in. I was upset, to say the least. But it didn't matter. I wasn't even mad at the gang either, I was mad that Marcus and TJ could've been tricked into all that. Maybe we could have integrated them into our gang? Maybe... I didn't have any other ways of looking at it anymore. I knew Leo was right and so was the Don. If Emmitt's brothers had turned, it'd only be a matter of time before Emmitt was convinced as well.

# Chapter Fifty One
## Monday, October 17th, 1977

That morning, Danny and I ate breakfast together before he went off to the warehouse alone. The Don told me I didn't have to work at the warehouse for a while, due to the fact that I had to figure out how to trade a human life for one that was taken. It was a daunting task, but I knew that I had to try.

As Danny finished up his homemade breakfast burrito, he said, "I admire you for trying to make peace, but I just... I don't know, Victor."

"I know what you mean," I said as I finished up a bowl of Wheaties.

"How do you plan to propose it? If you go to their side of town, you're a dead man."

"I'll just give them a call," I said with a shrug.

"Good luck with that," Danny said as he started walking out with Jacob.

"See ya, Victor," Jacob said.

"Bye guys."

They left me alone in the kitchen with Michelle as she cleaned the dishes. Somehow, all the clanging in the sink was soothing. It reminded me of when my mom did the dishes back home after we all ate a wholesome meal together...

But, as I remembered the grim reality of the current situation, I walked to the living room where a phone sat on a table next to the couch. I took a seat and looked around. Everyone else seemed to be busy doing their own thing and didn't pay any attention to me as they walked to and from the living room. I picked up the phone and dialed Emmitt's number by memory.

The phone rang several times, almost to a point where I thought I'd never get through. Finally, someone on the other end answered and said, "Who is it?"

"This is Victor," I said strongly. "I wanted to speak with Emmitt."

There was a pause, and then the unfamiliar voice on the other end said, "One moment."

I was put on a dead silent hold and I waited for someone to answer on the other end. When they did, it wasn't Emmitt.

"Victor, I had a feeling you'd call sooner or later."

It was Jackson Burose, Mr. Large and In Charge.

"Is Emmitt there?" I asked.

"No, he's not. But even if he was, I have strict orders for him to not speak to our enemies."

It already seemed as though Leo was right. It was only a matter of time until Emmitt became a part of it too. But instead of giving in, I decided to tell myself Leo wasn't right as I continued speaking with Jackson.

"Look, we don't have to be enemies."

"Is that so?"

"Yes."

"How do you figure that?"

"I have a way that we can make peace. The Don is allowing me to make you an offer in the meantime. If it doesn't work, then there will be no peace."

Jackson scoffed as he said, "If you kill Tyrel, my men and I will destroy you and your Don. You really think we're just going to hand over Tyrel? My nephew? Fuck you. I can't believe you'd even try and make that deal, Victor. I thought you were smarter than that."

"I know that it won't be easy. But that's the best offer I can give you for peace between us. You can keep your operation and we'll keep ours if we can work this out."

"There will be no peace, Victor. The last thing any of your people will see are my bloodthirsty eyes staring into their souls with a grin on my face."

Jackson's words chilled me to the core. I wasn't sure what else I could say to him. Then, a memory surfaced.

"I remember you, Jackson," I said to try and change the mood of the conversation. "A little longer than a year ago, you were in a bar that the Don controls and the bartender had us, me and Danny, throw you out. I felt bad for you. I didn't want to have to throw you out, but orders are orders. If that's why you hate us, then I just want to apologize. If I could take that back, I would. I wanted to say something at the time, but..."

"If you really felt bad, you would've said something right then and not now when it's too *fucking* late!"

I was dead silent, but it didn't matter. The phone clicked on the other end and the line started to buzz. I hung up the phone and cursed at myself. The frustration I felt made me want to cry. I couldn't believe how arrogant the Don and Jackson were being, but it didn't matter now. They were going to murder each other, no matter what I tried to do.

A few minutes later, Jordan stepped into the room and said, "Hey, Victor, some kid is on the phone for you."

I made a face at Jordan but he shrugged. When I lifted up the line, I could hear someone breathing on the other end.

"Hello?"

"Hey, Victor," Emmitt said quietly on the other end.

"Hey, Emmitt."

"So, you guys want to kill my cousin to make things right?" Emmitt asked.

His tone had changed to something different and harsh. It wasn't the way Emmitt usually talked.

"It's all I could convince the Don to do, besides the complete extermination of anyone linked to your father."

Emmitt paused a moment to choose his next words carefully.

"So, your Don agreed that if Tyrel was handed over, there would be no further actions taken?"

"Yes. He thinks that everyone in your family, including you, is involved in this. He doesn't understand that your father's gang does not consist of you or your brothers. I tried to tell him…"

Emmitt fell silent once more before he clarified, "Handing over Tyrel would convince your Don of that?"

"Yes, Emmitt, that's what I'm saying."

Emmitt's voice was so lifeless and dull. He didn't seem very happy about anything that was going on, but neither was I.

After I felt like I heard Emmitt talk to someone else with his hand over the phone, he said, "I think we should have a meeting. Not that I don't trust you, Victor, but sometimes it's hard to see if someone is lying when it's over the phone."

"I agree."

"You can bring someone with you, but I request that you both come unarmed. I'll call Friday with the place that we'll meet at. It'll be on our turf, but I can't guarantee your safety after you leave the meeting place, especially if my father catches on."

"I understand," I said.

"Good."

Silence fell between us. In a normal situation, I'd ask Emmitt how he was doing or if he wanted to hang out soon. But this was different. Everything was different.

"Until then," I ended up saying, and Emmitt immediately hung up the phone afterwards.

## Chapter Fifty Two
### Wednesday, October 19th, 1977

Eventually, the Don decided to have no one work at the warehouse any longer. He found other things for us (the Kids) to do while we were off. Luckily for me, the Don wasn't giving me much to do, because I was supposed to handle this peace agreement with Jackson Burose. Even though there didn't seem to be any hope in it, I didn't let the Don or Leo know. I still had faith there'd be a way to get Emmitt out of this alive, but he seemed different on the phone. I wasn't sure if there was any point in hoping for a happy ending.

"So, a meeting?" the Don asked after he called me into his office.

My breath still smelled of garlic from the spaghetti and meatballs that Michelle had cooked everyone for lunch.

"Yes," I replied, "The meeting takes place on Friday; they haven't disclosed a location yet. Emmitt said it would be on their side of town though."

"Are you sure it's not just a trap?" David asked, always standing by the Don's side.

"Honestly, I'm not sure. Emmitt said he can't guarantee my safety once the meeting is over."

The Don's face seemed to fall grim and pale, but he said, "Victor, I don't want you taking any unnecessary risks. If you think meeting with Emmitt is a bad idea, I suggest you don't do it."

At that moment, my mind started to wonder, hoping to find happiness somewhere. My mind was weary from all of this gang violence and talk of power. Not finding a memory that was satisfying enough, I looked around the office and started to wonder about the Platinum Briefcase, and questioned its existence. I wondered if it was in this very room. I thought I could feel its presence hidden behind the portrait of the Don's father. I seemed to think of the Platinum Briefcase every time things seemed gray. I wondered if it would help me, and what was even inside. If it was full of money, I would just use it to run away and hide for good. I wouldn't have to deal with this gang bullshit anymore.

Even though I was taught money doesn't buy happiness, I started questioning that. When my parents had money, everything seemed to be going okay. After my father's company got shut down... things went downhill, to say the least. I knew that money wasn't the source of all happiness, but it would damn sure make everything a little easier for me.

"Victor?"

The Don broke my concentration and I said, "Yeah, sorry Don. I don't think there's anything to worry about with Emmitt. I still consider him a friend of mine, so I don't fear any harm coming to me."

"You're a strong person, Victor, and a smart one at that. That being said, I'm convinced that I have to take your word," the Don answered with a sigh.

"Thank you for that; I admire you as well, Don Ponchello."

The Don gave me a faint smile and dismissed me. I left the room, but still felt the presence of the briefcase somewhere close.

If it were behind the portrait, I'd have to rip into it. But for that to happen, I think the Don would have to be dead.

I looked at my watch and saw that it was almost time for Chief Ramzorin to go to Michelangelo's. After I debated it in my head, I decided it was a good idea to go.

*****

Pulling up to the curb, I saw Chief Ramzorin sitting and drinking coffee alone. The restaurant looked still, and I felt as if I upset the air as I stepped out of my car. Darkness was already starting to fall across the city, and the streetlights and neon signs were the only light on the streets now.

I stepped into the restaurant, feeling completely uninvited. Chief Ramzorin turned to look and see who stumbled in, and he did a double-take. I started to walk toward him, ignoring all the bad vibes around me. As surprised as the Chief looked, I knew he didn't want me there.

I stepped up to the booth and stared at Chief Ramzorin. He stared back.

"Take a seat," he said plainly.

I shifted myself into the booth and I saw Antonio walking out of the kitchen.

"Shit, is that you, Victor? I haven't seen you in months!"

I had never really heard Antonio talk like that, but everything changes when you get older.

"Yes, it's me."

"What can I get you to drink?" Antonio asked, completely oblivious to the harsh conflict between me and the Chief.

"Coke would be good."

"Oh, and Antonio, I'd like more coffee," Chief Ramzorin requested.

"Yes, yes of course, coming right up, fellas."

Antonio walked to the kitchen as Chief Ramzorin and I looked like we had been thrown into wood chippers.

"Been busy?" Chief Ramzorin asked.

"Yeah, how about you?" I asked.

"Busy, of course. Lots of… murderous activity in the city."

"That's what I've heard."

Antonio brought me a Coke and Chief Ramzorin a refill of coffee.

"All right, and what will we have to eat?"

"Actually," Chief Ramzorin cut in, "Victor and I are just talking for now."

"Oh, okay guys, just call me over if you need anything else."

Antonio hurried away as some more people entered the restaurant. It was a family of five, all seeming happy and hungry.

I took a drink of Coke and Chief Ramzorin took a sip of the steaming coffee. That's when the gloves came off.

"So, you're working at the warehouse still?"

"Yes," I said.

"I see. Now, is that for Mark Ponchello, or Don Ponchello?"

I set my glass down hard and leaned in toward him.

"What the hell is that supposed to mean, exactly?"

"Don't patronize me, Victor. Do you think I'm stupid? You come in here with a fucking gun under your jacket and don't think I know what you're getting into? Or what you're already in?"

"Why do you care? When have you ever cared?" I argued. It was a typical teenage response.

"Don't say that to me! I've met you here every goddamn Wednesday trying to make sure you at least got one good meal a week."

There was a pause as Chief Ramzorin tried to quiet himself down.

"They're criminals, *Victor!* Why the hell do you want to be a part of that!?"

"They've been there for me a lot more than every Wednesday, I can tell you that."

The Chief scoffed. "What more did you want from me, Victor? I tried to do what I could. I gave you moral support; I fed you every week… I tried to help you, when you actually showed up."

"Yeah, you tried. But you didn't help me. My father was obviously assaulting me on a regular basis but I guess you just saw it as parenting."

"I work my ass off, Victor. Be glad that I could dedicate at least one day a week to you. I would have done more if I could, but I'm not some hoodlum who can just screw off at the expense of others whenever I want to."

"I don't feel like you did everything you could. I didn't expect you to be a second father to me, but I wished you could have put my good for nothing father away."

"You know I tried, I told you I tried. Besides, I even had a job lined up for you on the police force after you made it through high school. I planned on being a bigger part of your life at that point, but you decided to run off to be in the gang instead. And now they have you brainwashed into believing that what you're doing for them is right and what I do is wrong. When your parents were killed in the fire, I was ready to take full responsibility of you, but you just turned and walked away."

I was done talking with Chief Ramzorin.

"I wasn't good enough for you then, and I'm not good enough now. Coming here was pointless," I said, and I started to get up from the booth.

To my surprise, Chief Ramzorin didn't even try to stop me. Just like when my apartment was in flames, he only watched as I walked off and left him.

*****

After all of my anger passed to come back at another time, I still felt hungry so I decided to go to the diner. Once I stepped in, the atmosphere of the place hit me like a foreign planet. It was dirty looking, and almost all the tables had trash and dirty dishes on them. A waiter and waitress were just messing around with the busboy and they all stood around talking, not even paying attention to anything.

"Hello?" I said.

"Just sit wherever," the busboy said without even turning around.

I knew that the service would never be this bad if Emmitt and the others still worked here.

My face started turning red with anger and hate as I stormed over to the busboy and waiters. In pure rage, I grabbed the busboy by the collar. He thought I was just messing around at first, until I swung him around and into a table.

"Jesus Christ, what are you doing?" the waitress cried.

"Do you even know who I am?" I shouted. "Where is Sid?"

"He left for the night and has us as the closers. Rene is in the back doing dishes."

"Look around, looks like you guys have plenty more dishes to give her," I spat.

"Yeah, sorry, man, we'll start cleaning up."

"You'll be lucky if you're even working here tomorrow," I said as I looked at all three of them.

The busboy got himself up off the floor and went to grab his tub at the back. He scowled and started snatching all the plastic baskets and plates off the tables.

"Did you want to sit down and eat?" the waitress asked nicely, trying to regain high honor at the diner.

"Doesn't look like I have anywhere to sit," I said.

"I can clean you off a spot," the waiter said as he started to walk away.

"No, just get me a number three to go."

"With bacon, right Victor?" the waitress asked as she started walking off.

"Yeah," I said, out of breath and tired, "that's right."

*****

I made it back to the manor and wasn't exactly sure where I wanted to eat my dinner. I would eat in the kitchen, but I was now out of the mood to hear Michelle clanging dishes around. Eating in the dining room would be overkill. Well, that leaves...

I heard a *PING* noise coming from the living room and I smiled. That noise only meant one thing, and as I entered the room, I confirmed it.

Danny and Nick were playing Pong and I came in to sit and watch as I ate my dinner.

"Oh, hey, Victor, there you are," Danny said as he messed around with the joystick.

"Yeah, here I am."

"Did you get me a shake?" Danny asked.

"Did you get me some fries?" Nick asked.

"Geez, you two are pretty needy," I said as I plopped down and ripped into the sack. "Besides, I don't think you guys would want anything from that diner."

"Was it bad again?" Danny asked.

"Again?" I said, "There was a first time?"

"Yeah, I think I may finally have a talk with Sid. I ate there with Jacob on Monday and the service was terrible. For some reason, he has Rene working in the back all the time either cooking or doing dishes. She needs to be on the front counter to swoon in all the lonely teens."

"Hah, well you're right on the money. They were doing the same thing tonight," I said as I bit into my greasy burger.

"Gotcha!" Nick called out as he scored again on Pong.

"Dammit! Look what you made me do, Victor!" Danny said, jokingly.

I laughed and said, "I think you just suck, Danny."

Danny took a moment to punch my leg and I tensed up as a joke. When the laughing was done, I really started to wonder if I had ever told Danny...

"Danny," I said, in a strange sort of tone.

"Yeah, what is it, Victor?"

After thinking over the argument with Chief Ramzorin, I said, "Thank you. You know, for being there for me. At school, and now."

Danny turned back to look at me from the game of Pong and said, "Don't mention it, Victor. We're friends. That's what friends do."

As his head was turned to me, Nick managed to score again and Danny punched him in the arm. I stayed with my true friends for the rest of the night.

# Chapter Fifty Three
## The Meeting
## Friday, October 21st, 1977

The phone rang at the Ponchello manor around two PM and I was told to answer it. I heard Emmitt's voice on the other end of the line as soon as I said, "Yeah?"

"There's a meat market on the corner of 10th and Bladewake, across from a clothing store."

"Yeah, I know where that is," I said as Danny and the other Kids watched me answer the phone.

"Head there now. If you're not there in twenty-five minutes, the meeting is off."

"Understood."

*Click!*

I hung up the phone on my end as well and looked to my observers.

"10th and Bladewake, that one meat market across from the shitty clothing store down there," I said as I walked across the living room to get my jacket.

"Can you take someone with you?" Al asked.

"Yeah, originally I planned on Danny to come with me but…"

"I'd just get too pissed off, you know?" Danny explained. "My temper would really get the best of me, and I know that."

"I understand, trust me. I feel the same way right about now," I said as I pulled out my gun and made sure it was loaded.

"Well, I'll go with you, and we can take my car. I just don't wanna drive," Al said.

"Cool, that also works because it'll be a car they don't recognize; grab a pistol if you don't already have one."

"It's in my car," Al explained.

"Victor, didn't Emmitt request that you come unarmed?" Danny asked.

"Yeah, but that doesn't mean I'm going to," I said with a faint smirk.

After Al finished tying his shoes, we both went out to the garage and I got into the driver's seat of his brown 1972 Ford Maverick. Al climbed into the passenger's seat and checked his glove compartment.

"Yeah, it's there," Al said as he checked for his revolver.

"Good, let me put mine in there too. I want to show that we do want peace," I said as I reached under my armpit and pulled my gun out.

With both of our guns in the glove compartment, I started up the monster of a vehicle and started ripping down the driveway to the highway. Twenty-five minutes didn't give us much time to get there, but I knew we could make it if I was driving.

Anybody who was out for lunch was now heading home and the clock on Al's dashboard read 2:30. With five minutes till the meeting, I turned right at a red light and sped towards our destination.

"You nervous?" I asked Al.

Al turned his head to me and said, "You said Emmitt didn't guarantee our safety after the meeting, right?"

"Yeah, he did say that."

"Then you should know my answer."

With that being said, I pulled up to the curb next to the meat market and put the car in Park. As I stepped out of the car, I saw Emmitt standing in front of the meat market with his hands behind his back. The meat market was painted a dreary white color on the outside, and it was clear no one had taken the time to sweep in a long time. I just hoped the inside was cleaner for the customers' sake.

Emmitt had large black sunglasses on with black leather pants and a black leather jacket. He was also wearing one of the berets I had seen before, and the expression on his face was blank. He didn't look the same. He looked as if someone had taken over his mind and made him take orders from his tyrannous father.

Al and I stepped up to Emmitt and he spoke directly.

"I trust that we don't have to worry about any weapons."

"We're unarmed, just like you asked," I replied.

Emmitt nodded quickly and said, "Good. Follow me."

We walked behind Emmitt and entered the meat market. The black man behind the counter was dressed in a worn out white apron and stood there messing with the cash register. The freezer before him resembled what might be found in a bakery, with a glass display showing different cuts of beef and pork.

"We'll be in the back for a little bit, Harold," Emmitt said to the man at the cash register.

The man just nodded and motioned back to the curtain behind the counter. Emmitt walked behind and opened the curtain for us.

"Straight to the back, you'll see an office."

Al and I stepped through the opened curtain and started walking among the carcasses of cows and pigs. They all hanged from meat hooks, all skinned and left with no life. The air smelled of bleach and raw meat, and it made me reconsider what

I had for lunch.

When we stepped up to the plain white door, Emmitt motioned for me to go ahead and go on in. I turned the circular knob and walked in with Al, and I saw Tyrel sitting at the metal table.

Before I could even have another thought, a man grabbed me and pressed me up against the wall, and the same thing happened with Al. Emmitt stepped in after us and said, "I trust you about your weapons, Victor, but we must all take precautions."

"I understand," I said in a rough tone as I got the worst frisking I'd ever experienced.

When my face was peeled off the wall, I stepped back to where I could face Tyrel and Emmitt in the brightly lit room. Al stood next to me after his unpleasant frisk came to an end. Neither of the henchmen that frisked us were ones I remembered, but they wore sunglasses and black leather as well. Tyrel was the only one who dressed differently than them, wearing brown pants and a loose orange jacket. A small medallion was worn around his neck and he seemed to mess with it every once in a while, shuffling it between his fingers like a coin.

To start the pointless meeting, Emmitt spoke.

"I find it amusing that my father and Don Ponchello think that we can figure this out. Obviously, you and I are friends, Victor, or we once were. The two that hate each other are my father and your Don, or Danny's dad. Yet, I was told that an idea for peace instead of all-out war was in the works, so after talking to my father, he agreed this meeting should take place so I could see if you were really serious in your proposal."

Al knew not to say a word as I cleared my throat to begin.

"Well, the Don, generously enough, is willing to look the other way on some things that have happened and make peace if we can do a trade. For all of the damage that has already been done toward the Don, we would like Tyrel to be handed over."

"What!?" Tyrel shouted as he moved in his chair and let go of the medallion.

"Otherwise, the Don is wanting to go to war with your dad, and trust me, I don't want that."

"This is bullshit," Tyrel shouted as he stood up. "Is your father really considering doing this, Emmitt? I'm family!"

"Be quiet, Tyrel," Emmitt said tersely.

"No, fuck that. You and your Don are fucking crazy stupid if you think I'm just going to be handed over for execution like that. I'd rather go to war with you people rather than do that."

"I said be quiet, Tyrel!" Emmitt shouted back.

It was the first time any of us had heard Emmitt yell and I flinched when he did. Things were bad. I knew that; Emmitt knew that.

*This meeting was pointless. There was no way that a peace agreement could be made. Emmitt and I could make one easily, but the Don and Jackson…*

As soon as my thought passed, a secret door hidden in the wall behind Emmitt and Tyrel opened up and out came Jackson and two other henchmen with AK-47s raised. Jackson's cigarette had smoke billowing from it as he looked at me with hateful eyes. The two henchmen that had frisked us before walked away and stood behind Jackson and the others with pistols raised. Tyrel joined them, but Emmitt stood without a firearm.

"Hmm, it's the peacemaker, but not his best friend," Jackson said in a mildly disappointed tone.

"Jesus Christ, what are you doing!?" Al shouted.

Jackson seemed to smile as he said, "Well, Victor, I congratulate you for actually being able to hold your own, especially since your friend seems scared shitless."

There was a small laugh from the powerful group as they looked upon us with guns raised. This whole thing was a set-up.

"Jackson, Al and I are unarmed, just like Emmitt requested."

"Then you're a fool," Jackson said with a grin.

"You kill us, and you'll lose any honor that you might have had before."

Jackson scoffed incredulously and spat, "What's with you fucking mafia hoodlums with your honor and respect? I honor and respect my family, not my enemies."

"Dad, please, let them go," Emmitt pleaded, and I felt like the old Emmitt was back just for a split second.

Jackson could see it too, but we could tell the decision had been made as he said, "I am going to let them go, only because the one I really want to gun down is not here with you."

I knew he was talking about Danny, and now I was glad he didn't come.

"Tell your Don," Jackson started as he stomped out his cigarette, "nice try with the riot at my club. But because of that, there will be no more talks of peace. The next time my men see any of yours, it's over."

I nodded in defeat and signaled Al to start heading out of the meat market. There was some disappointing chatter from Tyrel as we headed out, and I gave one last look to Emmitt. With the look he returned to me, I knew our friendship really was over.

# Chapter Fifty Four

Al drove on the way back to the manor and I made sure to put my gun away in my holster after we got in his car. We knew we had to exercise caution, so Al drove around for a bit just to make sure no one was tailing us. I ended up keeping my head on a swivel. When it neared about 4:45, Al said, "Y'know Victor, I'm kind of hungry."

I pointed out a diner on the far west side of town where we both hoped there wouldn't be any push back. We ordered the food to-go and had to wait for a while. My eyes scanned the diner, looking for one of our enemies to pop out and attack. Emmitt's words from before about not guaranteeing our safety after the meeting kept ringing in my mind. Finally, when the food was handed over, we went back out to Al's car and he instructed for me to eat carefully so I wouldn't make a mess.

"Yeah I won't, don't worry," I said as I ripped into the sack and bit into an onion ring.

About halfway through the meal, Al asked, "So, you think we're going to be at war now?"

I kept staring forward at the diner as I said, "I don't think the Don will accept any other action."

"Do you still believe Emmitt is a good guy?"

"Well, he pleaded for his father to let us go."

"That's true."

There was silence for a moment, until Al asked, "What is it like? I mean, if we go to war with them."

Al started up his car as soon as he finished his meal and we started backing out. I took the last bite of my club sandwich as I said, "It won't be pretty. I mean, before your time with the gang, we took down another gang run by a man named Tandelli. We took his gang down the same way the Don wants to take down Jackson's. Except, we let Tandelli's wife and kids go. This time, the Don wants to kill all of them. And if we were to see each other on the street, there's going to be trouble, I can guarantee that."

Al drove down an unfamiliar street to throw off any pursuers. The sun was actually setting very early for the time of day, and most of the streetlights didn't work, so we were in a pretty dark area. I kept my eyes peeled but Al didn't seem to be too worried.

"I think up here, we can jump onto the highway," Al commented.

I nodded, hoping he was right.

Out of nowhere, I heard a loud pop and I jerked for my gun. When I looked to see Al was alright, I realized it wasn't a gunshot.

"Dammit, maybe this road was a bad idea. I think I just got a flat tire."

Al pulled over to the side of the road and I pointed out a payphone for him to get as close as possible to. The car came to a stop and Al smacked his hands against the steering wheel.

"Do you have a spare?" I asked.

"No, don't have much trunk space. Plus, Phil said these tires could withstand anything."

"I guess not," I said as I stepped out of the car.

I made sure to look around the abandoned streets and I didn't hear or see anything. The slam of the car door echoed down the street and I heard Al get out too.

"Wow, it's really torn up," Al said as he knelt down to look at his front left tire.

"Don't worry, I'll call the manor," I said as I stepped into the phone booth.

The phone booth reeked of several foul odors as I picked up the phone and started to insert a dime. I saw Al shaking his head as he examined the tire. The streetlight above us made Al's car shimmer, and I finally got an answer.

"This better be you, Victor," Danny said on the other end.

"Why, what's wrong?"

"You guys have been gone forever!"

I stared over at Al and knew that getting the food was a bad idea.

"Yeah, I know. Al was hungry so we stopped at a diner. We also started heading back on Amber Lane so anyone on our tail would get thrown off, but Al got a flat tire and he doesn't have a spare."

"A flat tire? There's no way," Danny said. "Those tires are supposed to be able to withstand anything."

"Well, we can bring the tire back home to show Phil if you'd like," I said, and Danny and I had a small laugh. "Is there a way you guys can come get us?"

I watched as Al still fiddled around with the torn up tire. Danny said, "Sure, it shouldn't be an issue. Amber Lane and...?"

"46th," I was able to say, before I watched part of Al's head fly up into the air and splash over the hood of his car.

I dropped the phone and cursed loudly. The bullet was silent and I tried to take what cover I could in the claustrophobic phone booth. The glass above me shattered and the silent bullets zipped above me. I kicked the door to the phone booth open while covering my face from the falling glass and heard Danny yelling on the other end of the phone. I didn't have time to yell back. I ripped out my gun and ran to the side of Al's car.

I was sure the shots came from the pitch black alleyway across the street. The street lamp above the alleyway would flicker on and off, and I was able to catch a glimpse of the end of a silenced rifle sticking out. When I waited for a second, I heard two indistinct voices talking for a brief second.

I jumped out from behind the hood and fired two deafening shots. Once the shots were just about done echoing between the walls of the buildings and all the way down the street, I heard a body thump onto the concrete. I peeked up out of cover and saw just the arm and the rifle in the street lamp's light. Several bullets hit all along the front of the car and I crawled back to the trunk. I heard a sizzle from the engine and some steam rose. Without giving it too much thought, I fired a bullet into the street lamp above me and the glass rained down as even more darkness surrounded me. On the other side of the street, my unknown opponent did the same thing to theirs with a silent bullet.

"Jesus Christ," I said to myself as I tried to decide what to do next. My eyes started to adjust to the dark and I waited.

No footsteps, no voices, nothing.

I figured it was only one-on-one at this point. I clenched my pistol and felt my grip getting weaker with sweat. I was out of whack; couldn't think straight. The image of Al's head exploding entered my mind again. I closed my eyes and shook my head to get it out.

Another burst of bullets came from the dark side of the alley and I saw the muzzle flash. I fired back twice in that area and didn't hear anything again. Not even the thud of my opponent's body.

It was getting darker outside and I didn't know how much time had passed. Ten minutes? Twenty minutes? An hour?

*Where the fuck is Danny?* I thought to myself.

Finally, a large amount of bullets smacked into the car, as if the other person had given up. Their patience was done. The front right wheel of Al's car flattened and I had to adjust my crouch with it. Right when I thought there would be silence again, I heard the person on the other end eject the magazine and they let it smack against the concrete. It was a fatal mistake.

I jumped up and fired five shots: One-two, one-two-three. When the fifth shot leapt from the end of my pistol, I heard a cry that sounded familiar. As I remained standing, I knew that I had won. I started feeling queasy as I ran across the street, trying to remember where I had heard that cry.

*Where had I heard it before?*

It then occurred to me as I saw the lifeless body of Marcus that it was the same cry I had heard TJ do when we played basketball together, what now seemed like a century ago. Marcus was the first person I had killed, and a deeply disturbing notion came over me as I saw it was TJ who received the last five shots.

TJ was still alive, but blood ran out of his mouth and he was shaking uncontrollably. I knew he'd be dead soon.

"No," I said as I knelt down to him.

He reached up to grab my shoulder and said, "We didn't know, it was you… Dad just said, to attack…"

That was it. That was all he could say before his eyes rolled back and his eyelids shut loosely. I stood back up as I noticed that I had knelt in a pool of Emmitt's only two brothers' blood.

# Chapter Fifty Five

The first house I ever lived in was really a magical place. In Brighton, that is. Brighton was a beautiful town about forty-five miles out from Detroit. A lot of rich folks had run out there when the real estate market was doing a lot better in the early fifties, especially with the invention of credit cards and credit lines. Who knew that using money you didn't actually have would ever get you in trouble?

Anyway, I was part of one of those snooty families that moved out there real quick, in the beginning. My parents had told me long ago that I had lived there since I was born. My father's business had just started booming before I was born, and with the news that my mother was pregnant, they moved out to that house; the one that I missed so much. The greenery was vibrant and made me feel awestruck just thinking about it. Each house in the circular neighborhood was built upon about three to four acres of land, and all the houses shared a small lake that people would take sailboats or small motorized boats out on. My father had a small boat to go fishing on sometimes, and I remember times when I would go out there with him.

Our golden retriever, Max, was the perfect dog. Hardly ever barked, knew how to entertain guests without getting his muddy paws all over them... haha.

My mom would plant some flowers and vegetables in the front and back gardens. The two-story house had large windows in the back and hardly any windows in the front. Our front door was large and majestic, almost like entering a castle. When I was really young, my father would be busting his ass at work while my mom fiddled in the garden. Max and I would run around and have adventures. He was my best friend.

"Max, what do you have there?" I remember my mom asking a long time ago.

A medium-sized turtle was hanging out of his mouth and I screamed so loudly that the neighbors started to look over. My mom shrieked too when she approached Max, but she calmly led him to the backyard, somehow pulled the turtle out of his mouth, and released it back into the water.

"Geez Mom, that was scary," I remember commenting.

She smiled with bright red lipstick and a straw hat on and said, "It gave me a fright, as well. Let's go make lunch..."

"Make sure to wash your hands!" I called back as we walked into the house.

Then I think of those moments that I didn't understand as a kid what was happening, but now I do.

My father was smoking a cigar on our back porch, watching as the sun was going down. Max had to go out and do his business, so I ran out with him to make sure he didn't go on the carpet like he would when he was little.

"Go, Max, go!" I cried, and then I only watched for a second. When he started going, I said, "Ewwwwww."

My father decided that laughing at me was better than giving me advice for the future. As he started to make a comment, I saw his face fall and he said, "Let's go back inside, Vic."

The only thing I could see was a boat out on the lake all alone. When my father picked up the phone and started complaining to one of the neighbors about his son and girlfriend in that boat... well, I now understand what was going on.

And then I remembered the times when my parents still got along, and when they weren't completely miserable drunks. I liked to cherish the memories I had of playing in the living room of our ridiculously colossal house, and I would hear my mom call out that dinner was ready.

Max would run off first, knowing the keyword "dinner", and I would linger for a second as I'd set down my action figures before bolting towards the kitchen.

"Hey, slow down there," my father would scold as I'd rush in.

I'd go quiet and pout, but I'd always feel better as soon as my mom would say what we were having for dinner. Plus, sometimes my dad would mention his belt coming off for a whipping. Eventually, the pouty face went away altogether.

There were a lot of other memories about that house that I liked. Sadly, they were scattered all over the place and I couldn't seem to get them all in order. They would just come to me at random times.

*****

"We have to go," the Don said sternly.

I felt the fifteen-year difference between then and now as I blankly stared at Al's headless body sprawled out on the hood of his car. We all took a quick moment to silently pay respects and we climbed into the car afterwards.

The Don sat by David and I sat by Danny. It was a normal routine by now. We looked at each other and Danny said he was glad I was alive.

At one point, I used to feel the same, but now I wasn't sure anymore.

## Chapter Fifty Six

The meeting took place in the dining room and everyone was present, including the Kids. Leo was even released from the hospital earlier that morning without anyone knowing.

Before the meeting began, I broke the news about Al to the Kids. All of them fell silent, and Jacob's eyes were red and teary as the meeting started.

The Don was actually seated while Leo stood next to the Don and got everyone to simmer down. Danny patted Jacob's shoulder and told him everything was all right. I wish he would've done the same for me.

"This is it," Leo said. "With the failure of the meeting and the attack on Victor and Al, this means war. Our plan is to go ahead and exterminate every last one of them. Victor was able to take out the two assailants, so that takes some of the muscle out of Jackson's arsenal."

"When do we kill 'em?" Charlie asked heartlessly.

I saw a faint smile on the Don's face after the question was asked and I felt sick to my stomach. I had to argue.

As I stood up, Leo said, "Victor, you've got to be fucking kidding me if you object to what I'm saying."

"It's not all of them. Emmitt's brothers weren't bad people."

"They attacked you. They tried to kill you, and they did kill Al."

I heard Jacob whimper softly and I said, "TJ's last words to me were him explaining they didn't know Al and I were in that car."

"Bullshit," Jordan said.

"Victor wouldn't lie," the Don stated plainly.

"They didn't know that I was in there. They wouldn't have attacked if they did."

"What about Al? Huh?" Leo argued. "Are we just turning a blind eye to that?"

"I'd like to be excused," Jacob said, even though Danny tried to comfort him.

"Grow a pair," Leo exclaimed.

"Fuck you," I said to Leo, which was not a good idea.

"What did you say to me?" Leo asked as he tensed up.

"Enough," the Don said quietly, mainly looking to Leo.

"It's all Jackson," I said before anyone could cut me off. "We should just take out Jackson, Tyrel, and a few other men that you deem necessary, but not every single one."

"Not Emmitt, you mean?" Leo asked.

"I said enough!" the Don exclaimed, turning to me and then Leo. I sat down and Leo actually did the same. The Don's face was red and hot as he stood up and stared me down.

"We have to kill all of them, not just the heads. This has been a fact throughout mankind. When there is power to this extent, someone will take it over if we don't take them all out. When a king is killed, his son will take over, even if he doesn't want to. But who doesn't want to be a king?"

The Don laughed strangely for a moment, and then grew serious once more. He took a walk around the room behind everyone and continued speaking.

"We have to kill all of them. Anyone associated with that gang, anyone wearing one of the berets, they have to go down. That's how I became the Don over all of you. When my mom and dad were killed under the hand of Thomas Hannigan, I swore vengeance. He didn't kill me out of respect, but it was a stupid mistake. I spoke to Mr. Dainov and we made a plan to kill him. It was done within the next week of my parents' murder, and I made sure none of his kids were left alive. Lo and behold, they never came into power again. All of the small parts of their operation started fighting with each other and they wiped each other out. It made me take control of my father's operation. When I killed a person of that importance, I had to accept what kind of person I was and who I would have to be today. If we just kill Jackson, Emmitt or someone else will rise to power. Did Emmitt act the same when you met with him? Did he act like a friend?"

I gasped slightly. I knew someone watched over us as we went to the meeting. I fell silent again and the Don shook his head.

"The assault will be Monday. Leo, we'll need you to call in our New York soldiers for this. As I understand, you said this will be quite a tough takeover?"

"Yes, quite," Leo started as the Don sat down. "Roy did some surveillance while I was out and found that Jackson overlooks some finances at a bar that is near our turf, but it's heavily guarded, inside and outside, on the ground and on the rooftops. Tyrel and the others usually hang out at a barbershop that's a little farther into their turf."

"So, the Kids will take care of the kids, and the adults take care of the adults?" Jordan asked with a disturbing levity.

"Basically," Leo said, and he looked over to Danny and me. "Think you guys can handle that?"

Danny nodded, but he also looked at me for approval. I didn't have a choice, unless I wanted to leave the gang. But, as everyone says, there's really only one way that most people can leave a gang, only they're not alive to tell the tale.

"We can handle it," I said in a deep and strong tone, and I saw Jacob nod as well.

Soon, everyone in the meeting room agreed that complete annihilation was the only option. Everyone, except for me.

# Chapter Fifty Seven
## The Weekend Before Halloween, 1977

That weekend, I was in a daze. On Saturday, the Kids and I decided to circle around and tell stories of Al; Jacob talked about how well they knew each other, even before the gang. I felt bad for Jacob, especially with what Leo said to him as well. It was messed up, and I didn't approve of Leo's mannerisms, as usual. Jacob had lost a good friend... hell, we all did.

Leo walked by our congregation at one point, and he gave me a dirty look. I didn't necessarily return one, but he knew it wasn't wise to approach me, especially with our emotions running high as we conversed about Al. And over time, as we started to talk about Al, we ended up reminiscing on Roger as well. He had just died last month, but it seemed like forever as we talked about it more and more.

Out in the backyard, where hardly anyone went, we had a cross in the ground for Roger next to the beginning of the forest. We finished up the one for Al, and Danny stuck it into the moist ground. A necklace was recovered from Al's room and placed over the cross. Jacob said it was Al's lucky necklace, one he had forgotten to wear the day he was killed.

I let the thought slide as we walked back into the house and sat around for the rest of the day as Leo, Roy, Jordan and David all brought in ammunition and weapons.

On Sunday, there was an eerie ring of the doorbell and we were all told to go to the front door. The Kids and I watched as five looming men came walking into the manor with overcoats on. The Don greeted them in a gracious manor, and they were then introduced to the rest of us. The New York soldier's names were Seth, Zack, Bill, Mason, and Alex. All of them, except Bill, were in their early thirties. Bill was the only one I liked, and he was nearing fifty. I liked him since he seemed like a more humble and genuine person, while the rest seemed like regulars from off the street. Jordan seemed to be pretty close to Seth and Zack though, and they all started joking around and talking about some old times.

Eventually, they were brought in the dining room and I followed for some reason. Jordan and David started giving them the run-down of the assault and I sat at the dining table with a blank face.

"Victor here, along with Danny, will lead an assault at the barbershop where some of the younger members hang out," Jordan explained to the New York soldiers.

"You guys can handle that?" Bill said in a low voice.

"We have before," I replied.

Bill gave me a pat on the shoulder and I saw Leo walk into the dining room.

"Hello, men, haven't been able to say much to you, but I wanted to welcome you all again," Leo said, and I remembered that these were men he had recruited after the Tandelli War ended.

Leo then turned to me but said to the others, "I hope Victor here isn't trying to make you fight for the other side."

The New York soldiers seemed confused and my face got heated. Instead of testing my luck again with an insult, I left the room to find Danny heading toward the basement.

"I hate Leo," I said as I stepped up to Danny.

"Yeah, I heard what he said to you," Danny said as he opened the door to the basement.

I started to follow him down there, but I heard the phone ringing in the kitchen. When I didn't hear it answered, I started to run to the kitchen and pick it up from the receiver.

Michelle smiled at me and apologized for not getting it as soap was covered all over her hands. I told her not to worry about it as I put the phone up to my ear.

"This is Victor."

"Victor!? I need someone to come get me."

"Why, what's going on?" I asked.

Roy spoke frantically as he said, "I was walking back to Studio 9 to start my guard duty again, but then, the fucking place blew up and took out my car! Michael is dead, the other guy I had watching the place is dead... it's a mess. I managed to go up north, hiding out at Magnificent Cakes."

"We'll come get you," I said, and I hung up the phone. Our dead pimp was the least of our worries. I just hoped they wouldn't attack Roy in the meantime.

Danny stepped up to me and I guess my distress was visible on my face.

"What happened?" Danny asked.

Not wanting to call the pimp by his nickname, I said, "Studio 9 was bombed; Michael is dead."

Leo bolted into the kitchen as well and said, "Is Roy okay?"

"You act as if you knew this would happen," I replied.

"It was inevitable. We are at war, Victor; now more than ever. You killed two of Jackson's sons."

I let his words cut through me but I tried to not act phased. Once I took a moment, I said, "Roy is fine, he just needs to get picked up at Magnificent Cakes."

"All right. How about you and Danny go do it and we'll secure the compound?"

I wanted to argue after what Jackson said at the meeting, but Danny didn't let me.

"Definitely. Let's go, Victor."

## Chapter Fifty Eight

Danny and I got into my car right away as the other men started running around the compound like chickens with their heads cut off. I hated this war more and more as each moment passed, but there was nothing I could do about it. It was out of my control. I didn't agree with either side at this point, which made it worse.

On the way to get Roy, Danny started talking to me.

"Did you really want to try and keep Emmitt alive?" Danny asked.

"Honestly? Yes, I do," I said as I stared forward at the highway.

"Y'know Victor, I feel the same way, sometimes."

I glanced over at Danny just to make sure he was serious, and then I wondered why I thought otherwise.

"So, why didn't you say anything at the meeting?" I asked.

"You said it yourself, Victor. When you met up with Emmitt at the meat packing plant, you said he acted different; that he dressed different; that his former self was gone. The only time you said it came back was when he pleaded to Jackson to let you and Al go, but that only worked for a few hours until they were ordered to attack you guys. At this point, Jackson has probably smacked Emmitt around and gotten him to believe in their cause."

I shook my head, hating to believe what Danny was saying, but he was right. Everyone was right, but in such a wrong way.

"I know, Victor. This sucks to hear, but better from me than Leo, right? The fact that Emmitt has probably been brainwashed is the only reason I feel okay with what we have to do. Otherwise, I'd be right there with you."

I exited from the highway and we neared Magnificent Cakes. Far in the distance, we could see black smoke billowing into the sky, and we only figured it was whatever was left of Studio 9.

"Jackson said he only let me go because you weren't there with me," I said.

"Oh. Then it probably wasn't a good idea for me to come with you then, huh?"

Danny's comment made us both laugh for a moment and it helped ease my stress. Danny always seemed to know how to make me feel better, even in terrible times like now.

We saw Roy standing out in the open at Magnificent Cakes and Danny honked my horn at him. Roy jumped, and saw that it was just us. He bolted toward my car and hopped in the backseat. He was panting heavily and sweat ran down his forehead.

"Roy," Danny started. "Calm down. We're getting you out of here."

I pulled away from the curb and Roy said, "No, you guys don't understand. I haven't seen explosives like that used since the war… Jackson has a goddamn arsenal!"

"Well, we'll make sure to beat him," Danny said with a smile.

*****

We made it back safely to the busy manor. Driving up to it was intimidating, even though we were all on the same side. Men with assault rifles stood outside and I even spotted a sniper on the roof. I eased into the garage (which was also heavily guarded) and we walked by Phil, who was working on getting the vans ready for assault.

Leo and Jordan were jogging toward us as we stepped out of the garage. Leo smiled for once and shook hands with Roy.

"We're glad you're okay," Leo said.

"I just hope the ringing leaves my ears soon," Roy replied.

We all walked into the manor and Roy started explaining everything in the living room.

"I'm telling ya, Leo, they used some type of explosives I haven't seen since 'Nam. It must've been C4, or SEMTEX," Roy explained as Michelle handed him a glass of water.

I wish I could be left as clueless about everything as Michelle. She was probably only told that Roy was upset and needed something to drink.

"Well, I got the shipment of ammo and some other guns yesterday," Leo said.

"I just don't know if it will be enough," Roy said. "When I did my surveillance, Jackson was a very heavily guarded man. His bar is not meant for the average customer."

"So, what do you want me to do? Act like Wile E Coyote and go to ACME for some explosives?"

"No, but I'm saying, if we can, we should get some bazookas, or LAW rockets."

"Are you fucking kidding me?" Leo asked with a scoff.

"No, I'm really not. The more I think about it, regular guns aren't going to do the trick. When we assault that bar, we're going to have to level it too."

There was silence, and the New York soldiers seemed to be enticed by the idea. The term war was not taken lightly this time around.

"All right," Leo said with all seriousness. "I'll give a call to Matthew."

## The Platinum Briefcase

Matthew was a man who didn't want to be bothered unless you really needed something bad and you had the cash to compensate him. I had heard the name in conversations before, but had never met the guy. I was told it wasn't too common to see him face-to-face. But within two hours, Matthew "Guns" came to the doorstep of the manor and said he had a very important package for us.

The Kids and I were instructed to bring in all the boxes and it reminded me of working at the warehouse. Except this time, we really had to be careful with the crates.

Matthew eventually came into the house and he looked like he was related to Roy. He wore a camo vest with plenty of pockets, cargo pants and a tank top, even though it was in the low forties that night. He had a slick brown pony tail and a full beard as well. The backpack he wore also made him look less professional. He wasn't one for games and tricks though. He was all business.

"All right, this is all you requested," he said to Leo through a tough voice. "Where's the twenty-five grand?"

The Don stepped out of nowhere and started to pull out a checkbook.

"Hey, hey, hey, now no disrespect Don, but you've gotta know how stupid that is for you to pull out a checkbook for this. I want cash, for the best of yours and my interests."

The Don nodded as he looked to David Weston and pointed back towards his office.

"Grab all of it," the Don instructed.

As David walked away, the Don said to Matthew, "I appreciate you being able to deliver at such short notice."

"You give me a lot of business. It's the least I could do."

"Yes, and I'm sure I haven't been your only client here recently," the Don said.

Matthew looked at the Don with a cold stare and said, "You know I don't discuss my other clients, and I know you'd appreciate that with how many times the police have questioned me. But, it is true that you're not the only one."

"How much would it take for you to tell me what Jackson Burose purchased from you recently?"

"I told you, I can't say."

"You can, for the right price. How much would it take?" the Don asked.

David came from the office and I saw him carrying a briefcase. A burst of excitement went over me as I thought it was the Platinum Briefcase, but it wasn't. It was just a regular tan leather one.

"Fifty grand," Matthew said. "Now that would be for the crates and the bribe."

"This isn't a bribe, it's for information."

"Sure."

David counted out fifty grand and handed it to the Don, who then handed it to Matthew. Matthew pulled his backpack to his side and started shoving the money in.

"He bought some C4 and some barrels of gasoline, though I can't tell you what they were used for."

"I could," the Don said, and then he ended with, "Thank you."

Matthew nodded and left without saying another word. The Don then turned to us (me and the Kids) and said, "All right, usually I wouldn't ask you to leave such dangerous weapons here in the living room but I'll allow it tonight. You don't think any of the Kids will be using these, do you?"

Leo and Roy both said no, so the Don continued, "Good. I suggest you Kids go on to bed and rest up. The war ends tomorrow."

With that, we all split off to go to our rooms and try to sleep. I fell asleep easily, but the only way that happened was by thinking about my night with Ashley, and how badly I wanted her in my arms again.

# Chapter Fifty Nine
## The Final War
### Monday, October 24th, 1977

At nine AM, everyone was ready to leave the manor and start the assault. The Don informed us that the police would not interfere at all, but I wondered how he could make such a guarantee. There was no way Chief Ramzorin was bribed by the Don... was there?

I didn't even eat before we left, neither did Danny. Michelle had made an excellent breakfast for everyone, but I couldn't do it. I felt sick at the thought of Emmitt getting killed today.

As the Kids and I headed out to one of the vans, we saw Roy giving another run down to the men of how to use the LAW rockets. We all had M16s with shoulder slings and our regular pistols as well. With Nick as the driver and Danny as the passenger, I sat in the back with Charlie, Blake and Jacob. We all looked anxious, but Jacob looked demented and thirsty for blood.

The van idled as we waited for the final command. Eventually, Leo ran out and gave it to us.

"Jackson's presence at the bar has been confirmed, along with the barbershop occupants."

Danny instructed Nick to put the van in drive and we drove on out first since the barbershop was farther away. Roy, Leo, Jordan, and the New York soldiers were in a van that wasn't too far behind us. This all seemed too familiar, too mundane. We had done this with Tandelli and Modellini... and now, it was time for me to kill one of my best friends.

I didn't think I could bring myself to do it. I tried to review it over and over in my mind, but I didn't think I could do it. Tyrel I could kill, but not Emmitt.

"Does everyone remember the plan?" Danny asked. Without getting an answer, he continued, "Victor and I are going to handle attacking the front. You guys need to run around the back and make sure they don't escape."

Everyone nodded. I continued to stare at the floorboard of the van and regret every decision I had made up to this point. There was no need to do this. No need to kill all of them. *Maybe I should have joined Chief Ramzorin, I thought to myself. Maybe I shouldn't have gone with Danny when my apartment burned down...*

But it was all too late now, and it was even more apparent as we headed down the street to the barbershop.

At first, the road seemed clear. I saw a few little kids playing hopscotch or jump rope: all African Americans, all minding their own business. One man stepped into a phone booth and started to make an important call. The phone booth was pretty close to the entrance of the barbershop, and I knew he'd get hit in the crossfire. I tried not to think about it, until I saw a figure run out into the street and aim down range at us. It was Tyrel. He saw us coming from a mile away and he began firing right at the front of our van with an Uzi. Nick jerked around in the front seat and blood erupted from his body. As Nick collapsed in a definite state of lifelessness, Danny crouched and took the wheel. It was too late to control the van by then. We ended up crashing head on into the wall of a pharmacy directly diagonal from the barbershop.

The van was totaled, which was quite apparent by the amount of smoke rising from the front. As I started to get myself up off the floor in the back, I heard the bullets slamming into the van. I knew we had to act fast.

"Bust out the top window and give me some covering fire!" Danny yelled as we heard the never-ending bullets hitting the outside of the van.

Charlie took the butt of his M16 and slammed it into the top window of the van. As the glass shattered and he popped up to start firing at the barbershop, Danny kicked his door open and jumped outside into the blinding sunlight. I climbed out behind him as Jacob and Blake started out the back door.

Once Danny and I were outside, we found cover behind someone's poor car parked next to the curb. I crouched beside Danny as he fired his M16 at the barbershop. He had blood on the side of his face, but I knew it was from Nick.

Tyrel was now inside the barbershop with everyone else and I peeked over the car to find Emmitt firing at us as well. The glass on the front of the barbershop was falling apart now, and I decided to start firing back. I didn't aim at anyone specifically; I just fired toward the shop. Several bodies were already littered on the street by Charlie's gunfire. I looked to the phone booth and saw it was indeed the last call that man would ever make. Danny and Tyrel kept exchanging gunfire and I watched as Blake, Charlie and Jacob ran to the back through the alleyway. Soon after they entered the alleyway, I heard them start shooting and I felt sick to my stomach. The screams of those injured and killed started echoing non-stop in my mind.

"Victor," Danny yelled, "C'mon, you gotta help me!"

I shook my head to clear it as I reloaded the M16. I didn't want to lose two close friends in one day, so I snapped out of it and started firing toward Tyrel with Danny.

Tyrel stood up and we saw him yelling as he fired at us, but we ripped him apart with our bullets and I watched in awe as he fell. Suddenly, I noticed that I didn't see Emmitt or anyone else in the barbershop, but I could still hear screaming and crying from nearby pedestrians.

"C'mon!"

Danny and I ran up to the barbershop and I looked over the damage as gun smoke rose into the air. Glass was shattered everywhere and I saw Tyrel's dead body next to one of the chairs. Two other people's bodies were filled with bullets as well, and I noticed one was a black girl in her mid-teens.

"The rest must be in the back with Charlie and the others," Danny said as glass crunched underneath his combat boots.

"Right," I said, dazed and confused.

I started running towards the back of the shop where I saw a back room. As soon as I passed the counter, the crazed and bloodied barber jumped out and tackled me with a straight razor in his hand.

"You muh'fucker, I'll fucking kill you, fucker!"

He was babbling like a madman and I tried pushing him off but his razor got closer and closer to my neck. I couldn't get him off of me, and I looked to try and find Danny.

Danny finally came up and pressed his foot up against the barber's side to make him fall on his back. I stayed lying down in terror as Danny fired a burst of shots into the barber's chest. I looked to my left and saw the lifeless eyes of the barber as blood fell over his face. Danny swung his M16 over his shoulder and reached his hand to me.

"Victor, you all right?" Danny asked.

I stared at the dead barber for a good long time. I couldn't even feel the massive cut from his straight blade on the front of my right shoulder.

*It should be me who's dead. He could've put me out of my misery...*

"Victor, get up!" Danny yelled.

I had to shake off the dark thoughts again and I let Danny help me up. As I brushed the glass and debris off of myself, Charlie actually ran into the shop from the back room.

"We got them, they're back here."

This was it. It was time for me to see Emmitt dead, and I didn't know how to deal with it. Part of me wanted to cry, but it was a part of me that died a long time ago.

I followed slowly behind Danny and Charlie as they ran back out to the alleyway. I hesitated to walk out, but I did when I heard Danny talking to someone.

"Well, well, well, looks like we got them pinned."

I immediately stepped outside and saw that Emmitt was not dead yet. He and five others stood facing us without any weapons or any hate in their eyes, only fear. Once I stepped out, Emmitt looked at me and I could tell it was the old Emmitt, not the changed one under Jackson's command. He was shaking, and I think I was too.

"Once we killed two of them that were running out, the rest surrendered. Not sure if they just surrendered because they're out of bullets or if they really mean it," Blake explained.

A disturbed look fell over Danny's face as he grabbed one of the remaining men by the back of the head and said, "You fuckers should've thought about surrendering before this war even began!"

Once Danny yanked the man out of the line, he began slamming his head against the brick wall of the barbershop. After a few blows to the head, Danny let the man slump to the ground and he shot him without hesitation.

Emmitt jumped at the sound of the gunshot and Charlie eagerly said, "What now, Danny?"

Danny didn't even take a moment to think it over.

"We're not here to take prisoners. Line them up against the wall."

One of the men started crying and pleading we let them go. Charlie told him to shut up and Danny looked at me.

"C'mon, Victor, we gotta execute them."

I could see that Emmitt was looking back to see what I'd say, but I shook my head.

"I can't, I'm sorry. I just can't."

Danny nodded and raised his pistol.

"Jacob, you get those two on the end of the wall. One bullet to the head apiece. I'll get Emmitt. Charlie and Blake, you get the two in the middle."

Danny and the Kids formed a line behind Emmitt and his friends. They all raised their pistols up, and I started to turn away.

"Wait!"

Emmitt's shout forced me to turn around and I saw that Danny was respectfully waiting. Emmitt was looking at me with sorrowful eyes and he made a final request.

"I want Victor to shoot me."

I shook my head and started to tear up. Danny turned to me too and Emmitt finished. "I'd rather have a friend do it than someone else."

I couldn't hold back the tears. They ran down my face but I didn't dare cry out loud. Danny stepped away and I pulled out my pistol slowly. Stepping behind Emmitt,

I saw him turn to the brick wall once more and I raised my pistol up. My hand was shaking; my heart was beating out of my chest. Everything seemed like a bad dream and I knew there was no escape.

I held my pistol up, and somehow found the unwanted strength to start pulling my trigger. The tears started to blur my vision, and I took a moment to wipe them away before firing.

And in the most terrible way possible, Emmitt jerked around to face me one last time and his final words were, "Remember what you said!"

It was in that moment that my finger finished pulling the trigger and the bullet leaped out, smashing itself into Emmitt's right eye. Blood and bits of his head splattered against the wall behind him and he started to fall toward the ground. It all happened so slowly, just to make it more traumatizing. I watched as my only good friend smacked onto the cold concrete and bled out of his hallowed head. I didn't even hear Charlie, Blake or Jacob fire their weapons and kill their victims; I only heard my shot. The worst part of it all was that I couldn't remember what I had said to Emmitt. Whatever angel that was still in me now left me for good; I was no longer human.

When reality struck me once again, I watched as Danny yelled at me to come with him.

"We have to go, Victor!" I could faintly hear him yelling.

The armored car had come to our rescue and we all climbed in to go back to the manor. The others seemed fine, but I was totally gone. One of them mentioned Nick's death but I didn't care about Nick. I cared about Emmitt. They would never know just how much this day had messed me up, and in some ways, I didn't even know if they'd care that it did.

# Chapter Sixty
Tuesday, November 1st, 1977
6 PM

Chief Ramzorin sat alone in his usual booth at Michelangelo's. He took a drink of straight black coffee and felt it burn all the way down his esophagus. He only drank black coffee because it faintly reminded him of alcohol in the way that it burned. But he had given up drinking a long time ago after his young fiancée had passed while they were in college. The scar on Chief Ramzorin's face was a reminder of how terrible drinking was, and it caused him to quit immediately after the incident. He'd think about that party they went to, and how afterwards, neither of them was fit to drive. He thought about that every single day, and how it almost cost him his spot at the police academy. Chief Ramzorin's father had pulled some strings though, and that's how the Chief was allowed to stay.

*Was it worth it, though?* the Chief would always wonder. *Did that really teach me a lesson?*

Ever since then, the scar -- along with the long hours he regularly worked -- had repelled other women from wanting to be with him. Sure, he had sex every now and again, but it wasn't the same. It'd never be the same as it was with Carolina.

Now as a police chief, he sought to do good deeds in the city of Detroit. However, too many terminal events kept happening. As he looked over his coffee stained newspaper, he saw the headline story was still about the murder of Jackson Burose. The headline read, "Race Turmoil or Gang Wars?" and pictures of the battered up bar and dead bodies followed, but were luckily in black and white. Chief Ramzorin shook his head, and read a part about the possibility of a rise in the Black Panthers under Jackson's command. It then showed that other members were killed at a barbershop farther south into town. Unlike the bar, the barbershop was only riddled with bullets as seen in the picture under and to the right of the headlining photo. There was one part of the article that showed an eyewitness saying they didn't see anything; it all happened too fast.

*So much for an eyewitness,* Chief Ramzorin thought as he took another drink of the blasphemingly hot coffee.

There was a ring at the front of the restaurant as someone stepped in. Chief Ramzorin wondered if it was that one family that seemed to come in every Wednesday now. He didn't really care, until his interest was piqued when he heard Antonio say, "Victor!"

***** 

Antonio's greeting to me was helpful but not welcome. I stepped into the diner feeling dead, wondering if I should turn around now. Antonio stepped up to me though, and I turned to look at Chief Ramzorin, who was staring me down.

"Glad you could make it," Antonio said.

"I'd like to discuss some things with the Chief alone," I said coldly as Antonio's happy look started to fade.

"Oh, sure, no problem. I'll leave you two be."

Antonio walked back toward the kitchen and I watched as Chief Ramzorin's cold eyes fell upon me. I knew he was a man who had experienced hurt as well, but I didn't know if he was the right man to go to.

*What am I thinking? He's the perfect one.*

I sat down and we didn't even say anything to each other. He folded up the newspaper and set it aside.

"Decided to come back, even after how last time ended?" Chief Ramzorin asked haughtily.

I stayed quiet. I didn't know exactly what to say, or how to say it.

"Have you finally realized I was right? That you made the wrong choice?"

I still stayed silent. I sat looking down at the table, the same one we always sat at. I wanted to feel normal; I longed to feel like my old self again, before all of this stuff with the gang.

"Jesus Christ. Are you really going to make me be a one man show and do all the talking? You came here for a reason, Victor, and I don't know what it is but I was hoping you'd apologize or tell me you came to your senses."

Finally, I couldn't hold back anymore. The tears started to flow down my face and I saw Chief Ramzorin's expression soften.

"I... they had me kill my one and only good friend."

I couldn't stop the tears now. Chief Ramzorin's face fell and he reached over to put his hand on my wrist.

"Victor, what happened? Tell me everything and we can fix this."

I kept crying; it was hard for me to form a sentence.

"I can't even remember," I started off saying.

"I believe you..." Chief Ramzorin replied, and I looked up at him. "What do you want me to do, Victor? What do you want to do? If you're saying what I think you're saying, I just want to tell you that I can get you a pardon. I can get you out of anything you've done. If you give me the necessary information, I can pull some strings. I just need to know what you're trying to say."

Finally, I was able to stop crying and I looked Chief Ramzorin dead in the eye. He gave me the same attentive look back and in a strong tone, I requested, "I want to take down Don Ponchello and his gang."

**The Platinum Briefcase**

# Part Three:

## An End To The Life

## The Platinum Briefcase

# Chapter Sixty One
## November 1977-October 1978

Men and women have passed judgment on each other for thousands of years. It's supposed to be part of our survival instinct. Animals will measure each other up and assess the situation at hand. They will determine if they were to fight, who would be the one to come out alive.

Human beings, on the other hand, think differently. We pass judgment on things like clothing, mannerisms, the value of someone's possessions, or the way they act. Some people even wonder if they could take others down, or maybe even kill them. That's the animal instinct I was talking about before.

I won't go into the whole nature versus nurture debate, but we do wonder those things, whether we want to or not.

After everything that's happened to me, the way I see it, it's just easier to fall into being a bad person. It may sound funny, but I think it starts with lies. The first lie most people are told is that Santa Claus exists. Or if you are one of many kids, the first lie you may be told is that your parents love you and your siblings equally. So when you realize you've been lied to, your world seems filled with lies and deception from that point on. Who could blame you for turning out bad?

Anyway, I've been doing a lot of thinking, and it occurred to me that I never really cared about all that shit... what people wore or how much money they had. I mean, it was cool riding in Danny's red Stingray for the first time, but I didn't see him as someone who was better than me because of it. All those people who were only after money and who had challenged Don Ponchello were dead now. And for what? That's the question I've been asking myself.

I didn't have an answer, or a good one, anyway, and that's why I finally turned to Chief Ramzorin. I needed his help because I realized throughout my life, I had only been worried about one thing: survival. Yeah – it seemed the best road to survival was siding with Chief Ramzorin instead of Danny or Don Ponchello or any of the rest of them.

So, Chief Ramzorin and I began our partnership in order to take down the Don, and we started in an aggressive manner.

"Victor, the best thing we can do is bug the Don's house and have you wear a wire," Chief Ramzorin stated.

I was tempted to agree with him, but I thought of reasons why that wouldn't work.

"Leo has already bugged the house. If I was to mess with his bugs..."

"Okay, bad idea... I was about to say, we could have a repairman go in and set them up... wouldn't have to be you, but..."

"Even if we were able to bug the house, they'd never let a repairman in. Leo and Jordan are pretty handy with things like the A/C and plumbing, electrical, all that."

We both sat in silence for a moment as we thought of different ideas.

"Who should we target first, since we don't have hard evidence necessarily linking anything to the Don?" I asked Chief Ramzorin.

Chief Ramzorin finished his coffee and said, "I mean, if we had two people telling the same story, it would be more believable. So, I thought you'd know who to target first."

I took a moment to think about it, and it hit me as soon as he raised the newspaper once more.

I told him everything about the New York soldiers, but I told him I only knew their first names. After some further research, the Chief was able to pull up more information on them. I did more investigating on my end, and found out they were leaving town soon.

"I think this is a good start, Victor," Chief Ramzorin said as we met up again toward the end of November, 1977. "But, what the hell are we supposed to arrest them for?"

"I don't know, you're the cop. Just make it a normal traffic stop. I'll notify you when they're leaving the manor and just have the highway patrol try and pick them up."

"How about you break one of their taillights?" Chief Ramzorin offered, but I shook my head.

As I thought about it, I ended up saying, "Well, I think they drive with false plates. Would there be a way to run them?"

"Yeah, we'd just have the patrolman call it in from his car."

*****

Around the end of December '77, the New York soldiers finally left the manor to return home. When they left, I made the call to Ramzorin, who then put out the APB on radio. I didn't know the results of what happened, until Leo demanded for me and Danny to change the channel to the news.

The news broadcast was horrendous, and it explained how the normal traffic stop went terribly wrong.

"... The officer began to approach the van again to hand back the driver's license, which is when we believe the gunfire was exchanged. Officer Pennington, along with State Highway Patrolman Reeves were both killed in the shootout. Officer Pennington's partner, Officer Valdez, ended the shootout and apprehended only one of the suspects alive. We are told this suspect, Bill Gash, who is a known gangster in New York City, is being taken to the hospital in critical condition and will be taken into custody and questioned as soon as he recovers from gunshot wounds to his head and chest."

"They're all dead?" I asked as we watched in disbelief. This helped cover up my involvement, but I was really more concerned about the officers.

It was strange to finally see (from a civilian standpoint) all the damage that the Don and his men could do. After discussing how terrible these men were with the Chief, I started to realize just how bad everything had been — and that it was only getting worse.

"Just about," Leo said, and he cursed to himself. "Bill won't make it. He's always been a fast bleeder."

Leo was right. Later that night, they reported Bill had bled out on the way to the hospital, leaving no one to bear witness against the Don, except for me.

As the New Year rolled around, the Chief and I met up again around the middle of January, 1978 to discuss other options.

"I'm so sorry about what happened to the highway patrolman, and Officer Pennington," I said in dismay.

"They knew what they were getting in to when I told them about that van. I warned them... Goddammit, I warned them," Chief Ramzorin said, and I could tell he blamed himself as well.

We both took a moment of silence for both men who had fallen in the line of duty, and I started to wonder if it was possible to take down the Don.

"I tried talking to the DA about you just testifying as an eyewitness to the events of the past few years," Chief Ramzorin started. My eyes widened and he calmed me down by saying, "Don't worry, I didn't say your name specifically. It was all hypothetical. But, it seems as though my fears were correct. They said that there's no way a case will hold up in court unless we really have some solid evidence. Otherwise, you testifying will just be some horror stories to tell around a campfire."

"And I told you, I'm not testifying yet," I argued.

I really wasn't trying to be difficult or anything; I just knew how these situations could play out. My idea with Chief Ramzorin was, we wanted to try and take down as many people as possible to lessen the Don's muscle and then try and take down the Don himself. Only then would I maybe feel safe, even though Chief Ramzorin guaranteed my safety if I was to go into protective custody. But my only other major problem was Danny.

I couldn't bring myself to tell him that I was siding with Chief Ramzorin at this point. I knew he would never go for that, but that was Chief Ramzorin's other option for me.

"If you could convince one other person to testify with you, then we wouldn't have much of a problem putting the Don away, even without the hard evidence. But two people telling the same story could get us grounds for a search warrant," Chief Ramzorin said.

"I'll never be able to convince anyone, even if it's their only option left to continue living," I said.

I started scratching at my face since I actually had facial hair growing in rather quickly. The Don liked us to be clean-shaven, but at this point I didn't care. Chief Ramzorin's mustache never changed. It always seemed to be the same stationary thing, almost like a piece of clothing. He made sure nothing was stuck in his mustache as I started to suggest a new option.

"The Don has underground gambling rings all over town, and some other venues of the sort," I said.

"Do you know where any of them are?" Chief Ramzorin asked.

"Yeah, there are three or four of them… I know where two are."

*****

After mapping out the two gambling rings that I knew of, Chief Ramzorin assembled an assault team that would take them down.

It was early February when Chief Ramzorin set his plan into action, and when the Don and Leo started suspecting someone in the gang was leaking information.

"There's just no way that anyone would've known about those hideouts… They were the two we just moved, weren't they?" the Don clarified with Leo, who nodded. "Then I don't understand."

At that point, I knew I had to start laying low. There was no way that I could continue leaving the manor for random reasons, because it would draw suspicion. The fact that everyone wasn't already pointing at me was a miracle on its own. We always met somewhere different though, and I knew no one ever followed me. I had debunked their theories a long time ago in reference to me being a traitor, so I hoped they wouldn't come up again.

I had to cut off communication with Chief Ramzorin for an excruciatingly long time. He knew I was alive. If he thought I was dead, the doors to the manor would've been busted down in a heartbeat.

My focus now was to stick with Danny as I had before. Unlike the times before the start of my defection, I didn't like being around him now. Danny seemed to be spiraling downward just like me, but we weren't going to end up in the same place.

Once spring rolled around, the Don's operation continued to weaken as every day passed. Sid's Diner closed due to poor staff and terrible service. Another reason was the fact that Sid wasn't paying property taxes. He kept the money stuck away in a safe and didn't let anyone near it. The police caught on and cuffed him. I never saw him again.

The venues in Las Vegas also started falling apart and losing customers; it was completely the Don's fault. He started having his men rig the machines so players would hardly ever win at slots. After an incident between a dealer and a player broke out – in which they ended up with bullets in each of their heads — customers had even more reason to stay away.

It was all becoming quite a mess, and the Don started to become desperate for cash. So desperate, he not only cut our wages almost in half, but he had us resort to more petty crimes. The Kids that were left started selling drugs on the streets in higher volumes, and the Don started having crack manufactured out in the back shed. It wasn't good crack, but it was cheap, and that drew in a lot of customers.

Next we started robbing random people in the streets downtown. Danny knew how to con people into giving him information, which would then lead to burglaries and even home invasions. Those became pretty profitable, and selling jewelry and other valuables on the streets made quite a turnaround for the gang.

Counterfeiting was also becoming common with the Don. Since we didn't have money, we made money. The bills appeared to be 100 percent real, but they didn't feel real. It didn't matter, though. Syphoning the money into our casinos as the payouts started out working beautifully. We kept all the real cash and the customers left with fake cash.

We also made connections with any Mexicans or Cubans trying to enter the country, and we traded their bills from home for our "American" money. It worked for a while as well, until Leo started to worry about the Treasury Department becoming involved. Our safest bet for getting cash was having Dave's Mechanical act as a chop shop. He made sure to treat his loyal customers the same, but any newcomers who broke down by his shop really got the definition of the "run around".

Laying low really started taking a toll on me. I felt lonely, and Danny, Jacob, Charlie, and Blake didn't seem to like me too much anymore. They could tell I was still down about Emmitt, and how we slaughtered him and his family. I couldn't stop thinking about it, though. I couldn't stop thinking about Emmitt, or his brothers, and how I ended all of their lives. I would never be the same, no matter what.

*Even if Chief Ramzorin and I can take them all down, I will never be the same... it won't change anything,* I would always think.

Two wrongs never make a right.

At one point, I convinced myself to leave the manor and try to meet up with Ashley. She always seemed to make me happy, so I had to rely on her.

But, to my disadvantage, I couldn't even break a smile around her.

"Victor, you look so down," she said as we sat at the table of a quiet restaurant downtown.

"There's so much I can't tell you. So much I want to, but I can't."

I know it sounds crazy, but I would get a sharp pain in my throat if I tried to tell her. It was a pain that ceased the existence of my voice. It was as if I was under some sort of curse.

"Just talk to me, Victor. Tell me anything that you want! I'm here for you, but you have to be here for me too."

I didn't even try anymore. She was making me worse, not better. I ended up leaving her there alone at the restaurant. I didn't even pay the tab. I just stood up, and left. Didn't even push my chair in, either, and she didn't stop me. She knew I was becoming dangerous.

Once I had reached that point of emotional desperation, I noticed that I started having dreams of the Platinum Briefcase. The dreams would cause me to sleep soundly and without interruption, because I would dream that the Platinum Briefcase could take away all of this misery. I dreamt of the Briefcase as a magical entity, almost like a new God. The Briefcase would speak to me in my dreams. I could hear a mystical voice telling me that I could find it and all would be okay. But every time I woke up, I lost all desire to search for it.

In the beginning of October 1978, the Don came down with some sort of illness. Of course, the Doctor was called in but he couldn't diagnose what the Don had. It was making him achy, feverish at times, and pale. The Doctor once believed it was walking pneumonia or mono, but he could never say for sure.

Finally, at the end of October, security around the manor started to fall and the need for me to hide out was unnecessary. I almost wanted to jump for joy, but I knew the fact that I could now leave the manor wasn't anything to really jump about, because I now had to communicate with Chief Ramzorin again.

"Chief, it's me," I said in a phone booth downtown.

"Victor..." he replied, and I could almost hear his smile. But I didn't reciprocate the feelings, and I knew he could hear my disgust.

"I had to lay low. The Don started to suspect someone in the gang was leaking information."

"I understand. It's good to hear from you though."

"We have work to do," I said, cutting out the bullshit. "When can we meet?"

Chief Ramzorin thought of the best setting for the meeting that he could. There was going to be a small celebration downtown for Veterans Day, and it was going to be surrounded by armed service members and cops. None of the Don's people, not even Roy, would go near it.

On November 11th, 1978, the Chief and I met up to discuss the next bust, but I really didn't know who to get next.

"I don't know, Chief... I thought I knew, but now I'm drawing a blank," I said sadly.

"That's alright, Victor. You'll think of something. The underground rings that we busted went off beautifully. They never saw it coming. You really have a knack for this stuff. Sting operations, that is."

"Are you saying I should've been a cop?" I asked.

"Maybe so. I think you would've been a great one," Ramzorin said.

I scoffed. Thinking back to when I chose Danny instead of the Chief, I'd never know what the other decision would've brought.

"How's Antonio?" I asked.

"He's good, he's good. He mentions you sometimes. Y'know, the last time we were there you didn't look so good to him."

"Crying to an officer is never usually a good sign," I said.

"No matter. We will take them down, and you'll figure out a way, I know you will," Chief Ramzorin said, and we heard the sounds of small fireworks as they were being fired off in the middle of the day.

## Chapter Sixty Two

At this point in time, I didn't have all that much to do. The gang seemed to be self-sufficient in the world of low-budget crime. I wasn't much of an asset anymore, but I was never told to do anything. I think the Don liked to keep an eye on me at the house. He wanted to make sure I wasn't really the traitor they had been looking for this whole time, and that I didn't get hurt.

"Victor, you are a valuable part of our operation. You and Danny, both. The others: Charlie, Blake, and Jacob.... I could care less. They are reckless souls to begin with. They're expendable. That's why I have them hustling drugs and selling stolen goods."

I hated to ask, but I had to keep up the image that I was still a dedicated member of the gang.

"What do you want me to do, then?" I asked. "There's only so much I can do around the house."

"I'd just like you to stay around here for the time being. Business has gotten rough out there, and I need you here as security. You're a good shot. David seems to comment on your abilities all the time."

Mostly what I did at the manor was go down to the basement and work on my aim. Firing a gun sickened me when I thought of Emmitt and his brothers, but I knew that if these busts went awry, I'd have to start shooting someone.

Knowing I wasn't satisfied with his remarks, he said, "Maybe on Wednesday you can accompany Danny on the bacon run. I'm sure he'd love to have you tag along."

I nodded in agreement at the time, but in my head I knew that was a terrible idea. Danny was changing, and he was changing in such a fast and deceleratory way that I couldn't even enjoy my time around him. The old Danny I knew who wanted to fight the bullies and keep a good friendship with me was slowly fading away. Now, he was the Danny Ponchello that wanted to be the bully, and was only friends with his fellow bullies.

Even after the raid on Emmitt and Tyrel at the barbershop, we didn't participate in any kind of ceremony after Nick's death. Finally, Charlie mentioned it a few months later, and we finally posted a stake in the backyard for him. The stakes were next to Roger, who had been killed first, and Al, whose head had disappeared before my eyes. Even after posting the stake for Nick, we didn't talk much or say anything on their deaths. At this point, it had become normal. Nick was just another dead man who fought for Don Ponchello's meaningless cause.

I remembered when Roger was killed at the hands of one of Modellini's men, it really struck us hard. I remember the loss I felt in the van as we headed back home to the manor. I remember how the Don even expressed sadness towards his loss. Once we returned to the manor and reported Nick's death, the Don could have cared less. It's as if… only killing the others was the important part. Only causing death and destruction to our enemies was the primary objective. If we lost a few men along the way, it didn't matter.

Even when the New York soldiers were killed, the Don felt little to no sympathy. Or at least, he didn't show it. When they said Bill may still make it, I knew the Don wished for him to die, that way the police would never get a word out of him.

My opinions of all these people I had lived with for the past two years had changed. I didn't like the Don anymore. I didn't like Danny. I never really cared for any of the Kids until one had died. I just couldn't. My survival told me to worry about myself, and no one else.

Since the Don didn't have me do much except sit around the house, it gave me plenty of time to think of my next bust. Who could I target, and why would I target them? Would it impact the Don's operation to the point where he would do something drastic? Or would it hurt his operation just enough to weaken it without total retaliation?

As I was plotting, Danny busted into the living room. Even his walk and general attitude had changed over the last year. It was almost like he had been downgraded.

"Ah, Victor, surprised to see you here," he said with utter sarcasm.

"Same to you," I said as it seemed to be kind of early for him to be home.

He shook his head as he strolled into the living room and sat down on the loveseat. He wore long black clothing and combat boots, along with some nice sunglasses. After sitting down, he started unlacing his boots and worked on taking them off.

"Man, you're really missing the action out there."

I nodded and said, "I know. But, Don's orders are to stay here."

"Yeah, but that sucks. You should've seen a grab we made today. Me and Jacob. People all over are getting rid of their vinyls and turntables. Now they want to get cassettes instead. Takes up less room, yadda, yadda, yadda. Anyway, Jacob and I found this pawnshop on the southeast side of town where everyone is turning in their record players and shit for cassettes and shit. The last turntable we had, some black guy bought it for a pretty penny. Not sure what they'd use it for, but I know there are more people that want to get their hands on one. So, Jacob and I nabbed some from the pawnshop and he's gonna start selling them ASAP. It'll bring in a lot of dough, and I know the Don will be happy to hear that."

"Cool, man," I replied.

My voice wasn't too convincing, and I found that out once Danny snapped back at me.

"So what did you do all day? Jerk off?"

The way he said it confused me; had he called me a jerk off or asked if that's what I did? Either way, I was bothered.

"No, I've been watching the house."

"Sounds like a chore."

"The Don says he wants me here as security," I argued.

"Yeah, in case the fucking rat we have here decides to have the cops knock on our front doorstep."

"In that case, I'll gun them down," I responded coldly.

Danny actually smiled at my comment.

"You know The Bobby Fuller Four said that's impossible to do. As much as I believe in this gang, the moment we start shooting at the police and live to tell the tales, that's when the fucking FBI will be swinging in on ropes."

"Well, your dad wants me to tag along with you Wednesday on the bacon run since I'm such a good shot."

Danny seemed to laugh and said, "C'mon, you're such a good shot? Really? That would be the case if you could've killed Johnny and the rest of 'em when they ambushed us at the warehouse. Instead, you just shot 'em in the leg."

"What the fuck, Danny?" I shouted, tired of everything. "I saved your fucking life!"

"Whoa, Victor, calm down man, I was only joking," Danny said, and I started to see his old self come back only through his voice.

My face had turned red hot in an instant and my heart rate accelerated to the highest it could be without killing me. There was a certain rage that was starting to take over me, and it was getting harder and harder to control.

"Maybe you do need to come with me on Wednesday, and get some of that anger out. Being cooped up in the house with nothing to do can get to you, I know that as well as anyone. Back when I was younger and we had the first war I experienced, I had to stay home from school… seemed like forever. It was hard to get any of my dad's men to play cards with me."

I continued breathing, just trying to get ahold of myself, but I nodded so Danny thought I was okay. He laughed slightly and came over to pat my back.

"The bacon run will be fun, don't worry. We'll have some laughs, and I'll make sure to put on a cassette while we drive around."

For some reason, it took me that long to think of the next bust. It had to be Jacob. Busting him for the illegal sales would hurt the Don, but not to the point where he'd do anything rash. I worried, though, as usual. Would it be too obvious to Danny that I was the rat if I told Chief Ramzorin about the opportunity right after Danny told me about their scheme with the pawnshop?

It was a risk I would have to take. Plus, I figured that Danny trusted me enough to believe I couldn't be the rat. We were friends. Even though he pissed me off a lot lately, he still thought of me as a close friend, and I had to make sure he thought I was still close to him too.

I was starting to become close to everyone at the manor, but it was only to eventually take them all down.

*That's it,* I thought, *Jacob is going down next.*

# Chapter Sixty Three
## Monday, November 13th, 1978

RING.... RING....

"Ramzorin here,"

"Chief, it's me."

"Victor? Good to hear from you, as usual."

"We need to meet up."

"The coffee shop downtown that we've been to before?"

"Perfect."

"See you there."

My anxiety was building as I headed to the coffee shop downtown to meet with the Chief. The escalating anxiety was caused by two factors: One, Jacob wasn't someone I could see surviving in prison. He had strange mannerisms that I didn't understand. He hated speaking up, and detested the current culture of today. I really didn't learn anything much about him until Al had been killed. That's when Jacob realized he had to consult with the rest of us on matters instead of his old friend. The Don had also once labeled Jacob as one of the "wussies" in our group. A long time ago, I felt bad for Jacob due to that fact, but now I didn't care. He changed so much after Al was killed; Al's death turned him into a terrible person.

Well, we were all terrible now. But his quiet attitude transformed after the death of Al; a lot of anger and evil started to rise from his heart.

And two, I wondered if because of how scared and intense Jacob was now, I could convince him to testify with me. I thought I could take advantage of his fear, but his intense loyalty to the Don and his pleasure at making money off of stolen goods was another story. If I had started taking down the Don early on, this whole thing would be another story.

But my decision had been made. I parked my car in an alleyway near the coffee shop, knowing Jacob was the best person to take down next. Although the worry of a rat was diminished, I still didn't want anyone spotting my Bel Air here. And with the sun covered by the dark and cool clouds that late fall likes to bring, my car was shadowed and not as easy to see as it would have been on the street.

I was wearing a dark hoodie to conceal my face as much as possible, along with some crappy sneakers and jeans so the wind wouldn't freeze my legs.

As I stepped into the coffee shop, I could smell the freshly roasted Colombian coffee beans brewing. I wasn't much of a fan of coffee, but theirs was very good. The Chief was the one who loved the place, and they knew him as a regular. Unfortunately, the owner always gave me a look that made his unacceptance of me very clear. I felt like he knew who I was, or what I was.

Towards the back next to a window was Chief Ramzorin. He was sipping away on some coffee that could've melted steel. I never understood how he could handle it, but he could. He sat still and didn't bat an eye as I walked up to him. It was almost as if he was in his own little world, wondering about everything going on. I almost felt bad for disturbing him, but we were meeting for a reason. Finally, as I pulled the seat out that was across from him on the other side of the small, circular table, he turned to face me.

"Still don't drink coffee, eh?" Chief Ramzorin asked.

"Not unless I want heartburn," I said.

"A kid like you shouldn't get heartburn. Have you not been as active lately?"

"Is this really what we came here to talk about? My intolerance for coffee?"

Chief Ramzorin didn't always like my new attitude, but I couldn't help it. Sometimes, I didn't think he took everything as seriously as he should. Besides, he wasn't the one leading a double life. That was all on me.

"Okay, so why did we meet up, Victor?" he asked sternly as he set his coffee down.

I sighed, feeling the rage that was slowly building and trying to escape from my insides. A man with funky glasses and a strange hat stood at the front counter and lit up a cigarette. I thought about reaching into my pockets for one, but I hated smoking.

"It's an idea for the next bust, but…"

"But what?"

"I'm not sure if it's really the best idea, mainly because of who it is."

"Is he too powerful? Too high up on the ladder?"

"No, you know our plan is to take out the smaller members first."

"Exactly. So who is it?"

"Jacob Flyman."

"Can't say I know the kid."

"Well, you're right on him being a 'Kid'. He's one of the recruits we got a year ago from New York. Just another fucking runaway, but he's an important one."

"How so?"

"He sells stolen goods on the streets, down toward the south side of the city."

"Like electronics and such?" Chief Ramzorin asked, and I felt as if he now knew who Jacob Flyman was.

"Yes. Turntables as of recent."

"Hmph… Well, I have some cops on a case that will be happy to hear that. Unfortunately, there were two people spotted leaving that pawnshop, but I'm sure you can't say who the other one is."

"The other one won't be there with the van full of goods," I said, still protecting Danny for whatever reason I could think of.

"I see. So, Jacob Flyman sells goods out of the back of a van on the south side of town. Do you have a street in particular?"

"Just south of 22nd on Bladewake, I'm pretty sure that's where he usually sets up. If not there, it'll be slightly down the street, about a block or two."

"Okay," Chief Ramzorin said as he started to pull out a pen and notepad. "22nd and Bladewake, or just south… Jacob Flyman, selling stolen goods out of a…"

Filling in the blank, I said, "Black GMC van."

"He will be alone, correct?"

"Yes."

"And when will he be doing this?"

"Well, today, actually. Right now till five or six tonight."

"Is this a bust we can do today? Will you have an alibi?"

"Is it really pertinent to do it today?"

"I was actually going to ask you the same thing."

I cracked my knuckles in slight agitation and said, "Well, yes and no. There are a lot of things that Jacob can't clear in one day. But if you're needing those turntables to link him to the pawnshop robbery, I'd say you need to get him today. He'll clear those by the end of the day, I guarantee it."

"But do you have an alibi if we were to do this bust today? Will they question if you were here or not?"

"I'm just getting lunch," I said to the Chief.

He gave me a hardened stare for a few moments before he decided to finish writing everything down. He knew I was a good liar, but it pained him.

"This is good, Victor. I think this will be just the bust that we need. What were you thinking would be bad about it?"

"Not sure…" I started. "He's a bit… crazy now. I don't want this bust to go like the one with the New York soldiers."

"It won't," Chief Ramzorin said. "I have a team in mind that can sneak up on him and take him away within seconds. No one will even know what happened, not even Jacob, until we fingerprint and book him."

The last sentence Chief Ramzorin spoke was accompanied with a smile, and I couldn't help but give a small smile of hope in return.

*****

It was around dinner time at the manor and I had just fixed myself some ramen noodles with chicken flavoring. Sometimes, due to how huge the manor was, it felt like there was an imbalance in the way the A/C or heater flowed. So as soon as the ramen came out of the microwave, my face moistened as the crazy amount of steam was a direct hit. I took the fork in my right hand and made the final stirring motions so the flavoring would mix in. Danny had just finished his bowl and he took it into the living room, so I decided to take mine into there as well. The gang of men I had been around for two long years stared at me with blank faces.

Still suffering of an unknown illness, the paled Don spoke first.

"Victor, it seems as though Jacob has been apprehended by the police."

I saw Leo and Danny watch for my reaction.

I said all I could think of. "Fuck," I started. "You mean, just now?"

Leo didn't seem satisfied with my response, but that seemed like a good thing.

"No, it was about three hours ago. Roy was driving around down there when he noticed the van was missing and no one had seen Jacob."

I let the bowl of Ramen burn my hands, as I knew taking a bite right now would be seen as inappropriate.

"I can't believe he got picked up," I commented.

"Honestly, I'm surprised it didn't happen sooner," David Weston mentioned as he stood by the Don. "I'm not an expert in selling stolen goods, but the kid was being cocky. He was selling them in the exact same place every day."

"It was a good location, though," Danny defended. "Those turntables would've been gone by the end of today."

"Well now it's all gone, including the money," Leo commented.

I went ahead and walked over to Danny so I could set my bowl on the coffee table and have a seat. Everyone adjusted to the change in tide and the Don spoke once again.

"At least we know it wasn't a snitch who gave the info."

"What?" Leo questioned and I could see the hurt in his eyes. "How do we know that?"

"Our man on the inside said that surveillance caught Jacob without his mask on as soon as he left the shop."

"Goddammit," Danny swore as he hit his fist on the couch, which made a hollowed sound. "I told him to leave it on, before and after the hit."

"Well then, let the cops have him. We don't need a fucking idiot like that on our side anyway," Leo sneered.

The Don sighed and started to slowly vacate the room. I couldn't figure out exactly what was wrong with him, and neither could the Doctor even though he was visiting almost once a week. And now, Jacob's imprisonment was really going to make a difference to our income.

Danny and I started to eat our ramen noodles and the other gangsters left to go do other things. Eventually, Danny turned on the TV, but that only made the silence between us even more obvious.

## Chapter Sixty Four
### Wednesday, November 15th, 1978

I sat in my room most of the day, wishing I'd slept better. The nightmares were still happening all too often and it was really affecting my everyday life. Monday night into Tuesday morning, I had only had about four hours of actual sleep. The rest was never-ending tossing and turning. Throughout Tuesday, it felt like it took ten times the normal exertion to climb up and down the stairs. I had to hold onto the rail to make sure I kept my balance. Tuesday night into this morning, I slept better, but it was only about six hours. I was used to getting eight or more most nights, until I had killed Emmitt. It all made my head hurt, badly.

At about three PM or so, Danny walked into my room without knocking and said, "Alright, time for the bacon run, hot shot."

I stood up and took my Smith and Wesson Model 39 out from under my pillow and tucked it into my belt.

We got into Danny's car and I remembered when he used to have the Stingray. I remembered the first time I stepped into his car and I felt like a million dollars. Everyone at school was so jealous, and for once, I felt like the cool kid. Now, getting into Danny's repaired Dodge Challenger, I didn't feel a thing.

Once I had my downfall after killing Emmitt, I noticed Danny had become closer to Jacob. With that observation in mind, Danny didn't seem all that upset about Jacob's imprisonment. He had just shown anger. I wondered if Danny was being consumed by hate and anger instead of sadness, or if he maybe didn't care. I was being consumed by all three with no way out.

But, our sad similarities gave me small hope that I could convince Danny to join me and Chief Ramzorin in taking down the Don, even though Don Ponchello was his father.

I glanced at Danny as he was driving, wondering if I could mention what was going on, and questioning if I could get him to side with us.

Throughout the bacon run, we would arrive at the destinations and Danny would get out and go grab the money. Then, he'd throw it to me and I'd count it. It was like the first time we had ever gone, but with no conversation in between the locations.

Fortunately, it gave me plenty of time to think over the possibility of asking him to join us. With two testimonies against the Don, Danny and I could get full pardons.

That's what the Chief promised for me, and I knew he could do the same for Danny.

"We haven't been short yet, right?" Danny asked me.

"No, no one has been short on their payment," I said.

"Good, good."

But I also knew Danny felt just as strongly about the possibility of there being a rat, like Leo did. What would he do if I was to admit to him that it was me all along?

*There's no way*, I could hear a voice say in my head. *Danny would kill you in your sleep. You thought it was annoying when he didn't knock earlier when he grabbed you for the bacon run you're on now? Just imagine him walking into your bedroom and cutting into your Adam's apple.*

The sinister voice left my head as quickly as it had arrived, and I noticed that we were making our last stop. Yet again, Danny hopped out of the car and ran to the drop location. I felt a sharp pain in the back of my head and I ended up smacking the area that was in pain to see if it would go away. For a few seconds more, the pain lingered, and then it went away.

Once Danny hopped back into the car, he tossed the money to me and said, "Okay hot shot, count it up."

"Is that my new name?" I asked.

"It could be, but I also picked up "52nd Street" by Billy Joel at the pawnshop the other day... so it's stuck in my head."

"Oh," was all I managed to say as I counted the money, not even correcting the song title.

Danny's eyes were pretty captivated on the money as I was counting it, and he finally said, "So, are we good?"

"Yeah, it's all here," I said as I put it back into the envelope.

"Great. I have to make one more stop if you don't mind."

"I don't have anywhere else to be."

That being said, Danny made a U-turn and we headed off to wherever he needed to go. I didn't really pay that much attention at first. My head was still hurting from the voice that had entered my head earlier. It didn't feel like a normal thought that I would have, and the voice didn't sound like mine. I started becoming paranoid, and wondered why it had happened. Maybe it was a warning. Maybe if God didn't want to help me, the Devil did.

And I decided to take it that way as I realized that we were approaching the pawnshop that Jacob and Danny had just robbed a few days prior.

Danny pulled up to it casually, but I saw rage burning in his eyes as he left his car running and ran through the front door. I snapped out of my worries and followed him in.

It was almost too late when I had entered. Danny was yelling at the top of his lungs and customers started running every which way as the owner argued back.

"... You tell the cops about my friend, Jerry?"

"They saw him on the tapes," the skinnier but yet still threatening owner argued back. "Besides, I should've mentioned you to them too."

"The fuck you would!"

Danny spat his words so forcefully it was almost comical, but now wasn't a time for laughter. The owner knew that too as he started reaching down behind the counter. In a matter of seconds, Danny had leaped over the counter and grabbed the owner by his long, greasy hair. The owner had a sawed-off in one hand, but he was holding it by the pump. I still pulled out my gun though, in case things really got out of hand.

Danny smashed the owner's face into the top of the glass display that he had stood behind and I saw the glass crack but not shatter. Next, Danny tossed the limp owner to the ground and began kicking him. I started to run and jump over the counter myself, but I knew I couldn't save the owner from enduring any pain. I knew Danny wore his steel toe boots; I should've known this was going to happen all along.

I tucked my pistol away and shouted, "Danny, c'mon man, what the fuck are you doing!? We need to go! Cops probably patrol here all the time now!"

I saw the owner spitting up blood and the shotgun had flown to the other side of the wall. Grabbing Danny's shoulders, he turned to me and said, "What, do you wanna swing at him, too?"

I stared at Danny for a moment, and I felt his rage pass over to me. All of the pain I had felt recently, and all of the sorrow I was cursed with, turned to anger. I accepted Danny's offer and I fell to my knees so I could take a few swings at the owner. I say a few swings to make myself feel better, but I can't actually remember how many swings it was. Once I was done with him, he was crying tears of blood, and Danny became the voice of reason.

"Alright, killer, let's go before the pigs show up."

I stood up and saw my reddened knuckles. It was almost impossible not to see them, and I could feel every muscle in my body tensing and relaxing over and over again. I was breathing heavily and felt like I had just been held underwater.

I took a second to shake it off and I followed Danny back to his car, where the owner was left in a bloody pulp.

## Chapter Sixty Five

Danny and I wiped our hands off in his car before heading back to the manor. He mentioned the sight of blood might worry his father of a possible scuffle with some new enemies.

"We don't want him thinking that. He has enough on his mind right now," Danny said, his voice normal and sincere for once.

The splitting pain I had once felt in my head was now completely gone without a trace left behind. My eyes couldn't look away from my reddened knuckles. The blood was all wiped up, but there was heat and friction occurring between the bone and skin, even though I wasn't tightening my fist at all. It was almost like my skeleton wanted to jump out and leave me behind.

The clouds loomed overhead, but they were too high up to precipitate. Danny was calmly cruising back to the manor and I was glad to see he wasn't totally wild.

"Victor, how long have we known each other now?" Danny asked.

"Well, I knew about you before I actually met you."

"Sure, but how long have we been talking?"

"I think next March will be three years."

"Wow, really? Feels like so much longer."

"I hope that's a good thing."

"Maybe."

I gave Danny a look, but the look he returned was different, and deeper.

"We've changed a lot, haven't we?" Danny asked.

"What makes you say that?" I asked, not wanting to fall into any traps.

"I'm serious. You used to take knuckle sandwiches from Johnny Fargo… I used to drive home alone every day after school, come home, try and talk with one of my dad's guys… Now we see each other just about every day."

"Yeah, for over two years I've had to see you every day. Don't you feel bad for me?"

Danny laughed, and I felt as if it had been months since a laugh of his wasn't sinister.

"I love you, Victor. You're like a brother to me. Remember that."

*****

We arrived to the manor in silence and Danny let me out near the front door so I could run all of the money to the Don. Blake pointed back to the office and I made my way with all of the envelopes. I walked up to the door and David was standing there to greet me.

"Everything go well with the bacon run?" David asked.

"Yeah, it's all good. I think we can still have turkey for Thanksgiving."

David seemed to be the only one I could joke around with anymore. Everyone else seemed to have their nose up my ass.

He flashed me a smile and opened the door to the Don's office without any warning to the two men inside.

Once I stepped in, I could feel the Don's eyes glare into me. After David shut the door behind me, The Doctor's eyes were next.

"Ah, Victor. Y'know," The Doctor said as he put the stethoscope around his neck, "I don't think I've ever had to treat you for any wounds."

"They're all internal," I replied.

"Pfft, looks like you got a Shakespearian fag in your gang," The Doctor said as he messed around in his doctor's bag.

I let him have his insult as the dazed and weakened Don looked to me. He wasn't dressed in his usual suit and tie. Instead, he wore a lush red robe with fur at the top. Underneath was a tank top to cover his chest.

"Is it all there?" the Don asked softly.

"Yes, it's all here," I replied as I set the envelopes on the desk.

"Good, good," he said as he wiped some sweat from his forehead. "You're dismissed."

And just like that, I was out of there. I heard that the Don feared of others getting sick, but he still had David by his side 24/7. I wasn't sure what to think of it all. It'd be a shame if he croaked right before he was thrown behind bars.

Walking through the hallway, I could feel the heat coming up from the vents below and I felt like taking off my jacket. As soon as I started towards the living room, Leo stopped me in the hallway.

"Whoa, where do you think you're going?"

His big hands were out, almost like he was ready to hug me. I thought about walking around him, but I knew that was a bad idea.

"Upstairs," I replied.

"What is there to do upstairs that you can't do right here?"

"Disrobe. But I'm sure you want to see it."

"Fuck off," Leo mumbled. "You got a light?"

I reached into my pocket and pulled out my Zippo. He had the cigarette ready in his mouth and I went ahead and lit it for him.

"Thanks. Say, why don't we get along?" Leo asked.

"Cause you're an asshole?"

"No, I think that's you. A stinky, lying asshole, to be exact."

*This Zippo can light more than your cigarette, baldy...*

"Okay, maybe that was too far," Leo retracted. "I know you think I'm out to get you, always thinking you're the rat."

"I thought there was no rat."

"Victor, c'mon, I thought you were smarter than that. Of course there's a rat. There's always a rat."

"Why's that?"

"Loyalty has gone to shit nowadays. Mobs used to only be made up of families. Now, look. We're just all of the leftovers of what could've been other empires. The Don trusts us, sure. But I have to give everyone a second look. I have to wonder whether or not everyone is on our side anymore. Because with the way things are going, someone has to be looking for a way out, you get what I'm saying? Someone is looking for forgiveness, for retribution, for a safe haven. Someone is looking to the cops for those things... haha!"

My blood was boiling. I felt like I knew exactly where this was going, but it took a hard left turn.

"I'm not saying it's even one of us."

"How does that make any sense?" I asked.

"We have other people in the gang, but they're not really in the gang, per se. They don't live here, they don't do any of the dirty work. But they're a part of us, unfortunately."

Without any more buildup, Leo finally said, "I think it's Peterson."

It was in that moment that I realized Leo had thought over what he had just said for a long time. I was always on the lookout for traps, no matter who I was talking to. Someone wanted to try and get me to spill the beans, but there was no way. I would never spill anything, only the blood of the others here at the manor if I had to.

So, very carefully, I replied, "Have you told the Don?"

He wasn't really expecting that answer, and I could see it in his face.

"No, I haven't. The Don's sick. Most of the time, he's not even in the mood to talk about business."

Leo let that thought stay in the air for a moment, before he asked, "So what do you think? Do you think it's Peterson? The Don would hate to hear that if it is...

wonder if Chief Ramzorin knows that he's been working for us this whole time."

*Bringing the Chief into this? You fucking bastard...*

I oppressed the voice inside and replied, "If that's who you think it is, I trust your decisions... even though you would never trust mine."

"Alright, then who do you think it is?"

I slightly ignored the question, but also offered more fuel to his flame.

"Have we heard anything on Jacob?"

Leo was disappointed in my lack of participation with his game. But, he reluctantly answered my question.

"No. Well, unless you didn't hear that he got away."

"What?" I asked.

"Yeah. When he was apprehended, they didn't put cuffs on him. So as soon as they went down the highway, I guess he jumped out of the fucking car and made a run for it."

"Are we going to look for him?"

"Well, the police are already looking for him. They got the dogs sniffing too. I'd say it's best if we don't get in the middle of it. My guess is, he's floating in the Detroit River by now."

Finally, I felt an opportunity to escape from Leo's presence and I made my way past him as he finished up his cigarette. I could feel his eyes on me as I entered the living room and went upstairs to my room. For some reason, I wasn't all that surprised that Jacob got away. He was quiet, but he was also crazy, and could snap in the blink of an eye. I knew he wouldn't come back to the gang, though. After what the New York soldiers did on the highway as they were leaving, I found out that wasn't too uncommon in gangs. In Don Ponchello's empire, being taken in by the police was a sign of weakness. It showed that you slipped up somehow, that you weren't as careful as you thought you were.

But with the information on Peterson, I felt like there was maybe more that could be done.

## Chapter Sixty Six
### Thursday, November 16th, 1978

They say when you're not sure about going through with something, you should sleep on it. Well...

Sometimes I wasn't so sure about keeping up this sting operation. Taking down the Don's crew was a daunting task, especially with Leo still around. But if Leo was taken down, or if it was even attempted, I knew everything would go to shit real fast.

I tried to think of someone else to take down, but I just couldn't. Besides my lack of sleep, my head also hurt from running through different scenarios and such. Last night was another sleepless night, filled with tossing and turning. I wondered about Jacob as well. I actually started to worry about him, almost like a parent does with their children even after they grow. When I first met him, he was so quiet and hungry for attention. The Jacob on the loose was a completely different person, however, and I tried to remind myself of that. But, it wasn't working. A thought kept floating around in my head, saying that continuing this partnership with the Chief was going to get me killed, one way or the other.

The Chief and I decided to meet up on the southern edge of town, which was now under a crazy amount of police surveillance. After Jacob and Danny robbing the pawnshop, and then Danny and I beating the owner just yesterday, fear was at an all-time high in the community.

I knew that if one of the Don's men found me out here, they'd try to attack immediately to make sure I didn't say a single word. And if they didn't attack immediately, oh well. I felt safer in the presence of Chief Ramzorin than I did before I put myself in this mess.

I walked into the unpopulated library and made my way to the other side. Outside, the sun was finally shining so brightly that my eyes couldn't adjust very well to the dimly lit scenery of books and dust. Chief Ramzorin and I decided to meet in the Western Non-Fiction section in hopes that we would not be bothered.

The front librarian greeted me as I walked in, but I ignored her. I wasn't in the mood for small talk anymore.

I spotted the Chief holding a book that I felt I had seen before. It looked like one my dad read a long time ago, before he became a stupid drunken mess. If I remembered correctly, it was about an outlaw that was believed to still be alive to this day; an outlaw who killed his way out of the Wild West and ended up slowing down in the Easy East. When the book first came out in the early sixties, it was probably quite believable. But now, almost twenty years later, the man would have to be resting quietly in the triple digits.

The Chief flipped through the book and I started making my way over to him.

"This isn't the easiest library to find," he said as I walked up to him.

"That's exactly what I hope the Don's men are thinking, too."

He closed the book and turned to me. Instead of putting it back on the shelf, he tucked it under his arm and said, "Now, you always make sure to check if you're being followed, correct?"

"Yes, I'm not stupid," I said like an annoyed little kid.

"Alright, Victor, calm down. Let's go have a seat over there."

We stepped out of the forgotten section of books and stepped over to a table and some chairs. Next to the table and chairs was an even darker hallway that led to a unisex bathroom. Instead of looking at this place as a sanctuary of stories and literature, this library was once a spot the gang considered selling drugs in, but the bathroom was too small and noticeable for two people to go into. Plus, the increase in crime around this area prompted us to look elsewhere. Now, with the pawnshop incidents and the busts so far, this location was out of the question. It was just another reason I felt safer meeting here.

The Chief and I sat down and silently scooted our small boxy chairs on the flat and faded carpet. Everything in this place had seen better days. Even the bookshelves looked worn. I knew Chief Ramzorin flipped through the book to check if anyone stuck gum in it. Providentially, they hadn't.

"You're actually going to get that book?" I asked, always unsure how to start our conversations.

"Yeah, I mean, it sounds interesting enough," he responded as he gave it a last look over.

I let him believe whatever he wanted to and I took another look around the library.

"I know I wasn't followed, but I thought I'd take another glance around before I start in."

"Can't be too careful."

I had made a decision in my mind, but I wasn't sure how to vocalize it. It had bothered me all night. So finally, I decided to spit it out.

"I don't think I want to do this anymore, Chief."

If we were at the coffee shop again and he had just taken a sip, it would've been all over me. His eyes darkened and he leaned in toward me.

"What do you mean? Do you really think you can just walk away at this point?"

"If you let me," I responded.

"You've got to be kidding me right now, Victor. Have you lost your head? My job is on the line right now enough as it is. Sure, I know you don't want to testify and that we may not have a real solid piece of evidence so far, but you're really about to break my back... I'm already bending too far backwards for you. You know how bad that makes me look, when I tell my men about a bust they can pull off but I can't tell them how I figured out that information? Do you know how obscure that really looks to everyone? Because I don't think you do. If I let you walk away and they found out that we had been talking all this time and that I was told everything about them... You're putting everything I have on the line, Victor."

"I'm not trying to fuck you over, I just don't see how this can continue."

"Why not? We still have plenty of people we can take down."

"Yeah, we do."

"What's wrong, Victor? What's changed your mind? Is the Don on to you?"

"I wouldn't even be here right now if that was the case."

The Chief cringed before he said, "What is it, then? I told you, I can guarantee a full pardon."

"But if I got someone else to testify with me, what would they get?"

"I could only do a reduced sentence for the other person... Not a full pardon."

"See, that's what worries me," I said. I leaned back for a second and then leaned in to explain. "Even if I was to get Danny to testify, who is the only person I can think of to try and convince, it wouldn't matter. He's loyal to his father. He's loyal to the gang now. If I was seen as a traitor, he'd kill me, before or after his prison time."

"Are you sure there's no one else you can convince? Not even the maid or mechanic?"

"They'd never betray the Don. Ponchello basically hired them when no one else would. Gave them a sustainable income and living."

"Shit."

"I just don't feel safe either, Chief... Leo was really grilling me just yesterday about the possibility of there being a rat."

The Chief gave me an odd look before he asked, "Well, if he thinks it's you, then why would he talk to you about it?"

"He was trying to lead me into a trap. They all are."

"Victor, quiet down..."

My last sentence had echoed a little more than I wanted it to. I tried to take a casual look around, and I saw that the kids who may have been looking at me before were now going back to their studies.

*My, my, you don't want everyone knowing you're crazy...*

My face was hot. My hands were shaking. I was slowly losing control. Chief Ramzorin knew something had to be done, so he grabbed my hands and said, "Look at me, Victor."

My eyes darted up to the Chief's lonesome but yet soothing eyes. With a tough edge to his voice, he said, "You're safe here with me. And the sooner we can get you out of the gang with those men in prison, the safer you'll be."

I closed my eyes, took a deep breath and shook my head.

"Okay. Okay, okay, okay..."

Chief Ramzorin slowly took his hands away from mine and said, "Now, as I'm sure you know, Jacob got away."

"Well, that was one of the things Leo and I talked about yesterday, which is when I knew he was trying to lay a trap. He was trying to get me to crack under pressure."

"How is he trying to do that?"

"First, he was trying to get me to say that I'm the rat, but once I kept my cool, he ended up saying who he thinks the rat is."

"Okay? And, who would that be?"

This was another moment where I was happy Chief Ramzorin wasn't drinking coffee.

"Peterson."

He looked confused, as if I was trying to bait him into a trap.

"Peterson? My Peterson? The cop?"

"Yes, Officer Peterson."

"He's actually a Corporal now... which makes your claim sicken me more."

"It's not my claim, it's Leo's."

"Still," Chief Ramzorin said, and he ran his hands across his face with a sigh.

"I'll be honest, I've seen him talking to some of our men on the streets, but I never thought he was a part of anything."

"So there was no mentioning of Peterson's involvement until yesterday?"

"No. There was always talk of an inside man, but Leo finally said who it was yesterday, with none of the others Kids knowing about it."

"And he wants us to act on that to see if you're the rat."

I nodded.

Chief Ramzorin seemed to mimic what I did earlier by closing his eyes, taking a deep breath and thinking everything over. I never thought of Peterson as being a bad guy, but we all have a dark side. Some just expose theirs more than others.

"I just can't believe what I'm seeing and hearing nowadays," Chief Ramzorin started. "It's sickening, really. I was just a Lieutenant when you were born, Victor. Never thought I'd have to dig you out of trouble like this. I thought we would take down the troublemakers together."

Tired of disappointing the Chief and feeling like a pansy, I said, "That's what we're doing now, Chief. We are going to take them down. You and me."

The Chief cracked a brief smile and said, "Your enthusiasm seems forced, but I'll go along with it."

"No, I mean it. We will get the evidence we need and take them down."

I started to get out of the chair as my mind raced, but Chief Ramzorin wanted me to stay put.

"Where are you going, Victor? We haven't agreed to the next course of action?"

"I'm going to have to do it alone," I replied to the Chief as I walked out. "I'll keep in touch though, don't worry."

And as I walked out, I felt as if I heard him say, "Too late."

# Chapter Sixty Seven
## Friday, November 17th, 1978
## 8 PM

My idea that wasn't to be shared with Chief Ramzorin wasn't complicated or anything like that. It was just better for me to do it alone. No cops, no big scenes, or even little scenes. Just me and Peterson, head-to-head.

I remembered as I talked to the Chief that Peterson liked to gamble on Friday nights at one of the Don's underground rings, the one that didn't fuck everyone over in their winnings. Only two were operational anymore, one for lower income players and one for medium to higher income players. Peterson liked to play the largest stakes possible, and I didn't blame him. That always brought in more thrills and more women, but also bigger losses.

I hadn't been gambling in a long time. Honestly, I wasn't all that good anymore. My confidence in playing had diminished. Peterson loved to play Texas Hold'em with a man named Nelly Worchester. Once upon a time, the Don got aggravated and accused them of setting up the games for failure and having one walk away with all the money. But, they were both just very skilled card players, and they didn't split any earnings at the end of the night.

As soon as Danny got home from whatever he was doing, I asked him if he wanted to go out to the high stakes ring.

Danny grinned as he still took off his coat. "Feel like losing some money tonight?"

"Nah, Nelly and Peterson are going to be there and I wanna see if I can beat them."

"So the answer to my question should've been yes," Danny replied as he started putting his coat back on. I stood up and started walking over to him. "But, I'd appreciate it if you drove."

"Oh I will. I know how much you love to knock back the cocktails."

Danny gave me a friendly punch in the arm and we made our way out to my Bel Air. Before I could get in, Danny hopped into the passenger seat and was all ready to go. I strapped myself in and turned on my car. The radio came on and "Peg" by Steely Dan started playing as we headed down the manor. Danny signaled Scott with his headlights so he'd open the gate.

Once we made it out onto the highway, Danny started up a small conversation.

"How much are you bringing, Victor?"

"I have five-hundred in my wallet."

"Five-hundred dollars!?"

"What else would I keep in my wallet?"

"I don't know, maybe a reminder that says you don't need to spend everything you have."

I laughed at that as the song came to the end. The next song came on, but I couldn't recognize it. Sounded like one of the Gibb's was singing, though.

"I have five-hundred as well, but I think I'll only spend a hundred."

"That's a good idea."

"Oh yeah, and if you're playing against Peterson and Nelly, you'll need five-hundred. Hahaha!"

I didn't really care about losing my money. I just wanted to make sure I could talk to Peterson and see what he says about his life in this world. Otherwise, Leo was just talking out of his ass.

We pulled up to the Chinese restaurant that housed our gambling ring in its basement. Danny seemed excited as he hopped out and made his way around back, but I took my time to lock the car and make sure our windows were up all the way. My pistol stirred in the small of my back, as if it was excited. I kept my hands away from it and made my way down with Danny.

The entrance to the ring was not a flattering one. It resembled the door to a storm shelter and was usually covered in some trash. There was a way into the ring by going inside the restaurant as well, but that was for the members we wanted to keep an eye on. This entrance was for anyone wanting to sneak in, or just not wanting to take the normal way.

Danny flipped the door open and it slammed to the right of us, exposing a well-lit smoky atmosphere that we descended into. Danny always let me go first so he could pull the door closed, which he did after we stepped into the creaky musky stairwell.

"Go on, Victor. Don't want to breathe in the asbestos for too long."

I stepped down to see one of the guards standing at the end of the entrance. He gave us a nod and we proceeded into the ring.

The gambling area was about nine-hundred to a thousand square feet of tacky red and yellow carpet. It made sure to keep your eyes up and looking for the next table to play at. On the far side near the normal entrance was the cash-out booth. That was the best place to get your chips, for the Don even let people trade their valuables for chips. A lot of Jordan and Leo's watches were purchased from the cash-out booth, and it made the business run a lot easier. Of course, the chips handed out were slightly lesser in value that the item given, and once you were at a table, cash or chips only. The other thing that was different about our ring was we offered slot machines. They were some of the most unforgiving, however, and most of them were just there to waste electricity. The slots were all across the walls while the tables were in the middle of the playing area. The games included roulette, baccarat, poker, and blackjack. The max bet on the blackjack table was one hundred and fifty bucks. If you had that kind of money for each hand, you may come out a rich man.

Completely diagonal of the cash out booth was the bar. That's where the cocktail waitresses would serve the free booze, and only get paid about fifteen a day plus tips. The Don used to have several waitresses employed, but after all of the other cuts he had to make, most of the waitresses had to go as well.

I didn't really care to learn their names, but they were very attractive women. If I remembered right, the Ballz had recruited them when he was still alive. Now he was blown to a million pieces, which wasn't all that unsettling to me.

"Alright, which table first?" Danny asked.

I looked to the poker tables and tried to find Nelly, but I didn't see him. Usually, if I could find Nelly, I could find Peterson, but that method wasn't working out this time around.

"Well, I told you I wanted to play against Peterson but I can't find him."

"Is that him at the blackjack table?"

It sounded odd when Danny first said that, but lo and behold, there was Peterson. His hair was greasy and curled but short, and he wore black dress pants with a thin blazer, a white button up that was exposing his chest, and a faded bronze wedding ring. I'd heard a rumor of his divorce, but he still wore the ring with little pride. His face was beaten down and angry looking as he leaned back in his high chair and watched the cards dance on the table to their next partner. As he lit up another cigarette, I saw there was another seat open at the table and it was on the opposite end to where we could talk to each other at a distance.

Now was my chance. I left Danny alone and walked up to the empty seat with as normal of a demeanor as I could exert. Once I sat down, the dealer was preparing a new deck of cards to be dealt. It was the perfect time for me to throw down my Benjamin and show that I was game.

Peterson's head tilted back slowly as the smoke flowed from his cigarette. The other people I sat by were absolute scum. They smelled badly, reeking of body odor. All they did was work out in the fields all day to come blow it all every Friday night. Most of them had families, but they didn't care. They lived in broken homes that would never be mended. It made me wonder if my father ever came out here.

"Little Victor, is that you?"

One of the men at the table laughed as Peterson stared me down from his side of the table.

"Yeah, it's me. Still losing, Peterson?"

"Hah, I'm losing something. Not sure if it's my money, or my marbles."

"I don't see any marbles on this table," I replied.

"Exchanging a hundred!" the female dealer called out as she lifted the bill to the camera above.

Once the money was tucked away in a lockbox, the dealer gave me mostly chips of ten, but finished off with chips in increments of five. Once I received my chips, the dealer loaded the new cards into the dispensary and made sure they were in there tightly.

"Antes and bets, antes and bets," she said twice in the same tone as before.

"Now remember, Victor," Peterson said to me in a creepy tone, "we're on the same team here."

I wondered how many he had knocked back so far. If he was already this close to saying something, I needed him to drink more. If Peterson was spilling information to both sides, or even just to the Don, he'd be trapped. There'd be no good way to get out of his situation if I was to turn him in. He was my only possible ally in my mind, and I was his only savior, especially for the sake of his daughter back home.

"I know, don't worry," I said, and I turned to see Danny talking to one of the cocktail waitresses.

While Danny continued with the innuendo towards the waitress, I watched as the dealer yanked the first card out for Peterson and then proceeded down the table to me.

"Aces are high and low," the fat lowlife next to me said before belching.

"I know how to play," I replied.

"Alright, 'Little Victor'."

There was a small laugh around the table and I stood content. The card facing the ceiling that the dealer had was a five. That meant the most she could have was sixteen, which is where she had to stop hitting. As I had said before, I knew how to play, and I was ready to play.

Since Nelly was gone, the other men played like amateurs. They were way too cocky. The table shuffled with different men trying their best, but Peterson and I were the only ones winning every other hand or so. After about an hour of playing, this man insisted he had to hit on seventeen. We all told him not to, but it's hard to stop a man with such determination.

"Twenty-seven, bust," she said with glee as she pulled his chips away.

The man seemed upset and surprised as he stood up and I noticed those were his last chips.

*What a fat fuck... should've used his money to buy himself a cheeseburger instead.*

Now it was my turn, again. I wondered if I should even waste the time or money to double down now that the fat slob had taken my card. I looked at Peterson, who seemed to still be smiling.

"That would've been a good play, Little Victor. Now, I'm not so sure."

"If I make the right move, will you stop calling me that?"

"Sure. I'd like to see you dig yourself out of this one."

With Peterson's encouraging words entangled with his cigarette smoke, I put down another five and said, "I'm still doubling down."

Peterson laughed and said, "This ain't a competition."

But I wasn't surprised when the dealer threw a seven my way and said, "Eighteen."

I waved my hand to show I was done and she nodded as she flipped her card up and said, "Dealer has, fifteen, twenty-five, bust."

"All right, Victor!" Peterson said with a lame clap.

The dealer paid me what was owed and I pulled my chips over to me. Peterson's eyes kept staring at me and I wondered how to converse with him. I decided to wait a few more games before I tried to talk to him. I won two more times, lost once, and then won. He won the same amount, but in a different order that I can't remember. And just as I started wondering who would talk first, to my liking, he started.

"How did you learn to play like that?" Peterson asked. "Or was it just luck?"

"Isn't that all blackjack is?" I asked as I set up my next bet.

"I suppose. In poker, you just need to be a good liar."

"Where's Nelly?" I asked.

"He's sick. Said he caught a fever out there in the cold today. It was pretty brisk, wasn't it?"

"It has been the last few days."

"I guess it has," Peterson said as he requested to stay. "How's your life, Victor?"

"Interesting," I said as I asked for a card. I was up to twenty and I told the dealer I'd stay. The dealer flipped her cards and beat us both out with twenty-one.

"Gah, dammit. Oh well, being Corporal sure makes a difference in the pay."

"How is the life of a cop?" I asked.

"I'd figure you know, by talking to the Chief."

Maybe my deceptive skills were no match to Peterson's slimy persona. I didn't let him know that his words hit me wrong as I replied, "Eh, we're just good friends, the Chief and I. We go way back. The Don knows that."

"Is that so?"

"Yeah, unlike how the Chief doesn't know anything about your doings."

Peterson finished up his cigarette with a sly smile and shook his head. I could tell I was getting to him. I was starting to rethink doing this here, but it made sense. The Don's men were around, he couldn't hurt me.

"Oh, Victor. You and I aren't so different."

"I was kind of thinking the same thing."

Peterson's face fell to a place of darkness and despair as he tried to signal the Lord above for help.

"Like me, you're drinking clean water out of a stained glass, my friend. It helps keep you going, but there's still something wrong with it; something that may bite you later on. You have no idea what bacteria or parasite you might be hosting now."

"It doesn't have to be that way," I replied, trying to signal a way out for the both of us.

Peterson's sorrowed expression changed to fear in a flash as we heard a loud bang from the main entrance above. I knew it wasn't a gunshot; I figured it was the door itself as Leo, Jordan, and Roy came down the steps in a hurry. I watched as they approached me and Peterson. Leo spoke first.

"Victor, Mika, step away from the table. Danny, come over here. Everyone else needs to scram."

The dealer and I knew better than to question Leo, but Peterson didn't.

"Fellas, what's this all about?"

"Your days are over," Leo said bluntly as the last people left the underground ring.

"Oh yeah? Why's that?"

"What? You think we wouldn't catch on? You think you're the only man we have inside the force?"

Leo's statement was unsettling to me, since I thought Peterson was the only man in the force.

"You didn't trust me, baldy?" Peterson asked with almost a smile.

"Enough bullshit," Roy stated as he lifted up his handgun. "You sold out the information on the New York soldier's departure, the underground rings, and Jacob!"

I feared what Peterson would say next, but I don't think he was drunk enough to tell the truth, or what he thought was the truth.

"You really think I'd do that? I've been with you guys since you came out here to this shithole!"

"So why'd you do it then? Were you tired of it? Tired of getting free money for the info we needed?"

"You guys are crazy, you know that? Organized crime my-"

The next thing I knew, Roy pounced on Peterson, pushed his head onto the table and fired one round that went in one ear and not very cleanly out the other. I shuttered as Roy breathed heavily over Peterson's dead body. I had no feeling or emotions whatsoever, just an unsettling stillness inside.

"Roy, we weren't supposed to do it here!" Leo shouted. "That table is ruined now."

Roy leaned back and let go of Peterson's neck. The body that once housed Peterson's soul slumped to the ground and I glanced to see the playing cards riddled in dirty blood.

"He was reaching for his gun... I saw him reaching."

Leo nodded and said, "Yeah, I know... it had to be done."

*Did it? Why did they think Peterson was the rat?*

*You're fucked now, Victor. Really fucked. Peterson was your last hope, and now... well, look at him.*

"Victor! Are you listening?"

I jerked up to see Leo and the others staring at me.

"Sorry," I said as I patted the side of my head, "my ears were ringing."

"You, Danny, and Roy need to head to the manor, now. The boss has something to discuss. Something important. I wouldn't keep him waiting much longer."

After Leo made the command, he walked over to Peterson's body and Jordan started to unravel a trash bag. Roy looked to us with his wild eyes and said, "Let's go."

## Chapter Sixty Eight

The little voice inside was troubling me. There wasn't any conversation between me and Danny on the ride to the manor, but there was plenty going on in my mind.

*They just killed him. Didn't even present any proof or nothing. Is that the way you want to die, Victor? A gun pushed into your ear like some kind of mechanical Q-tip?*

The night lights were dashing across my windshield as I made my way down the highway, trying to ignore the voice. Danny was just staring ahead, still quiet. I feel like he was also jarred by Peterson's death.

*There's no hope now. Who the hell am I supposed to take down next, or try to convince to be on my side?* I wondered.

Danny would never agree to it. I knew he wouldn't. Especially when he finally started talking as we hauled ass.

"Peterson had it coming to him. You fuck with us, you screw us over, you're done."

"You have no doubt of what he was doing?" I asked.

"Victor, we don't kill cops for nothing. That's a big deal. It's a big mess to clean up, even with the dirty ones. I'm just glad they don't still think it's you, like Leo always says."

I had to mentally take a step back for a second, and move back into the Victor that I appeared to be to Danny.

"Yeah, I hate how he's always saying it's me."

"Me too. Kinda pisses me off, but hey, I'm not gonna say anything to him."

The car burned across the front entrance and we parked out by the front door instead of pulling the car into the garage. It felt strange, until I thought about how serious Leo was when he said we needed to get back to the manor. What did the Don have in mind?

I wasn't putting it past me that the Don may want to go ahead and go to war with the police. After Jacob was apprehended, the Don fell in to despair. The Don was so desperate at this point, I really couldn't think of anything that didn't sound ridiculous. Tandelli was a threat, so we killed him. Next was Modellini, who the Don had us Kids take care of; then Jackson Burose and his followers/family. Now, our threat was the local law enforcement, due to my involvement with them. At this point, I believed the Don would go to war against a God if he felt the need to; someone just needed to set up the battlefield.

I followed behind Danny into the manor, as I had many times before. I really didn't know what to expect or prepare for. The Don wanted to do something big, I knew that much. This meeting was important enough to leave two of the head guys behind at the casino to clean up the highly illegal mess.

As I was about to close the front door, Roy stepped in and nodded for me to go ahead. He was shaking, afraid of what was to come. I wondered if Leo had already given him a briefing of sorts, but I decided not to ask.

Entering the Don's office at David's request, I could feel the Don's growing sickness ease out of the room and scatter into the hallway. It felt as if a humidifier had been left on too long. Usually, the office was very dull and serious, but this time, Don Ponchello still wore a dark red robe with fur stitched down the inside. His face was growing paler, and I could sense that his sickness was not an easy one to overcome, though none of us knew what it was.

After we stepped in and gave the room a moment to breathe, David closed the door behind us and Roy scooted to the side of the Don's desk as we stood before it.

"Victor and Danny, my sons."

His opening line creeped me out, but I tried to bear through it.

"I don't feel as if we've had a good talk in awhile, but now's a better time than any. I don't think it's necessary for me to say, but things are bad, boys. We have taken a gross and tremendous downturn in our income. It forced me to sell the casinos in Vegas, Phil and Michelle were let go earlier this morning, and my ability to bribe officials has become less and less possible. Tell you the truth, Jacob's gig out on the streets was making us quite a bit of money, if you can wrap your mind around that. But after he was taken in, well…"

The Don began coughing into a worn handkerchief and we waited for him to finish.

"Heh! Excuse me. Anyway, I'm not worried that we will be able to recover. In fact, I have found an investment opportunity that sounds very promising, but they just need us to give them some cash to make the investment. The money I made selling the casinos is being saved as pension money for my men, otherwise I would go ahead and use that. Now, I've been told that Peterson was killed at the Chinese casino, is that correct?"

"Yes, Don," Roy responded.

"At your slippery hands?"

"… Yes, Don."

"I heard he was reaching for his gun, is that correct?"

The Don looked to Danny and me for clarity. I knew I wasn't the right choice for any clarification at this time.

"Yes, that's right," Danny said.

"Don't worry, you won't get Roy in any trouble, I just needed to know. We had to get rid of Peterson for this next job, but I was hoping we could do it a little cleaner."

*The next job? Ooo, how fun. Maybe he'll have you burn down an orphanage... you know he wouldn't be opposed if the orphanage housed the sons of Tandelli or Jackson.*

The Don's next sentences almost sounded like a high school gossip rushing up to the most popular lunch table.

"Was Peterson surprised? Did he know we were going to take him away?"

"I don't think so; he and Victor were just playing blackjack against the dealer."

I was worried the Don would think too much of that sentence, but he didn't. I knew Leo would if he was here, even after being told that Peterson was the snitch.

"Haha, I can't even image the look on that slimy fuck's face."

Danny laughed with his father for a brief moment. It was their new way of bonding, to see who had less of a heart.

"Anyway, we creamed Peterson for this next job, which is a big one. Probably the biggest one you Kids will ever be a part of."

The sickness I felt before as I entered the room had now moved to my stomach and didn't want to stay there, but it had to.

"Leo has reports that an armored vehicle is picking up tons of cash at the Federal Exchange Bank downtown this weekend that is to be moved Monday afternoon. Our plan is to do the heist while the money is being moved out of the vaults on Monday so we don't have to worry about any safe cracking nonsense. You Kids are the manpower on this heist, due to the fact that the police still don't know you all are a part of my syndicate."

"What are we going to do with the armored guards who are taking the money out?" I asked.

"You're going to kill them."

The Don's statement was spoken with no feeling, but he elaborated as he said, "Anyone with a gun or anyone who is a part of security at that bank, you kill them. We can't have any threats in there. All the other civilians... just make sure they hit the ground and put their hands behind their heads. I would have you and Charlie check the bathrooms, while Blake and Danny secure the civilians and make sure no one does anything stupid."

*You're the ones doing something stupid. This is suicide, don't you see, Victor? It's not that the*

*Don's losing his mind. That process started years ago. Now it's just completely gone.*

"Roy will be our getaway driver and Jordan will be listening to the police radio and act as a backup if needed. Leo will show you your weapons here shortly. I told them not to dedicate too much time to the disposal of Peterson's body."

*Don't dedicate too much time to the disposal of Peterson's body?* I wondered.

*He's being careless, Victor. Can't you see? Get out of here, NOW!*

"After you take their bags of money, you'll exit the bank and meet Roy in an alleyway about two blocks away. That should throw off the police's pursuit. I'll be honest, this won't be easy. As soon as you leave the bank, be prepared for resistance. I trust you and Danny will inform the other Kids of the plan. Roy will explain the route to take also."

Suddenly, the Don broke out into a major coughing fit that sounded like he was trying to cough up a train. Danny's excited face fell slightly and I even took a step back. Once the Don finished, he waved his arms around and said, "Don't worry, it's just a cold or something... That's what the Doctor told me. But, I think it's about time I headed upstairs and got some rest."

I glanced at the clock above his desk and saw it was nearing eleven PM. The Don made his way past us and David led him out of the room. The three of us followed them out and headed to the basement. Roy still looked frightened and fidgety, but to my surprise, Danny appeared to be as excited as ever.

"Damn, Victor! This is going to be like a Wild West gig or something! Go in guns blazing and leave with the cash! Hah!"

Like a parent, I wanted to scold Danny for what he was saying. How could this be exciting to him? Killing innocent people? I was starting to believe that Danny and his father weren't only financially bankrupt, but morally as well.

I didn't have to do the scolding, though.

"I hope you are all taking this seriously," Leo said as he walked down the hallway to take us to the basement.

"Yeah, but I've never pulled off a heist like this! My dad used to talk about these kinds of jobs a long time ago, but I never got to experience it myself until now."

"Well, times are different now," Leo said, seeming as thrilled about the plan as Roy and I were. "They used to cover their faces back then, but that was for the sketch artists. Now you got cameras in these banks and major security. That's why we gotta give you Kids armor piercing rounds."

"Armor piercing?" I asked.

"Yeah," Roy said, "These security guys will have body armor under their white dress shirts, so you all won't have to worry about getting headshots if you have the armor piercing rounds."

"Roy's right. This is military grade stuff you'll be dealing with, so we don't need you Kids dicking around with it."

Once we got to the bottom of the basement, Leo opened up a small lock box and we set our eyes on some small submachine guns.

"These are Mac-10s. I had them fine-tuned for accuracy, and their high rate of fire will scare anyone into not messing with you. They're forty-five caliber and we have the armor piercing rounds in them and ready to go. I'd suggest loading up two or three extra mags, because these fire off quick. They'll be used for the primary assault on the bank. Afterwards, we'll have you use M16s with armor piercing rounds for the police officers who may roll up. These will put a stop to their engines or hearts real quick, trust me. Under the Mac-10s are some bulletproof vests. You Kids will need these, but I don't think Roy or Jordan will need them very badly."

"Is Roy going to drop us off and pick us up?" I asked.

"No," Leo said plainly, which seemed to relieve Roy. "You Kids will be taking a van and leaving it behind. If you have enough time, try and set it on fire or something. I have a map all drawn up over there with your route of escape, but Roy will be hiding in an alleyway ready to get you guys and leave. Jordan will be in another car over on this side of town, just in case things really go wrong."

"This ain't my first time as a getaway driver, so don't worry too much," Roy said, even though he seemed to be the one who needed to chill out.

"The hardest parts are going to be the initial attack and keeping the civilians calm. They can be a real pain in the ass, and the minute some guy decides to play hero, you put a bullet through his head. We're not fucking around with anyone trying to be Clark Kent, eh?"

Leo's comment made Danny laugh, but I wondered if Superman could fly me out of here.

"Okay, now I know it's late, but you Kids like to stay up anyway, so how about you practice shooting a little before you go to bed, and then I expect you to tell Charlie and Blake about the plan and get them prepared. This won't be a walk in the park, but I know we can pull it off."

Danny picked up a Mac-10 and walked over to the range. I stared at the Mac-10 for a long time. As I stared, the screams of innocent men and women ran rampant in my mind and the only way I could silence them was to finally load the Mac-10 and start unloading on the targets.

# Chapter Sixty Nine

On Saturday morning, Danny and I revealed the plan to Charlie and Blake. Blake, like Danny was before, seemed very excited about the plan. Danny started getting excited about it again as soon as Blake expressed his enthusiasm, but Charlie was more on the indifferent side. I was completely against it, but it didn't matter. If I started voicing my feelings on it, everyone would turn against me. I think my lack of interest was expressed in my facial expressions, but it didn't matter. As long as I didn't vocalize it, no one would know. I hoped.

The fear of the whole thing going south just kept coming to my mind. I worried about my own life more than anyone else's. I also worried that the idea of the heist would make Chief Ramzorin go ballistic, or that he would make sure to beef up security and police forces there. It was one bust that I didn't think I could tell him about. It was too dangerous, especially since we'd all be wearing black ski masks. There'd be no way to tell us apart.

"Also," Leo said, late in the day on Saturday, "don't call each other by your first names or last names. Make up codenames."

After little discussion of the matter, we decided to go with animals. Danny would go by "Duck", Charlie came up with "Camel", Blake insisted on the name "Anaconda", and I decided on "Velociraptor" or "Velo" for short.

"What about Vulture?" Danny asked, and then they all started laughing.

*They all think this is a joke. They all think it's a game of cops and robbers. Well, it is. But the pop guns are real, and some won't be able to stand in the end.*

It was at that point that I thought Chief Ramzorin may be able to help me. If the Kids didn't take this seriously, and we could get the cops to take some of us in peacefully, we could talk some sense into them and convince them into being witnesses. I knew Danny still wouldn't budge, but maybe I could convince Charlie since he seemed to be indifferent on the entire heist anyway.

*****

It was Sunday after lunch when I decided to leave the manor and meet with the Chief. The Chief invited me to a bar, saying it wasn't open for business and the bartender would let us talk there alone. I agreed, but it seemed a little strange. We usually went to a public place with other vehicles and other people, but I decided not to think too much of it as I made my way there.

The bar was on the far eastern edge of town where I could look out and see Belle Isle sitting in the middle of the Detroit River. I had never really been over there before, but I never had a reason to go. Supposedly there were some family-friendly activities over there, but I wasn't a part of that lifestyle anymore. Any activity I was a part of required a gun or dirty money.

I stepped out onto the quiet street and looked ahead at the bar. It was a pretty basic bar, with neon advertisements on both sides of a dark blue door. To the side of it was a black sedan that I had never seen before, but I figured it was the owner's.

As I walked up to the bar, the blue door clicked and swung open. In the doorway was Chief Ramzorin, all dressed up in his uniform.

"Come on in, Victor."

I hurried in and the Chief closed the door behind me. My eyes began to adjust from the bright outside light to the murky indoor lighting. Once they did, I looked around the bar to see that no one else was here. It made me feel safer as the Chief sat down in a booth next to the center of the bar. I took a seat before him, and our eyes slowly made a connection.

"What brings us together today, Victor?"

"Well, I'm sure by now you know that Peterson was killed."

"Yes," Chief Ramzorin said with a large sigh. "I put two and two together."

"But, it was so weird. He was cornered by the Don's men, who accused him of being the one who has spilled the beans on the last few operations, and he didn't deny any of the accusations."

"That was actually my doing, Victor."

I stared at the Chief for a second as I tried to process what he said. When it still wouldn't process, I asked, "What? How?"

"There was a man in the same department as Peterson, named Officer O'Connell, who I feared was also being bribed and conditioned under the Don's orders. I called him into my office personally and told him what I thought about Peterson, but no one else in the force ever learned what he said."

"Oh, wow," I said blankly. "That was a good idea."

"Sort of. Last night, a few minutes before midnight, some necking teens found his body under some brush in a park. Said they could smell something foul, so the idiot boyfriend wanted to check it out."

"They found Peterson's body?" I asked.

"No, O'Connell's, the officer I told about Peterson."

I sat there for a second to try and process that as well. It wasn't making any sense, or I didn't want it to make sense.

"Who would've killed O'Connell?" I asked.

"Take a wild fucking guess," Chief Ramzorin spat.

My face started to heat up and my palms were sweating. Chief Ramzorin seemed to prepare himself for my outburst.

"Easy for you to say, asshole! You weren't the one who had to watch as they shot Peterson in the fucking head, and then all they cared about was the blackjack table getting dirty!"

"These are the kind of people you're working with, Victor. I've been trying to tell you this for two fucking years now and you still don't get it! I fear you still live in this fantasy world where Danny's your best bud and the Don helped you in life!"

"Y'know, I had some real good information to share, but I think I'll just hold on to it. I don't need your help or insults. I'm done here."

I slid myself out of the booth and started making my way to the front door. Unlike the other times I had walked away from Chief Ramzorin, he didn't even try to stop me.

But, a mysterious new voice did.

"I had a feeling you'd say that."

I stopped dead in my tracks. The voice seemed to come from directly behind me. I wondered if I should go ahead and pull my gun, or if I should turn and face whoever the man was first.

I decided to face the mystery man and I wasn't sure it helped my decision much.

He stood tall and lanky at about six-foot two-inches. His face was plain and creamy white with bold aviator sunglasses to conceal his eyes. His dirty blond hair was cut short, like someone coming out of the Marines. I could tell his finely tailored suit covered large muscles and that he wasn't someone to mess around with. Leo once said, "Your opponent will either be fat and strong, or skinny and fast." He seemed to be the best of both.

A smile spread across the asshole's face as he popped out a cigarette and continued staring me down. As he lit the cigarette, I knew that he could still have me dead in a mere second. It looked as if he and David Weston would be best friends, but I knew they weren't.

Even with all of that in mind, I started to rip out my gun from behind my back and point it at the man.

"No, Victor, *don't!*" Chief Ramzorin shouted.

"No, it's alright. Go ahead kid, shoot me and the Chief can take you where you belong."

He finished lighting his cigarette and then put his hands up to surrender. After taking his first puff, he pointed to his upper arm.

"What is that? A forty caliber? A forty-five? Yeah, lemme hold out my arm and you can put a bullet right here. That way it doesn't break my arm off."

I felt I knew the answer, but I panicked and asked Ramzorin anyway.

"Who is this guy?"

The man lowered his arms and pulled the cigarette away from his mouth. "Why don't you talk to me, Victor? You don't seem to be too happy with the Chief right now, anyway. Maybe we can be friends instead."

Chief Ramzorin said in a parental way, "Put your gun away right now, Victor."

"Yeah, otherwise I may have to take my gun out. And trust me, when I take my gun out, it never goes back into its holster feeling cold."

"What about mine?" I asked. "What makes you think I don't have the same rule?"

"Because you don't have a holster, duh."

The man's change from super serious to silly made me loosen up a little bit, or enough to where I knew my gun wasn't necessary. Just as the Chief was about to request me to put my gun away again, I tucked it away and raised my hands up to show I wasn't a threat anymore.

"Good. We can be civilized," the man said.

"So can you tell me who you are?" I asked.

"Maybe you should sit down first, and I'll grab you a towel if you think you may piss yourself."

His sarcasm oozed out of him like a hot tube of toothpaste that was stuck in your car too long on a hot summer day.

I did as he said and began to sit back down into the booth. He took another puff of his cigarette and I saw Chief Ramzorin stare at me with his sore eyes.

"To your Don and his other men, I'm their worst nightmare. But if you haven't figured that out yet, then I'll just spell it out for you: F. B. I."

My stomach churned and I almost gasped.

"You called in the FBI!?" I yelled at Chief Ramzorin.

"No, no, he didn't call me," he said as he walked over to our booth and stood at the end. "Y'see, my job title is kind of… nonexistent."

"To answer your question, this is Special Agent Darnell of the FBI," Chief Ramzorin cut in.

"Yeah, that's my name. Anyway, kid, Victor Carez, age twenty, working for Don

Ponchello, I'm usually a part of the Treasury Department or some kind of liaison of sorts, and as I was doing that work, we found some counterfeited bills down in Florida. You know where Florida is? It's a lot nicer than it is here, I'll tell you that. And you can't smell burning rubber there all the time, unless you're in the clubs. Point is, I found those bills, which really led to the casino in Vegas that the Don owned. Unfortunately, if you didn't catch that last part, I said, 'owned', meaning he doesn't own it anymore. Kinda bummed me out, and I didn't even know it was from the Don who resides out here, until I got an anonymous tip that there was some… interesting, and mildly threatening, activity out here in your little town, so I moseyed on over and met up with the Chief here to discuss what the fuck was going on."

"So what? You're here to take me in, make me talk, and grab someone else and get a case going?"

Special Agent Darnell made a face and said, "Oh, I mean, we can do that if you want? Is that what you want me to do? I don't mind putting you in prison where you'll get butt-fucked the rest of your life. From what it sounds like, you've already fucked Chief Ramzorin's ass enough."

"Simmer down," Chief Ramzorin warned as my face started to redden.

"Sure, Chief. But no, Victor, that's not what I'm here to do. Because I don't have a definitive title, I'm really more of a… I don't know what to call it exactly."

"An asshole?" I commented.

"Well, that too. But, I'm here to assist the Chief here in any way that I can or see fit. Basically, I hired myself to be his help, but I'm not allowed to do anything without his consent. So, as much as I would like to just wrap this whole thing up and send you and your buddies to jail, I'm afraid I can't until the Chief tells me in writing that I can. I know this little deal you two have going on, about the pardon and all, but we really need you to act, Victor. Use that thing inside your head. I got the same advice when I was your age, but it didn't resonate until I was in my late twenties. But, I hope we can convince you earlier on in your life."

"Convince me to do what, exactly?" I asked. "Am I not getting a pardon anymore?"

"I never said that. I'm saying that I need you to give us that last bit of evidence, that last bust that we need to get everything straightened out. You don't need to hold out anymore."

"I'm not holding out!" I shouted.

Darnell sighed.

"I find that hard to believe. I find it hard to believe that you don't have a single shred of evidence that you could provide for us. Or even a name. For instance, here's an easy one for you, Victor: Who killed Peterson? You claim to have been there; didn't you see who did it? Give me that guy's name, just his fucking name, and we can pick him up in a matter of minutes. Then I'll bust him around a little bit, make him feel safe, and get him to start talking."

"I... I can't do that," I said, not trusting Darnell at all. He was too cocky, too arrogant. I gave the Chief a look of disappointment and despair, but he reciprocated Darnell's views.

"Victor, how many more people have to die before you realize this needs to stop now?" the Chief asked.

"Yeah, Victor, I mean, the Don has to be running out of funds now. What's his next plan? Sell a new drug? Open a new club? Rob a bank?"

"You're right about the last one," I said slyly.

This made Chief Ramzorin and Special Agent Darnell perk up and pay attention. Darnell seemed to finally lose the tough guy attitude; he became a little more concerned and empathetic.

"Tell us about it, Victor. Tell us what's happening, when, where, how?" Darnell questioned.

"Wouldn't you like to know, Special Agent Darnell?" I asked, feeling powerful.

"Just call me Detective Darnell for now. I like the ring it has to it, plus I don't feel all that special yet."

"Victor, stop playing around and tell us what's going on?"

"We're hitting the Federal Exchange Bank downtown."

"When?" Darnell asked.

"Tomorrow."

"What time?"

"Not sure. Afternoon sometime."

"I need specifics, dammit."

"Look, that's all I know, okay?" I lied, not trusting Darnell for a second. "It was nice to meet you and all, but I gotta go."

I started walking away and Darnell decided to go back to his old methods.

"Ah, c'mon, Victor. Gimme a fucking break. I told you, you don't have to hold out anymore. Stop teasing me and give it all to me."

"You'd like that, wouldn't you?"

"Victor, stop."

Chief Ramzorin's command made me think twice before I opened that blue door to go back out into the fresh air.

I turned to the two men and said, "I gave you the info I know, do what you want with it."

And with that, I swung the door open and left the two men to bicker alone.

## Chapter Seventy
### The Heist
### Monday, November 20th, 1978

"Guns?"

"Check."

"Vests?"

"Check."

"Is the van all loaded up and ready?"

"Yes."

"Roy, are you ready to go?"

"Ready as I'll ever be."

"Jordan, you're listening on the radio?"

"Just for you."

Danny lowered the walkie-talkie and looked to me, Charlie, and Blake.

"All right, the heist is on. We should be there in about twenty minutes."

Danny lowered the radio and we all piled into the plain white GMC van. I had done this so many times that it was practically muscle memory at this point. First Tandelli, then Modellini, followed by Emmitt... and now I hoped this would be the last time.

We were all armed to the teeth with bulletproof vests, black combat clothing, combat boots, Mac-10s, M16s, and plenty of ammo. Our ski masks rested on top of our heads so our faces could breathe in the meantime before the heist.

I was nervous, to say the least. I felt like I hadn't slept for years. It was driving me crazy. Nothing made sense anymore. I even worried that Darnell and the Chief weren't going to do a damn thing about the heist. If they did, I just hoped they would capture me and Charlie alive. That was the plan in my mind, but I couldn't tell Darnell and the Chief about it. I didn't feel safe enough to. If Danny and Blake were killed, I'd take down Charlie and surrender ourselves to the police.

*Well done, Victor. You may have found a way out after all. One that may keep you alive.*

I had debated it in my mind all night last night. Kill Danny to take Charlie in. It made the most sense to me, but I hated to think about it too much.

*Oh, Victor, will you even be able to pull the trigger when the time comes?*

We rumbled down the highway and sped past all the other vehicles. Danny was driving as Blake sat in the front seat and Charlie sat in the back with me.

Charlie and I were both staring down at the ground, waiting for everything to unfold. Danny and Blake would mutter to each other every once in a while and have a laugh. They enjoyed the idea of this heist way too much. It sickened me.

"Alright, everyone, we're about halfway there; time to pull down your masks if you haven't already."

I pulled mine the rest of the way down, and so did Charlie. As we did, Blake said, "Yeah, you don't want to pull a Jacob!"

The reference to Jacob's downfall actually made Charlie laugh, but it struck a nerve with Danny.

"Hey, that's fucked up, man," Danny seethed.

"Sorry, Danny, but I was just saying."

"Yeah, well shut your fucking mouth."

Blake didn't dare speak again as we headed down the highway and Roy talked on the walkie.

"Okay, Kids, I'm right where I need to be. Remember, you're only going to have about two minutes to secure the cash and get out of there before the pigs come running to the trough."

"Yeah, yeah, don't worry."

Now we were downtown, and I could feel my hands start to moisten my gloves. The cold air outside was making the back of the van feel like a walk-in fridge. So now, my fingers were a bunch of frozen popsicles.

I felt better that way. Made me think that I may not have to fire my gun at anyone, because I physically couldn't.

We made our final left turn onto Madison Street and I could tell where the bank was from the times I had passed by it before.

This was it. No backing out. No running away.

We neared the bank, but I noticed that Danny wasn't exactly slowing the van down.

"Danny, we're coming up on it," I said.

"I know," he said, and then he glanced back at me in his black ski mask. "You remember how I said this was going to be like the Wild West?"

I didn't respond, but then he said, "Well, I decided to modernize that idea. Hold on."

I didn't have to wonder anymore as Danny pulled onto the sidewalk, gained speed, and pulled a hard right. The van, because of the basic laws of physics, crashed through the tinted glass doors and walls of the bank and sent glass everywhere. The van's front was demolished by the thresholds, and it caused the van to slowly roll to a stop.

"Stay down," Danny said, completely unphased by what had happened.

We stayed as low as we could and waited for whatever would happen next. Smoke started to rise from the front of the van and I could hear the customers outside of the van wondering what had happened. The consensus I heard was that they thought we were just some joyriding kids who accidentally crashed into a federal building, but little did they know of our real intentions. I didn't feel scared or anxious the entire time. I just felt numb.

"You gonna check it out, Jack?" I heard someone yell; sounded like security.

"Sure thing."

I could almost see a smile from Danny's face as we heard the jingling of keys coming up to his door. When the smile faded, Danny turned with his Mac-10 pointed to his side window and he whispered, "Get ready."

Charlie and I ducked by the back doors of the van, ready to pile out and start shooting. Blake prepared to swing his door open as well. We all seemed ready for what was to come, unlike anyone outside of the van.

The older gentleman, who was a part of security, stuck his head over the driver side window and in the next moment, it was gone. Danny fired a burst from his Mac-10 and then kicked the door open. Charlie and I piled out and I stood on the same side with Blake as we began firing at the three armored guards. They tried to take out their Glocks, but it was too late. Gunning them down was almost too easy.

Once Danny and Charlie finished on their side, all we could hear was the screaming of all the civilians and tellers in the bank.

"Everybody get down! I said 'get down' once already; don't make me say it again!" Danny yelled violently with saliva coming out of his mouth.

The screams started turning into whimpers as the men and women in the bank started to kiss the floor. On my side, I saw a woman get to the floor and tuck her child under her. As soon as Blake saw this, he said, "Hey lady, get your fucking hands on your head or I'll make your stupid kid an orphan."

"Anaconda, forget about it," I said, sticking to his stupid codename.

"Whatever, Velo."

"Hey, guys, up here!"

We met at the front of the van and Danny said, "Camel, Velo, check the bathrooms."

"Got it," I said as we made our way to the bathrooms on the far side of the lobby.

I started reloading my Mac-10 as Danny said, "Okay everyone, while my accomplices check the bathrooms, the rest of you need to just stay still and keep your hands on your heads. The cops will be here soon, so then you won't have anything to worry about. We'll only kill ya if you do something stupid. Like if you try to be a hero."

Charlie chose the ladies' bathroom and kicked the door open in the darkened hallway. I looked back in the plain, light brown bank and watched as Blake climbed onto the marble countertop and watched over the civilians from a higher ground.

Taking a deep breath with my Mac-10 ready, I kicked open the men's bathroom door and prepared for anything. I was lucky I did.

A security guard that just finished taking a leak fired at me twice and I fell back. As I did, I squeezed the trigger on my Mac-10 until it was completely empty. I watched as the unarmored guard was ripped apart and fell into a plastic stall that gave way. His blood was all over the bathroom and the door started to swing closed.

"Velo!"

I turned to see Danny running toward me but I waved him off.

"Stay there! I'm fine. He hit my vest!"

Charlie left the ladies' room and ran over to help me stand up. I could feel the bruising start to form on my chest, and when I reached down to push the bullets off my vest, I noticed the guard had aimed at my heart.

*Nice try, but it's gone. Don't know when it'll be back...*

I reloaded my Mac-10 and headed out into the lobby with the others.

Danny was back behind the counter grabbing two thick black duffle bags of money that were waiting to be picked up by the dead armored men. As he started stepping out, he said, "Velo, grab two of the bags from those dead guys right there. Camel, you grab that other one."

I stepped up to the dead armored men, grabbed their bags of money and swung them around behind me. They weighed about ten pounds each, and I knew we were making a really good heist.

Danny started to make his way out and found a fourth bag on the way. I looked to Charlie, who appeared to be as ready as I was to get the fuck out. Danny went ahead and ran over to me and Charlie, looked to Blake and said, "Hey, get that fourth bag, and then let's get out of here, Blake."

The slip of Blake's name caused him to start bitching.

"Hey, it's Anaconda, remember?"

Before he could say anymore, a stray bullet from across the bank slammed into Blake's head and sent him flying behind the counter. I heard a teller scream as I saw a man in casual clothing standing on the far left of the bank with a smoking gun.

"FBI, freeze!"

The man didn't even finish saying "freeze". Danny whipped around and fired upon him in an instant. The agent fell to his death and Danny started yelling, "We gotta move, now!"

Danny ran out first, then me, and then Charlie brought up the rear to make sure no one else jumped up. As we stepped outside into the blinding sun, I saw a stray police car making its way toward us with its sirens blaring.

"Switch to the M16s!" Danny yelled as he threw his Mac-10 to the ground.

Charlie did the same and readied his M16 at the police car. He fired short bursts as I threw my Mac-10 over my shoulder and readied my M16 as well.

"Roy, we're on our way!" Danny yelled into the walkie.

Charlie's fire upon the police car caused it to fly into the phone booth across the street. I knew the driver was dead, and the passenger in the police car was probably too wounded to do anything to us. Danny ran out to the right of the bank and we made our way to where the map said Roy would be.

"I'm here waiting," Roy said shakily.

"Besides that car that one of you just fired on, there're two more cruisers coming your way," Jordan said.

I heard the screams as people saw us running down the sidewalk to the other side of the street. We were a virus to these people, and they were trying to escape any way they could. Danny fired a few shots in the air and yelled, "Everyone get the fuck out of the way!"

"I can't believe they got Blake," Charlie yelled through his panting as we made our way down an open alleyway.

"He was being a shithead. We couldn't have that today."

*It's okay, his death helps our plan, doesn't it, Victor?*

Danny finished turning and we saw one of the cop cars stop at the other end of the alley and the officers started getting out with shotguns ready. We all fired upon the vehicle and Danny kicked open the service door next to us.

"Go this way! I think this is a dry cleaners!"

Charlie jumped in first and I ran behind him. Danny stopped firing on the police car and ran in with us. I heard the officers firing their shotguns as we ripped through the ridiculous amount of clothing hanging up all over the place. The owner of the store started to yell at us, until he saw our guns.

We made our way to the front of the dry cleaner and Charlie looked out the glass door frantically to make sure there weren't any cops waiting on us. Once he figured it was clear, he held the door open and I ran out with Danny behind me. After we stepped out and headed east, Charlie fired into the back of the dry cleaners and I figured that the cops from the alleyway were on our tail.

"Just fire a few more shots and then we gotta just run!" Danny yelled as he skipped the shooting to start running.

Charlie fired in and yelled, "Got one! Fucker!" and then started running down the street with us.

"You guys need to hurry. There are tons of cops getting word of what's going on!" Jordan yelled on the walkie.

"Ah, fuck you, Jordan, we know what we're doing," Danny said aloud without picking up the walkie as we sprinted down the street to the next alleyway.

We were really close to where Roy was stationed. The map showed that after we ran across the street, we'd enter the next alleyway, turn left between the east and west buildings, and there would be Roy in his crappy station wagon ready for us to load in and get out of there.

The civilian drivers were doing all sorts of random things, though. Some would halt and let us pass; others would step on the gas and practically run us over. About halfway across the four-lane highway, Danny started firing upon the ones who wouldn't stop so they'd jerk away.

"Well, traffic's terrible as usual!"

I didn't know how Danny could make a joke at this time. Especially since the cops were on us and wanting our blood. But as I looked around, I didn't see any police cars or officers.

"I think we may get off scot-free," I said with a smile.

We entered the alleyway and we could see where the two buildings split on the left, and on the other side would be Roy.

"I think so too. And I bet you're glad you wore a vest."

I started to scoff as we turned the corner, but I saw that Danny was coming to a dead halt. We finished walking between the two buildings and made it out on the other end to where Roy's car was supposed to be but it wasn't there. Instead, I could see some fresh tire marks where Roy had peeled out and left us to die.

Danny yanked the walkie up from his belt and said, "Roy, where the fuck are you?"

There was silence on the other end and we waited for a response. Now, Danny sounded sad as he said, "Roy?"

"Guys, what's going on?" Jordan asked.

"Roy's not here!" Danny practically screamed.

My finger danced about the trigger, knowing that it may be as good of a time as ever to put Danny out of his misery and make Charlie surrender.

*C'mon, do it, Victor. You know you've always wanted to come out on top.*

It bothered me that the voice didn't decide to come to me until I was done killing people. Why did it ask for constant madness?

As soon as I had made up my mind to kill Danny, a police officer rounded the corner and shot Charlie in the neck twice, making his head tilt and almost rip completely off. In a sudden rage, I turned to the officer and fired the M16 at him. As the shells flew to the ground, I started screaming at the top of my lungs, wishing I could be in Charlie's or Blake's place instead. Nothing worked out.

The officer sat there in a bloody pulp as I heard Jordan say, "I'll be on Mechanic and Beaubien, not too far from you guys, and there aren't any cops here."

"Victor, c'mon!"

Danny and I started running northeast to where Jordan was waiting, and I had little to no hope that we would make it. I had a feeling the cops weren't talking on the same radio signal anymore. I didn't know if it was just the police, or if more FBI agents were going to come in with better weapons and armor than us.

We were close to where Jordan claimed to be and my legs were just about ready to give out. Danny was running toward an alleyway and I was following behind him, but then, Danny said, "I'll go this way and you go around the alleyway on the other side! I'll meet you in front of that construction store!"

Danny made his way down the alley and I took a left and ran to the other side. As I turned the corner and headed toward the construction store where Danny was supposed to meet me, I noticed that there weren't as many civilians or traffic around.

*Awfully quiet around here for a Monday during lunch, don't you think, Victor?*

I kept running until I stepped in front of the hardware store and turned to look through the thin glass. I could hear my final footsteps thud as I saw something that sent a violent chill over my whole body.

Danny was on the ground, surrounded by about four police officers, one of which had him pinned to the ground with his knee between his shoulder blades. I started to run, but I saw that Danny was lifting his head to look at me and the cop ripped his mask off. Danny stared at me for a few seconds with a look of sadness and defeat. The old Danny was finally coming back, but it was too late. He would be taken in for the man that the police saw him as: A man who's a crook, and killed people for fun, rather than a man who cared about friendship and trust.

"Run, Victor!"

He yelled at the top of his lungs and I saw an officer look up and start to fire his pistol. I ran as the glass of the store rained down diagonal to where Jordan said he'd be.

*This is all wrong. Everything went wrong.*

As I made my toward the alleyway, I turned and shot at the officer who fired upon me. I didn't even want to hit him; I just wanted to scare him off as I made my getaway.

Finally, after all the running and worrying, I saw Jordan in a plain sedan with the engine idling.

"C'mon!" I heard him yell as he waved his hands.

Breathless, I made my way to the car and threw whatever I could to the floor board. As soon as I was in, I said, "I'm all that's left, let's go!"

He didn't react to what I said until we were halfway down the highway. By then, the madness had come to a temporary stop.

## Chapter Seventy One

For the longest time, Danny Ponchello was my only friend. When I started going to school in Detroit, nobody really wanted to be my friend. I heard that in small towns, it was easy for everyone to make friends. Here in the city, though, it was a lot tougher. No one liked each other unless they had a reason to. You needed to be the kid who packed a lot of lunch money; the kid who could make everyone laugh in class; or the one everyone feared. That's why it was so strange when Danny first ever approached me – he was feared. But it was then that I realized we had more in common than I had ever thought. He was an outcast, no one talked to him; no one wanted to. I was an out-of-towner whose father once had a multi-million dollar company that collapsed overnight. Some of the kids I went to school with had parents who had lost their jobs and despised the Carez family. So, much like with political views, their parents' views of my family started me on a downward spiral of acceptance.

But Danny had given me a chance. Danny had saved me multiple times. Danny kept me sane when the Don began killing anyone and everyone in his way. Now, I wasn't so sure how to feel.

I knew it'd be near impossible for Danny to ever get out of prison. He had killed police officers today; I had killed police officers today. Chief Ramzorin kept promising a pardon, but I wasn't sure it would stay that way after today's antics. Several cops were dead, FBI agents were dead... Danny was going to hang in the town square, I knew it. And if they had caught me, I'm sure I'd be saying my last words with him.

Jordan looked me over several times as we headed back to the manor. His eyes were beady and crazed. I stared out the front windshield, wondering where we had gone wrong. Was it the fact that we didn't keep the van intact so we could make our own getaway, or was it that Roy fled the scene?

*Maybe it's the fact that you were born at all... I can see that as a reason everything went wrong... Heh.*

The stronger and more powerful voice in my head sounded like a man had spoken into my left ear. I turned to see if there was someone there, but I only saw Jordan, looking ahead at the traffic and then staring at me.

His expressions genuinely worried me, but I didn't let it show. My head tilted down and I lifted my hands up. My left arm was covered in blood. Whose blood, I had no idea. The desire to take a shower had never been so prevalent.

"You're telling me no one else got away? There wasn't a split or nothing?"

I slowly shook my head, as if an artist was making a caricature of my face and he had already told me once to stay still.

"Blake got a bullet to the head; Charlie's head ripped off after getting two shots in the neck."

"Jesus Christ… and Danny?" Jordan hesitated to ask.

"He's alive, for all I know, but the cops got him."

I hated to explain everything now, because I knew the Don would demand an explanation as well. Jordan backed off and let me keep my silence for now. He knew that I'd have to explain the entire situation to the Don, but he wanted the first scoop.

*Isn't it sickening, Victor? They make you risk your life to get them money, and that's really all they want? No guarantee of safety, no feelings shared? Plus, they want the juicy story of how two of your friends were practically beheaded and your closest friend was taken to prison? Or, you only hope he was taken to prison. He might get his head beaten in while he's in the cruiser getting transferred for booking. You never know.*

My hand contorted and I started clawing into the back of my head from one side to the other, slowly. I felt a searing pain, but thought that it might silence the voice.

Jordan gave me one last concerning look before I stepped out of his car at the front of the manor and threw my ski mask on the floorboard of his car.

No one was outside waiting for me. No one welcomed me in or held the door open for me: the one crook who got away.

I stepped up to the front door and pushed it open myself. Jordan was more concerned about grabbing the money bags and bringing them in behind me. The M16 could stay in his vehicle for all I cared. I didn't want to touch it ever again.

Once I stepped in, I made my way to the Don's office in silence.

No one in the living room, no one making a late lunch, nothing… absolutely nothing.

*Wonder if anyone is even home.*

Without knocking or giving any other warning, I pushed the Don's office door open and made my way in. David Weston turned to face me and I could tell he had started to reach for his gun. The Don, sitting sickly in his chair, lifted his head to face me.

"Victor, you made it back. The others are bringing in the money?"

His initial statements shocked me, but didn't at the same time. He didn't care if anyone had died. Why would he?

"Jordan is bringing it in."

"Oh? Did you and the others return the same time Jordan did?"

My blood started to boil as I realized he didn't keep a walkie on while the whole operation happened. He lived in a fantasy world at this point, where he was the ruler and we were all his peasants.

"No. Roy wasn't there to pick me up."

The Don finally started to grasp onto what happened. I could see it as some sort of care start to flow over his dead face.

"Just you?"

"Charlie and Blake were too busy catching bullets."

The Don didn't care about them.

"And Danny?"

I waited for a second, and tried to word my next sentence in the most optimistic way possible.

"The cops got him and he told me to run. It was a little after we found out Roy wasn't there for us. Charlie was killed, and then Danny and I made our way to Jordan's pick up point. Danny suggested that I go around the hardware store while he goes through it, and that's where they apprehended him. I got away with two bags."

The Don's depressed look even made David cringe in fear. Crime bosses were usually very straight-faced until it came to a loss in their family. I knew Danny was alive, but he was as good as dead. No matter what the Don tried to do to pull him out of prison, it wouldn't work.

But even though Danny was taken into police custody with a ridiculous amount of evidence against him, the Don stayed relatively cool as he said, "That's terrible to hear, but I'm glad you made it back, Victor. We'll find Roy as soon as possible and see what the hell happened with him."

Before I could start yelling at the top of my lungs in sheer anguish, the Don began coughing the very deep cough that had now become a signature of his. David started to lean over and hit his back, but the Don lifted his hand and said, "This news seems to be stirring up my illness even more. I think I'm going to go lie down. Victor, I suggest you clean yourself up. Find Leo if you have any wounds and he'll patch you up."

And… that was it. The Don began to stand up and David made sure he didn't need any assistance. I stood and watched for a few seconds.

*Hmm, it's nice to see this high and mighty ruler falling short in some way…*

It was the first time I agreed with the voice that randomly made its way into my head just months ago. But I felt that if I agreed too much, my descent into madness would only gain more momentum.

After watching for a bit, I walked out of the office and next thing I knew, I was in the shower with blood running down the drain. Anything in between was a complete blur.

It was the longest shower I had ever taken. The skin on my fingers and toes was past wrinkling, but I didn't want to leave. Part of my reason for staying was due to a voice convincing me that the grass wasn't greener on the other side.

*What's the point of leaving, Victor? You don't have any friends, you don't have anyone to save you except yourself.*

The voice sounded like it was down at the bottom of a well. But for once, as the water ran down my face, I decided to go ahead and reply to the voice aloud.

"What about Ramzorin? He can help me."

*Really? You think after that robbery you pulled, Ramzorin will still save you?*

"Why wouldn't he?"

*Great question… well, it would be, but you didn't use your head. Why do you think Darnell is in the picture?*

"Because he put himself there."

*He's going to take over the operation, Victor. I don't care about what he said before about assisting the Chief if he can. He's going to take over and make sure you don't make it out alive. He was sent here to clean everything up.*

"You really think he'd do that?"

*As you said before but in a different context, Victor: Why wouldn't he?*

I took a moment to soak in the information, but I was already too soaked from the water falling upon me. Why the hell was I listening to this voice? Where did it come from?

I didn't feel like asking these questions, because I felt as if the voice was just a reaction to some deeper worries and anxieties of mine. I had heard about it happening to those who experienced extreme trauma. I guess I needed to join that club.

I yanked the nozzle and turned the water off. Steam lifted from the shower drain and I opened the glass door to step out. The steam swayed with me as I reached out for my towel and wrapped it around my waist. I got dressed once the wrinkling subsided and I felt like leaving my room to get some food. I was praying to whoever was listening that I'd sleep tonight, but I didn't think it would work.

As I stepped into the kitchen, I saw the last person who I wanted to see.

Leo.

He kept preparing his food, but his head turned and stared me down. But unlike his previous looks, his sorrow was more apparent. He didn't seem crazy about how today played out, but that just made two of us.

Honestly, I thought he'd start grilling me on how I was the only one that got away. As I walked up to the fridge to see if any leftovers were around, I heard Leo start in.

"We don't have all that much to eat; I found that out the hard way."

"I think I can manage," I said as I dug around.

Leo finished cutting up green beans and tossed them into some soup that was boiling on the stove.

"I'm making my chicken noodle soup," Leo said.

I didn't respond. I could feel my stomach turn and my body turn hot.

"You can have some if you want."

"I don't want any of your *fucking* soup."

Leo was standing right beside me when I said it and I closed the door to the fridge calmly. We were both dangerous people to mess with. I didn't used to be, until I reached this new state of mind: A change that Danny was a part of.

"Hey, Victor... I'm sorry about Danny. I really am. It's not easy seeing your friend, or best friend, being taken into the pen."

For now, I decided to play nice.

"Yeah... I just know we could've been fine if you were our getaway driver."

Leo stood still at first, but then he nodded.

"What about Roy? I haven't seen or heard anything about him."

Leo's face darkened, but it was a darkness that had fallen over me long ago.

"I thought you had heard."

"Heard what? Did he get taken in too?"

Leo sighed and said, "No, he wouldn't let them. The police found him parked in that alleyway and they chased him all over downtown, until he cornered himself in an alleyway, and he..."

I thought I knew where his story was going, but I was wrong.

"... he jumped out of his car, put his revolver to his head, admitted to killing Peterson, and blew his head off on live TV."

If today hadn't been so bad already, I would've been surprised. I couldn't be, though. There was no way. From the first mention of the bank robbery, Roy seemed sketchy about it. He was always worried about the next big thing going on. I can't say that I was surprised, because I really wasn't. But, I could feel the weight being pressed down harder and harder on my heart. My appetite ran screaming out of the kitchen, and I could feel tears slowly forming. I couldn't show this side to anyone, especially not Leo. So, I nodded at what he told me and walked out.

# Chapter Seventy Two

The next step after pulling off one of the worst robberies in history was to lay low. For once I actually wanted to, since going outside seemed like a terrible idea at this point. I wouldn't have to see Ramzorin or Darnell, and I wouldn't have to explain myself for a while. It gave me an ample amount of time to try and clear my head.

Once I'd heard the news of Roy's death, the voice inside silenced itself for a little while. I was able to lie around the house in peace and quiet, but it made me long for the sound of Danny's voice. Or even Charlie's voice, or Blake's. The fact that only adults surrounded the house bothered me. There was no one my age that I could talk to or hang out with. David Weston was the only one who slightly interested me, but he was too busy taking care of the Don and watching out for him.

"He worries that if the news of his illness goes around, an old enemy of his may try and take him down," David said.

"I figured all of his enemies were dead," I said as we passed in the hallway.

"I guess not."

If you counted the police as one of the Don's enemies, my statement would be false.

Danny's absence really started to bother me as time passed, especially when photos of him were splattered all over the news. At one point in the day, I saw the story on the national news, and it included an interview with Blake's parents back in New York.

"He was such a good kid with us," Blake's mom said. "But one day, he just up and left. We never knew where he went…"

Leo was bothered about the mother's story, since the Don always said he picked up kids who were orphaned or homeless.

"He told me his parents were in Mexico but he was able to make it all the way to the Big Apple. Maybe the lack of an accent should've been a giveaway that his story was far-fetched."

Nothing we could do about it now. Blake was dead, and Charlie was dead. His parents didn't appear on the news at all. We could only assume his story of refuge was real.

Although the peace and quiet in my mind was nice, I felt that it originated from becoming numb to any more death or destruction. I was used up. There was nothing more to be shocked or sad about. Or at least, that's what I thought, until I started trying to get a better night's sleep.

Monday night after the robbery into Tuesday night, I had a dream that started off with a fire in the middle of an everlasting darkness. It was a distant fire at first, but I realized it was coming closer and closer. Looking out on the scene through my own eyes, I watched as my mom and dad came out of the fire with their skin melting off of their bodies. Smoke poured off of them as they stepped out, but they walked out towards me in a very slow and undisturbed way. The dream looked as though it was going to end with just the flames, but then it restarted. This time, there were quite a few changes. One change that I'm not sure how to explain was, I could smell their burning skin during the dream, which smelled of burning pork chops and blood. On top of that, they started saying all kinds of different things to me. My mom would mutter things about my childhood and how she still thought I was a child, while my father made random hate-filled statements about me, my mom, and anything else he could think of.

Before my parents could reach me, Chief Ramzorin ran out from the sidelines and was making turkey noises as he put his thumbs in his ears and wiggled his hands around in a silly way. Surprisingly, the Chief scared my parents off and I didn't have to watch their pain any longer. He then turned to me with quite a large grin. He clapped his hands together and continued laughing. I feel like I started to laugh with him, but what was once the fire now became a different scene; one I thought I had overheard the Chief talk about before. It was a major car accident, and I looked at the vehicle to see a woman straddled across the front hood in a sick and twisted fashion. Her head had smashed violently into a stiff oak tree and I watched as Chief Ramzorin went from his silliness to a state of irregular mourning. The dream then came to a sudden end.

Tuesday night into Wednesday morning, I had a new nightmare. It took place in a large black space that was very plain and empty, but ahead of me was Emmitt. I knew it was Emmitt, even though he wouldn't turn around. I still knew it was him, and I started to calmly say his name at first, but by the end of the dream, I was yelling it. When I woke up Wednesday morning, my throat was dry and burned, and I knew I had been screaming his name throughout the night.

Wednesday night into Thursday morning, the dream of Emmitt started again. Only this time, I didn't have to start yelling Emmitt's name. He turned around after a while to face me, but a gaping hole appeared where his right eye was and the hole was filled with pure blackness. Blood was all over his face and he slowly started walking towards me. I wanted to step back in the dream, but I couldn't move. And once his face was right in front of me, he whispered, "Remember what you said!"

I felt liquid splash onto my face from Emmitt's wound and I jumped up in my bed. As I looked around, I saw my glass of water from the night before had fallen over on my night stand and simulated the feeling of his blood. Once I wiped my face off, I turned to the alarm clock and saw the time was four AM.

Five hours was the most sleep I had gotten in days. And although the dreams creeped me out and made me paranoid, the sleep really helped stabilize my brain and help me move through the day. I realized I was still disconnected from the real world, and how I figured that out was by walking downstairs that morning and going into the kitchen to fix a bowl of cereal. It was the way David greeted me that rocked my world.

"Happy Thanksgiving," he said.

I figured he wasn't saying what he meant to, but the calendar in the kitchen was unable to falsify his greeting.

"You too," I replied quietly before pouring the cereal and milk.

With Michelle gone and the morale of the manor being so low, the Thanksgiving meal we ended up consuming was a joke. Leo took a pool of money and went to go get Chinese take-out downtown. He came back with steamy bags of fat and MSG, which were distributed across the dining room table. I thought we'd all eat together, but I noticed that as each person fixed a plate, they scattered around the house. There was no togetherness anymore.

*Wow, this is pathetic...*

The gruff voice returned to my mind, but I was pretty sure I felt the same way. It was a pathetic meal, and it made me miss the last few years we all had Thanksgiving together... especially when Michelle made a turkey for everyone.

I remembered me and all the Kids sitting at the smaller table in the kitchen, laughing and making jokes at one another's expense. As I stepped by the kitchen, I felt that I could hear our conversations in the distance. When I looked over at the table, I saw I was fooled.

We would have all eaten together, I think. But since it was announced that the Don didn't feel well and wanted David to bring the food up to him, it caused everyone to lose interest in congregating.

"I don't know what he has," David said as he made the plate. "I don't think it's contagious though. Fuck, I hope it's not contagious."

I really didn't care that the Don was sick. It made me wonder if he might die before the police were able to finally nab him. That thought actually made me laugh aloud, and I had to stop myself before everyone started looking over at me.

It seemed like the day was coming to a boring end, until the intercom in my room buzzed.

"Victor, you have a phone call. It's Danny."

I hopped up out of bed and grabbed the phone off of the receiver. Once I did, I heard Danny start in right away.

"Victor?"

"Hey there, Danny."

"Jesus Christ, it's good to hear your voice, man."

Danny sounded excited and full of life at first, but as the conversation continued, his mood dwindled.

"You doing alright?"

"Yeah, as good as I can be doing. You?"

He sounded like the old Danny, and it made my eyes water.

"Yeah, I just miss ya."

"Oh, don't get all sappy on me, Victor. You know what they'll do to me in here if they think I'm a romantic."

The subject matter didn't make me laugh, and I was glad it didn't make Danny laugh either.

"So, after some beatings by the guards for what I did to some police officers, they said I'll be able to have visits starting this weekend."

"Really?"

"Yeah."

"What about a court date?"

" I went ahead and plead guilty at the recommendation of my father. That made them sentence me to fifty years, but I know my dad is working on getting me a really great lawyer that can pull some strings to get me out sooner."

I thought about how my original plan was to swoon Charlie onto my side and have him testify against the Don, but with Danny in his situation, I wondered if I could swoon him instead.

"That's a lot of strings they'll have to pull for a crime that you were caught red-handed in."

"Well don't say that, Victor. Maybe I was just out for a jog with my M16 and a ski mask. It was all a fashion statement."

"Hah," I replied.

There was an awkward silence that was only filled by the buzzing of the hardline. Eventually, Danny said, "My dad definitely won't be coming to see me while I'm here, what with his sickness and all the heat on the gang now."

"We still don't know what he has," I replied.

"I know... But I was wondering if you would come see me, Victor."

The simple request was like a cry for help. I wanted to see Danny, especially if I could convince him to testify against the gang — the gang that put him where he was now. My chances of doing that still seemed pretty small, but at this point, it was worth a shot.

"I don't think I will this weekend, but I definitely will in a week. Does it have to be during the weekend?"

"No, you could come a week from today if you want to. That'll probably be a good time, anyway."

He didn't have to explain why.

"Okay, I'll come down next Thursday."

"Sounds good. Hey, I think this phone may cut us off soon, but tell my dad I love him again."

"Will do."

"Thanks. Hope your-"

That was it. Without any warning, the phone connection was lost and I started to worry for Danny's safety. Even worse, I never went to tell the Don that Danny loved him. He already had, but maybe saying it again would've made his dad feel better.

And I didn't want that.

## Chapter Seventy Three

Technically, I wasn't allowed to leave the manor. No one was, unless it was for medicine or food. But as the night grew darker and darker, I felt more and more of a need to speak with Chief Ramzorin. But, I knew I couldn't call on the phones inside the house. I knew that the phones were tapped.

That's when I started thinking about the detached garage and remembered there was an emergency phone out there with a completely different hook-up and phone number.

So, before it got to be too late at night, I snuck past the cricket choir of the night and opened the small side door into the garage so no one would hear me go in. There was a work lamp that was always kept on at the other side of the structure, so I decided not to turn on any of the other lights.

My feet were cold and wet in my socks and I rubbed them on the smooth concrete to try and clean them up. I then stepped up to the phone next to the tool cabinets and dialed the number for the downtown police station, hoping Chief Ramzorin would still be there.

"Detroit Police Department."

"I need to speak to Chief Ramzorin."

"Who's calling?"

"A friend."

"Look, I ain't sending over any prank callers. Give me your name."

"Victor Carez."

The irritated receptionist said no more as I was put on hold and transferred straight over to the Chief. It didn't take long for the other end to be picked up, but I started to regret calling as soon as he answered.

"They say that dead men can't operate equipment of any kind."

"I'm not dead," I replied.

"Dead to rights, is what he means," I heard Darnell argue in the background.

"Chief, I just want to talk to you, not that asshole."

"Oh, I'm the asshole?" Darnell shouted. "Says the kid who refuses to tell us full details on a murder-robbery of a bank. Now I've lost an agent."

"You should have sent a better guy to stop us."

"You know what Victor Carez rhymes with?" Agent Darnell said, "Jail."

Chief Ramzorin decided to cut in.

"Victor, just whose side are you on, anyway?"

"You don't understand, Chief. I'm trying to play both sides."

"You better reword your sentences before I knock your goddamn head off," Darnell spat.

"I mean that I have to keep up a persona with the people here while trying to help you guys bust the Don. You can't even start to understand how fucking paranoid I am! I can't believe you sent an agent in there to murder us."

"I'll admit, Victor, I wasn't too happy about that either," Ramzorin said.

"Oh, c'mon, what is this? The grand cousin-fucking convention where everyone is fine and dandy with wrong-doings?" Darnell argued. "I don't admit to any wrong-doing in regards to sending that agent in. He was ordered to try and apprehend you unless things got violent. And boy, did they get violent. Well, his family had to find out a few hours later just how violent that robbery became."

"You don't understand. I had an idea for how to end all of this."

"Why didn't you tell us that before, then!?"

"Because! I didn't have it fully fleshed out yet."

"What was this genius plan of yours? I'd love to hear it."

*God, this Darnell guy really likes to bust your balls, doesn't he? Makes you kinda wonder his sexuality, eh?*

"I was going to kill Danny and take Charlie as a prisoner to testify with me. I was willing to do that based on the idea that Charlie would crack under pressure."

"So this kid, Blake... What were you going to do with him? Or did you not figure out this plan until my man had killed one of your criminal buddies?"

I had tried to hold back the distress in my voice before, but now there was no way.

"Look, I'm just going to tell you the truth, okay? I know I fucked up, but for the longest time, I couldn't think straight. I couldn't sleep at night. Last night, I got the most sleep I've gotten in a while but that was only five hours. But even with those five hours, it was filled with nightmares, as were the nights before. I couldn't think straight, until I was in the middle of the fucking robbery and we were on the run. It was when Roy wasn't at the pickup zone that I had the idea to kill Danny and take Charlie in, but then a cop rounded the corner and practically took Charlie's head off. Charlie was going to be my partner. I don't have any evidence to give. If I take any of that money we got, they'll find me."

"You are the evidence, Victor!" Darnell argued. "I know Ramzorin told you that your testimony wouldn't be enough, but at this point, I hate to even give you any more chances. You are killing people, Victor. One-by-one. The longer you drag this out, the more people are going to die and the less we'll have to work off of. Is that what you want? Everyone to walk away scot-free? Because that's the outcome you're currently heading towards."

"No… I have an idea, just hear me out, please."

The other end of the phone went quiet and I took another breath.

"You guys took Danny in, and we all know he's dead to rights as we stand now. But if you give me something to work with, I'm going to try and convince him to turn his father in."

"Bullshit. He'll never do it."

"Quiet," Ramzorin urged.

I could tell Darnell was pissed for being told to keep quiet, but it really worked.

"You really think you can convince Danny?" Ramzorin asked.

"I feel like it's a possibility. I just really have to work on how I word it to him and how I think he'll take it."

There was silence on their end, until Darnell said, "Whatever floats your boat, Chief. If you trust this kid, go for it."

The Chief sighed as he said, "As long as you're not going to go shoot up the place or anything, you have my permission to try. But if you feel at any moment that he's going to turn that information on you, don't spill anything to him. I don't doubt that you'd be killed in a matter of seconds if he decided to turn you in to the Don."

"I mean, that wouldn't be so bad," Darnell said, and I could feel his grin through the phone.

"Fuck you," I seethed.

*Bash his head in, cut it off, and roast him like a turkey.*

"When are you going to see Danny?"

"A week from tonight."

"Well, prepare a speech in the meantime. Otherwise, you may lose him."

# Chapter Seventy Four
## Tuesday, November 28th, 1978

It was tough to try and find something to do around the manor. The Don, through Leo and David, had given me the okay to leave the manor on Thursday to go see Danny; I wasn't all too crazy about it, but I couldn't stand sitting around the manor anymore. Especially with all the nightmares I kept having, the lack of sleep, everything. I really couldn't take it anymore, and it was finally on Tuesday that I ran off from the manor and decided to find something to do downtown during lunch time.

My first idea was to drive around and see if I could find any damage from the robbery still scattered about. I drove around slowly, seeing if I could spot any bullet holes or other distress from the route we took. Some bullet holes were still apparent; others were sloppily covered up with paint or plaster of some sort.

Next I drove to the bank, which was practically spotless from the mess before. Banks had to operate. There was no way that one could be shut down for too long, even after what we had done.

I drove to the edge of downtown where I had heard about a good burger place that had just opened up. When I finished parking my car on the curb and paying the parking meter, I stepped away and accidentally bumped into someone. When I looked up to see it was a woman, I turned my manners back on.

"Oh, gosh I'm sorry," I said.

"No, it was my fault."

I didn't face her for the reply, I just kept walking down the sidewalk. Before I could even take two steps, the woman called out my name.

"Victor?"

Her voice did sound familiar, so it didn't take me long to turn around.

"Do you remember me?" she asked.

The woman wore a very nice red conservative dress with painful four-inch heels on. Her handbag draped down from her dainty shoulder but I could tell she could hold her own. That's when it finally clicked.

"Kassidy…" I muttered as a flurry of memories came back to me.

It's weird to think that about a year ago at this same time, I was fussing and worrying about if I'd ever see her again. In all of my sadness and despair, I thought that maybe approaching Ashley for comfort was the best way to go. When I looked into her eyes and she faintly smiled, the presence of the voice that had been bringing me down seemed to be nonexistent.

I had lost my virginity to her. And even though it's common to think most guys don't take it to heart when that happens, I know I did. I thought back to the party at the manor with Danny and the other kids from school, and I thought about how, after several drinks, Kassidy and I woke up next to each other naked and afraid of the Don.

She looked very different and reserved from how I had known her before, but she was still a magnificent beauty that was hard to find. She didn't even look embarrassed or upset that we were just now meeting for the first time in…

"How long has it been?" she asked as she came in for a hug.

As we embraced, it gave me time to think about how long it really had been.

"I wanna say two years or more," I responded.

To twenty year olds, that was a long time.

Eventually, we parted from our embrace and she looked me over. I was glad that I got cleaned up pretty well, but she still seemed to not be impressed.

"You look exhausted," she said.

"Oh… Haha. Just been working a lot," I said.

"I can tell. Where have you been working?"

The warehouse story seemed to be old at this point, but I stuck to it.

"Danny's dad owns a warehouse that houses a bunch of liquor for the stores around town. We move the boxes over from the semis and then take them where they need to go."

"Hmm," she said flatly.

"What about you?" I asked.

"I'm a secretary for the VP of Billings Oil."

"Hey! That's really cool, awesome."

"I like it a lot. Are you off work today? Is that why you're out here?"

"Well I was actually going out for lunch."

"Alone?"

She made it seem like it was a bad thing.

"Yeah, everyone else is working today."

"Well, I wouldn't mind getting lunch with you! I'm on my lunch break right now."

"Well sure!"

So we went to a restaurant with a ton of lunch specials. Men in suits and ties dominated the crowd, but there were a few other women who were eating lightly in their dainty dresses. Kassidy and I were seated pretty quickly and I figured I would hurry up on deciding what I wanted to eat, since I didn't want her being late to work from lunch.

"I'll have the turkey club," I said after Kassidy ordered a chicken Caesar salad.

"Sounds good, I'll be back with your drinks shortly," the cookie-cutter waiter said.

After he walked away, I thought about Kassidy's friend who went to the party with her.

"Do you still talk to Tiffany?" I asked.

"No... she wouldn't grow up. She kept running around from job-to-job at different diners and such... never wanted to settle down. She also left the apartment one day to be with some rock star as he went on tour. It was hell getting out of that lease."

"Oh, I bet... Sorry to hear that."

"Yeah... What about your friend, the one Tiffany got with? Geez, I don't know why I can't think of his name, and I feel like you said it earlier..."

"You mean Danny?"

"Yeah, Danny!"

Right after she said that, her face turned into a horrified expression as she said, "Oh my God... He robbed that bank just a few blocks away, didn't he?"

*Well, so much for the warehouse story...*

I sighed.

"Yes, they caught him running from the scene."

"Dear Lord... I can't believe that. They said one person ended up fleeing the scene and is still at large."

"Hmm," I replied as the waiter brought over our drinks.

I took a sip of water immediately. I started to feel antsy as the time passed.

"I can't believe it's been so long," I mentioned, avoiding the topic of the bank robbery.

"I know... Hah. I was pretty wild back then, though."

At the mention of the word "wild", I remembered what The Ballz had told me that disheartened me from seeing Kassidy ever again.

*"...I found her a long time ago, but I just didn't have the heart to tell you... she's owned."*

That was only about a year ago... it was then I realized that neither of us were telling the full truth. But now that we were talking to each other, my old feelings started to rise once again. I had finally found her... and it was completely by accident.

"Victor, are you okay?"

She was staring into me with her dark lovely eyes and I felt safe.

"Yeah, I was just thinking about our time together before."

A strange disconcerting and awkward look moved over her face as she said, "Oh, Victor... you know we can't do that ever again."

*Why, 'cause she has herpes?* the voice interjected.

"I'm not saying we have to wake up next to each other naked, I just thought we could go out on a more formal date."

Kassidy sighed and shook her head in a disapproving way. Once I started to speak again, she said, "Victor, I'm engaged."

As her hand started to rise to show me the ring, my heart started to fall. And once my heart was about to hit rock bottom, I felt an angry lava start to boil up inside of me.

It was an anger that Kassidy tried to contain by saying, "Did you really think after all this time that we could just pick things up where we left off? It's not that easy, Victor. And you can do so much better than me. I was a mess back then. Sometimes I'm still a mess now. I can't believe you'd wait around for me. You're better than that, Victor."

Her words were failing to soothe me. I felt the anger rising and my ears were turning red. There was no way I could hold back.

From the darkest depths of my inner soul, I spat, "You bitch."

"Excuse me?"

I noticed that some people had turned around when I had called her a bitch, but the gloves had come off and I was coming unglued.

"I loved you, Kassidy. I loved you from the moment I laid eyes on you. But I see how you are now, even as you try to cover up working for Jackson Burose's pimp."

"Victor, stop."

"You just want to fuck your way to the top, huh? You liked fucking me since I was some kind of bad boy, then you had a 'hard time' getting out of that lease by fucking any guy who'd pay even a dime to get in those nice jeans you used to wear. Yeah, I bet something hard was going in and out of you so you could get out of that lease, eh? And now you tell your fiancé that you're the sweetest girl on the face of the earth and that you'd love to be with him for the rest of your life, 'cause the road you have down there is riddled with tire marks that no one else wants to drive on. That's not how it works, Kassidy. I mean, it's nice to hear that you're a sex-retary now. But you gotta work hard, not blow hard."

"What do you suggest, Victor?" she asked as tears rolled down her face. "Being a murderer and robbing banks with your best friend?"

"Fuck you," I growled menacingly. "You were my first, and I thought that was something special. But now that I'm reconsidering everything and wondering why I thought about you all this time, I realize that I just liked the thought of you and nothing more. Because the real you is sick, and I don't want to even be near you anymore."

My eruption was over. I watched as Kassidy made my wish come true and she bolted out of the restaurant bawling her eyes out. My anger had been released for once, and it felt really good. It was as if my words had formed into a sauna and I had all of the steam come out of me. I felt powerful; freed of one stress that had plagued me for so long.

What I didn't notice was that the waiter was standing there the entire time with our food in his hands. When I finished steadying my breath, I turned to him and I saw fear-filled eyes staring back.

"Look, man, I just try to make a decent living here. I can't handle any ill words towards me."

"Just sack up the food for me and I'll make it worth your while," I said as I dropped a fifty on the table.

# Chapter Seventy Five
## Thursday, November 30th, 1978

"Tell him to be safe, and careful... and that I love him," the Don instructed before I walked out the front door.

On that morning, it was easy to stand up, dress myself and eat some food, but it wasn't easy to get mentally prepared for seeing Danny in the pen.

Even though his attitude had changed over the last year and he was bringing my morale down with his anger, not having Danny at the manor was like going to an arcade without any quarters. As I drove to the prison, I started to think about everything we'd been through.

I missed him, especially after talking to him on the phone and hearing his voice; his old voice, I might add. It brought a sense of comfort to me when I thought about it. It made me think of "Still the Same" by Bob Seger... or maybe that applied more toward Kassidy.

After talking on the phone with him from prison, I noticed Danny — although filled with anger and hate — seemed to be a lot more like the Danny I met two years ago: the one who helped save my life. I guess I owed Jordan and Leo credit as well, but Danny was the one who really made the initial effort. I felt happy as I remembered when he offered for me to come to his house for the first time ever after school. Initially, I was scared to death. I thought my father would cut me down for sure. But we made it work, and once we had hung out the first time, there was no way to stop it from continuing. We understood each other; we related on so many different levels. Even the fact that his mother had run off so long ago actually drew us closer to each other instead of further away. I felt safer with Danny. I felt like I could tell Danny anything that I wanted to. Anything that came to mind, I could tell Danny. It didn't matter what it was.

Then I thought about when our friendship started to hit the harder times with Modellini and Johnny Fargo attacking us at the warehouse. When Danny was shot, I knew that the entire game had changed. We weren't just "the Kids" anymore. It threw us into a new set of responsibilities. When Danny and I had helped kill Tandelli and the rest of his men, it was more like shooting rats in a barrel. But when I told the Don that we could take care of Modellini and his men, the rats then were armed and ready to shoot back.

As I made my way towards the jail, I noted that it seemed as if small towns were always cursed with large penitentiaries, but it was one of those... large, small towns, if that made any sense.

The downtown area looked like something out of an old western. Although the sights were semi-enjoyable, the trip there and the meaning behind it brought my mood down.

A few older gentlemen watched in awe as I drove by in my Bel Air. They sat on their porches and watched the day and my car roll on by. It was relaxing to them, but it'd drive me crazy.

Once I started reaching the end of the town, I noticed the maximum security prison in the distance. As soon as I saw it, a cold feeling went down my spine.

*Wonder if this is where they'd take the Don when you get Ramzorin to bring him in... haha,* the voice wondered.

The hard part was going to be trying to convince Danny. I didn't follow the Chief's instructions of making a script, but I did think about it a lot before making the hour and a half drive out to the prison. Was it really the best way to go? Trying to get Danny to testify against his own father? He'd only go for it if it meant he'd get a full pardon, but that was never going to happen. He killed too many people, and they caught him red-handed. No way he could just walk away from it all.

The parking spots were marked for different staff members and such, and I finally found one that specified it was for visitors. Once I parked my car and tucked my pistol and holster in the glove box, I stepped out and headed into the prison.

The first gate I stepped up to was a see-through gate while the one behind it was a large slab of concrete and metal with little wheels under it. Once I stepped up to the first gate, I heard a buzz and it started rolling open. As I stepped to the next gate, two officers stared me down. One of the officers held a leash with a stunning German Shepard at the end. I knew not to reach my hand out toward it, but I saw that the dog was getting excited, and wondered if it'd be gnawing on my ass by the time I left here.

"Heel, Buster," the officer said directly.

The other officer looked me over and said, "You here for a visit?"

"Yeah, Danny Ponchello."

"You'll tell that to Officer Daniels inside. Can I have you place your hands on the gate over here and I'll pat you down. Then we're going to have the dog sniff you."

I stepped up to the gate and placed my hands flat on it. I couldn't help but stare at the dog as he panted and whimpered as he waited to sniff me.

"Buster, are we gonna have to put you through training again?" the officer asked as he patted me down. "He seems to be excited to sniff you. Hope you're not carrying anything."

"Y'know, I don't know that I ever fed him breakfast this morning," the officer with the leash said, trying to intimidate me.

"Let's hope so," the other officer said as he finished patting me down. "I'm now gonna ask you to stand still."

Standing perfectly still, I felt as the dog's nose went places that the officer's hands hadn't been. Once the dog was done, he stepped back and still whined.

"Aw, poor thing was hoping to munch on your balls," the officer with the leash said.

"Well I feel bad for you and him," I said, expressing my distaste in his words.

The officer who patted me down waved at the tower above and I heard the gate in front of us start to move.

"Like I said, Officer Daniels will get you checked in and stuff. And, as always, enjoy your visit."

I nodded and the cop with the leash gave me one last dirty look before I headed inside.

After walking across about a half-mile of solid concrete and freshly mowed grass surrounded by barbed wire, a guard opened the plain glass door and let me into a lobby area. I stepped in and looked ahead to two officers sitting at a semi-circle desk with multiple monitors before them. Only one of the officers looked up at me and I read his tag that said "Daniels".

"Who are you here to see?" he asked.

"Danny Ponchello," I said.

"Do you know his unit or number?"

"No, sorry."

"Most people don't. Go ahead and step through that metal detector and I'll make a quick call."

Today didn't seem to be the usual day for visits. Once I stepped through the metal detector just fine, I looked out and saw some prisoners running around in a recreational area, but they were quite a distance from the lobby. If someone had made it to this point in their escape, they'd either be covered in blood because they had to go through so many barbed wire fences, or because they had to bust so many skulls to get to this point.

"Hey, Vernon, got a kid here wanting to see the Ponchello boy. Isn't he in B unit?"

There was a pause, and then Daniels said, "Well bring him to the visit room. We'll use the one we throw the attorneys into with their clients, since no one else is here."

He hung up and said, "It's your lucky day. You won't have to talk so loud over the sound of everyone else's conversation. Once Vernon gets Ponchello, he'll take you to see him. You can have a seat over there if you want."

I was more of a standing person, but I could tell by his tone that he meant "You need to have a seat." I walked over to the hard metal chair and waited for only a minute or two before Vernon opened one of the terribly painted solid steel doors and said, "Come this way."

I followed him down a dimmed hallway and a creepy vibe was coming off of the walls. I felt that several people had been beaten down or even killed in this hallway, but I had no idea how many were cops and how many were prisoners.

Once I started looking at the signs next to the doors, I saw that one said, "Visiting Room #2" and I figured we were nearing our room.

"Okay, we're going to lock the both of you into room number five. I don't feel that I should have to say this, but there's no physical contact during the visit. That includes high-fives, hugs, kisses, ass grabbing, whatever. You're educated on the phrase physical contact, right?"

"Yeah."

"Okay, so I don't have to explain too much. You get the idea. You'll have fifteen minutes. I suggest you make the most of it. I'll be waltzing in when that time is done, okay?"

"I understand."

Without further adieu, he opened the door and I walked in. Only the half of the room with Danny was lit and I heard Vernon step in for a second so the lights on my side could be turned on as well. After he turned them on, I walked over to the table where Danny was and I heard the door slam behind me.

Danny watched with a small smile as I walked over to him. He wore a baggy gray jumpsuit with cuffs on his hands and legs, all of which were connected with chains. If we were to hug, it wouldn't be easy.

"Victor, I'm glad you could make it," Danny said softly.

As soon as I sat down, I looked up at Danny's paled face and replied, "No problem. Quite a drive, though."

"I know… Well, I mean I've only made the trip once, but it seemed to take forever."

Danny laughed and I tried to laugh with him, but it made me think of what the

Don had said.

"Your dad says he loves you, and he hopes you're being careful."

"Of course. Right when I walked in, they handed me the survival guide."

Danny's levity was a bit out of place. He seemed crazed and cold as he looked around in the room as if someone was watching us. Come to think of it, I wasn't sure if anyone was or not, but I'd hate to ask.

"I'm surprised they put us in this room. They don't have any recording equipment in these rooms, since they're for attorneys and clients."

"Speaking of that, who is your attorney?" I asked.

"His name is Mahan Varsochi. Kind of an odd character from New York, but he can supposedly get anyone out of anything."

"Did he guarantee that?" I asked, trying to gather information before I decided to spill my own.

"Well, not exactly. But they think they can get me a lesser sentence. Ten years at least."

"That's not too bad for what happened," I said, hiding my skepticism.

"You're telling me. It also depends on if the Judge takes tips."

I laughed a bit and sat back as much as I could.

"What's been going on with you, Victor? I'd talk more about stuff here but nothing really changes."

"Oh, well…" I started, and I thought about what I could say.

I didn't particularly want to talk about the voice that has been visiting me lately, but I did think of one topic.

"I saw Kassidy on Tuesday."

"Really?" Danny asked, seemingly surprised. "How was that?"

"Well, when you're right, you're right," I replied as I sat forward again. "She has a fiancé; tried to play the sympathy game with everything she did with Jackson Burose."

"What did I tell ya, man?" Danny said with a forbidden grin. "She was bad news, totally not worth your time."

"I'm glad I saw her though… I got to tell her off."

"Hah! Good. Bitch deserves it."

I tried to think of something else that happened, but I couldn't. That was about it. Anything else would sound like I was whining.

"Did you hear about Roy?" I asked.

Danny didn't seem too happy anymore as he said, "Yeah… crazy coot. I'm gonna miss him."

"Me too," I said, and I decided to try and play on Danny's emotions to bring him to my side. "And Blake and Charlie."

"Yeah... and now I'm stuck here in the pen."

I thought about how Chief Ramzorin asked me how many more people had to die before I realized something needed to be done.

"We've lost everyone, Danny."

"Well there's still Leo, Jordan, Scott, David..."

"No, I mean all of the Kids. They're all dead except you and me."

That seemed to strike a chord in Danny, but he fought back.

"They knew what they were getting into. They were sworn in by Leo. Modellini was a piece of shit... he started our digression. If it wasn't for him doping around, we could've had a pretty good team for the heist."

"I don't feel it's his fault, Danny."

"Oh yeah? Then who do you blame for everything? I know you won't blame yourself."

"Y'know, in some ways, I do. I blame myself for trying to get close to Emmitt and not seeing what his family started to become. But most of all, I blame your father."

"You better watch what you say, Vic. I know we're friends, but you better watch yourself."

"Peterson said something to me that has always stuck."

"Peterson was an un-loyal dog, only helping the next person who gave him a bone."

I could tell I was taking the wrong route for this conversation. I started to wonder what the right route was.

"Look, all I'm saying is, your dad had us do an operation that not even Leo and the others could've pulled off. We needed more manpower. We needed more stability."

"How would that have helped? That FBI agent still would've jumped up and capped any of us, even if we had more people."

"With more eyes, we could've seen him jump up."

"Ah, what do you know, Victor? I've been in the gang longer than you. I know that no matter what, that was a tricky job and there was no way it was going to go clean. But it should have. There's no reason the fucking Feds should've been on our asses."

"But your dad acted out of desperation, you can't deny that."

"Yes I can. We needed that money. With all the cutbacks, and with Jacob out of the picture, how could we even make our money?"

"The operation could've gone a lot smoother in my opinion."

"Stop, Victor, just stop, okay? I trust my dad. I love my dad. He did what he thought was best."

*Even though it caused his only son to be imprisoned?* the voice almost had me retort.

But I was done arguing with Danny, and it was after our argument that I realized convincing him to join me, Darnell and Ramzorin was impossible. He loved his father and trusted his father. Why wouldn't he? He was bound to two separate but equally powerful loyalties, his family and the gang. There was no way I could convince him to jump out of that loop and join me. The only loyalty we had was friendship, and I had seen that fail so many times before.

But as I started to lose my hope, the one thing that still kept me going returned to my mind again.

"What about the Platinum Briefcase?"

"Huh? What are you talking about?"

The fact that Danny seemed to forget his mother's bedtime story filled me with sadness, but then he remembered.

"Oh, hah, the one my mom told me about?"

I nodded.

"What about it?"

"Well, if we would've just looked for it instead, we could have helped the Don."

Danny smiled and said, "Victor, if you find that thing, you better use it to bust me out of prison."

"And then what? We'll run away together?"

"Yeah, we can buy an island and bring some girls with us; some really nice girls, not Kassidy and Tiffany, but some backup dancers off of Broadway or a cabaret."

"Now you're talking," I said.

Our conversation surprisingly ended in a laugh as the guard stepped in behind Danny and told us the visit time was over. Danny's smile seemed to fade, but it was still apparent as he said, "Thanks for coming, Victor. Tell everyone that they don't need to worry about me. I'll become the king of this place before long."

And as he was pulled away, I nodded, thinking that his desires would come true. But a few weeks from our visit, I'd find out we were both terribly wrong.

## Chapter Seventy Six
### Lucent Skies Penitentiary
### December 1st-15th, 1978

Danny Ponchello awoke from a deep slumber in the middle of the night, the day after Victor's visit. At first, he had forgotten what woke him up. It always surprised him when it happened, but he knew one day it wouldn't be a surprise.

"Roll call, roll call, everyone up and at'em!"

Danny sighed and started to get out of his top bunk. His lanky cellmate on the other side, James Stein, rolled out of bed as well and they saw their cell door open. These type of roll calls happened once a week. Most often, the guards would just check each cell with a flashlight and move on.

Danny and James stepped out with all the other convicts and they formed a single-file line that faced the other single-file line before them. The line was formed on a straight red line that went from one end of the cells to the other, and the two lines were far enough apart that the guards could walk safely between them to observe all the prisoners.

As the guards started the count, Danny turned to his left and saw the man who tried to talk to him sometimes, a man he only knew by the name Kirby.

"Fuck this shit, I was in the middle of a wet dream," he said to Danny.

"Oh yeah, who was it with?" Stein asked.

"Your mother," Kirby replied in his deep bellowing voice.

"No chit-chat, Kirby!" the guard yelled.

The guards slowly made their way down the line, making sure that every prisoner was accounted for. Danny turned and looked to his right to watch the guards shine the flashlight in each prisoner's face. A black man in about the middle of the line was finally fed up with the counts.

"Man, get that fuckin' light out of my face," he said as he batted the flashlight away.

The guard, without any hesitation, turned the flashlight around and used it to bash the man's nose in. Danny watched in horror as the man fell flat on his back, and Danny was convinced he was dead.

"Jesus Christ, you niggers used to mind so well, and now you get all uppity whenever you get a chance," the guard said.

The guard in question was notorious for beating prisoners who gave him any kind of lip or pushback. His name was Travis, and Danny learned early on that he was not the right person to mess with.

Another guard came out and started dragging the black prisoner away to God knows where. Danny would never see the man again.

"Hey Christoph, what was that you said the other day about niggers being all uppity?" Travis asked as he joyously continued down the line with the flashlight shining into everyone's faces.

"I said that Lincoln caused it," Christoph, a rather large guard said as they walked side-by-side.

"No, no, you said something else but I can't remember."

"Oh, I said that like Lincoln, they seem to get so excited and uppity that their heads almost explode."

In any other context, Danny might have laughed at the joke, but with what had just happened to the black man and with what hour of the morning it was, it wasn't funny at all.

Travis finally stepped up to Danny and raised his flashlight into his face.

"Hey there, Ponchello," Travis said. "You settling in nicely?"

Danny watched as the other end of the flashlight had blood drip off of it from the man's nose and he replied, "Yessir."

Travis was irked at the fact that Danny refused to play along with the others and cause trouble. Instead, Danny acted like the golden boy once he reached the other side of the prison.

"Well good. Looks like we'll be having nigger soup in about ten hours, so I hope you all are hungry around lunch time."

Travis finished up the count as Christoph tried to compose himself, and then they said, "Okay, back in your cells!"

After seeing the man's face bashed in, Danny found it hard to fall back to sleep. Stein seemed to be the same way.

Once the sun was up, the guards came around with trays of breakfast and passed them through the one rectangular opening in the bars. Danny stood at the ready for the breakfast and devoured his biscuit in seconds. Stein eventually came to and walked over to his breakfast.

Their cell had two empty bottom bunks but no one had been moved in with them yet. They both dreaded the day that it would happen, since there wasn't much say in who your celly could be.

Danny had sort of lucked out with Stein being his cellmate. Instead of a rapist or murderer, Stein was found guilty of a major embezzlement scheme at his uncle's bank. He was sentenced to thirteen years with probation for life afterwards. He was in his mid-thirties and wore slightly tattered glasses. He spoke in an intelligent tone, but it bothered Danny at times.

"You seem hungry," Stein commented.

"You're always the observer, Stein," Danny said as he took a drink of milk from the small carton.

"I just thought you'd want to save room for the nigger soup later."

"You're sick, Stein."

"No, I'm serious. I don't doubt that they're going to use that man for it. Who's going to miss him? He's probably another runaway."

"I'm trying to eat."

"You're going to be here a long time, Danny. Might as well get used to these jokes and topics."

"I won't be in here for long," Danny said. "My dad will get me out of here."

"You're quite an optimist, especially for someone who robbed a bank during the middle of the day, killed people, and plead guilty to it."

Danny's relationship with Stein was purely a love-hate relationship. Stein seemed to think that Danny was a rude person, but Stein would never admit any wrong-doing on his end. But at times, when Danny was obviously perturbed, Stein would try and fix it.

"Fuck off, Stein. I'm not in the mood for you to point out all my mistakes, again."

"No, no, Danny, c'mon now. I'm not pointing out your mistakes. I'm just saying, you are quite the optimist. I was given thirteen years and I don't think I'll ever get out of here any sooner."

"See, that kind of talk brings me down."

"The talk of a realist brings you down?"

"No, you're a pessimist."

In the classic way that Stein had established, he tried complimenting Danny but would insult him at the same time, like so.

"Have I mentioned you have quite a big vocabulary for a gangster?"

"Yes, you have, actually."

"Well good, just thought you should know that."

Later that day, their cell doors were opened from noon to five with a count at three. Danny leapt from the cell and made his way to the kitchen for lunch. He arrived and saw the rounded metal pot steaming as the chef, who was a fellow inmate, stirred.

Danny saw that it was soup on the menu for the day, and it sickened him.

"Looks like Travis wasn't kidding," Kirby said as he stepped up to Danny.

Kirby was quite an intimidating black man, but Danny was glad that they didn't resent one another. Instead, Kirby had Danny's back and Danny had his, if Kirby even needed it. He really was a man who could take care of himself.

He was imprisoned for having sex with a minor, but it was a cute blond girl who never shared her real age until it was too late. She made buckets of money that way and Kirby had fallen into it.

"I'm going outside," Danny said.

Danny went without lunch and made his way out to the courtyard. The courtyard appeared to be a very open and free place, but gangs and other cliques had marked their territory early on. It was a dangerous place to roam around, but Danny didn't care too much. He just wanted to be free from Stein's comments and questionings.

He watched as some men started playing basketball, and it reminded him of when he and Victor had met up with Emmitt and his brothers to play. One man who was playing appeared to be a Vietnam veteran who had mixed himself into the wrong crowd. He wore a bandana and was always playing basketball any chance he got. As Danny observed him, the ball rolled out of bounds and headed toward Danny.

"Hey kid, can you throw that back here?" the man asked.

Danny didn't hesitate. He reached down as the basketball neared his feet and started to pick it up, until he was pushed down to the ground. Danny fell forward but twisted so he'd fall on his back and be able to see who did it.

It was someone who Danny hadn't seen before, but the black man was large and in charge, and he had a threatening crew backing him.

"Lucius, I'm surprised you're talking to this pussy," the large man said in a bellowing voice.

"That's not very nice, Richardson. Plus, he was about to hand me back my ball," Lucius said in a slighted tone.

"You don't have a good hold of your balls anymore?" Richardson asked, and his crew laughed with him.

Now Lucius had a crew behind him of all kinds of mixed races, and Richardson's group stayed strong. Danny, unfortunately, was right in the middle of it all.

"Fuck off, Richardson," one of Lucius' men said.

This riled up Richardson and his gang. Danny stood on his feet, but didn't know where to lean.

"Hey, quiet down," Lucius said as he turned and exposed a neck tattoo of a skull being held by a devil woman. "I'm just asking you to leave the kid alone, alright?"

"Why should I be afraid of some little kid? Or why should I even be afraid of you, Lucius?"

"I know you don't fear me, but this is Ponchello's kid right here."

Instead of making Richardson fear Danny, it made his resent grow.

"Ponchello… that sounds familiar. Makes me kinda wanna cream him even more."

Danny knew there wasn't a good way out of this now. And as Richardson and his gang started to walk in towards him, Lucius and his gang started to step in as well.

Finally, it was all ended by a stray bullet hitting near the group. The shot was then heard and they all jumped back. The guard from the tower lifted a megaphone and said, "I can grab more ammo from the tower if I need to and gun all of you down."

Richardson's group started to walk away and Lucius didn't seem too crazy about letting Danny into their group, but eventually, he said, "Wanna shoot some hoops with us?"

"No," Danny decided. "But thank you."

Danny tossed the ball back to Lucius and headed back inside. At this point, he'd rather have Stein harass him more.

*****

Somehow, Danny was able to stay out of trouble until Wednesday, December 6th when Mahan Varsochi decided to pay him a visit with more updates.

"Alright, tell me you have some good news," Danny said.

Mahan, an eastern Italian man, wore a finely tailored suit that stuck to him like print on paper. He took a seat across from Danny and put his tan briefcase on the table. The man did not play around, he didn't have much of a sense of humor, and he always dressed to impress. Unlike other people associated with mobs, he didn't curse very often, either.

Danny found these things out as Mahan opened his briefcase, pulled out some meaningless papers and said, "Well, Danny, after speaking to the courts and trying to figure out what we're going to be able to do…"

"Yeah? Go on," Danny said.

"I told you before that ten years would be the minimum."

"Yes?"

"It's looking to be about fifty now."

Danny's jaw almost unhinged as it practically fell to the floor. He felt all the life within him start to slowly die as he said, "Fifty fucking years?!? Are you kidding me?"

"The police have more evidence than we thought," Mahan said. "They can link the footage of you and what you were wearing to how they caught you. It shows you kill at least one of the armored guards and then the FBI agent. Fifty years is the least we can get it reduced to. Otherwise, it would be one hundred-fifty years."

"Jesus fucking Christ Almighty… What the fuck is my dad paying you for if these are the results you're going to give? You said pleading guilty would help!"

"You don't understand, you spoiled brat. I can't clap my hands and make evidence disappear. Your father mentioned being able to pull some strings, but with something like this…"

Danny always liked to look around before he said anything incriminating.

"My father can send someone into the police station and have that evidence wiped out."

"Nope. Not a chance. The evidence has been spread out between three different departments, not to mention replicas of the footage have already been made. We have no way to do anything like that."

"I'm sure Leo could."

"He's not going to. Your father is not going to take any crazy chances right now. The police are practically breathing down his neck as we speak."

"Yeah, well, whatever saves his ass, I guess."

Mahan looked disgusted as he said, "Your father loves you and cares for you very much. Every time I head over here, he makes sure that I pass that along to you."

"When's our appeal date, or whatever?" Danny asked.

"They keep messing with us. Sometimes they say a year, sometimes two years."

"So it could take two years for me to even get any kind of deal to get out of here?"

"Unless you wanna stick with the fifty year deal, yeah."

"Nope, not gonna happen."

"Danny, be reasonable. The evidence is very much alive."

"Yeah, I'm done talking to you. Let me know when the appeal date is, or when you can work your magic and convince a judge to get me outta here early."

*****

Danny tried so hard to cope with what was going on for the next few days, but he couldn't. He felt as if the world around him was slowly crumbling.

"Fifty years isn't too bad for what you did. Considering you also killed some police officers and whatever else you did before you even robbed that bank," Stein said while stirring around his instant mashed potatoes on the cafeteria tray.

"Shut up, Stein. I don't want to hear it."

"I'm serious. Hell, in fifty years, you'll still be kicking no problem. I can see you still being able to live it up at seventy years old."

"Jesus Christ, I said stop!"

Danny was stricken with terror every time he thought of how long that would be. He couldn't imagine being around in prison for fifty years. But if he hadn't plead guilty in the first place, he would've gotten around 150 years...

Danny was shaking after his outburst and Stein's face showed instant remorse.

"Danny, I'm really sorry. I know your dad will pull through for you, I know he will. He'll think of something, I promise."

Danny tried to calm himself before he had another panic attack, and he was able to do it successfully. The guard started to step up to the cell as Danny exhaled deeply.

"Quiet down in there, Stein and Ponchello."

Danny nodded and waited for the guard to walk away once more. After he did, Danny turned to Stein and said, "I'm sorry I'm just... freaking out."

"I know," Stein replied softly.

*****

On Sunday, December 10th, Danny attempted to go outside in the courtyard once more with a long sleeve shirt under his jumpsuit. It was cold and windy, which caused every group outside to stick together for warmth.

For some reason, Danny had a desire to speak with Lucius about wanting to stand up for him. When Danny approached them, Lucius looked up from the group and gave him a look of acceptance.

"Ponchello."

"Lucius."

"Would you like a cig?" Lucius asked with smoke escaping his lips.

"Definitely."

Lucius pulled up another cigarette from his pack and handed it over to Danny, who didn't even need to request a lighter. In a matter of seconds, he had the cigarette lit and puffed once into his lungs. An overwhelming feeling of relaxation was flowing over him and he felt fine.

"There, that'll loosen you up," Lucius said.

Danny faintly smiled and Lucius continued, "What's got you so down?"

"They're saying I need to hold out in here for another two or so years to get a reduced sentence, or I can be stuck here for fifty years."

"Jesus, kid... what did you do?"

"Held up the Federal Exchange Bank in Detroit and killed a few cops."

Lucius stared at Danny and said, "So that was you making the big getaway. What about your partner? Is he the one who visited you a few weeks ago?"

"Yeah, he got away. I told him to run. Our original getaway driver-"

"Got away too soon?" Lucius interrupted.

"Exactly."

"Yeah, I think that was my old friend Roy Harrison if I remember right."

"You knew Roy?" Danny asked as he took another long puff.

"Yeah, we were in 'Nam together. Served under the thirty-ninth Infantry. We were active duty... hell, everyone was active duty at one point or another."

"What did you do?" Danny asked.

Lucius hesitated a second, but ended up saying his next sentence with a small smile.

"I don't know, Ponchello, I just couldn't stop killing people I guess."

It chilled Danny to see someone talk of death so freely, but he remembered doing it once himself.

*****

Soon, Lucius and Danny became pretty close. Danny would try and sell things that Lucius brought in from the outside world, and it made their partnership flourish. At one point, Danny felt bad that he hadn't talked to Victor in a while, even though Victor had upset him before. Victor had seemed semi-delusional and paranoid when he came to visit Danny, but they were still friends. On the night of the fifteenth, Danny made sure to make the call before he headed on to bed.

"Victor, it's me, Danny."

"Danny... are you doing okay?"

"Yeah Victor, I'm fine. I made some friends here in prison... besides my cellmate and the guy in the next cell over."

"That's good."

"What about things there, Victor?" Danny asked.

"Oh, not much really... I was given the all clear to leave the manor, but I really have nowhere to go."

"What happened to Sid's Diner?" Danny asked.

"It's funny you ask that," Victor started. "I drove by it yesterday and it's turning into a McDonald's."

"No way... that's a disgrace," Danny said.

"Yeah... but hey, the Don said Mahan visited you recently. How did that go?"

Danny didn't want to ever repeat what Mahan Varsochi had said, so he replied, "Oh, he didn't say much. He said the courts are fucking with my case all the time. Can't figure out an appeal date or anything like that, yet. I don't even understand half of this shit."

"Oh, that sucks. I miss ya, man."

"I miss you too, Victor."

"Want me to come see you again?"

"Of course, how about this weekend? Like, Sunday or something?"

"Sure, I can do that."

There was a brief silence before Danny continued, "Victor, I've been thinking about what you said... about my father being selfish."

"Oh, I don't mean for that to upset you, Danny."

"No, no, I think you're right, Victor. I think my father is being selfish in a way. This guy, Mahan... he's not pulling miracles out of his ass like he's usually been known to do. This guy could've had me out on bail if he wanted to, but he's not giving his A-game. I think my father is responsible for it."

Victor went quiet on the other end, but Danny wasn't sure why. Isn't this what Victor was wanting to hear this whole time?

"Danny, maybe we should talk about this more on Sunday."

"I think that's a good idea, Victor. But hey, before I go, I have a question?"

"Yes?"

"Have you found the Platinum Briefcase yet?"

They shared a laugh and Victor admitted that the Platinum Briefcase had yet to be found. When they were done with their laugh, Danny said his goodbyes and hung up the phone.

*****

As Danny lay in his bed in the middle of the night, he slept peacefully. At one point in his dream, he saw his mother in a flowery dress, running around in high grass. It brought joy to him as he slept, and it distracted him from the evil that was about to consume him in the conscious world.

The cell door buzzed but didn't slide open. The noise made Danny stir, but he didn't completely wake up. Instead, he continued dreaming about his mother who he hadn't seen in so long.

Once Lucius and his men made sure that Stein and Ponchello were still asleep, he pulled the cell door open and held his knife at the ready. He turned to look at his men, who all readied their shanks, and Lucius began the carnage.

He lifted Danny's right arm and stabbed under his ribcage into his lung. With the lung punctured, Danny was no longer able to scream or shout but he did try. Lucius then yanked Danny off the bed and he thudded to the cold hard ground.

"Sorry Danny, but I can't say no to extra money for my commissary."

Once Lucius made the final statement, he stepped back so the other men could begin stabbing Danny to death.

Danny stared up at the ceiling of the cell with his mouth opened wide, desperate to make some sort of sound, but he couldn't. The men stabbed into Danny until their shanks were practically dull, and then they started in on Stein. Danny was dead by the time they started in on Stein, but for one last measure to make sure Danny was dead, Lucius slowly slit Danny's throat from left to right and then tucked the knife away once more.

All of the men had bedsheets tucked around their arms so blood would only get on their hands and not their clothes. When they were done with the stabbing, they threw the pillowcases to the floor and covered Danny's blood soaked corpse for the guards to find in the morning.

## Chapter Seventy Seven
### Saturday, December 16th, 1978
### The Ponchello Manor

I woke up at about noon and felt that I had wasted most of my day. But, I really didn't have anything I could do, so maybe it wasn't so bad.

I went outside of the manor and took a jog, a stress-relieving technique that Chief Ramzorin had suggested for me to try after I told him that the conversation with Danny didn't go as planned. He understood, and said he would try and stall Darnell in the meantime.

"Why do you help me so much, Chief?" I asked.

"Because I care about you, Victor, and I don't want you ending up like all the others."

The relaxing jog took me around the manor grounds, although passing by the sticks where we commemorated Roger, Al, and Nick made it a more somber experience. But as I passed by those graves, I remembered that I had two more that needed to be placed there: Charlie and Blake.

I made my way over to the woods and grabbed the sticks that were available. Then, I ran back to where the others were and placed the sticks for them.

I hoped they were all resting in peace, and then I continued my run around the manor.

I made a few laps around the garage, and then decided to take a jog across the front grounds, which were quiet and empty. As I ran around the front of the manor, I realized how bad the ivy had gotten on the front. It had started to brown and deteriorate but it wasn't completely gone yet. As I finished my run, I took a few minutes to stand outside so the air would cool me off. I saw Jordan come out and light up a cigarette.

"Hey, Victor."

"Doing alright, Jordan?"

"Yeah, yeah I think so."

Jordan seemed a little shaky, but it didn't appear to be because of the wind alone.

"You okay?"

"Didn't you just ask that?"

"Yeah but I think you're lying."

"Well," Jordan said, "I kind of am."

"Tell me what's going on."

Jordan let out a long sigh and said, "Michelle called me from Rhode Island… that's where she moved when the Don cut her pay and everything. She has family there. She said I'm going to be a father."

Deep inside I knew that I was about to bring this whole operation to an end and everyone would be imprisoned. But for the sake of the moment, I smiled and said, "What? Jordan, that's great! Don't be down about that."

"It's not that I'm down about it, I just… now is a bad time to be told that."

"Should've worn a raincoat."

"She said she was on protection… helped regulate her… stuff."

Jordan's queasiness over the female reproductive system made me laugh. He shot me a look and I decided to stop laughing.

"Look, we should go out and get drinks!"

"No, the Don asked me to stay here. I think you're the only one with permission to leave the grounds."

"Fine, lemme go get a bottle and then I'll come back so we can celebrate."

I drove down to the warehouse and walked over to where they put the busted crates. It reminded me of when Danny and I stockpiled for the party we had at the manor. Not sure if we could have a party tonight, but whatever reason I could make up to get my hands on a drink would work for now.

I grabbed three bottles of vodka and then drove over to the convenience store and grabbed some Root Beer, Coke, and Dr. Pepper. My excitement started to build as I made it back to the manor, but then I noticed how dead the manor looked when I returned.

When I walked through the front door, I saw quite a few people standing in the living room, murmuring amongst themselves.

"… something like this was not supposed to happen."

"… do we know who did it?"

"… Jesus Christ."

I saw that Jordan was in the crowd, and I was hoping they were talking about Michelle being pregnant with his child. They all heard my paper bags rattling as I walked by and they turned around to face me. Their faces were filled with sadness.

"Victor, have a seat, please," Leo said with dim eyes.

I placed the paper bags at the entrance of the living room and I made my way to my favorite loveseat. All of the other men remained standing as Leo waiting for me to sit down. The minute I did, Leo broke the news.

"Victor, Danny's dead."

The same old train that had hit me so many times in the past few years of my life had made another stop right into my heart. Not seeing Danny for a few weeks made it even harder to believe. I had almost predicted that something would happen to Danny. There was no way that a cop killer would survive in prison.

My mouth felt dry, my hands started to turn cold. I looked at someone for comfort, but I knew that out of the group that stood before me, none of them could offer it.

Before anything else could be said, I walked out of the room and made my way to my car. I don't even remember the drive into downtown; I just knew that I needed to go to a bar.

The bar I ended up going to was one the gang migrated to once Studio 9 was destroyed by Jackson Burose and his gang. It was simple, and the owner didn't mess with anyone in the gang.

The bartender could see the tears on my face, so he didn't even bother to ask me how it was going.

"What's the strongest that you have?"

"We're out of Everclear, so how about some whiskey?"

"That's what I want."

The bartender started to prepare it, but then he asked, "Have you eaten anything?"

"I don't need to."

I knew he was going to suggest having the drink mixed, or that I should have some bread or nachos, but I didn't care.

*That's right, let it go straight to your liver...* the voice egged me on.

The bartender finished preparing the straight whiskey in his smallest shot glass and I downed it in one swift motion. I could tell he was partially amazed and fully worried about why I was drinking, but I wouldn't talk. Instead, I continued taking as many shots as I could, until I faintly remember the bartender practically throwing a trashcan at me. I'm pretty sure I ended up falling into a steaming pile of my own vomit in the men's bathroom and sleeping until about four AM, when I was awakened by David Weston.

"Victor, my God... let's get you home."

I never knew why they sent David to get me, but I was glad they did. He actually understood me and knew what I needed to feel better. After he set me up in his car, he gave me two chew tablets and said, "Bartender said you were drinking straight whiskey, these should help."

I chewed the chalky substance and wanted to gag, but David was prepared for it. "Have a little water, too," David said.

I took a few sips and I felt the chalky tablets work their way down to my empty stomach and ease my pain. I finished taking the sips of water from the bottle and I screwed the cap back on. David looked at me and said, "I'm sorry, Victor. I know Danny was your best friend."

"Don't be sorry," I replied as I put the water bottle between my legs. "I'm not surprised it happened, I just can't believe it."

## Chapter Seventy Eight
### Sunday, December 18th-24th, 1978
### Ponchello Manor

It was hard to stay alive at this point in my life. Not because I really had any outstanding threats, but because I couldn't think of a reason to live. My judgement was blurry, nothing made sense. Even with Christmas approaching, I really didn't have a care in the world. I knew there was nothing I could do to make myself feel in the holiday spirit. Everyone I wanted to talk to or spend time with was dead.

I wasn't the only one feeling down, however. There was no holiday spirit in the Ponchello manor. Michelle, Phil, and a few others used to decorate the household with tinsel and ornaments. The couch in the living room was moved out to the front area for a Christmas tree and presents, but not this year. It didn't matter. With Danny dead, and with the Don feeling ill 24/7, there was no need to have a traditional Christmas.

Everyone seemed to be moping around the house just like me. Because of the Don's forbidden sadness, none of us wanted to be happy. We all felt that Danny's death was somehow our fault.

One day in the kitchen as David went to make the Don some food, he said to Leo and me, "I've never seen the Don cry until I told him about Danny... and even then, it took him a few hours before he finally broke."

"He lost his one and only son, what can you expect?" Leo asked.

"He definitely shouldn't take shots of whiskey..."

They both turned to me at my morbid joke, but I grasped my stomach as I felt a burn in my lower intestine that had started ever since the night I chugged so much of it. I looked at them and the voice spoke in my mind.

*Ah, fuck off. We needed to loosen up, didn't we, Victor?*

"Yeah, I'd recommend never doing that again, kid," Leo commented.

David nodded in agreement and took the microwave dinner out for the Don. When he left the room, Leo asked, "Feeling any better, Victor?"

"I've been better, but it's not as bad as it was."

"Good... you really gave us quite a scare when you left, I'll tell ya."

"I had to leave... I couldn't think of a reason to stay here."

Leo seemed to understand what I was saying, but I ended up leaving before the conversation went any further.

*****

On Christmas Eve, the snow was coming down like it was the next ice age. I stared out my window at the back yard practically all day, and it made me start to feel the holiday spirit. I wasn't going to go make a snowman or anything, but I really wanted to meet up with Chief Ramzorin. I didn't think he could make me feel better, but he was really the only friend I had left.

I walked through about two inches of settled snow to make it over to the garage. Upon arrival, I walked in and grabbed the phone next to the tool cabinets.

After dialing Chief Ramzorin's direct number to his office, I waited for him to answer.

"Ramzorin here."

"Chief, hey…"

"Victor. What a… surprise, I guess."

"Chief, do you think we could meet up?"

"Do you have something on the Don?"

I thought about lying, but it would do no good.

"No, I don't."

"Then why would we meet up?" Chief Ramzorin asked blatantly.

"I just… I need a friend."

I heard Chief Ramzorin go completely silent on the other end, until he finally said, "Okay. Let's meet at Michelangelo's, like old times."

"Sounds good to me. I'm leaving now."

I opened up the garage door and started up my car. I wasn't sure that my tires would do very well in the snow, but from what I listened to on the radio there wasn't any ice so I felt that I could make it.

Luckily, my car was able to plow through the snow like a tank. But I was surprised to see Leo step out and make his way over to my car.

"Victor, where are you going in the snow?" he asked. "It's going to start getting really bad. The sun hasn't been out all day."

"I ran out of deodorant," I said, trying to think of anything that I could. "I don't want to stink up the house if we get snowed in."

"Well you can change that if to a when," Leo said sternly. "But okay, I know I won't be able to stop you. If you don't mind, I think we're low on milk. Can you grab some?"

Leo handed me two dollars and I nodded. He patted my car and watched as I drove to the front gate that we were now leaving open so it wouldn't get stuck with the snowy and icy weather.

Hopping onto the highway, I started thinking about how many times I had taken this trip downtown before. It seemed like way too many. It would be much easier to just live downtown, but moving out of the manor was always seen as a sign of betrayal, as if I hadn't betrayed the Don enough already.

That thought made me laugh, knowing he'd regret giving me this car if he knew I ratted out so many operations and other accomplices.

*The Don would use any strength he has left in him to strangle your neck dry, I'll tell ya that.*

"I wonder if he even has all that much strength. He's been stuck in his room for days," I replied to the voice in my head.

*I know the perfect Christmas present for you, Victor... having the Don drop dead.*

I laughed at the way the voice said that. It made it seem like it was a cartoon.

*You laugh, but I know that's what you'd like to see happen.*

"Chief Ramzorin... no, *Darnell* would be so pissed if that happened."

*Hahaha, I can only imagine. Then, who'd he have to bring in? A bunch of henchmen?*

"Pretty much," I replied.

At no point did speaking aloud to this voice ever bother me since I had replied to it in the shower. I felt like it was keeping me company as I pulled off of the plowed and salted highways and made my way into the snowier streets. I watched in glee as other cars continued to struggle through all of the snow on the grounds. Other shops around the downtown area had their own Christmas trees and ornaments that I could look at, but it didn't feel the same. None of it did.

At last, I pulled in front of Michelangelo's and put my car in park with the emergency brake to back it up. I saw Chief Ramzorin at our usual booth sitting alone, and I was hoping Darnell wouldn't be around.

I stepped in, feeling the cold slowly lift off of my back as the warm restaurant made me feel safe and welcomed. Chief Ramzorin didn't look up from his coffee as I approached him, but I didn't blame him. For the first time in a long time, I approached him with optimism. But when I sat down, he made it clear he didn't feel the same.

"Chief, thank you for meeting me," I said.

"I can't say 'no problem' because I hit a slick spot on the way here and almost broke my neck."

I grimaced and watched as he kept drinking the coffee.

"Where's Antonio?" I asked.

"I told him and the others to stay in the back. They're technically closed right now for the holiday."

"Oh, I feel bad then."

Chief Ramzorin seemed shocked at my remorse and I felt him analyze me over and over again.

"So, Danny was killed in prison."

I felt the glee leave my body as I slowly nodded.

"We haven't talked much since after you saw him. Do you really not have any other leads?"

"What are you doing for Christmas, Chief?"

My change in the topic made Ramzorin's face turn blood red as he started in on me.

"Great question, Victor. I wish I could say that I'd be feeling safe at home for Christmas. I wish I could say that the Don was imprisoned along with all his other men and maybe they'd piss off some prison folk and get murdered as well. I wish I didn't have to talk to some kid I used to respect and admire and try to convince him of the seriousness of this conversation. I wish I could say all of those things, but it turns out I can't."

"Y'know what I'd like for Christmas, Victor?"

I turned to my right to see Darnell stroll out of the bathroom and throw his used paper towel in the trash receptacle at the front of the bar.

"A new dildo so you can fuck yourself?" I asked.

"Close! I'd really like it if a Mr. Don Ponchello could be behind bars."

"The Don is ridiculously ill, I think he's gonna croak any second now."

"Well then we really need to go ahead and get him! If we do, then I can get to self-sodomizing at home!"

"You just fall for anything I say, don't you?"

"I guess the Chief taught me well."

"Tell him what you really wanted to tell him, Darnell," Chief Ramzorin argued.

"Yeah, what would that be, Darnell?" I asked.

Detective Darnell's smile and cheerfulness seemed to disappear from his face as he said, "We found your buddy Jacob, finally."

"Really?" I asked, feeling hope for a partner to testify with.

"Yeah, or parts of him, anyway. He appeared to be attacked by wild dogs as he was on the run. The patrol car had to scare them off before we were able to recover the body."

"Thanks for getting my hopes up for another person to be able to testify," I said as I felt sickness in my stomach.

"Victor, at this point, you're just obstructing justice. We need to have you testify against Don Ponchello ASAP. I don't know if you guys have big plans for your gangster Christmas bullshit where everyone gets a hooker and a new TV, and so you want to wait for all of that first, but we need your testimony and we need it now. Can't you see, Victor? The Don and his men are all cursed. The Don's getting sick, Danny was horrendously murdered, Jacob was killed, all the other members of the Kids were killed, and you're the only one left. But I've found that your curse is that you're too stupid to see that the only way out is to testify against this prick and his organization... or what's left, anyway."

"Does it really still matter that much to you?" I asked.

"Well, *duh*. Otherwise, I came out here for no reason, and my boss will chew my ass out like saltwater taffy."

"They're going to kill me... if they get a chance and any of them make bail, they'll kill me. Don't you both understand that?"

"We do," Chief Ramzorin said. "But we can protect you. When you agree to testify, we can have them arrested by the next morning. Darnell has some people in Washington who are very eager to bring this to a close. He can have all the documentation in a matter of seconds and we can get these guys, Victor. We can keep you at the police station in protective custody."

"Yeah, and once you testify, we can have you in Jamaica under some new name with girls and their massive tits smacking your thighs while they blow you, how does that sound?"

"Do you really mean that?" I asked.

"Yeah, they have nice tits down there in Jamaica."

"No, I mean about the new name."

Darnell seemed upset by my lack of interest in the women down there, but he finally said, "Oh, well, yeah we'd have to change your name. Otherwise, someone could find you real quick if any of the Don's loyal members were still out there."

I started to think about the tailor, Mr. Dainov, but I doubted he even had the will or strength to find and kill me. But it wasn't a worry of mine. When he said my name would be changed, I started feeling excited about the whole entire thing. I had always wanted to change my name to something different, but I never found a way to do so without going through the legal system and making it obvious. If we were to do it this way, maybe no one would be able to find me ever again.

"But, it'd be better if we had any kind of evidence we can get," Chief Ramzorin said. "Is there any money from the bank robberies left?"

"I think so... and they wouldn't notice if I took any at this point," I answered with a new hope rising.

"Great! Then I think we're all on board to have this closed out by tomorrow morning, right?" Darnell asked with a sincere smile.

"Yes, I'm ready to have this all lifted off my shoulders," I replied.

Chief Ramzorin gave me a smile of encouragement as well as I stepped away from the booth and made my way to the door.

"Victor, I think we'll assemble a team to storm the manor tomorrow. If you can, I'd suggest getting a hotel room at the Hilton downtown after grabbing the money and I'll call ahead so they can put the room under a different name. Otherwise, things may get ugly when we breach."

"No, I am completely fine with that. Let me get the cash, and then I'll check in to the Hilton downtown."

I left the restaurant with high hopes of what was to come. All I had to do was take the money and run.

But of course, that was all set up in a fashion that was way too easy.

"Victor."

I was outside and just about to get in my car when the haunting voice spoke my name. I knew who it was before I even turned around, and I almost let loose of my bladder.

I turned around to face Leo, who had the passenger window rolled down and a smug look on his face.

"Come over here to my car, Victor. We're going to take a little drive."

# Chapter Seventy Nine

"I can't fucking believe it, after all this time, I always knew!"

Leo was almost crying in joy at his discovery of my meeting with Chief Ramzorin and Detective Darnell. My entire body was numb. I had no idea what to do or say. Everything had been going well just minutes before, and now...

"I really did catch you red-handed, didn't I? Oh, I knew I would."

He was driving down roads that would eventually lead to the Detroit River, where I figured he'd be dumping my body either dead or alive. It was all ruined; there was no way out.

"Man, you really have nothing to say, do you? Don't worry. I recorded on tape everything you just said with your friends in there, followed by taking some photos of you with the Chief of Police here in the shitty metropolis of Detroit. I really got you, Victor. You have to admit. This has been going on for a while, hasn't it? Jesus… I told the Don over and over again. It's Victor, it's gotta be Victor. But no, I was told that I was bothering you too much and making you resent the gang. I told him so many times… I said, 'What about the New York soldiers, boss? No one knew they'd be leaving today, and they just coincidentally got stopped?' And then Jacob was taken in, but you threw me off with the whole beating up the owner routine you did with Danny. Then I just wondered if you were schizophrenic, which, in my opinion, became overwhelmingly apparent when the bank robbery went down. I mean, FBI? They don't just appear magically, but that makes sense with that Darnell guy being in the restaurant with the Chief. What is he doing here, Victor? Huh?"

*Yup, you got me, Leo, you bald-headed fuck. Got me fair and square.*

I couldn't bring myself to speak. My fear was slowly turning into rage and hate towards Leo, feelings that had always been there but were now growing exponentially. I couldn't stand him talking anymore. He was driving me insane. I heard a sharp ringing in my brain, like a teapot that was done brewing, and I knew that my retaliation was coming, I just wasn't sure how.

Leo was driving to a snowy construction area. I knew I had to act fast.

"You don't have to talk, Victor. I just got one question: Of all the people that were taken down, why haven't you told the Chief about me?"

I felt something snap in my brain as I shouted, "Because you're next!"

"No, Victor, wait!"

My pistol was just begging to be fired and I made its wishes come true. I disturbed it from its comfortable slumber under my left armpit with my right hand, grasped the handle, and started yanking the trigger. The bullets started flying through my coat and into Leo's side. Leo's defense was to try and put his hand up at me with the palm facing out, but I wasn't going to stop. After I had fired almost the entire clip into his side, I felt the car jerk forward as we slowly ran into a light pole.

I had my seatbelt on, but Leo didn't. He slammed forward into the steering wheel and spit up blood onto the console. After all the shots that I had fired, it didn't take long for him to bleed out. I heard a suppressed moan of exhaust and old age flow out of his mouth with the blood, and he remained still with his eyes facing forward at the construction site. I glanced down to see a small fire starting on my coat, so I pulled it off and threw it down on the floorboard.

Blood was all over the nice interior of his car, and I thought back to what he said right before I started firing.

His right hand moved across the dash slowly, until he ran out of room to drag it and it fell in front of the glove box, making a bloody handprint quite prevalent on it.

I turned to the glovebox, and then turned back to Leo's lifeless body. I had a feeling he was trying to show me something. Without wasting too much time, I pulled the glove box down and saw a silver silenced pistol waiting to be used inside. Next, I saw a weird black walkie-talkie that just had static on the other end and no way to talk to the person on the other side. But the best part of it all was a collection of cassette tapes that were in a Ziploc baggie.

When I was very confident that Leo was deader than dead, I pulled out the Ziploc baggie and read what the Sharpie said on the front:

### Evidence against the Don

I took a moment to turn back to Leo and stare at him with a slight sense of anger and regret.

*That son of a bitch… he was going to say he wants to testify with you… but he let his pride of catching you get in the way. He knew the gang was coming down, and he figured there had to be some way out. Little did he know, that way out would be with his least favorite person in the gang.*

I opened the baggie as that thought passed by and I saw a tape labeled "Bank

Robbery Plans". I popped the cassette into Leo's tape player on the console and pressed play. Right away, I heard Leo's voice.

"So, let me get this straight. You're going to have Victor, Danny, Charlie and Blake do the robbery, and no one else?"

I then heard the Don speak.

"Yes. We need the money, Leo, and I don't want you being in the middle of this. That's why Roy will be the getaway driver and Jordan will be the backup."

"How are we going to do this? How are we going to pull it off?"

"That'll be the Kids job… Your job is to kill Peterson before he rats us out on something again."

"I don't think it's Peterson, Don."

There was silence, but then I heard the Don speak again.

"You dare question me, Leo? You still want to go on about how you think it's Victor? It's bullshit. He and Danny are too good of friends. Victor wouldn't turn him in, or any of the rest of us."

"He hasn't yet but he will. I guarantee it. And I fear that by the time you figure that out, it'll be too late."

The tape stopped playing and I rewound it. As I waited for it to stop, I looked at Leo again and shook my head.

"Son of a bitch…"

But it was right then that I realized, I had evidence against the Don. Leo had provided the evidence that I needed to put the Don away.

I reached over Leo's body and pulled his handle towards me to open his door. Once I did, I pushed Leo out of the car with my feet and turned the car off.

Leo's body hit the snow and it practically buried him. I took my coat and draped it over his body. It was the least I could do.

Finally, I looked around and saw what I desperately needed.

A payphone.

# Chapter Eighty

"What? Are you serious?"

"As serious as I can be."

"Do I even ask what happened to Leo Morton?"

I looked over at his body in the snow and said, "I'd rather not talk about it."

"Jesus Christ… well, I'm glad you found what you did. That's exactly what we need to take down the Don," Chief Ramzorin said.

"Great job, Victor! I knew you could do it," Darnell shouted in an overly dramatic way.

"We knew something had happened when your car stayed there at the restaurant for so long, but we knew you could pull through whatever it was."

"Okay, enough of this cheerleading shit," I said. "What are we going to do?"

"What do you mean? Darnell is done getting the arrest warrant for any and all residences of the Ponchello manor. We've won, Victor. You just need to make your way to the hotel and wait there. Otherwise, we're afraid you'll get stuck out in the snow."

"We're going to arrest the Don Christmas morning?" I asked.

"Did you think I was kidding?" Darnell asked.

Chief Ramzorin sighed and said, "I'm not really crazy about the timing either, Victor, but it's now or never."

"I understand," I responded.

"Good. Now get out of that phone booth and get to the hotel. Otherwise you're going to freeze to death."

We ended the conversation on that note and the line went quiet. I hung up the phone, and then started thinking in the frozen glass box.

*David Weston doesn't deserve any of what's coming*, I thought.

*Ah… you grew a soft spot for David, did you?*

I couldn't deny it. David had helped me out so many times and been the one who really seemed to show care towards me. He was the one they sent to get my drunken ass just a few days ago, so I felt that I owed him a warning.

I picked up the payphone once more and made the call to the manor. To my luck, he was the one who answered.

"Who is this?"

"David, it's me."

"Victor?"

"Yeah, it's me, Victor."

"Hey, are you almost home? The snow keeps coming down."

"You need to leave."

David was silent on the other end for a moment, and then asked, "Why?"

"Look, Leo found out that the cops are going to raid the manor in the morning and now he's on the run. He told me to do the same, and to call you and have you run too."

"Whoa, whoa, whoa, wait Victor, you're speaking gibberish."

"No, I think I'm speaking clearly."

"But you're not telling me the truth."

Even through the phone, David could tell I was lying. I was relieved he hadn't confronted me before about being the rat.

"David, it's been me this whole time."

"As the rat?"

"Yes."

David waited a bit before he inquired further.

"And Leo? Where is he really?"

I glanced over at Leo's body again, still feeling regret for killing him, but also a sense of accomplishment.

"Depending on his religious views, he's either in Heaven, Hell, or eternal darkness."

David did a strange kind of sigh on the other end of the line, and then composed himself.

"Look, David, I have a ton of cash saved up under my mattress at the end of the footboard. I've never told the cops anything about you or what you do, or that you even exist. I want you to take all that money I have saved up and just, disappear."

"I can do that," David replied confidently. "But, why me, Victor? Why warn me?"

"Does it really matter?" I asked. Before he could respond, I added, "You could do better, David. And you were really not a part of this to begin with. You've just been the one who protected the Don this whole time, and I don't want you getting killed when the cops raid tomorrow. You were a hired gun to begin with, and now I'm paying you to leave."

"Well, Victor, I do appreciate it. I suppose we'll never see each other again, but it was nice knowing you."

"Same to you, David."

And David ended the call with a simplistic, "Goodbye, then."

## Chapter Eighty One

It all seemed to finally be coming to an end. After so many people were killed in the process, mostly by my hand or the police, I now felt safer as I drove around in Leo's blood-soaked car. I was trying to clear my mind, really bring everything to a close. It was all over. By tomorrow morning, the Don would be in police custody.

For some reason, I didn't feel like getting to the hotel room just yet. I felt like a drive around town in the snow would soothe me and bring me to a place of rest and relaxation.

Beside me was the silenced pistol, the Ziploc baggie of tapes, and the walkie-talkie that continued to buzz with no voices or anything else, but I felt paranoid about turning it off.

*Well done, Victor. You finally cleared yourself of the Don and his men and you'll be in Jamaica before you know it.*

I smiled at the thought of it, but I wondered why I still had this voice in my head that talked to me. It seemed as though if all of the madness had come to an end, the voice should too.

*Do you not like me, Victor? I was really starting to think we were getting along, but maybe not. That's okay though, you don't have to like me.*

"Then leave," I said.

*Oh, but as you said, I will not leave until the madness is over.*

"What the hell are you talking about?" I asked aloud. "It is over. The Don is dead to rights."

*No, no, the madness is not over... it will never end. It is only just beginning, you see... You're too naïve, Victor. It's quite bothersome.*

"Who are you, anyway?"

*That's a silly question. I am you. I am your id, your primal instinct, the one who can drive you to a point of wanting to kill your own best friend so you can get away with it all.*

"It was a last minute idea... it made sense in my head."

*Lots of things make sense to lots of different people, but society may argue which things make the most sense, and which things are not acceptable. For instance, when you joined the gang. It made sense to you back then, but what about now? That's not even society arguing your ideas, that's YOU from WITHIN.*

"Danny had to go; he'd never join me in the trials."

*Of course not. He was loyal to his father till death, which was finally bestowed upon him. I'm not arguing with you, Victor. I'm simply showing you that the madness will not end. You have not completed the madness that is in store for you.*

"Why do you say that?"

I was in the middle of the downtown area when I started driving by the police station that Chief Ramzorin worked at. Unexpectedly, the walkie-talkie started crackling, and then I heard two male voices speaking faintly to one another. I slowed the car down, and wondered if I should turn the volume up or not.

*Go ahead, see what they're chatting about.*

There was no way I was going to ignore the conversation inside, so I reached over to the walkie and turned up the volume.

"I can't believe the little bastard finally got us exactly what we need," I heard Darnell say.

"It was pretty incredible when I picked up the phone and I heard him on the other end. I was sure that he had been picked up and fed to the same dogs that Jacob was," Chief Ramzorin replied.

"Goddamn, I must say… it took a lot out of me to not knock that kid's teeth down his fucking throat when he wouldn't cooperate, even from day one."

"Well I'm glad you didn't do that."

"Eh, I still want to, but I'll try to continue to hold back."

Darnell's voice infuriated me as I listened in on their conversation.

"By the way, Ramzorin, I've been meaning to ask you."

"What would that be, Special Agent Darnell?"

Darnell took a deep breath and asked, "You know you can't really give Victor a full pardon for everything that he's done, right?"

I felt myself hold my breath for the answer.

"Yes, of course I know that. But how else was I going to get him to cooperate?"

Once Darnell started laughing about the story of Jamaica and everything else, I grabbed the walkie and smashed it on the front of the car.

*Victor, Victor, Victor…*

I was panting. My anger could no longer be contained at all. Everyone I loved was gone. No one was my friend anymore. Even Chief Ramzorin, of all people, had only been using me.

I looked at the silenced pistol and thought about taking it into Chief Ramzorin's office…

*NO! You're going after the wrong target.*

"Then who do I have to kill?"

*Whoever is left at the Don's manor.; anyone that will be brought into police custody tomorrow morning and put on trial. You have to kill them, Victor, not the Chief or Darnell. You go in there to kill Darnell, the Chief is going to have to put you down whether he wants to or not. You must go after the real enemy, although seeing Darnell without any blood left in his system would be nice.*

"I have to kill all of them? Everyone at the manor?"

*Yes. Because the second that you leave one of them alive for the police to apprehend tomorrow, and the second they find out it's you that is putting all of them away, they will have you killed in an instant. I guarantee someone is going to pull some strings and have you looking awful similar to Danny Ponchello.*

The conversation went on and on as I continued driving downtown until the darkness really started to engulf the city. As I jumped back on the highway to fulfill my new mission, my new slaughter, my final slaughter, I could feel that instead of having an angel on one shoulder and a devil on the other, both shoulders were weighed down by the devil.

I drove with my left hand on the steering wheel and my right hand gripping the silver silenced pistol. I couldn't keep my thoughts straight. Voices of people from my past were shouting in my mind and I had to shake my head every once in a while to try to get them out.

*Go ahead and kill them all, son... I knew you'd turn out to be a screw up,* I heard my father shout.

*They ruined you, my poor sweet Victor... this is the way it has to end,* my mother's voice echoed.

I saw Johnny Fargo's face and his voice bellowed, *Man, I didn't know beating you up on a daily basis would have me end up like this...*

*You could have saved me, Victor, but you let me die instead,* Charlie's voice boomed.

*Don't do it, Vic. That's my father in there. You're really going to kill my dad?* Danny asked.

*I was going to be on your side, kid... oh well, you always got all the attention anyway,* Leo said plainly.

*It seems that the only person you don't want to kill is yourself,* Emmitt's voice said to end them all.

When I pulled past the front gate of the manor, the voices went completely silent. There was only the small voice deep in the back of my mind, softly but hoarsely repeating the words, *kill, kill, kill.*

I stepped out of Leo's blood-soaked car and slammed the door behind me. My clothes were starting to crisp in the freezing air as I walked up to the manor; the silver pistol binding to my hand from the cold. The snow fell like it was never going to end.

*Even though David is gone, you're going to have to be careful of the others.*

"I know," I whispered, and I reached out to open the door with my left hand and stepped into the manor.

I was now inside and I felt the warmth of the manor start to defrost my body. I felt that my fingers could move freely once again and I quietly closed the front door. Very softly in the back of my mind, the voice continued to say, kill, kill, kill. When the door was closed, I heard the TV blaring in the living room with some sort of Christmas special on rerun.

*There's your first target, probably not expecting what's coming for him.*

I walked up to the entry way of the living room and the man watching the TV had his back facing me. I was pretty sure it was Scott, but it didn't really matter who it was.

I started to raise the pistol, and without much hesitation, I fired a shot through his head.

The silent bullet made things a little loud when it hit the TV and caused sparks to fly about and glass shattered to the floor.

"Hey, Victor?"

I turned to my right and saw Jordan walking with some steaming ramen noodles in a porcelain bowl from the kitchen.

"Hey, don't just go pointing that wherever you-"

The first bullet I fired went through his ramen and then through his spine, causing him to crumble to the ground. As he started to say something else, I fired through his head and mixed his brain matter with the noodles.

*You're doing well... That should be all of the men downstairs.*

I turned back into the living room like a robot and stepped toward the stairs. But right before I started heading up them, a man who didn't look too familiar came down with his pistol drawn. He didn't realize it was me doing the killing until I aimed up and fired once through his shoulder. The blood spattered on the wall behind him and he blindly fired two shots toward me, which both missed terribly. I finished him off with a shot through the head and he tumbled down the rest of the stairs.

*His shots weren't silenced. You may have to up your game now.*

The pistol had a ridiculously extended clip, so I wasn't worried about running out of ammo. I felt like that should've been most of the henchmen, but it was possible there were more.

Climbing up the rest of the stairs, I had my pistol up and ready for whatever else was to come. I stared down the long hallway and didn't see or hear a soul.

*Not a creature was stirring, not even a mouse... but the rat was the one doing the killing in this house.*

I moved quickly to the other end of the hallway and then peeked around the corner at the Don's room. His two doors at the corner of the hallway were closed, but I still didn't hear anyone.

*Let's hope David's not waiting in there for you.*

"He won't be," I whispered confidently as I continued forth towards the Don's room.

As I got closer and closer to the double doors, I could feel my heart racing like crazy.

*Didn't even know you still had a heart, Victor.*

I thought about opening the double doors slowly, but I knew that was a bad idea. So instead, I readied myself for a tremendous kick.

The semi-thin doors cracked open loudly and I jumped in with the pistol up and ready. I cleared the room as fast and accurately as I could to find that no one else remained, except for the Don.

I walked past his desk, over to the last set of double doors that were slightly opened, and entered into the abyss of illness.

The Don was waiting calmly for me in his bed, with the lamp on at his bedside table. He was extremely pale, practically near death from what I could tell. He didn't seem surprised at all when I came in with the pistol drawn and ready to fire. He actually seemed delighted to see me, and in this moment, I was delighted to see him too. We were all alone.

"Victor, I must say, this was quite foreseen by Leo."

"Yeah, well he's dead," I said as I slightly lowered the pistol.

"I can tell, by all the dark blood on you. Leo always had a darker tint of blood than most people."

*Even in his last moments alive, he's still lying to you.*

"Victor, you were supposed to be my successor…"

"Why me?" I asked. "I don't want to run this gang!"

"No, you wanted to destroy it… why, I do not know. We gave you everything we could."

"You took everything away from me, and tried to fill those holes with money and power!"

The Don slowly smirked and said, "You really don't know just how accurate that statement really is, do you?"

"What are you talking about!?" I shouted. "Why wouldn't you let Danny run the gang?"

"Victor, I had Danny killed in the prison."

His words were so lifeless, so cold. I felt a great deal of shock overcome me, but I had to have answers as a tear ran down my frozen face.

"You're his father... and he was your only son... how could you?"

"I had to... for the sake of our safety. He would spill everything eventually, so I hired Lucius and his men on the inside to do it. It's what they do in prison. They kill others who know too much."

"Jesus Christ, he was family."

"He always will be my family, Victor. Just like Adrianna."

"You did kill her, didn't you?"

The Don shook his head sadly.

"No... she really did run off one day, and I could never find her again. At one point, I thought maybe she had returned to Detroit and was ruining my operation as revenge, but I knew that Leo and the others wouldn't agree with it."

The voices chanting *kill, kill, kill* started to build in my head once more as I asked, "But, what about Jacob?"

"Yes, he finally called us and we had him killed as well... I was trying to clean the pallet for you, Victor. The new Ponchello gang would be more powerful than ever before. Only the strongest would survive to see it."

"I think it'd be the Carez gang at that point," I corrected.

"No, you became a Ponchello the day your parents were killed and engulfed in flames."

I studied his words carefully with his last sentence and I said, "What makes you say they were killed and then burned?"

The Don, in all his sickness and weakness, was still able to smile and couldn't hold back a laugh. It all started to come together and I vocalized my realization.

"You killed my parents..."

"I basically did the same thing that was done to the German people under Hitler's command... they had nothing. So, he wiped away the nothingness they had and he gave them everything."

The voices were getting louder and louder. I could barely hear myself talk.

"Comparing yourself to Hitler? Do you even hear what you're saying? Is this sickness of yours shrinking your brain?"

He ignored me as he said, "I mean, it works... time and time again."

"Well it's over now, Don!"

As soon as I started to fire, a gunshot rang out from under the Don's comforter and I felt the hot lead plow through the side of my stomach. I stood tall and began unloading the entire clip on the Don. Three shots hit his chest, then two bullets hit both sides of his forehead causing his face to contort, and the rest of the bullets were laid into his torso. The Don squirmed around at first until the two bullets cracked his skull open, and it was almost impossible to see where the blood was since his sheets were already red.

I felt my neck start to hurt and I realized I had been screaming the entire time I fired upon him, but I didn't even hear it. All of a sudden, as I looked down at the wound in my stomach, I realized that the madness was finally over. The voice, along with all the other voices, had escaped my mind. I felt refreshed and alert, almost like my old self once more. I would have been joyous if it wasn't for the gunshot wound or the tattered dead body before me.

It was in that moment that some words of my own about the Platinum Briefcase came to light.

*If it was behind the portrait, I'd have to rip into it... for that, I think the Don would have to be dead.*

With the Don now deceased, I made my way back down the stairs with the silenced pistol hanging by my side. When I saw the dead man on the stairs, Scott slumped over on the couch, and Jordan dead in the hallway, I had to think back and remind myself that I had killed them.

I walked past Jordan's body and made my way to the Don's office. I stepped inside and placed the pistol on the desk so I could move the portrait of the Don's father. But when I placed my hands on the side of the portrait and tried to move it, it wouldn't budge.

I stepped back for a second and saw a signed baseball bat that the Don had treasured. It appeared to be what I needed to get the job done.

I steadied the bat in a batting position and I took a swing at full force. The bat escaped from my hands and flew into the wall. I almost fell to the ground from the pain of the gunshot wound, but then I stood back up and saw a large black hole where the original Don's face once was.

I smiled in amazement and I used my bare hands to rip through the rest of the portrait. When I had ripped out almost the entire portrait, I found what I had been seeking for so long.

The Platinum Briefcase was lying before me in all its glory. The briefcase was very thin and I didn't worry about it being heavy as I lifted its handle. I could almost see my reflection in the thin coating of shiny platinum, and I carried it over to the Don's desk and pushed off any paperwork that was in the way.

There was no combination lock, no key locks, nothing. Just a button next to a latch on each side and that was it. I released the right latch first, and then the left latch second.

"Okay…" I told myself as I had to take a breath. "One… two… three!"

I yanked up the lid and the ridiculous amount of excitement I once had started to fall. Inside the lid of the Platinum Briefcase was…

Me.

I was staring into a very high quality mirror that had been specially fitted for the briefcase. At first, I felt like just closing the briefcase and throwing it aside, but I was captivated by how different I looked in this mirror. I mean, before and after taking a shower, I had glanced at the mirror, or even when I shaved. But in this moment, I started to think about how much had changed throughout my life, and how much I had changed. I had turned into a monster, and what I had done here at the manor was a monstrous thing. I let myself fall into madness, I let myself give into my inner deepest thoughts, and I regretted it all.

But I found that the Platinum Briefcase had a much more profound purpose than guilt.

I finally looked down from the mirror and when I did, I saw a small hand written note that I hadn't noticed before. When I held it up to the light, the words hit me like nothing had before:

**The one who seeks the Platinum Briefcase seeks a new life.**
**-Adrianna Ponchello**

I couldn't believe it… This entire time, she was telling Danny this bedtime story as a hint. That was the point of the Platinum Briefcase. It was so Danny and his mother could run away from all the pain and misery that the Don had caused… and now, I had inherited the briefcase instead.

But, maybe I was supposed to end up with the briefcase all along. I mean, the message didn't specify it was for Danny… it's for whoever seeks a new life. Ever since I had killed Emmitt, I felt any angel trying to guide me had left. But now I realized Adrianna was the angel who accompanied me and led me to the briefcase.

As I started to put the note back on the grey felt, it started to wrinkle and I could tell there was something under it.

And boy, was I right.

I pulled the cover away to find stacks of hundred dollar bills wrapped in labels that stated each stack was ten thousand dollars. I was baffled and shocked, but not as much as the mirror shocked me.

I figured the money was to help me build a new life… but where would I go?

Even after I had pulled back onto the highway in Leo's bloodied car with the Platinum Briefcase beside me and one hand over my bullet wound, I never really decided just where I was going. But one thing was for sure.

My next stop needed to be anywhere but here.

# Chapter Eighty Two
## Monday, December 25th, 1978
## The Raid

Chief Ramzorin didn't have a wife, didn't have a family; didn't have any kids. For him, Christmas was just another holiday he spent alone. Did he prefer it that way?

Not exactly.

At one point, he wondered if he had taken in Victor, whether or not they would've celebrated Christmas together, and Halloween, and their birthdays. He'd gotten so used to being alone, that he didn't care too much for the idea of celebrating all the time. Being alone had, however, made him a stronger person. Especially since when he tried to get close to Victor, Victor ended up joining a gang.

But now, at 8:45 on Christmas morning, Chief Ramzorin finished getting dressed and holstered his revolver by his side. He never really used it anymore, but it was always a good thing to have, especially during a police raid.

He climbed into his black Ford sedan and noticed that most of the snow was melting now that the sun was out.

Chief Ramzorin was happy as he drove down to the Ponchello manor, because he knew that the organization – which had been preying on the citizens of Detroit for about fifteen years – was about to finally come to an end. All thanks to Victor Carez.

The Chief thought about calling Victor in his hotel room last night, but he didn't get around to it. He thought about calling Victor this morning, but then he remembered how Victor hadn't slept well for so long. He wanted the kid to get some rest, he deserved it.

Without any coffee in hand, Chief Ramzorin was closing in on the Ponchello manor and his anticipation was perpetually growing. He couldn't wait to see the look on Don Ponchello's face.

But as he pulled off the highway and started to approach the front gate of the manor, he knew something wasn't right. The SWAT team appeared to be pretty relaxed and the front door to the manor was wide open with snow melting in the entryway.

"What the...?"

Chief Ramzorin stepped out of his sedan and tried to find Darnell, but Darnell found him.

"Ramzorin!"

Darnell's shout from across the manor grounds could have awakened all the dead inside the house. Ramzorin turned his head to see a highly distraught Special Agent Darnell practically racing towards him.

"What happened here?" Chief Ramzorin asked as he stepped into the manor with Darnell.

CSI had swarmed the place just moments before the Chief had arrived, putting markers and tape down anywhere they could.

"Your boy blew a fucking fuse, that's what fucking happened!"

"What are you talking about?"

"Victor! Victor Carez! Victor the-fucking-ender-of-my-career Carez!"

"Calm down, Darnell."

"Calm down? Can you not see what's right before your eyes?"

Chief Ramzorin looked at Jordan's lifeless body first, followed by Scott's in the living room and then the man on the stairs. It was at that moment Ramzorin understood what had happened.

"They're all dead."

"Yup! Bingo! Yahtzee! Fucking brilliant! He killed every single person who was here last night."

"Including the Don?"

"Of course!"

"I... I can't believe this."

"I'm kind of surprised that you're not a part of it, Chief."

Chief Ramzorin stared into Darnell's eyes and said, "You better watch what you're saying."

"Or what? You're going to pull a Victor and kill me and everyone else here?"

The rest of the crew at the crime scene turned their heads at Darnell's hysteria and then went back to work.

Darnell finally took a deep long breath and said, "Okay, Ramzorin, I'm just going to ask you this once, okay? Where is Victor Carez now? Because he's not in his hotel room, and he's not among the dead."

Suddenly, Chief Ramzorin felt an overwhelming emotion flow through him; one of absolute relief. He felt the voice in his head, one that had been bothering him for months now, finally leave him be. It was unlike anything he had ever experienced, but it was too good to share. He knew that.

And with one last sigh at the treachery before them, Chief Ramzorin collected his thoughts and replied, "He's safe now, that's all that matters…"

The End.

## **About the Author**

Henry Cline was born in 1994 in Oklahoma City, Oklahoma. He has been writing since he was seven and started writing novels at the age of eleven. His other passions include playing the electric guitar, cooking, and baking. His first album, Resilience, was released September of 2016, and The Platinum Briefcase is his first novel. More books are on the way!